ONCE AGAIN— WITH TRUMPETS!

Starring:

POUL ANDERSON

JAMES TIPTREE, JR.

FREDERIK POHL

CLIFFORD D. SIMAK

MICHAEL G. CONEY

T.J. BASS

W. MACFARLANE

ROBERT J. TILLEY

VERNOR VINGE

PHYLLIS MacLENNON

Continuing the tradition of excellence earned by the long and distinguished series of the world's best science fiction anthologies edited by Donald A. Wollheim.

Anthologies from DAW

Wollheim's WORLD'S BEST SF

Series Two

Edited by

DONALD A. WOLLHEIM

with Arthur W. Saha

Formerly titled:

The 1973 Annual World's Best SF

DAW BOOKS, INC.

DONALD A. WOLLHEIM, PUBLISHER

1301 Avenue of the Americas
New York, N.Y.   10019

For
"Ted" Carnell
in memoriam

FIRST PRINTING, MAY 1973

4 5 6 7 8 9

PRINTED IN U.S.A.

Table of Contents

INTRODUCTION

Several years ago an anthology was published bearing the unusual title, *Science Fiction for People Who Hate Science Fiction*. The premise of the collection was not to give such people further grounds for hating it but to show them what fascinating, literate stories the field could encompass, and show them also something on the wonderful ideals and marvelous visions they were missing. The book contained, as you might reasonably expect, a careful sampling of tried-and-tested favorites by tried-and-tested writers.

Lately there has been a rising tide of what we are coming to think of as Science Fiction *by* People Who Hate Science Fiction. These volumes of new stories generally begin with editorials assaulting the old masters, accusing them and those who follow their lead of being outdated, and demanding the application of avant-garde styles of narration to go with the presumed avant-garde ideas of science fiction. There have been quite a few such collections, occasionally with some interesting innovations but much more likely to be laden with snide, open-ended, implausible, and sometimes plotless writing —and occasionally works that are offensively and pointlessly obscene. Simultaneously there has been a rash of critical essays by the same people and their hangers-on praising this type of stuff, knocking the "old" science fiction, and proclaiming what amounts to a crusade to bring what they call SF into a merger with the mainstream (whatever that is).

At the same time it is to be noted that many of these obscurantists have augmented their income by making the circuits of colleges and schools as lecturers or even "teachers" of their type of SF.

That this rise of the incomprehensible should be taking

place alongside the discovery of science fiction as a literature of ideas by the academic world is truly unfortunate. Colleges and many high schools all over America—and in other lands as well—are presenting courses in science fiction . . . what it is, who are its masters, what is it telling us? Workshops are coming into existence wherein young talents are trying their wings under the guidance of supposedly knowing instructors. Unfortunately too many of these instructors are not well versed on their subject—faculty members who have hastily boned up on the subject—and have too often been taken in by the self-advertising of these avant-garde editors and writers.

In the past year we have noted a rising tide of anthologies specializing in new stories—stories written to order for a book editor, rather than for the magazine editors, who have hitherto provided the prime market for short stories and novelettes. In many cases these anthologies are being directed by obscurantists and produce volumes that do not measure up to the type of science fiction enjoyed by the majority of its faithful.

Several of the new-story anthologies assume a periodic form . . . and last year saw the demise of two of the most incomprehensible and offensively snobbish. But more of the same are likely to be coming into existence.

The biggest news of the coming year is likely to take the form of an avalanche of new-story collections in book form —an idea which seems suddenly to have overwhelmed book publishers. We have seen reliable reports that one free-lance editor alone has placed over forty contracts for anthologies with a dozen publishers new to the field and is working to create even more such anthologies. Other free-lance editors are in busy competition, trying to reap a quick harvest before the blight of overproduction sets in, as it is sure to do.

Now in all this new material there must be some good stories and even some good new writers. But the task of locating them amid the mass of mediocre or hastily written-to-order jobs by "name" professionals is going to be exceedingly hard . . . and possibly not worth the effort.

The fact is that the good stuff is still being found in the established magazines: *Analog, Galaxy, If, Fantasy & Science Fiction, Amazing*. In reading for this annual of the best, we have found that even the seconds from those magazines, the stories we did not ultimately select, were generally superior in plot and sense-of-wonder than what was being touted in the new-story anthologies.

Orbit, formerly the best of the American books of that sort, seems to have fallen deeper into the temptation of "new-wavism" more than in previous editions—we could not enthuse over any of its offerings the past year. On the other hand, the original new-story collection, John Carnell's *New Writings in SF,* of British origin, continued to represent the good taste of a fine editor and continued to prove a rewarding reading experience. The death in 1972 of its editor, Edward John Carnell, was a loss comparable to those of John W. Campbell and August Derleth the year before. We are happy to report that both Carnell's famous literary agency and the anthology series are being continued by competent Old Hands.

1972 also saw the publication of the second massive collection of new writings masterminded by the dynamic Harlan Ellison, *Again Dangerous Visions.* Unfortunately it was the opinion of your editors that this was not the equal of its predecessor, *Dangerous Vision,* and that, while there were some outstanding pieces in it, too many were either incomprehensible or slight. Here we made a deliberate policy decision not to attempt to select anything from this remarkable book for this annual. Let others try, if they wish, but we think readers should judge it as a whole, especially since the entire work is glued together by Ellison's always delightful and always lengthy introductions and the authors' own afterthoughts.

Meanwhile the rise of European science fiction continues, though still at a slow pace. The first European convention took place in the summer with a good attendance and a mixed report. It seems to have been a far more serious gathering than the huge American "world" conventions. This "Eurocon" initiated the presentation of regional awards for the best stories of each country. Other European conferences are scheduled for this and future years. As they gather experience, we expect that the Eurocons will become factors to be reckoned with.

Here now is our selection of the best of the year in science fiction. Once more it is confined to works written originally in English—though several stories were submitted from abroad, none had that extra quality demanded of a "world's best." As we have also indicated, most of these stories came from the magazines, still the most reliable source of real science fiction.

What the next year and the years after will hold remains to be seen. Changes are in the offing—and we hope that some of the opinions of those who criticize the old will be demonstrated in stories we can applaud.

—*Donald A. Wollheim*

GOAT SONG

POUL ANDERSON

It often happens that an author has grave doubts about the very story that others will acclaim as his finest. Whether this is Poul Anderson's finest is anyone's guess, but few will deny that it is among the best this brilliant writer has ever produced. Yet in his introductory note to the magazine publication, Poul admits that he held the manuscript back for several years being unsure of it. The readers and writers who are nominating it for a Nebula are not so unsure. Nor will you be.

Three women: one is dead; one is alive; One is both and neither, and will never live and never die, being immortal in SUM.

On a hill above that valley through which runs the high-road, I await Her passage. Frost came early this year, and the grasses have paled. Otherwise the slope is begrown with blackberry bushes that have been harvested by men and birds, leaving only briars, and with certain apple trees. They are very old, those trees, survivors of an orchard raised by generations which none but SUM now remembers (I can see a few fragments of wall thrusting above the brambles)—scattered crazily over the hillside and as crazily gnarled. A little fruit remains on them. Chill across my skin, a gust shakes loose an apple. I hear it knock on the earth, another stroke of some eternal clock. The shrubs whisper to the wind.

Elsewhere the ridges around me are wooded, afire with scarlets, brasses, bronzes. The sky is huge, the westering sun wan-bright. The valley is filling with a deeper blue, a haze whose slight smokiness touches my nostrils. This is Indian summer, the funeral pyre of the year.

There have been other seasons. There have been other lifetimes, before mine and hers; and in those days they had words to sing with. We still allow ourselves music, though, and I have spent much time planting melodies around my rediscovered words. *"In the greenest growth of the Maytime —"* I unsling the harp on my back, and tune it afresh, and sing to her, straight into autumn and the waning day.

> *"—You came, and the sun came after,*
> *And the green grew golden above;*
> *And the flag-flowers lightened with laughter,*
> *And the meadowsweet shook with love."*

A footfall stirs the grasses, quite gently, and the woman says, trying to chuckle, "Why, thank you."

Once, so soon after my one's death that I was still dazed by it, I stood in the home that had been ours. This was on the hundred and first floor of a most desirable building. After dark the city flamed for us, blinked, glittered, flung immense sheets of radiance forth like banners. Nothing but SUM could have controlled the firefly dance of a million aircars among the towers: or, for that matter, have maintained the entire city, from nuclear power plants through automated factories, physical and economic distribution networks, sanitation, repair, services, education, culture, order, everything as one immune immortal organism. We had gloried in belonging to this as well as to each other.

But that night I told the kitchen to throw the dinner it had made for me down the waste chute, and ground under my heel the chemical consolations which the medicine cabinet extended to me, and kicked the cleaner as it picked up the mess, and ordered the lights not to go on, anywhere in our suite. I stood by the vieWall, looking out across megalopolis, and it was tawdry. In my hands I had a little clay figure she had fashioned herself. I turned it over and over and over.

But I had forgotten to forbid the door to admit visitors. It recognized this woman and opened for her. She had come with the kindly intention of teasing me out of a mood that seemed to her unnatural. I heard her enter, and looked around through the gloom. She had almost the same height as my girl did, and her hair chanced to be bound in a way that my girl often favored, and the figurine dropped from my grasp and shattered, because for an instant I thought she was my girl. Since then I have been hard put not to hate Thrakia.

This evening, even without so much sundown light, I would not make that mistake. Nothing but the silvery bracelet about her left wrist bespeaks the past we share. She is in wildcountry garb: boots, kilt of true fur and belt of true leather, knife at hip and rifle slung on shoulder. Her locks are matted and snarled, her skin brown from weeks of weather; scratches and smudges show beneath the fantastic zigzags she has painted in many colors on herself. She wears a necklace of bird skulls.

Now that one who is dead was, in her own way, more a child of trees and horizons than Thrakia's followers. She was so much at home in the open that she had no need to put off clothes or cleanliness, reason or gentleness, when we sickened of the cities and went forth beyond them. From this trait I got many of the names I bestowed on her, such as Wood's Colt or Fallow Hind or, from my prowlings among ancient books, Dryad and Elven. (She liked me to choose her names, and this pleasure had no end, because she was inexhaustible.)

I let my harpstring ring into silence. Turning about, I say to Thrakia, "I wasn't singing for you. Not for anyone. Leave me alone."

She draws a breath. The wind ruffles her hair and brings me an odor of her: not female sweetness, but fear. She clenches her fists and says, "You're crazy."

"Wherever did you find a meaningful word like that?" I gibe; for my own pain and—to be truthful—my own fear must strike out at something, and here she stands. "Aren't you content any longer with 'untranquil' or 'disequilibrated'?"

"I got it from you," she says defiantly, "you and your damned archaic songs. There's another word, 'damned.' And how it suits you! When are you going to stop this morbidity?"

"And commit myself to a clinic and have my brain laundered nice and sanitary? Not soon, darling." I use *that* last word aforethought, but she cannot know what scorn and sadness are in it for me, who knows that once it could also have been a name for my girl. The official grammar and pronunciation of language is as frozen as every other aspect of our civilization, thanks to electronic recording and neuronic teaching; but meanings shift and glide about like subtle serpents. (O adder that stung my Foalfoot!)

I shrug and say in my driest, most city-technological voice, "Actually, I'm the practical, nonmorbid one. Instead of running away from my emotions—via drugs, or neuroadjustment, or playing at savagery like you, for that matter—I'm about to implement a concrete plan for getting back the person who made me happy."

"By disturbing Her on Her way home?"

"Anyone has the right to petition the Dark Queen while She's abroad on Earth."

"But this is past the proper time—"

"No law's involved, just custom. People are afraid to meet Her outside a crowd, a town, bright flat lights. They won't admit it, but they are. So I came here precisely not to be part of a queue. I don't want to speak into a recorder for subsequent computer analysis of my words. How could I be sure She was listening? I want to meet Her as myself, a unique being, and look in Her eyes while I make my prayer."

Thrakia chokes a little. "She'll be angry."

"Is She able to be angry, anymore?"

"I . . . I don't know. What you mean to ask for is so impossible, though. So absurd. That SUM should give you back your girl. You know It never makes exceptions."

"Isn't She Herself an exception?"

"That's different. You're being silly. SUM has to have a, well, a direct human liaison. Emotional and cultural feedback, as well as statistics. How else can It govern rationally? And She must have been chosen out of the whole world. Your girl, what was she? Nobody!"

"To me, she was everybody."

"You—" Thrakia catches her lip in her teeth. One hand reaches out and closes on my bare forearm, a hard hot touch, the grimy fingernails biting. When I make no response, she lets go and stares at the ground. A V of outbound geese passes overhead. Their cries come shrill through the wind, which is loudening in the forest.

"Well," she says, "you are special. You always were. You went to space and came back, with the Great Captain. You're maybe the only man alive who understands about the ancients. And your singing, yes, you don't really entertain; your songs trouble people and can't be forgotten. So maybe She will listen to you. But SUM won't. It can't give special resurrections. Once that was done, a single time, wouldn't it have to be done for everybody? The dead would overrun the living."

"Not necessarily," I say. "In any event, I mean to try."

"Why can't you wait for the promised time? Surely, then, SUM will recreate you two in the same generation."

"I'd have to live out this life, at least, without her," I say, looking away also, down to the highroad which shines through shadow like death's snake, the length of the valley. "Besides, how do you know there ever will be any resurrections? We have only a promise. No, less than that policy."

She gasps, steps back, raises her hands as if to fend me off. Her soul bracelet casts light into my eyes. I recognize an embryo exorcism. She lacks rital; every "superstition" was patiently scrubbed out of our metal-and-energy world, long ago. But if she has no word for it, no concept, nevertheless she recoils from blasphemy.

So I say, wearily, not wanting an argument, wanting only to wait here alone: "Never mind. There could be some natural catastrophe, like a giant asteroid striking, that wiped out the system before conditions had become right for resurrections to commence."

"That's impossible," she says, almost frantic. "The homeostats, the repair functions—"

"All right, call it a vanishingly unlikely theoretical contingency. Let's declare that I'm so selfish I want Swallow Wing back now, in this life of mine, and don't give a curse whether that'll be fair to the rest of you."

You won't care either, anyway, I think. None of you. You don't grieve. It is your own precious private consciousness that you wish to preserve; no one else is close enough to you to matter very much. Would you believe me if I told you I am quite prepared to offer SUM my own death in exchange for It releasing Blossom-in-the-Sun?

I don't speak that thought, which would be cruel, nor repeat what is crueler: my fear that SUM lies, that the dead never will be disgorged. For (I am not the All-Controller; I think not with vacuum and negative energy levels but with ordinary Earth-begotten molecules; yet I can reason somewhat dispassionately, being disillusioned) consider—

The object of the game is to maintain a society stable, just, and sane. This requires satisfaction not only of somatic, but of symbolic and instinctual needs. Thus children must be allowed to come into being. The minimum number per generation is equal to the maximum: that number which will maintain a constant population.

It is also desirable to remove the fear of death from men. Hence the promise: At such time as it is socially feasible, SUM will begin to refashion us, with our complete memories but in the pride of our youth. This can be done over and over, life after life across the millennia. So death is, indeed, a sleep.

—*in that sleep of death, what dreams may come*—No. I myself dare not dwell on this. I ask merely, privately: Just when and how does SUM expect conditions (in a stabilized society, mind you) to have become so different from today's that the reborn can, in their millions, safely be welcomed back?

I see no reason why SUM should not lie to us. We, too, are objects in the world that It manipulates.

"We've quarreled about this before, Thrakia," I sigh. "Often. Why do you bother?"

"I wish I knew," she answers low. Half to herself, she goes on: "Of course I want to copulate with you. You must be good, the way that girl used to follow you about with her eyes, and smile when she touched your hand, and—But you can't be better than everyone else. That's unreasonable. There are only so many possible ways. So why do I care if you wrap yourself up in silence and go off alone? Is it that that makes you a challenge?"

"You think too much," I say. "Even here. You're a pretend primitive. You visit wildcountry to 'slake inborn atavistic impulses . . .' but you can't dismantle that computer inside yourself and simply feel, simply be."

She bristles. I touched a nerve there. Looking past her, along the ridge of fiery maple and sumac, brassy elm and great dun oak, I see others emerge from beneath the trees. Women exclusively, her followers, as unkempt as she; one has a brace of ducks lashed to her waist, and their blood has trickled down her thigh and dried black. For this movement, this unadmitted mystique has become Thrakia's by now: that not only men should forsake the easy routine and the easy pleasure of the cities, and become again, for a few weeks each year, the carnivores who begot our species; women too should seek out starkness, the better to appreciate civilization when they return.

I feel a moment's unease. We are in no park, with laid out trails and campground services. We are in wildcountry. Not many men come here, ever, and still fewer women; for the region is, literally, beyond the law. No deed done here is punishable. We are told that this helps consolidate society, as the most violent among us may thus vent their passions. But I have spent much time in wildcountry since my Morning Star went out—myself in quest of nothing but solitude—and I have watched what happens through eyes that have also read anthropology and history. Institutions are developing; ceremonies, tribalisms, acts of blood and cruelty and acts elsewhere called unnatural are becoming more elaborate and more expected every year. Then the practitioners go home to their cities and honestly believe they have been enjoying fresh air, exercise, and good tension-releasing fun.

Let her get angry enough and Thrakia can call knives to her aid.

Wherefore I make myself lay both hands on her shoulders, and meet the tormented gaze, and say most gently, "I'm sorry. I know you mean well. You're afraid She will be annoyed and bring misfortune on your people."

Thrakia gulps. "No," she whispers. "That wouldn't be logical. But I'm afraid of what might happen to you. And then—" Suddenly she throws herself against me. I feel arms, breasts, belly press through my tunic, and smell meadows in her hair and musk in her mouth. "You'd be gone!" she wails. "Then who'd sing to us?"

"Why, the planet's crawling with entertainers," I stammer.

"You're more than that," she says. "So much more. I don't like what you sing, not really—and what you've sung since that stupid girl died, oh, meaningless, horrible—but, I don't know why, I *want* you to trouble me."

Awkward, I pat her back. The sun now stands very little above the treetops. Its rays slant interminably through the booming, frosting air. I shiver and wonder what to do.

A sound rescues me. It comes from one end of the valley below us, where further view is blocked off by two cliffs; it thunders deep in our ears and rolls through the earth into our bones. We have heard that sound in the cities, and been glad to have walls and lights and multitudes around us. Now we are alone with it, the noise of Her chariot.

The women shriek, I hear them faintly across wind and rumble and my own pulse, and they vanish into the woods. They will seek their camp, dress warmly, build enormous fires; presently they will eat their ecstatics, and rumors are uneasy about what they do after that.

Thrakia seizes my left wrist, above the soul bracelet, and hauls. "Harper, come with me!" she pleads. I break loose from her and stride down the hill toward the road. A scream follows me for a moment.

Light still dwells in the sky and on the ridges, but as I descend into that narrow valley, I enter dusk, and it thickens. Indistinct bramble bushes whicker where I brush them, and claw back at me. I feel the occasional scratch on my legs, the tug as my garment is snagged, the chill that I breathe, but dimly. My perceived-outer-reality is overpowered by the rushing of Her chariot and my blood. My inner-universe is fear, yes, but exaltation too, a drunkenness which sharpens instead of dulling the senses, a psychedelia which opens the reasoning mind as well as the emotions; I have gone beyond myself, I am embodied purpose. Not out of need for comfort, but to voice what Is, I return to words whose speaker rests centuries dust, and lend them my own music. I sing:

> "—Gold is my heart, and the world's golden.
> And one peak tipped with light;
> And the air lies still above the hill
> With the first fear of night;
>
> Till mystery down the soundless valley
> Thunders, and dark is here;
> And the wind blows, and the light goes,
> And the night is full of fear.
>
> And I know one night, on some far height,
> In the tongue I never knew,
> I yet shall hear the tidings clear.

They'll call the news from hill to hill,
Dark and uncomforted,
Earth and sky and the winds; and I
Shall know that you are dead.—"

But I have reached the valley floor, and She has come in sight.

Her chariot is unlit, for radar eyes and inertial guides need no lamps, nor sun nor stars. Wheelless, the steel tear rides on its own roar and thrust of air. The pace is not great, far less than any of our mortals' vehicles are wont to take. Men say the Dark Queen rides thus slowly in order that She may perceive with Her own senses and so be the better prepared to counsel SUM. But now Her annual round is finished; She is homeward bound; until spring She will dwell with It Which is our lord. Why does She not hasten tonight?

Because Death has never a need of haste? I wonder. And as I step into the middle of the road, certain lines from the yet more ancient past rise tremendous within me, and I strike my harp and chant them louder than the approaching car:

> *"I that in heill was and gladness*
> *Am trublit now with great sickness*
> *And feblit with infirmitie:—*
> *Timor mortis conturbat me."*

The car detects me and howls a warning. I hold my ground. The car could swing around; the road is wide, and in any event a smooth surface is not absolutely necessary. But I hope, I believe that She will be aware of an obstacle in Her path, and tune in Her various amplifiers, and find me abnormal enough to stop for. Who, in SUM's world—who, even among the explorers that It has sent beyond in Its unappeasable hunger for data—would stand in a cold wildcountry dusk and shout while his harp snarls:

> *"Our presence here is all vain glory,*
> *This fals world is but transitory,*
> *The flesh is bruckle, the Feynd is slee:—*
>
> *The state of man does change and vary,*
> *Now sound, now sick, now blyth, now sary,*
> *Now dansand mirry, now like to die:—*

No state in Erd here standis sicker;
As with the wynd wavis the wicker
So wannis this world's vanitie:—
Timor mortis conturbat me.—?"

The car draws alongside and sinks to the ground. I let my strings die away into the wind. The sky overhead and in the west is gray-purple; eastward it is quite dark and a few early stars peer forth. Here, down in the valley, shadows are heavy and I cannot see very well.

The canopy slides back. She stands erect in the chariot, thus looming over me. Her robe and cloak are black, fluttering like restless wings; beneath the cowl Her face is a white blur. I have seen it before, under full light, and in how many thousands of pictures; but at this hour I cannot call it back to my mind, not entirely. I list sharp-sculptured profile and pale lips, sable hair and long green eyes, but these are nothing more than words.

"What are you doing?" She has a lovely low voice; but is it, as, oh, how rarely since SUM took Her to Itself, is it the least shaken? "What is that you were singing?"

My answer comes so strong that my skull resonates, for I am borne higher and higher on my tide. "Lady of Ours, I have a petition."

"Why did you not bring it before Me when I walked among men? Tonight I am homebound. You must wait till I ride forth with the new year."

"Lady of Ours, neither You nor I would wish living ears to hear what I have to say."

She regards me for a long while. Do I indeed sense fear also in Her? (Surely not of me. Her chariot is armed and armored, and would react with machine speed to protect Her should I offer violence. And should I somehow, incredibly, kill Her, or wound Her beyond chemosurgical repair, She of all beings has no need to doubt death. The ordinary bracelet cries with quite sufficient radio loudness to be heard by more than one thanatic station, when we die; and in that shielding the soul can scarcely be damaged before the Winged Heels arrive to bear it off to SUM. Surely the Dark Queen's circlet can call still further, and is still better insulated, than any mortal's. And She will most absolutely be recreated. She has been, again and again; death and rebirth every seven years keep Her eternally young in the service of SUM. I have never been able to find out when She was first born.)

Fear, perhaps, of what I have sung and what I might speak?

At last She says—I can scarcely hear through the gusts and creakings in the trees—"Give me the Ring, then."

The dwarf robot which stands by Her throne when She sits among men appears beside Her and extends the massive dull-silver circle to me. I place my left arm within, so that my soul is enclosed. The tablet on the upper surface of the Ring, which looks so much like a jewel, slants away from me; I cannot read what flashes onto the bezel. But the faint glow picks Her features out of murk as She bends to look.

Of course, I tell myself, the actual soul is not scanned. That would take too long. Probably the bracelet which contains the soul has an identification code built in. The Ring sends this to an appropriate part of SUM, Which instantly sends back what is recorded under that code. I hope there is nothing more to it. SUM has not seen fit to tell us.

"What do you call yourself at the moment?" She asks.

A current of bitterness crosses my tide. "Lady of Ours, why should You care? Is not my real name the number I got when I was allowed to be born?"

Calm descends once more upon Her. "If I am to evaluate properly what you say, I must know more about you than these few official data. Name indicates mood."

I too feel unshaken again, my tide running so strong and smooth that I might not know I was moving did I not see time recede behind me. "Lady of Ours, I cannot give You a fair answer. In this past year I have not troubled with names, or with much of anything else. But some people who knew me from earlier days call me Harper."

"What do you do besides make that sinister music?"

"These days, nothing, Lady of Ours. I've money to live out my life, if I eat sparingly and keep no home. Often I am fed and housed for the sake of my songs."

"What you sang is unlike anything I have heard since—" Anew, briefly, that robot serenity is shaken. "Since before the world was stabilized. You should not wake dead symbols, Harper. They walk through men's dreams."

"Is that bad?"

"Yes. The dreams become nightmares. Remember: mankind, every man who ever lived, was insane before SUM brought order, reason, and peace."

"Well, then," I say, "I will cease and desist if I may have my own dead wakened for me."

She stiffens. The tablet goes out. I withdraw my arm and the Ring is stored away by Her servant. So again She is faceless, beneath flickering stars, here at the bottom of this shadowed valley. Her voice falls cold as the air: "No one can be brought back to life before Resurrection Time is ripe."

I do not say, "What about You?" for that would be vicious. What did She think, how did She weep, when SUM chose Her of all the young on Earth? What does She endure in Her centuries? I dare not imagine.

Instead, I smite my harp and sing, quietly this time:

> *"Strew on her roses, roses,*
> *And never a spray of yew.*
> *In quiet she reposes:*
> *Ah! would that I did too."*

> *"Her cabin'd, ample Spirit*
> *It flutter'd and fail'd for breath.*
> *To-night it doth inherit*
> *The vasty hall of Death."*

I know why my songs strike so hard: because they bear dreads and passions that no one is used to—that most of us hardly know could exist—in SUM's ordered universe. But I had not the courage to hope She would be as torn by them as I see. Has She not lived with more darkness and terror than the ancients could conceive? She calls, "Who has died?"

"She had many names, Lady of Ours," I say. "None was beautiful enough. I can tell You her number, though."

"Your daughter? I . . . sometimes I am asked if a dead child cannot be brought back. Not often, anymore, when they go so soon to the crèche. But sometimes. I tell the mother she may have a new one; but if ever We started recreating dead infants, at what age level could We stop?"

"No, this was my woman."

"Impossible!" Her tone seeks to be not unkindly but is, instead, well-nigh frantic. "You will have no trouble finding others. You are handsome, and your psyche is, is, is extraordinary. It burns like Lucifer."

"Do You remember the name Lucifer, Lady of Ours?" I pounce. "Then You are old indeed. So old that You must also remember how a man might desire only one woman, but her above the whole world and heaven."

She tries to defend Herself with a jeer: "Was that mutual, Harper? I know more of mankind than you do, and surely I am the last chaste woman in existence."

"Now that she is gone, Lady, yes, perhaps You are. But we— Do You know how she died? We had gone to a wild-country area. A man saw her, alone, while I was off hunting gem rocks to make her a necklace. He approached her. She refused him. He threatened force. She fled. This was desert land, viper land, and she was barefoot. One of them bit her. I did not find her till hours later. By then the poison and the unshaded sun— She died quite soon after she told me what had happened and that she loved me. I could not get her body to chemosurgery in time for normal revival procedures. I had to let them cremate her and take her soul away to SUM."

"What right have you to demand her back, when no one else can be given their own?"

"The right that I love her, and she loves me. We are more necessary to each other than sun or moon. I do not think You could find another two people of whom this is so, Lady. And is not everyone entitled to claim what is necessary to his life? How else can society be kept whole?"

"You are being fantastic," She says thinly. "Let me go."

"No, Lady. I am speaking sober truth. But poor plain words won't serve me. I sing to You because then maybe You will understand." And I strike my harp anew, but it is more to her than Her that I sing.

> "If I had thought thou couldst have died,
> I might not weep for thee;
> But I forgot, when by thy side,
> That thou couldst mortal be:
> It never through my mind had past
> The time would e'er be o'er,
> And on thee should look my last,
> And thou shouldst smile no more!"

"I cannot—" She falters. "I did not know such feelings existed any longer."

"Now You do, Lady of Ours. And is that not an important datum for SUM?"

"Yes. If true." Abruptly She leans toward me. I see Her

shudder in the murk, under the flapping cloak, and hear Her
jaws clatter with cold. "I cannot linger here. But ride with
Me. Sing to Me. I think I can bear it."

So much have I scarcely expected. But my destiny is upon
me. I mount into the chariot. The canopy slides shut and we
proceed.

The main cabin encloses us. Behind its rear door must be
facilities for Her living on Earth; this is a big vehicle. But here
is little except curved panels. They are true wood of different
comely grains: so She also needs periodic escape from our
machine existence, does She? Furnishing is scant and austere.
The only sound is our passage, muffled to a murmur for us;
and, because their photomultipliers are not activated, the
scanners show nothing outside but night. We huddle close to a
glower, hands extended toward its fieriness. Our shoulders
brush, our bare arms, Her skin is soft and Her hair falls loose
over the thrown-back cowl, smelling of the summer which is
dead. What, is She still human?

After a timeless time, She says, not yet looking at me:
"The thing you sang, there on the highroad as I came near—I
do not remember it. Not even from the years before I became
what I am."

"It is older than SUM," I answer, "and its truth will outlive
It."

"Truth?" I see Her tense Herself. "Sing me the rest."

My fingers are no longer too numb to call forth chords.

> "—Unto the Death gois all Estatis,
> Princis, Prelattis, and Potestatis,
> Baith rich and poor of all degree:—
>
> He takis the knichtis in to the field
> Enarmit under helm and scheild;
> Victor he is at all mellie:—
>
> That strong unmerciful tyrand
> Takis, on the motheris breast sowkand,
> The babe full of benignitie:—
>
> He takis the campion in the stour,
> The captain closit in the tour,
> The ladie in bout full of bewtie:—

He sparis no lord for his piscence,
Na clerk for his intelligence;
His awful straik may no man flee:—
Timor mortis conturbat me."

She breaks me off, clapping hands to ears and half shriek-
ing, "No!"

I, grown unmerciful, pursue Her: "You understand now, do
You not? You are not eternal either. SUM isn't. Not Earth,
not Sun, not stars. We hid from the truth. Every one of us. I
too, until I lost the one thing which made everything make
sense. Then I had nothing left to lose, and could look with
clear eyes. And what I saw was Death."

"Get out! Let Me alone!"

"I will not let the whole world alone, Queen, until I get
her back. Give me her again, and I'll believe in SUM again.
I'll praise It till men dance for joy to hear Its name."

She challenges me with wildcat eyes. "Do you think such
matters to It?"

"Well"—I shrug—"songs could be useful. They could help
achieve the great objective sooner. Whatever that is. 'Optimi-
zation of total human activity'—wasn't that the program? I
don't know if it still is. SUM has been adding to Itself so
long. I doubt if You Yourself understand Its purposes, Lady
of Ours."

"Don't speak as if It were alive," She says harshly. "It is a
computer-effector complex. Nothing more."

"Are You certain?"

"I— Yes. It thinks, more widely and deeply than any human ever did or could; but It is not alive, not aware, It has
no consciousness. That is one reason why It decided It needed
Me."

"Be that as it may, Lady," I tell Her, "the ultimate result,
whatever It finally does with us, lies far in the future. At present I care about that; I worry; I resent our loss of self-deter-
mination. But that's because only such abstractions are left
to me. Give me back my Lightfoot, and she, not the distant
future, will be my concern. I'll be grateful, honestly grateful,
and You Two will know it from the songs I then choose to
sing. Which, as I said, might be helpful to It."

"You are unbelievably insolent," She says without force.

"No, Lady, just desperate," I say.

The ghost of a smile touches Her lips. She leans back, and

murmurs, "Well, I'll take you there. What happens then, you realize, lies outside My power. My observations, My recommendations, are nothing but a few items to take into account, among billions. However . . . we have a long way to travel this night. Give Me what data you think will help you, Harper."

I do not finish the Lament. Nor do I dwell in any other fashion on grief. Instead, as the hours pass, I call upon those who dealt with the joy (not the fun, not the short delirium, but the joy) that man and woman might once have of each other.

Knowing where we are bound, I too need such comfort.

And the night deepens, and the leagues fall behind us, and finally we are beyond habitation, beyond wildcountry, in the land where life never comes. By crooked moon and waning starlight I see the plain of concrete and iron, the missiles and energy projectors crouched like beasts, the robot aircraft wheeling aloft: and the lines, the relay towers, the scuttling beetle-shaped carriers, that whole transcendent nerve-blood-sinew by which SUM knows and orders the world. For all the flitting about, for all the forces which seethe, here is altogether still. The wind itself seems to have frozen to death. Hoarfrost is gray on the steel shapes. Ahead of us, tiered and mountainous, begins to appear the castle of SUM.

She Who rides with me does not give sign of noticing that my songs have died in my throat. What humanness She showed is departing; Her face is cold and shut; Her voice bears a ring of metal; She looks straight ahead. But She does speak to me for a little while yet:

"Do you understand what is going to happen? For the next half year I will be linked with SUM, integral, another component of It. I suppose you will see Me, but that will merely be My flesh. What speaks to you will be SUM."

"I know." The words must be forced forth. My coming this far is more triumph than any man in creation before me has won; and I am here to do battle for my Dancer-on-Moonglades; but nonetheless my heart shakes me, and is loud in my skull, and my sweat stinks.

I manage, though, to add: "You *will* be a part of It, Lady of Ours. That gives me hope."

For an instant She turns to me, and lays Her hand across mine, and something makes Her again so young and untaken that I almost forget the girl who died; and She whispers, "If you knew how I hope!"

The instant is gone, and I am alone among machines.

We must stop before the castle gate. The wall looms sheer above, so high and high that it seems to be toppling upon me against the westward march of the stars, so black and black that it does not only drink down every light, it radiates blindness. Challenge and response quiver on electronic bands I cannot sense. The outer-guardian parts of It have perceived a mortal aboard this craft. A missile launcher swings about to aim its three serpents at me. But the Dark Queen answers— She does not trouble to be peremptory—and the castle opens its jaws for us.

We descend. Once, I think, we cross a river. I hear a rushing and hollow echoing and see droplets glitter where they are cast onto the viewports and outlined against dark. They vanish at once: liquid hydrogen, perhaps, to keep certain parts near absolute zero?

Much later we stop and the canopy slides back. I rise with Her. We are in a room, or cavern, of which I can see nothing, for there is no light except a dull bluish phosphorescence which streams from every solid object, also from Her flesh and mine. But I judge the chamber is enormous, for a sound of great machines at work comes very remotely, as if heard through dream, while our own voices are swallowed up by distance. Air is pumped through, neither warm nor cold, totally without odor, a dead wind.

We descend to the floor. She stands before me, hands crossed on breast, eyes half shut beneath the cowl and not looking at me nor away from me. "Do what you are told, Harper," She says in a voice that has never an overtone, "precisely as you are told." She turns and departs at an even pace. I watch Her go until I can no longer tell Her luminosity from the formless swirlings within my own eyeballs.

A claw plucks my tunic. I look down and am surprised to see that the dwarf robot has been waiting for me this whole time. How long a time that was, I cannot tell.

Its squat form leads me in another direction. Weariness crawls upward through me, my feet stumble, my lips tingle, lids are weighted and muscles have each their separate aches. Now and then I feel a jag of fear, but dully. When the robot indicates *Lie down here,* I am grateful.

The box fits me well. I let various wires be attached to me, various needles be injected which lead into tubes. I pay little attention to the machines which cluster and murmur around me. The robot goes away. I sink into blessed darkness.

I wake renewed in body. A kind of shell seems to have grown between my forebrain and the old animal parts. Far away I can feel the horror and hear the screaming and thrashing of my instincts; but awareness is chill, calm, logical. I have also a feeling that I slept for weeks, months, while leaves blew loose and snow fell on the upper world. But this may be wrong, and in no case does it matter. I am about to be judged by SUM.

The little faceless robot leads me off, through murmurous black corridors where the dead wind blows. I unsling my harp and clutch it to me, my sole friend and weapon. So the tranquillity of the reasoning mind which has been decreed for me cannot be absolute. I decide that It simply does not want to be bothered by anguish. (No; wrong; nothing so humanlike; It has no desires; beneath that power to reason is nullity.)

At length a wall opens for us and we enter a room where She sits enthroned. The self-radiation of metal and flesh is not apparent here, for light is provided, a featureless white radiance with no apparent source. White, too, is the muted sound of the machines which encompass Her throne. White are Her robe and face. I look away from the multitudinous unwinking scanner eyes, into Hers, but She does not appear to recognize me. Does She even see me? SUM has reached out with invisible fingers of electromagnetic induction and taken Her back into Itself. I do not tremble or sweat—I cannot—but I square my shoulders, strike one plangent chord, and wait for It to speak.

It does, from some invisible place. I recognize the voice It has chosen to use: my own. The overtones, the inflections are true, normal, what I myself would use in talking as one reasonable man to another. Why not? In computing what to do about me, and in programming Itself accordingly, SUM must have used so many billion bits of information that adequate accent is a negligible subproblem.

No . . . there I am mistaken again . . . SUM does not do things on the basis that It might as well do them as not. This talk with myself is intended to have some effect on me. I do not know what.

"Well," It says pleasantly, "you made quite a journey didn't you? I'm glad. Welcome."

My instincts bare teeth to hear those words of humanity used by the unfeeling unalive. My logical mind considers replying with an ironic "Thank you," decides against it, and holds me silent.

"You see," SUM continues after a moment that whirrs, "you are unique. Pardon Me if I speak a little bluntly. Your sexual monomania is just one aspect of a generally atavistic, superstition-oriented personality. And yet, unlike the ordinary misfit, you're both strong and realistic enough to cope with the world. This chance to meet you, to analyze you while you rested, has opened new insights for Me on human psychophysiology. Which may lead to improved techniques for governing it and its evolution."

"That being so," I reply, "give me my reward."

"Now look here," SUM says in a mild tone, "you if anyone should know I'm not omnipotent. I was built originally to help govern a civilization grown too complex. Gradually, as My program of self-expansion progressed, I took over more and more decision-making functions. They were *given* to Me. People were happy to be relieved of responsibility, and they could see for themselves how much better I was running things than any mortal could. But to this day, My authority depends on a substantial consensus. If I started playing favorites, as by recreating your girl, well, I'd have troubles."

"The consensus depends more on awe than on reason," I say. "You haven't abolished the gods, You've simply absorbed them into Yourself. If You choose to pass a miracle for me, Your prophet singer—and I will be Your prophet if You do this—why, that strengthens the faith of the rest."

"So you think. But your opinions aren't based on any exact data. The historical and anthropological records from the past before Me are unquantitative. I've already phased them out of the curriculum. Eventually, when the culture's ready for such a move, I'll order them destroyed. They're too misleading. Look what they've done to you."

I grin into the scanner eyes. "Instead," I say, "people will be encouraged to think that before the world was, was SUM. All right. I don't care, as long as I get my girl back. Pass me a miracle, SUM, and I'll guarantee You a good payment."

"But I have no miracles. Not in your sense. You know how the soul works. The metal bracelet encloses a pseudo-virus, a set of giant protein molecules with taps directly to the bloodstream and nervous system. They record the chromosome pattern, the synapse flash, the permanent changes, everything. At the owner's death, the bracelet is dissected out. The

Winged Heels bring it here, and the information contained is transferred to one of My memory banks. I can use such a record to guide the growing of a new body in the vats; a young body, on which the former habits and recollections are imprinted. But you don't understand the complexity of the process, Harper. It takes Me weeks, every seven years, and every available biochemical facility, to recreate My human liaison. And the process isn't perfect, either. The pattern is affected by storage. You might say that this body and brain you see before you remembers each death. And those are short deaths. A longer one—man, use your sense. Imagine."

I can; and the shield between reason and feeling begins to crack. I had sung, of my darling dead:

> *"No motion has she now, no force;*
> *She neither hears nor sees;*
> *Roll'd round in earth's diurnal course,*
> *With rocks, and stones, and trees."*

Peace, at last. But if the memory-storage is not permanent but circulating; if, within those gloomy caverns of tubes and wire and outer-space cold, some remnant of her psyche must flit and flicker, alone, unremembering, aware of nothing but having lost life— No!

I smite the harp and shout so the room rings: "Give her back! Or I'll kill You!"

SUM finds it expedient to chuckle; and, horribly, the smile is reflected for a moment on the Dark Queen's lips, though otherwise She never stirs. "And how do you propose to do that?" It asks me.

It knows, I know, what I have in mind, so I counter: "How do You propose to stop me?"

"No need. You'll be considered a nuisance. Someone will decide you ought to have psychiatric treatment. They'll query My diagnostic outlet. I'll recommend certain excisions."

"On the other hand, since You've sifted my mind by now, and since You know how I've affected people with my songs— even the Lady yonder, even Her—wouldn't you rather have me working for You? With words like, *'O taste, and see, how gracious the Lord is; blessed is the man that trusteth in him. O fear the Lord, ye that are his saints: for they that fear him lack nothing.'* I can make You into God."

"In a sense, I already am God."

"And in another sense not. Not yet." I can endure no more. "Why are we arguing? You made Your decision before I woke. Tell me and let me go!"

With an odd carefulness, SUM responds: "I'm still studying you. No harm in admitting to you. My knowledge of the human psyche is as yet imperfect. Certain areas won't yield to computation. I don't know precisely what you'd do, Harper. If to that uncertainty I added a potentially dangerous precedent—"

"Kill me, then." Let my ghost wander forever with hers, down in Your cryogenic dreams."

"No, that's also inexpedient. You've made yourself too conspicuous and controversial. Too many people know by now that you went off with the Lady." Is it possible that, behind steel and energy, a nonexistent hand brushes across a shadow face in puzzlement? My heartbeat is thick in the silence.

Suddenly It shakes me with decision: "The calculated probabilities do favor your keeping your promises and making yourself useful. Therefore I shall grant your request. However—"

I am on my knees. My forehead knocks on the floor until blood runs into my eyes. I hear through stormwinds:

"—testing must continue. Your faith in Me is not absolute; in fact, you're very skeptical of what you call My goodness. Without additional proof of your willingness to trust Me, I can't let you have the kind of importance which your getting your dead back from Me would give you. Do you understand?"

The question does not sound rhetorical. "Yes," I sob.

"Well, then," says my civilized, almost amiable voice, "I computed that you'd react much as you have done, and prepared for the likelihood. Your woman's body was recreated while you lay under study. The data which make personality are now being fed back into her neurones. She'll be ready to leave this place by the time you do.

"I repeat, though, there has to be a testing. The procedure is also necessary for its effect on you. If you're to be My prophet, you'll have to work pretty closely with Me; you'll have to undergo a great deal of reconditioning; this night we begin the process. Are you willing?"

"Yes, yes, yes, what must I do?"

"Only this: follow the robot out. At some point, she, your woman, will join you. She'll be conditioned to walk so quietly you can't hear her. Don't look back. Not once, until you're in the upper world. A single glance behind you will be an act of rebellion against Me, and a datum indicating you can't really be trusted . . . and that ends everything. Do you understand?"

"Is that all?" I cry. "Nothing more?"

"It will prove more difficult than you think," SUM tells me. My voice fades, as if into illimitable distances: "Farewell, worshiper."

The robot raises me to my feet. I stretch out my arms to the Dark Queen. Half blinded with tears, I nonetheless see that She does not see me. "Good-bye," I mumble, and let the robot lead me away.

Our walking is long through those murky miles. At first I am in too much of a turmoil, and later too stunned, to know where or how we are bound. But later still, slowly, I become aware of my flesh and clothes and the robot's alloy, glimmering blue in blackness. Sounds and smells are muffled; rarely does another machine pass by, unheeding of us. (What work does SUM have for them?) I am so careful not to look behind me that my neck grows stiff.

Though it is not prohibited, is it, to lift my harp past my shoulder, in the course of strumming a few melodies to keep up my courage, and see if a following illumination is reflected in this polished wood?

Nothing. Well, her second birth must take time—O SUM, be careful of her!—and then she must be led through many tunnels, no doubt, before she makes rendezvous with my back. Be patient, Harper.

Sing. Welcome her home. No, these hollow spaces swallow all music; and she is as yet in that trance of death from which only the Sun and my kiss can wake her; if indeed, she has joined me yet. I listen for other footfalls than my own.

Surely we haven't much further to go. I ask the robot, but of course I get no reply. Make an estimate. I know about how fast the chariot traveled coming down. . . . The trouble is, time does not exist here. I have no day, no stars, no clock but my heartbeat, and I have lost the count of that. Nevertheless, we must come to the end soon. What purpose would be served by walking me through this labyrinth till I die?

Well, if I am totally exhausted at the outer gate, I won't make undue trouble when I find no Rose-in-Hand behind me.

No, now that's ridiculous. If SUM didn't want to heed my plea, It need merely say so. I have no power to inflict physical damage on Its parts.

Of course, It might have plans for me. It did speak of reconditioning. A series of shocks, culminating in that last one, could make me ready for whatever kind of gelding It intends to do.

Or It might have changed Its mind. Why not? It was quite frank about an uncertainty factor in the human psyche. It may have reevaluated the probabilities and decided: better not to serve my desire.

Or It may have tried, and failed. It admitted the recording process is imperfect. I must not expect quite the Gladness I knew; she will always be a little haunted. At best. But suppose the tank spawned a body with no awareness behind the eyes? Or a monster? Suppose, at this instant, I am being followed by a half-rotten corpse?

No! Stop that! SUM would know, and take corrective measures. Would It? *Can It?*

I comprehend how this passage through night, where I never look to see what follows me, how this is an act of submission and confession. I am saying, with my whole existent being, that SUM is all-powerful, all-wise, all-good. To SUM I offer the love I came to win back. Oh, It looked more deeply into me than ever I did myself.

But I shall not fail.

Will SUM, though? If there has indeed been some grisly error . . . let me not find it out under the sky. Let her, my only, not. For what then shall we do? Could I lead her here again, knock on the iron gate, and cry, "Master, You have given me a thing unfit to exist. Destroy it and start over."—? For what might the wrongness be? Something so subtle, so pervasive, that it does not show in any way save my slow, resisted discovery that I embrace a zombie? Doesn't it make better sense to look—make certain while she is yet drowsy with death—use the whole power of SUM to correct what may be awry?

No, SUM wants me to believe that It makes no mistakes. I agreed to that price. And to much else . . . I don't know how much else, I am daunted to imagine, but that word "recondition" is ugly. . . . Does not my woman have some rights in the matter too? Shall we not at least ask her if she wants to be the wife of a prophet; shall we not, hand in hand, ask SUM what the price of her life is to her?

Was that a footfall? Almost, I whirl about. I check myself and stand shaking; names of hers break from my lips. The robot urges me on.

Imagination. It wasn't her step. I am alone. I will always be alone.

The halls wind upward. Or so I think; I have grown too weary for much kinesthetic sense. We cross the sounding river, and I am bitten to the bone by the cold which blows upward around the bridge, and I may not turn about to offer the naked newborn woman my garment. I lurch through endless chambers where machines do meaningless things. She hasn't seen them before. Into what nightmare has she risen; and why don't I, who wept into her dying senses that I loved her, why don't I look at her, why don't I speak?

Well, I could talk to her. I could assure the puzzled mute dead that I have come to lead her back into sunlight. Could I not? I ask the robot. It does not reply. I cannot remember if I may speak to her. If indeed I was ever told. I stumble forward.

I crash into a wall and fall bruised. The robot's claw closes on my shoulder. Another arm gestures. I see a passageway, very long and narrow, through the stone. I will have to crawl through. At the end, at the end, the door is swinging wide. The dear real dusk of Earth pours through into this darkness. I am blinded and deafened.

Do I hear her cry out? Was that the final testing; or was my own sick, shaken mind betraying me; or is there a destiny which, like SUM with us, makes tools of suns and SUM? I don't know. I know only that I turned, and there she stood. Her hair flowed long, loose, past the remembered face from which the trance was just departing, on which the knowing and the love of me had just awakened—flowed down over the body that reached forth arms, that took one step to meet me and was halted.

The great grim robot at her own back takes her to it. I think it sends lightning through her brain. She falls. It bears her away.

My guide ignores my screaming. Irresistible, it thrusts me out through the tunnel. The door clangs in my face. I stand before the wall which is like a mountain. Dry snow hisses across concrete. The sky is bloody with dawn; stars still gleam in the west, and arc lights are scattered over the twilit plain of the machines.

Presently I go dumb. I become almost calm. What is there left to have feelings about? The door is iron, the wall is stone fused into one basaltic mass. I walk some distance off into the wind, turn around, lower my head and charge. Let my brains be smeared across Its gate; the pattern will be my hieroglyphic for hatred.

I am seized from behind. The force that stops me must needs be bruisingly great. Released, I crumple to the ground before a machine with talons and wings. My voice from it says, "Not here. I'll carry you to a safe place."

"What more can You do to me?" I croak.

"Release you. You won't be restrained or molested on any orders of Mine."

"Why not?"

"Obviously you're going to appoint yourself My enemy forever. This is an unprecedented situation, a valuable chance to collect data."

"You tell me this, You warn me, deliberately?"

"Of course. My computation is that these words will have the effect of provoking your utmost effort."

"You won't give her again? You don't want my love?"

"Not under the circumstances. Too uncontrollable. But your hatred should, as I say, be a useful experimental tool."

"I'll destroy You," I say.

It does not deign to speak further. Its machine picks me up and flies off with me. I am left on the fringes of a small town further south. Then I go insane.

I do not much know what happens during that winter, nor care. The blizzards are too loud in my head. I walk the ways of Earth, among lordly towers, under neatly groomed trees, into careful gardens, over bland, bland campuses. I am unwashed, uncombed, unbarbered; my tatters flap about me and my bones are near thrusting through the skin; folks do not like to meet these eyes sunken so far into this skull, and perhaps for that reason they give me to eat. I sing to them.

> *"From the hag and hungry goblin*
> *That into rags would rend ye*
> *And the spirit that stan'd by the naked man*
> *In the Book of Moons defend ye!*

> *That of your five sound senses*
> *You never be forsaken*
> *Nor travel from yourselves with Tom*
> *Aboard to beg your bacon."*

Such things perturb them, do not belong in their chrome-edged universe. So I am often driven away with curses, and sometimes I must flee those who would arrest me and scrub my brain smooth. An alley is a good hiding place, if I can find one in the oldest part of a city; I crouch there and yowl with the cats. A forest is also good. My pursuers dislike any place where any wildness lingers.

But some feel otherwise. They have visited parklands, preserves, actual wildcountry. Their purpose was overconscious —measured, planned savagery, and a clock to tell them when they must go home—but at least they are not afraid of silences and unlighted nights. As spring returns, certain among them begin to follow me. They are merely curious, at first. But slowly, month by month, especially among the younger ones, my madness begins to call to something in them.

> *"With an host of furious fancies*
> *Whereof I am commander*
> *With a burning spear, and a horse of air,*
> *To the wilderness I wander.*
> *By a knight of ghosts and shadows*
> *I summoned am to tourney*
> *Ten leagues beyond the wide world's edge.*
> *Me thinks it is no journey."*

They sit at my feet and listen to me sing. They dance, crazily, to my harp. The girls bend close, tell me how I fascinate them, invite me to copulate. This I refuse, and when I tell them why, they are puzzled, a little frightened maybe, but often they strive to understand.

For my rationality is renewed with the hawthorn blossoms. I bathe, have my hair and beard shorn, find clean raiment, and take care to eat what my body needs. Less and less do I rave before anyone who will listen; more and more do I seek solitude, quietness, under the vast wheel of the stars, and think.

What is man? Why is man? We have buried such questions; we have sworn they are dead—that they never really existed, being devoid of empirical meaning—and we have dreaded that they might raise the stones we heaped on them, rise and walk the world again of nights. Alone, I summon them to me. They cannot hurt their fellow dead, among whom I now number myself.

I sing to her who is gone. The young people hear and wonder. Sometimes they weep.

> *"Fear no more the heat o' the sun,*
> *Nor the furious winter's rages;*
> *Thou thy wordly task hast done,*
> *Home art gone; and ta'en thy wages:*
> *Golden lads and girls all must*
> *As chimney-sweepers, come to dust."*

"But this is not so!" they protest. "We will die and sleep a while, and then we will live forever in SUM."

I answer as gently as may be: "No. Remember I went there. So I know you are wrong. And even if you were right, it would not be right that you should be right."

"What?"

"Don't you see, it is not right that a thing should be the lord of man. It is not right that we should huddle through our whole lives in fear of finally losing them. You are not parts in a machine, and you have better ends than helping the machine run smoothly."

I dismiss them and stride off, solitary again, into a canyon where a river clangs, or onto some gaunt mountain peak. No revelation is given me. I climb and creep toward the truth.

Which is that SUM must be destroyed, not in revenge, not in hate, not in fear, simply because the human spirit cannot exist in the same reality as It.

But what, then, is our proper reality? And how shall we attain to it?

I return with my songs to the lowlands. Word about me has gone widely. They are a large crowd who follow me down the highroad until it has changed into a street.

"The Dark Queen will soon come to these parts," they tell me. "Abide till She does. Let Her answer those questions you put to us, which makes us sleep so badly."

"Let me retire to prepare myself," I say. I got up a long flight of steps. The people watch from below, dumb with awe, till I vanish. Such few as were in the building depart. I walk down vaulted halls, through hushed high-ceilinged rooms full of tables, among shelves made massive by books. Sunlight slants dusty through the windows.

The half memory has plagued me of late: once before, I know not when, this year of mine also took place. Perhaps in this library I can find the tale that—casually, I suppose, in my abnormal childhood—I read. For man is older than SUM: wiser, I swear; his myths hold more truth than Its mathematics. I spend three days and most of three nights in my search. There is little sound but the rustling of leaves between my hands. Folk place offerings of food and drink at the door. They tell themselves they do so out of pity, or curiosity, or to avoid the nuisance of having me die in an unconventional fashion. But I know better.

At the end of the three days I am little further along. I have too much material; I keep going off on sidetracks of beauty and fascination. (Which SUM means to eliminate.) My education was like everyone else's, science, rationality, good sane adjustment. (SUM writes our curricula, and the teaching machines have direct connections to It.) Well, I can make some of my lopsided training work for me. My reading has given me sufficient clues to prepare a search program. I sit down before an information retrieval console and run my fingers across its keys. They make a clattery music.

Electron beams are swift hounds. Within seconds the screen lights up with words, and I read who I am.

It is fortunate that I am a fast reader. Before I can press the *CLEAR* button, the unreeling words are wiped out. For an instant the screen quivers with formlessness, then appears:

I HAD NOT CORRELATED THESE DATA WITH THE FACTS CONCERNING YOU. THIS INTRODUCES A NEW AND INDETERMINATE QUANTITY INTO THE COMPUTATIONS.

The nirvana which has come upon me (yes, I found that word among the old books, and how portentous it is) is not passiveness, it is a tide more full and strong than that which bore me down to the Dark Queen those ages apast in wildcountry. I say, as coolly as may be, "An interesting coincidence. If it is a coincidence." Surely sonic receptors are emplaced here.

EITHER THAT, OR A CERTAIN NECESSARY CONSEQUENCE OF THE LOGIC OF EVENTS.

The vision dawning within me is so blinding bright that I cannot refrain from answering, "Or a destiny, SUM?"

MEANINGLESS. MEANINGLESS. MEANINGLESS.

"Now why did You repeat Yourself in that way? Once would have sufficed. Thrice, though, makes an incantation. Are You by any chance hoping Your words will make me stop existing?"

I DO NOT HOPE. YOU ARE AN EXPERIMENT. IF I COMPUTE A SIGNIFICANT PROBABILITY OF YOUR CAUSING SERIOUS DISTURBANCE, I WILL HAVE YOU TERMINATED.

I smile. "SUM," I say, "I am going to terminate You." I lean over and switch off the screen. I walk out into the evening.

Not everything is clear to me yet, that I must say and do. But enough is that I can start preaching at once to those who have been waiting for me. As I talk, others come down the street, and hear, and stay to listen. Soon they number in the hundreds.

I have no immense new truth to offer them: nothing that I have not said before, although piecemeal and unsystematically; nothing they have not felt themselves, in the innermost darknesses of their beings. Today, however, knowing who I am and therefore why I am, I can put these things in words. Speaking quietly, now and then drawing on some forgotten song to show my meaning, I tell them how sick and starved their lives are; how they have made themselves slaves; how the enslavement is not even to a conscious mind, but to an insensate inanimate thing which their own ancestors began; how that thing is not the centrum of existence, but a few scraps of metal and bleats of energy, a few sad stupid patterns, adrift in unbounded space-time. Put not your faith in SUM, I tell them. SUM is doomed, even as you and I. Seek out mystery; what else is the whole cosmos but mystery? Live bravely, die and be done, and you will be more than any machine. You may perhaps be God.

They grow tumultuous. They shout replies, some of which are animal howls. A few are for me, most are opposed. That doesn't matter. I have reached into them, my music is being played on their nerve-strings, and this is my entire purpose.

The Sun goes down behind the buildings. Dusk gathers. The city remains unilluminated. I soon realize why. She is coming, the Dark Queen Whom they wanted me to debate with. From afar we hear Her chariot thunder. Folk wail in terror. They are not wont to do that either. They used to disguise their feelings from Her and themselves by receiving Her with grave, sparse ceremony. Now they would flee if they dared. I have lifted the masks.

The chariot halts in the street. She dismounts, tall and shadowy cowled. The people make way before Her like water before a shark. She climbs the stairs to face me. I see for the least instant that Her lips are not quite firm and Her eyes abrim with tears. She whispers, too low for anyone else to hear, "Oh, Harper, I'm sorry."

"Come join me," I invite. "Help me set the world free."

"No. I cannot. I have been too long with It." She straightens. Imperium descends upon Her. Her voice rises for everyone to hear. The little television robots flit close, bat shapes in the twilight, that the whole planet may witness my defeat. "What is this freedom you rant about?" She demands.

"To feel," I say. "To venture. To wonder. To become men again."

"To become beasts, you mean. Would you demolish the machines that keep us alive?"

"Yes. We must. Once they were good and useful, but we let them grow upon us like a cancer, and now nothing but destruction and a new beginning can save us."

"Have you considered the chaos?"

"Yes. It too is necessary. We will not be men without the freedom to know suffering. In it is also enlightenment. Through it we travel beyond ourselves, beyond Earth and stars, space and time, to Mystery."

"So you maintain that there is some undefined ultimate vagueness behind the measurable universe?" She smiles into the bat eyes. We have each been taught, as children, to laugh on hearing sarcasms of this kind. "Please offer me a little proof."

"No," I say. "Prove to me instead, beyond any doubt, that there is *not* something we cannot understand with words and equations. Prove to me likewise that I have no right to seek for it.

"The burden of proof is on You Two, so often have You lied to us. In the name of rationality, You resurrected myth. The better to control us! In the name of liberation, You chained our inner lives and castrated our souls. In the name of service, You bound and blinkered us. In the name of achievement, You held us to a narrower round than any swine in its pen. In the name of beneficence, You created pain, and horror, and darkness beyond darkness." I turn to the people. "I went there. I descended into the cellars. I know!"

"He found that SUM would not pander to his special wishes, at the expense of everyone else," cries the Dark Queen. Do I hear shrillness in Her voice? "Therefore he claims SUM is cruel."

"I saw my dead," I tell them. "She will not rise again. Nor yours, nor you. Not ever. SUM will not, cannot raise us. In Its house is death indeed. We must seek life and rebirth elsewhere, among the mysteries."

She laughs aloud and points to my soul bracelet, glimmering faintly in the gray-blue thickening twilight. Need She say anything?

"Will someone give me a knife and an ax?" I ask.

The crowd stirs and mumbles. I smell their fear. Street lamps go on, as if they could scatter more than this corner of the night which is rolling upon us. I fold my arms and wait. The Dark Queen says something to me. I ignore Her.

The tools pass from hand to hand. He who brings them up the stairs comes like a flame. He kneels at my feet and lifts what I have desired. The tools are good ones, a broad-bladed hunting knife and a long double-bitted ax.

Before the world, I take the knife in my right hand and slash beneath the bracelet on my left wrist. The connections to my inner body are cut. Blood flows, impossible brilliant under the lamps. It does not hurt; I am too exalted.

The Dark Queen shrieks. "You meant it! Harper, Harper!"

"There is no life in SUM," I say. I pull my hand through the circle and cast the bracelet down so it rings.

A voice of brass: *"Arrest that maniac for correction. He is deadly dangerous."*

The monitors who have stood on the fringes of the crowd try to push through. They are resisted. Those who seek to help them encounter fists and fingernails.

I take the ax and smash downward. The bracelet crumples. The organic material within, starved of my secretions, exposed to the night air, withers.

I raise the tools, ax in right hand, knife in bleeding left. "I seek eternity where it is to be found," I call. "Who goes with me?"

A score or better break loose from the riot, which is already calling forth weapons and claiming lives. They surround me with their bodies. Their eyes are the eyes of prophets. We make haste to seek a hiding place, for one military robot has appeared and others will not be long in coming. The tall engine strides to stand guard over Our Lady, and this is my last glimpse of Her.

My followers do not reproach me for having cost them all they were. They are mine. In me is the godhead which can do no wrong.

And the war is open, between me and SUM. My friends are few, my enemies many and mighty. I go about the world as a fugitive. But always I sing. And always I find someone who will listen, will join us, embracing pain and death like a lover.

With the Knife and the Ax I take their souls. Afterward we hold for them the ritual of rebirth. Some go thence to become outlaw missionaries; most put on facsimile bracelets and return home, to whisper my word. It makes little difference to me. I have no haste, who own eternity.

For my word is of what lies beyond time. My enemies say I call forth ancient bestialities and lunacies; that I would bring civilization down in ruin; that it matters not a madman's giggle to me whether war, famine, and pestilence will again scour the Earth. With these accusations I am satisfied. The language of them shows me that here, too, I have reawakened anger. And that emotion belongs to us as much as any other. More than the others, maybe, in this autumn of mankind. We need a gale, to strike down SUM and everything It stands for. Afterward will come the winter of barbarism.

And after that the springtime of a new and (perhaps) more human civilization. My friends seem to believe this will come in their very lifetimes: peace, brotherhood, enlightenment, sanctity. I know otherwise. I have been in the depths. The wholeness of mankind, which I am bringing back, has its horrors.

When one day
the Eater of the Gods returns
the Wolf breaks his chain
the Horsemen ride forth
the Age ends
the Beast is reborn

then SUM will be destroyed; and you, strong and fair, may go back to earth and rain.

I shall await you.

My aloneness is nearly ended, Daybright. Just one task remains. The god must die, that his followers may believe he is raised from the dead and lives forever. Then they will go on to conquer the world.

There are those who say I have spurned and offended them. They too, borne on the tide which I raised, have torn out their machine souls and seek in music and ecstasy to find a meaning for existence. But their creed is a savage one, which has taken them into wildcountry, where they ambush the monitors sent against them and practice cruel rites. They believe that the final reality is female. Nevertheless, messengers of theirs have approached me with the suggestion of a mystic marriage. This I refused; my wedding was long ago, and will be celebrated again when this cycle of the world has closed. Therefore they hate me. But I have said I will come and talk to them.

I leave the road at the bottom of the valley and walk singing up the hill. Those few I let come this far with me have been told to abide my return. They shiver in the sunset; the vernal equinox is three days away. I feel no cold myself. I stride exultant among briars and twisted ancient apple trees. If my bare feet leave a little blood in the snow, that is good. The ridges around are dark with forest, which waits like the skeleton dead for leaves to be breathed across it again. The eastern sky is purple, where stands the evening star. Overhead, against blue, cruises an early flight of homebound geese. Their calls drift faintly down to me. Westward, above me and before me, smolders redness. Etched black against it are the women.

THE MAN WHO WALKED HOME

JAMES TIPTREE, JR.

Selecting a story by Tiptree to be represented in this collection is hard, because just about all the stories this new writer has produced are original, talented, artistic and memorable. However, we chose this one because its presentation of time travel is realistically different.

—Transgression! Terror! And he thrust and lost there— punched into impossibility, abandoned, never to be known how, the wrong man in the most wrong of all wrong places in that unimaginable collapse of never-to-be-reimagined mechanism—he stranded, undone, his lifeline severed, he in that nanosecond knowing his only tether parting, going away, the longest line to life withdrawing, winking out, disappearing forever beyond his grasp—telescoping away from him into the closing vortex beyond which lay his home, his life, his only possibility of being; seeing it sucked back into the deepest

maw, melting, leaving him orphaned on what never-to-be-known shore of total wrongness—of beauty beyond joy, perhaps? Of horror? Of nothingness? Of profound otherness only, certainly whatever it was, that place into which he transgressed, certainly it could not support his life there, his violent and violating aberrance; and he, fierce, brave, crazy—clenched into one total protest, one body-fist of utter repudiation of himself there in that place, forsaken there—what did he do? Rejected, exiled, hungering homeward more desperate than any lost beast driving for its unreachable home, his home, his HOME—and no way, no transport, no vehicle, means, machinery, no force but his intolerable resolve aimed homeward along that vanishing vector, that last and only lifeline—he did, what?

He walked.

Home.

Precisely what hashed up in the work of the major industrial lessee of the Bonneville Particle Acceleration Facility in Idaho was never known. Or rather, all those who might have been able to diagnose the original malfunction were themselves obliterated almost at once in the greater catastrophe which followed.

The nature of this second cataclysm was not at first understood either. All that was ever certain was that at 1153.6 of May 2, 1989 Old Style, the Bonneville laboratories and all their personnel were transformed into an intimately disrupted form of matter resembling a high-energy plasma, which became rapidly airborne to the accompaniment of radiating seismic and atmospheric events.

The disturbed area unfortunately included an operational MIRV Watchdog bomb.

In the confusions of the next hours the Earth's population was substantially reduced, the biosphere was altered, and the Earth itself was marked with numbers of more conventional craters. For some years thereafter the survivors were existentially preoccupied and the peculiar dust bowl at Bonneville was left to weather by itself in the changing climatic cycles.

It was not a large crater; just over a kilometer in width and lacking the usual displacement lip. Its surface was covered with a finely divided substance which dried into dust. Before the rains began it was almost perfectly flat. Only in certain lights, had anyone been there to inspect it, a small surface marking or abraded place could be detected almost exactly at the center.

Two decades after the disaster a party of short brown people appeared from the south, together with a flock of somewhat atypical sheep. The crater at this time appeared as a wide shallow basin in which the grass did not grow well, doubtless from the almost complete lack of soil micro-organisms. Neither this nor the surrounding vigorous grass were found to harm the sheep. A few crude hogans went up at the southern edge and a faint path began to be traced across the crater itself, passing by the central bare spot.

One spring morning two children who had been driving sheep across the crater came screaming back to camp. A monster had burst out of the ground before them, a huge flat animal making a dreadful roar. It vanished in a flash and a shaking of the earth, leaving an evil smell. The sheep had run away.

Since this last was visibly true, some elders investigated. Finding no sign of the monster and no place in which it could hide, they settled for beating the children, who settled for making a detour around the monster-spot, and nothing more occurred for a while.

The following spring the episode was repeated. This time an older girl was present but she could add only that the monster seemed to be rushing flat out along the ground without moving at all. And there was a scraped place in the dirt. Again nothing was found; an evil-ward in a cleft stick was placed at the spot.

When the same thing happened for the third time a year later, the detour was extended and other charm-wands were added. But since no harm seemed to come of it and the brown people had seen far worse, sheep-tending resumed as before. A few more instantaneous apparitions of the monster were noted, each time in the spring.

At the end of the third decade of the new era a tall old man limped down the hills from the south, pushing his pack upon a bicycle wheel. He camped on the far side of the crater, and soon found the monster-site. He attempted to question people about it, but no one understood him, so he traded a knife for some meat. Although he was obviously feeble, something about him dissuaded them from killing him, and this proved wise because he later assisted the women to treat several sick children.

He spent much time around the place of the apparition and was nearby when it made its next appearance. This excited him very much, and he did several inexplicable but apparently harmless things, including moving his camp into the crater by the trail. He stayed on for a full year watching the site and was close by for its next manifestation. After this he spent a few days making a charmstone for the spot and then left, northward, hobbling, as he had come.

More decades passed. The crater eroded and a rain-gully became an intermittent steamlet across one edge of the basin. The brown people and their sheep were attacked by a band of grizzled men, after which the survivors went away eastward. The winters of what had been Idaho were now frost-free; aspen and eucalyptus sprouted in the moist plain. Still the crater remained treeless, visible as a flat bowl of grass, and the bare place at the center remained. The skies cleared somewhat.

After another three decades a larger band of black people with ox-drawn carts appeared and stayed for a time, but left again when they too saw the thunderclap-monster. A few other vagrants straggled by.

Five decades later a small permanent settlement had grown up on the nearest range of hills, from which men riding on small ponies with dark stripes down their spines herded humped cattle near the crater. A herdsman's hut was built by the streamlet, which in time became the habitation of an olive-skinned, red-haired family. In due course one of this clan again observed the monster-flash, but these people did not depart. The stone the tall man had placed was noted and left undisturbed.

The homestead at the crater's edge grew into a group of three and was joined by others, and the trail across it became a cartroad with a log bridge over the stream. At the center of the still-faintly-discernible crater the cartroad made a bend, leaving a grassy place which bore on its center about a square meter of curiously impacted bare earth and a deeply-etched sandstone rock.

The apparition of the monster was now known to occur regularly each spring on a certain morning in this place, and the children of the community dared each other to approach the spot. It was referred to in a phrase that could be translated as "the Old Dragon." The Old Dragon's appearance was always the same: a brief, violent thunderburst which began and cut off abruptly, in the midst of which a dragon-like creature was seen apparently in furious motion on the earth although it never actually moved. Afterward there was a bad smell and the earth smoked. People who saw it from close by spoke of a shivering sensation.

Early in the second century two young men rode into town from the north. Their ponies were shaggier than the local breed and the equipment they carried included two boxlike objects which the young men set up at the monster-site. They stayed in the area a full year, observing two materializations of the Old Dragon, and they provided much news and maps of roads and trading-towns in the cooler regions to the north. They built a windmill which was accepted by the community and offered to build a lighting machine, which was refused. Then they departed with their boxes after unsuccessfully attempting to persuade a local boy to learn to operate one.

In the course of the next decades other travelers stopped by and marveled at the monster, and there was sporadic fighting over the mountains to the south. One of the armed bands made a cattle-raid into the crater hamlet. It was repulsed, but the raiders left a spotted sickness which killed many. For all this time the bare place at the crater's center remained, and the monster made his regular appearances, observed or not.

The hill-town grew and changed and the crater hamlet grew to be a town. Roads widened and linked into networks. There were gray-green conifers in the hills now, spreading down into the plain, and chirruping lizards lived in their branches.

At century's end a shabby band of skin-clad squatters with stunted milk-beasts erupted out of the west and were eventually killed or driven away, but not before the local herds had contracted a vicious parasite. Veterinaries were fetched from the market-city up north, but little could be done. The families near the crater left, and for some decades the area was empty. Finally cattle of a new strain reappeared in the plain and the crater hamlet was reoccupied. Still the bare center continued annually to manifest the monster and he became an accepted phenomenon of the area. On several occasions parties came from the distant Northwest Authority to observe it.

The crater hamlet flourished and grew into the fields where cattle had grazed and part of the old crater became the town park. A small seasonal tourist industry based on the monster-site developed. The townspeople rented rooms for the appearances and many more-or-less authentic monster-relics were on display in the local taverns.

Several cults now grew up around the monster. Some held that it was a devil or damned soul forced to appear on Earth in torment to expiate the catastrophe of two centuries back. Others believed that it, or he, was some kind of messenger whose roar portended either doom or hope according to the believer. One very vocal sect taught that the apparition registered the moral conduct of the townspeople over the past year, and scrutinized the annual apparition for changes which could be interpreted for good or ill. It was considered lucky, or dangerous, to be touched by some of the dust raised by the monster. In every generation at least one small boy would try to hit the monster with a stick, usually acquiring a broken arm and a lifelong tavern tale. Pelting the monster with stones or other objects was a popular sport, and for some years people systematically flung prayers and flowers at it. Once a party tried to net it and were left with strings and vapor. The area itself had long since been fenced off at the center of the park.

Through all this the monster made his violently enigmatic annual appearance, sprawled furiously motionless, unreachably roaring.

Only as the fourth century of the new era went by was it apparent that the monster had been changing slightly. He was now no longer on the earth but had an arm and a leg thrust upward in a kicking or flailing gesture. As the years passed he began to change more quickly until at the end of the century he had risen to a contorted crouching pose, arms outflung as if frozen in gyration. His roar, too, seemed somewhat differently pitched and the earth after him smoked more and more.

It was then widely felt that the man-monster was about to do something, to make some definitive manifestation, and a series of natural disasters and marvels gave support to a vigorous cult teaching this doctrine. Several religious leaders journeyed to the town to observe the apparitions.

However, the decades passed and the man-monster did nothing more than turn slowly in place, so that he now appeared to be in the act of sliding or staggering while pushing himself backward like a creature blown before a gale. No wind, of course, could be felt, and presently the general climate quieted and nothing came of it all.

Early in the fifth century New Calendar three survey parties

from the North Central Authority came through the area
and stopped to observe the monster. A permanent recording
device was set up at the site, after assurances to the townfolk
that no hardscience was involved. A local boy was trained to
operate it; he quit when his girl left him but another volun-
teered. At this time nearly everyone believed that the apparition was a man, or the ghost of one. The record-machine boy
and a few others, including the school mechanics teacher, referred to him as The Man John. In the next decades the roads
were greatly improved; all forms of travel increased and there
was talk of building a canal to what had been the Snake River.

One May morning at the end of Century Five a young
couple in a smart green mule-trap came jogging up the highroad from the Sandreas Rift Range to the southwest. The
girl was golden-skinned and chatted with her young husband
in a language unlike that ever heard by the Man John either
at the end or the beginning of his life. What she said to him
has, however, been heard in every age and tongue.

"Oh Serli, I'm so glad we're taking this trip now! Next
summer I'll be so busy with baby."

To which Serli replied as young husbands often have, and
so they trotted up to the town's inn. Here they left trap and
bags and went in search of her uncle who was expecting them
there. The morrow was the day of the Man John's annual
appearance, and her Uncle Laban had come from the Mac-
Kenzie History Museum to observe it and to make certain
arrangements.

They found him with the town school instructor of mechanics, who was also the recorder at the monster-site.
Presently Uncle Laban took them all with him to the town
mayor's office to meet with various religious personages. The
mayor was not unaware of tourist values, but he took Uncle
Laban's part in securing the cultists' grudging assent to the
MacKenzie authorities' secular interpretation of the "monster," which was made easier by the fact that they disagreed
among themselves. Then, seeing how pretty the niece was, the
mayor took them all home to dinner.

When they returned to the inn for the night it was abrawl
with holiday makers.

"Whew," said Uncle Laban. "I've talked myself dry, sister's
daughter. What a weight of holy nonsense is that Morsha female! Serli, my lad, I know you have questions. Let me hand
you this to read; it's the guide book we're giving 'em to sell.

Tomorrow I'll answer for it all." And he disappeared into the crowded tavern.

So Serli and his bride took the pamphlet upstairs to bed with them, but it was not until the next morning at breakfast that they found time to read it.

" 'All that is known of John Delgano,' " read Serli with his mouth full, " 'comes from two documents left by his brother Carl Delgano in the archives of the MacKenzie Group in the early years after the holocaust.' Put some honey on this cake, Mira my dove. 'Verbatim transcript follows; this is Carl Delgano speaking.

" 'I'm not an engineer or an astronaut like John. I ran an electronics repair shop in Salt Lake City. John was only trained as a spaceman, he never got to space, the slump wiped all that out. So he tied up with this commercial group who were leasing part of Bonneville. They wanted a man for some kind of hard vacuum tests; that's all I knew about it. John and his wife moved to Bonneville, but we all got together several times a year, our wives were like sisters. John had two kids, Clara and Paul.

" 'The tests were all supposed to be secret, but John told me confidentially they were trying for an anti-gravity chamber. I don't know if it ever worked. That was the year before.

" 'Then that winter they came down for Christmas and John said they had something new. He was really excited. A temporal displacement, he called it; some kind of time effect. He said the chief honcho was like a real mad scientist. Big ideas. He kept adding more angles every time some other project would quit and leave equipment he could lease. No, I don't know who the top company was—maybe an insurance conglomerate, they had all the cash, didn't they? I guess they'd pay to catch a look at the future; that figures. Anyway, John was go, go, go. Katharine was scared; that's natural. She pictured him like, you know, H.G. Wells—walking around in some future world. John told her it wasn't like that at all. All they'd get would be this kind of flicker, like a second or two. All kinds of complications'—Yes, yes, my greedy piglet, some brew for me too. This is thirsty work!

"So . . . 'I remember I asked him, what about the Earth moving? I mean, you could come back in a different place, right? He said they had that all figured. A spatial trajectory. Katherine was so scared we dropped it. John told her, don't worry, I'll come home. But he didn't. Not that it makes any difference, of course; everything was wiped out. Salt Lake too. The only reason I'm here is that I went up by Calgary to see Mom, April twenty-ninth. May second it all blew. I didn't find you folks at Mackenzie until July. I guess I may as well stay. That's all I know about John, except that he was an all-right guy. If that accident started all this it wasn't his fault.

" 'The second document'—In the name of love, little mother, do I have to read all this! Oh very well; but you will kiss me first, madam. Must you look so ineffable? . . . 'The second document. Dated in the year eighteen, New Style, writter by Carl'—see the old handwriting, my plump pigeon. Oh, very well, very well.

" 'Written at Bonneville Crater. I have seen my brother John Delgano. When I knew I had the rad sickness I came down here to look around. Salt Lake's still hot. So I hiked up here by Bonneville. You can see the crater where the labs were; it's grassed over. It's different, it's not radioactive, my film's OK. There's a bare place in the middle. Some Indios here told me a monster shows up here every year in the spring. I saw it myself a couple of days after I got here but I was too far away to see much, except I was sure it's a man. In a vacuum suit. There was a lot of noise and dust, took me by surprise. It was all over in a second. I figure it's pretty close to the day, I mean, May second, old.

" 'So I hung around a year and he showed up again yester-day. I was on the face side and I could see his face through the faceplate. It's John all right. He's hurt. I saw blood on his mouth and his suit is frayed some. He's lying on the ground. He didn't move while I could see him but the dust boiled up, like a man sliding onto base without moving. His eyes are open like he was looking. I don't understand it anyway, but I know it's John, not a ghost. He was in exactly the same position each time and there's a loud crack like thunder and another sound like a siren, very fast. And an ozone smell, and smoke. I felt a kind of shudder.

" 'I know it's John there and I think he's alive. I have to leave here now to take this back while I can still walk. I think somebody should come here and see. Maybe you can help John. Signed, Carl Delgano.

" 'These records were kept by the Mackenzie Group but it was not for several years—' Etcetera, first light-print, etcetera, archives, analysts, etcetera—very good! Now it is time to meet your uncle, my edible one, after we go upstairs for just a moment."

"No, Serli, I will wait for you downstairs," said Mira prudently.

When they came into the town park Uncle Laban was directing the installation of a large durite slab in front of the enclosure around the Man John's appearance-spot. The slab was wrapped in a curtain to await the official unveiling. Townspeople and tourists and children thronged the walks and a Ride-For-Good choir was singing in the bandshell. The morning was warming up fast. Vendors hawked ices and straw toys of the monster and flowers and good-luck confetti to throw at him. Another religious group stood by in dark robes; they belonged to the Repentance church beyond the park. Their pastor was directing somber glares at the crowd in general and Mira's uncle in particular.

Three official-looking strangers who had been at the inn came up and introduced themselves to Uncle Laban as observers from Alberta Central. They went on into the tent which had been erected over the enclosure, carrying with them several pieces of equipment which the town-folk eyed suspiciously.

The mechanics teacher finished organizing a squad of students to protect the slab's curtain, and Mira and Serli and Laban went on into the tent. It was much hotter inside. Benches were set in rings around a railed enclosure about twenty feet in diameter. Inside the railing the earth was bare and scuffed. Several bunches of flowers and blooming poinciana branches leaned against the rail. The only thing inside the rail was a rough sandstone rock with markings etched on it.

Just as they came in a small girl raced across the open center and was yelled at by everybody. The officials from Alberta were busy at one side of the rail, where the light-print box was mounted.

"Oh, no," muttered Mira's uncle, as one of the officials leaned over to set up a tripod stand inside the rails. He adjusted it and a huge horsetail of fine feathery filaments blossomed out and eddied through the center of the space.

"Oh *no*," Laban said again. "Why can't they let it be?"

"They're trying to pick up dust from his suit, is that right?" Serli asked.

"Yes, insane. Did you get time to read?"

"Oh yes," said Serli.

"Sort of," added Mira.

"Then you know. He's falling. Trying to check his—well, call it velocity. Trying to slow down. He must have slipped or stumbled. We're getting pretty close to when he lost his footing and started to fall. What did it? Did somebody trip him?" Laban looked from Mira to Serli, dead serious now. "How would you like to be the one who made John Delgano fall?"

"Ooh," said Mira in quick sympathy. Then she said, "Oh."

"You mean," asked Serli, "whoever made him fall caused all the, caused—"

"Possible," said Laban.

"Wait a minute," Serli frowned. "He did fall. So somebody had to do it—I mean, he has to trip or whatever. If he doesn't fall the past would all be changed, wouldn't it? No war, no—"

"Possible," Laban repeated. "God knows. All *I* know is that John Delgano and the space around him is the most unstable, improbable, highly charged area ever known on Earth and I'm damned if I think anybody should go poking sticks in it."

"Oh come now, Laban!" One of the Alberta men joined them, smiling. "Our dust-mop couldn't trip a gnat. It's just vitreous monofilaments."

"Dust from the future," grumbled Laban. "What's it going to tell you? That the future has dust in it?"

"If we could only get a trace from that thing in his hand."

"In his hand?" asked Mira. Serli started leafing hurriedly through the pamphlet.

"We've had a recording analyzer aimed at it," the Albertan lowered his voice, glancing around. "A spectroscope. We know there's something there, or was. Can't get a decent reading. It's severely deteriorated."

"People poking at him, grabbing at him," Laban muttered. "You—"

"*Ten minutes!*" shouted a man with a megaphone. "Take your places, friends and strangers."

The Repentance people were filing in at one side, intoning an ancient incantation, "mi-seri-cordia, ora pro nobis!"

The atmosphere suddenly took on tension. It was now very close and hot in the big tent. A boy from the mayor's office wiggled through the crowd, beckoning Laban's party to come and sit in the guest chairs on the second level on the "face" side. In front of them at the rail one of the Repentance ministers was arguing with an Albertan official over his right to occupy the space taken by a recorder, it being his special duty to look into the Man John's eyes.

"Can he really see us?" Mira asked her uncle.

"Blink your eyes," Laban told her. "A new scene every blink, that's what he sees. Phantasmagoria. Blink-blink-blink— for god knows how long."

"Mi-sere-re, pec-cavi," chanted the penitentials. A soprano neighed "May the red of sin pa-aa-ass from us!"

"They believe his oxygen tab went red because of the state of their souls." Laban chuckled. "Their souls are going to have to stay damned a while; John Delgano has been on oxygen reserve for five centuries—or rather, he *will be* low for five centuries more. At a half-second per year his time, that's fifteen minutes. We know from the audio trace he's still breathing more or less normally and the reserve was good for twenty minutes. So they should have their salvation about the year seven hundred, if they last that long."

"*Five minutes!* Take your seats, folks. Please sit down so everyone can see. Sit down, folks."

"It says we'll hear his voice through his suit speaker," Serli whispered. "Do you know what he's saying?"

"You get mostly a twenty-cycle howl," Laban whispered back. "The recorders have spliced up something like *ayt*, part of an old word. Take centuries to get enough to translate."

"Is it a message?"

"Who knows? Could be his word for 'date' or 'hate.' 'Too late,' maybe. Anything."

The tent was quieting. A fat child by the railing started to cry and was pulled back onto a lap. There was a subdued mumble of praying. The Holy Joy faction on the far side rustled their flowers.

"Why don't we set our clocks by him?"

"It's changing. He's on sidereal time."

"*One minute.*"

In the hush the praying voices rose slightly. From outside a chicken cackled. The bare center space looked absolutely ordinary. Over it the recorder's silvery filaments eddied gently in the breath from a hundred lungs. Another recorder could be heard ticking faintly.

For long seconds nothing happened.

The air developed a tiny hum. At the same moment Mira caught a movement at the railing on her left.

The hum developed a beat and vanished into a peculiar silence and suddenly everything happened at once.

Sound burst on them, raced shockingly up the audible scale. The air cracked as something rolled and tumbled in the space. There was a grinding, wailing roar and—

He was there.

Solid, huge—a huge man in a monster suit, his head was a dull bronze transparent globe holding a human face, dark smear of open mouth. His position was impossible, legs strained forward thrusting himself back, his arms frozen in a whirlwind swing. Although he seemed to be in a frantic forward motion nothing moved, only one of his legs buckled or sagged slightly—

—And then he was gone, utterly and completely gone in a thunderclap, leaving only the incredible afterimage in a hundred pairs of staring eyes. Air boomed, shuddering, dust roiled out mixed with smoke.

"Oh, oh my God," gasped Mira, unheard, clinging to Serli. Voices were crying out, choking. "He saw me, he saw me!" a woman shrieked. A few people dazedly threw their confetti into the empty dust-cloud; most had failed to throw at all. Children began to howl. "He *saw* me!" the woman screamed hysterically. "Red, Oh Lord have mercy!" a deep male voice intoned.

Mira heard Laban swearing furiously and looked again into the space. As the dust settled she could see that the recorder's tripod had tipped over into the center. There was a dusty mound lying against it—flowers. Most of the end of the stand seemed to have disappeared or been melted. Of the filaments nothing could be seen.

"Some damn fool pitched flowers into it. Come on, let's get out."

"Was it under, did it trip him?" asked Mira, squeezed in the crowd.

"It was still red, his oxygen thing," Serli said over her head. "No mercy this trip, eh, Laban?"

"Shsh!" Mira caught the Repentance pastor's dark glance. They jostled through the enclosure gate and were out in the sunlit park, voices exclaiming, chattering loudly in excitement and relief.

"It was terrible," Mira cried softly. "Oh, I never thought it was a real live man. There he is, he's *there*. Why can't we help him? Did we trip him?"

"I don't know; I don't think so," her uncle grunted. They sat down near the new monument, fanning themselves. The curtain was still in place.

"Did we change the past?" Serli laughed, looked lovingly at his little wife. He wondered for a moment why she was wearing such odd earrings. Then he remembered he had given them to her at that Indian pueblo they'd passed.

"But it wasn't just those Alberta people," said Mira. She seemed obsessed with the idea. "It was the flowers really." She wiped at her forehead.

"Mechanics or superstition," chuckled Serli. "Which is the culprit, love or science?"

"Shsh." Mira looked about nervously. "The flowers were love, I guess . . . I feel so strange. It's hot. Oh, thank you." Uncle Laban had succeeded in attracting the attention of the iced-drink vendor.

People were chatting normally now and the choir struck into a cheerful song. At one side of the park a line of people were waiting to sign their names in the visitors' book. The mayor appeared at the park gate, leading a party up the bougainvillea alley for the unveiling of the monument.

"What did it say on that stone by his foot?" Mira asked. Serli showed her the guidebook picture of Carl's rock with the inscription translated below: WELCOME HOME JOHN.

"I wonder if he can see it."

The mayor was about to begin his speech.

Much later when the crowd had gone away the monument stood alone in the dark, displaying to the moon the inscription in the language of that time and place:

ON THIS SPOT THERE APPEARS ANNUALLY THE FORM OF MAJOR JOHN DELGANO, THE FIRST AND ONLY MAN TO TRAVEL IN TIME.

MAJOR DELGANO WAS SENT INTO THE FUTURE SOME HOURS BEFORE THE HOLOCAUST OF DAY ZERO. ALL KNOWLEDGE OF THE MEANS BY WHICH HE WAS SENT IS LOST, PERHAPS FOREVER. IT IS BELIEVED THAT AN ACCIDENT OCCURRED WHICH SENT HIM MUCH FARTHER THAN WAS INTENDED. SOME ANALYSTS SPECULATE THAT HE MAY HAVE GONE AS FAR AS FIFTY THOUSAND YEARS AHEAD. HAVING REACHED THIS UNKNOWN POINT MAJOR DELGANO APPARENTLY WAS RECALLED, OR ATTEMPTED TO RE-

TURN, ALONG THE COURSE IN SPACE AND TIME THROUGH WHICH
HE WAS SENT. HIS TRAJECTORY IS THOUGHT TO START AT THE
POINT WHICH OUR SOLAR SYSTEM WILL OCCUPY AT A FUTURE
TIME AND IS TANGENT TO THE COMPLEX HELIX WHICH OUR
EARTH DESCRIBES AROUND THE SUN.

HE APPEARS ON THIS SPOT IN THE ANNUAL INSTANTS IN
WHICH HIS COURSE INTERSECTS OUR PLANET'S ORBIT AND HE
IS APPARENTLY ABLE TO TOUCH THE GROUND IN THOSE IN-
STANTS. SINCE NO TRACE OF HIS PASSAGE INTO THE FUTURE
HAS BEEN MANIFESTED, IT IS BELIEVED THAT HE IS RETURNING
BY A DIFFERENT MEANS THAN HE WENT FORWARD. HE IS ALIVE
IN OUR PRESENT. OUR PAST IS HIS FUTURE AND OUR FUTURE IS
HIS PAST. THE TIME OF HIS APPEARANCES IS SHIFTING GRADU-
ALLY IN SOLAR TIME TO CONVERGE ON THE MOMENT OF 1153.6
ON MAY 2ND 1989 OLD STYLE, OR DAY ZERO.

THE EXPLOSION WHICH ACCOMPANIED HIS RETURN TO HIS
OWN TIME AND PLACE MAY HAVE OCCURRED WHEN SOME ELE-
MENTS OF THE PAST INSTANTS OF HIS COURSE WERE CARRIED
WITH HIM INTO THEIR OWN PRIOR EXISTENCE. IT IS CERTAIN
THAT THIS EXPLOSION PRECIPITATED THE WORLDWIDE HOLO-
CAUST WHICH ENDED FOREVER THE AGE OF HARDSCIENCE.

*—He was falling, losing control, failing in his fight against
the terrible momentum he had gained, fighting with his human
legs shaking in the inhuman stiffness of his armor, his soles
charred, not gripping well now, not enough traction to brake,
battling, thrusting as the flashes came, the punishing alterna-
tion of light, dark, light, dark, which he had borne so long,
the claps of air thickening and thinning against his armor as he
skidded through space which was time, desperately braking
as the flickers of earth hammered against his feet—only his
feet mattered now, only to slow and stay on course—and the
pull, the beacon was getting slacker; as he came near home it
was fanning out, hard to stay centered; he was becoming, he
supposed, more probable; the wound he had punched in time
was healing itself. In the beginning it had been so tight—a
single ray in a closing tunnel—he had hurled himself after it
like an electron flying to the anode, aimed surely along that
exquisitely complex single vector of possibility of life, shot
and been shot like a squeezed pip into the last chink in that
rejecting and rejected nowhere through which he, John Delgano, could continue to exist, the hole leading to
home—had pounded down it across time, across space, pump-*

ing with his human legs as the real Earth of that unreal time
came under him, his course as certain as the twisting dash
of an animal down its burrow, he a cosmic mouse on an interstellar, intertemporal race for his nest with the wrongness of
everything closing round the rightness of that one course, the
atoms of his heart, his blood, his every well crying Home—
HOME!—as he drove himself after that fading breath-hole,
each step faster, surer, stronger, until he raced with invincible
momentum upon the rolling flickers of Earth as a man might
race a rolling log in a torrent! Only the stars stayed constant
around him from flash to flash, he looked down past his feet
at a million strobes of Crux, of Triangulum; once at the height
of his stride he had risked a century's glance upward and
seen the Bears weirdly strung out from Polaris—But a Polaris
not the Pole Star now, he realized, jerking his eyes back to his
racing feet, thinking, I am walking home to Polaris, home!
to the strobing beat. He had ceased to remember where he had
been, the beings, people or aliens or things he had glimpsed
in the impossible moment of being where he could not be;
had ceased to see the flashes of worlds around him, each flash
different, the jumble of bodies, walls, landscapes, shapes, and
colors beyond deciphering—some lasting a breath, some
changing pell-mell—the faces, limbs, things poking at him;
the nights he had pounded through, dark or lit by strange
lamps; roofed or unroofed; the days flashing sunlight, gales,
dust, snow, interiors innumerable, strobe after strobe into night
again; he was in daylight now, a hall of some kind; I am
getting closer at last, he thought, the feel is changing—but he
had to slow down, to check; and that stone near his feet, it
had stayed there some time now, he wanted to risk a look
but he did not dare, he was so tired, and he was sliding, was
going out of control, fighting to kill the merciless velocity that
would not let him slow down; he was hurt, too, something
had hit him back there, they had done something, he didn't
know what back somewhere in the kaleidoscope of faces, arms,
hooks, beams, centuries of creatures grabbing at him—and his
oxygen was going, never mind, it would last—it had to last,
he was going home, home! And he had forgotten now the
message he had tried to shout, hoping it could be picked up
somehow, the important thing he had repeated; and the thing
he had carried, it was gone now, his camera was gone too,
something had torn it away—but he was coming home! Home!
If only he could kill this momentum, could stay on the failing

course, could slip, scramble, slide, somehow ride this avalanche down to home, to home—and his throat said Home!—said Kate, Kate! And his heart shouted, his lungs almost gone now, as his legs fought, fought and failed, as his feet gripped and skidded and held and slid, as he pitched, flailed, pushed, strove in the gale of timerush across space, across time, at the end of the longest path ever: the path of John Delgano, coming home.

OH, VALINDA!

MICHAEL G. CONEY

Changing residence from one island on one edge of the Western hemisphere (Antigua) to another at the other edge (Vancouver) may be part of that spiral which is bringing this high talent to the top of current science fiction writers. Coney's first novel, MIRROR IMAGE, was published in 1972 and he will have three more equally striking ones in 1973, if all go according to plan. Here, in this unusual story we see again his talent for human characterization amid alien surroundings —that still retain a relationship to the problems of our own modern Earth.

The rigid wind hissed around Skunder's helmet as he stood, shivering despite the protection of thick fur, on the blinding Cantek ice cap. Powdery snow was drifting about his boots and he shuffled nervously, watching the two Earthmen as they fiddled with their instruments, clumsy with gloved hands.

The shorter of the two men, the captain, spoke. "There's a definite trace down here. Right below us, depth about three hundred feet, I reckon. A big one."

"You sure?" the other, taller man queried; his voice was cynical as always. "I mean, we'd look silly if we drifted out to sea on an unpropelled floe, Erkelens."

"Rosskidd"—the short man's voice was deliberately patient —"I've been transporting floes for a few years now. I know a trace when I see one." He indicated the screen. "See that shadow?" The two men crouched over the large rectangular box. "That's a bergworm, about four hundred yards long. A good worm."

Rosskidd chuckled dryly. "I suppose you can tell me which end the head's at?"

Erkelens glanced around, his gaze taking in the dazzling snowfields rising with distance into the blue haze of the floating polar ice-mountains. Turning, he regarded the ocean, gray and silver and raw, tossing from the horizon toward them, disappearing from sight beneath the edge of the glacial cliff some forty yards away. He moved back to the screen and indicated with a gloved finger.

"That's the head," he stated definitely. "Facing northeast, against the flow of current."

Skunder, still silently watching them, wondered why these Earthmen always insisted on placing such faith in their electronic gear. He, Skunder, a native-born Cantek—he *knew* the bergworm was down there. He had told them where to look. As soon as the helicopter passed over this spot, he had sensed the presence of the giant marine worm; sensed it as a tingling in his bones, a nervous void in his stomach. Sensed the obscene warm fatness of phosphorescent death buried deep within the ice, pulsing, drawing in huge quantities of water, filtering out plankton and larger fish, jetting out the torrent of denatured water from its monstrous anal opening. Hanging in the underside of the floating ice cap like an inverted U; its phosphorus-rich body cooled, its cavernous mouth questing free and murderous in the dark water. Skunder shuddered.

"You, Cantek . . . Skunder. Set up the tent."

He untied, unwrapped and laid out flat the flaccid folds of pink polythene and awkwardly screwed in the nozzle. As the two Earthmen moved away to survey their new property he jerked the stiff lever and air hissed, the tent rising and crackling, soon standing taut and dome-shaped like a mature breast on the niveous body of the snow-plain.

Skunder grinned to himself. From time to time he would be amazed at the technological supremacy of Earth over Cantek; the plastics, the atomics, the mere perfection of machinery. And then he would think to himself: yet they need *me* to control the bergworm. So he would smile and for a moment himself feel superior, despite knowledge of his home planet's oil-based economy and polluted seas.

But they were clever, these Earthmen who had bought the option on the Cantek polar ice cap a century ago. They had been farsighted, their judgment based on experience of their own world; while Cantek had laughed and sold what it thought was a useless waste of floating ice.

Skunder shrugged and carried the equipment and provisions into the tent, stowing them neatly, setting up the two beds. Himself, he preferred to sleep outside in a minidome, away from the company of the two men who mostly ignored him, thereby making his loneliness more intense.

Oh, Valinda . . .

So he set up his minidome and walked over to where Erkelens and Rosskidd had begun to drill and the ice was fountaining steam as the laser beam sank deep. To act as general laborer was a part of the deal and the men of Earth paid well.

Rosskidd looked up. "Ah, Cantek. You can drop the charges in. Make sure they go right to the bottom. Follow us along with the leads. Mind you don't break any. Got that?"

"Skunder's done this before," said Erkelens mildly.

"No doubt, but I'm an explosives expert, Skipper. That's why you hired me, remember? After that trouble you had last trip, when you split the berg and killed the worm . . . I'm not blaming you, but you've got to watch Canteks all the way, or they'll fall down on the job. I know."

In the course of the next few hours they drilled innumerable shafts deep in the ice, delineating an area roughly one hundred yards square based on the estimated size of the worm beneath. Skunder followed behind, dropping the charges, trailing the wire. At last they were finished; they returned to the dome and connected up the control unit.

Erkelens glanced at the sky. Cantek's yellow sun was

well above the horizon; the long polar day would last for a few more weeks. "No point in doing too much," he said. "We'll turn in for a while. Detonate in six hours."

Rosskidd yawned; in the warmth of the dome he had removed his top clothing and stood bearlike and hairy in long underpants. Skunder suppressed his distaste for the uncouth, animal appearance of the man and said good night politely, stepping through the lock to the snow. Erkelens muttered tiredly but there was no reply from Rosskidd. Skunder hadn't expected one. He crawled into his minidome and slept.

He was awakened within an hour by a harsh chattering from above. Pushing his head through the flap of the dome, he looked up. Stark against the blue mist of the sky was the dragonfly outline of a helicopter whirling west. He withdrew into the tent and tried to sleep again but his thoughts were whirling with the rotor blades in a vortex of hate. It was not the chartered helicopter which had brought them here. He had recognized the white insignia on the underbelly of the machine, however; the image remained on his retina for several hours.

Asleep at last, it seemed only minutes before he was awakened again by a rough hand on his shoulder. He opened his eyes wearily; Rosskidd was bending over him, his face unshaven and expressionless with contempt.

"You. Up."

Skunder rolled his legs off the bed, stood, and already fully dressed, followed the Earthman out of the dome. Erkelens was emerging from the larger dome, dragging the detonating equipment. He glanced at them briefly, then scanned the horizon.

"Everything ready?" he queried, a note of uncertainty in his voice. There was something very final, irreversible, about the operation of blasting clear.

Rosskidd looked at him. "All ready," he said.

"Right." Erkelens depressed a button and the ice trembled as the charges fired one by one at microsecond intervals. Little puffs of snow rose in a rectangular mist around the camp, apparently simultaneously. The three men waited, not looking at each other, standing square on the ice and waiting for their feet to tell them whether the operation had been successful.

"We're free," said Erkelens with relief as he detected motion beneath him. Imperceptibly, the ice was rocking.

Grinding noises began, rose to tortured shrieks as the new berg began to move clear of the ice cap. "Start cutting the control shaft, Skunder." He disconnected the detonator and dragged it back into the dome.

Skunder wheeled the pump and laser to the seaward end of the new berg. He erected the laser drill downward-directed, hung from a tripod, and set the control to throw a beam two feet wide by a thousandth of an inch thick. He flicked the switch and checked the rotary propulsion unit with a test circuit. The two-foot thread of light focused on the ice and described a slow radius. Soon Skunder was standing beside a neat circular pool of steaming water, four foot six in diameter. He started the synchronized pump and watched as the ribbon of steam circled the flexible six-inch pipe. Satisfied, he relaxed as the unit drove the shaft rapidly downward, the generator puttering evenly, the water flowing from the outlet of the pump, away across the snow.

He walked back to the camp. Erkelens and Rosskidd were preparing breakfast on a portable stove; a whiff of bacon arose.

"I saw Lejour's helicopter last night," Skunder said.

The effect of his remark was immediate. Erkelens sprang to his feet, upsetting the frying pan.

"Where? Which way was he headed?"

"West."

"West. God . . ." Erkelens stared at Rosskidd. "He could be on the same run as us. He could be going to Alkar. It's the only sizeable city in this direction."

"We've got a start on him."

"Not if he's blasting free downcoast, we haven't. He's taking the shortest route. We've got to follow the ice cap for thirty miles before we strike off across the Polar Sea. I thought we'd got plenty of time; I was more interested in finding a good worm. If Lejour's already got a worm lined up . . . He'll be ahead by the time we reach his departure point."

"So if he beats us to Alkar, he gets the best market," Rosskidd said slowly. "We have to take a giveaway price. And we can't hang around bargaining, with the berg melting under us in the warmer waters."

"Christ." Erkelens slumped to his collapsible chair, threw the spilled bacon back into the pan and stirred it moodily.

"We have a good worm," Skunder ventured. "We can beat him."

"I hope so." Rosskidd looked at the Cantek meaningly.

Skunder decided he would be better out of the picture, so he muttered something about seeing to the laser and walked quickly away.

The hole was deep, the bottom out of sight in a mist of steam. He watched for a while, his thoughts straying, then felt the unmistakable distant jolt as the bergworm sensed the presence of the approaching laser beam. He switched off, removed the tripod, strapped the smaller, portable laser on his back and threw the collapsible ladder down the shaft. He began to descend.

At the foot of the shaft the flexible pipe was sucking air, a noisy gobbling sound. He shrugged the laser from his back, thumbed the switch and began to enlarge the shaft into a chamber, his breathing harsh in the steamy atmosphere. When he had melted enough ice to permit free movement he drove away to one side, playing the laser on the glittering ice-wall, kicking the hose before him as he moved forward. He drove a narrow tunnel about twenty feet horizontally into the ice, then began to slope downward, gradually doubling back, to run parallel to, but many feet below his original course.

An hour later he could make out a dark shadow beyond the scintillating reflections of the laser beam. He turned the instrument to low output and carefully melted away the remaining ice, exposing a rough leathery wall at the extremity of the tunnel.

This was the flank of the giant bergworm. He tried a full-power pulse. The hide contracted, the flesh bubbled. The berg lurched, a vast heave under his feet. The worm was a good one, huge and strong.

Skunder shuddered.

He crawled back to the chamber at the foot of the shaft and repeated the operation, driving a tunnel to the opposite flank of the worm. He tested the creature's reactions then, satisfied, climbed the ladder and eventually emerged into daylight.

Erkelens and Rosskidd were waiting for him.

"Everything OK?" Erkelens' face was lined with anxiety.

"Fine. It's a good worm. We'll be all right."

He looked around. They had left the ice cap and were

drifting in the open sea. Behind them yawned the gap in the glacier, a behemoth's bite.

"There is no right of property in a floating berg." Erkelens sat outside the dome on a folding chair, oiling his rifle, watching the shimmering cliffs slide by. "Once it has left the ice cap, possession is what counts. Occupancy."

"Scared of piracy?" Rosskidd glanced at the gray horizon.

"Of Lejour. He's got more resources than me. He can pull some queer tricks, and he's got the cash to back them up. He can afford his own helicopter—and you ought to see his submarine. It's a bit different from that can over there."

He indicated the small craft hanging from automatic davits at the lip of the berg. A patched ovoid of gray metal, it measured some twenty feet in length and contained cramped accommodation for one man in dangerous proximity to an ancient miniature reactor.

Skunder's eyes followed Erkelens' finger and his heart constricted at the thought of the claustrophobic blackness within.

The image remained with him as he made his way to the control shaft to correct a slight course deviation. As he played the laser at low power on the tough hide of the worm, he imagined the huge head swinging below the dark water, swinging to the right as the beast's muscles contracted in response to the heat irritant. He imagined the cavernous mouth sucking, blindly questing for sustenance in the depths.

He remembered Valinda.

He remembered Lejour ("Get down there, you Cantek, and find out what's wrong—I don't want to see you back until we're moving again.") and Valinda as she stood beside him, holding his hand as the Earthman raved about loss of profits for late delivery, inefficiency of his Cantek worm expert; while the berg heaved idly on the gray sea. So he and Valinda climbed into the midget submarine and swung wildly out from the face of the berg while Lejour overrode the automatic, freewheeling the davits with heedless speed.

He remembered the jarring impact as they hit the water, the sudden blackness in the viewport turning to abrupt viridescence when he switched on the floodlights and illuminated the side of the berg as they sank slowly. He remembered Valinda's hand on his in a tender attempt to quell his uncontrollable trembling ("Don't let him get you down, darling;

just remember the bonus at the end of this trip.") And his feeling of gratitude because she *knew* he was shivering from fear, not anger.

And then the sight of the bergworm . . . oozing segmented from the base of the berg like a monster maggot, glowing phosphorescent in the black water, a gigantic tube of mindless evil. Hanging low, too low; two thirds of its tunnel it was preparing, for unknown reasons, to quit the berg.

It had to be driven back. The head had to be forced upward and backward; the brute's present forward creep through the berg had to be reversed. Hovering with Valinda in the midget submarine, he released oxygen from the forward vents and watched as the bubbles were drawn into the maw of the worm. They disappeared and the mouth gaped further in a silent roar of pain as the gas coursed through the phosphorus-rich body. But it did not retreat.

He remembered his sudden shock when he found that Valinda was no longer beside him. Knowing that he would have refused her, she had taken the initiative; he felt the click as the airlock closed and he moved too late to stop her. Presently her rubber-suited figure appeared in the viewport, moving steadily toward the bergworm, drifting fast in the current of inhaled water. In one hand she held a jetpack, the straps swinging loose; in the other hand, a small mine.

She reached the lip of the worm's mouth and hung there, a tiny black figure in the nightmare phosphorescence, while she pulled the lever which sank barbs deep into the coarse flesh at the same time arming the mine. Then she began to swim back, kicking strongly with her legs against the current, the jet pack streaming bubbles as she hugged it to her breast.

He remembered Lejour's careless attitude over the time-setting on the mines. He remembered wishing he had had a chance to check the delay factor before Valinda had left. He remembered holding his breath as he watched her struggling toward him; and he inched the submarine as close to the yawning mouth as he dared.

He remembered the flash, the sudden star-shaped ragged wound appearing on the worm's mouth edge. He remembered Valinda's body tossing in the shock wave, remembered the jolt through the submarine, the flickering of the lights, the sight of Valinda spinning slowly head over heels, unconscious, out of control, drifting into the mouth of the worm as it convulsively withdrew into the berg.

And he remembered, a recollection colored with the crimson fury of murder, Lejour's later remark:

"You won't have to split your percentage now, will you?"

Oh, Valinda . . .

Rosskidd's voice was in his ear and he returned to the present.

"I don't know what you think you're doing down here, but we're out of control. The berg's spinning." The big man was regarding him furiously, and behind the rage was terror; the pale eyes flickered to the exposed flank of the worm.

Skunder considered. A spinning berg could mean several things. It was possible that, lost in memories, he had overcorrected with the laser, but he didn't think so. Again, the worm could have withdrawn its head into the berg, allowing the tail to hang free in the water, jetting aimlessly. This was unlikely; he would have noticed that the area of skin at the control point had altered.

The third possibility was a near certainty. "Sometimes a worm will become aware that it is being used," he informed Rosskidd. "It senses the presence of men on the berg and the constant use of the laser irritates it. As a rule, the worms are almost mindless, but you can get one which turns rogue."

"So what's happening?"

"It's doubled its head back, and it's burrowing toward the surface of the berg. We've lost propulsion. We're drifting with the tide and spinning with the wind."

"Great," said Rosskidd sarcastically; his voice was soft and he smiled mirthlessly, as though dealing with a child. "So what do you suggest we do now, Mr. Skunder?"

The Cantek shrugged. "Wait," he replied simply. "After a while the worm will double back and work through to the water again. It will probably finish up facing in the other direction. This often happens, but it's rare that a worm leaves the berg altogether. At this stage in the life cycle they have to keep cool. Sometimes the heat of the worm's body melts the ice around it, making it difficult to get a grip to propel the berg, so the worm merely drives a new tunnel."

"You're quite an expert." The Earthman's voice was dangerously quiet and Skunder shivered inwardly. Why were they all like this? What was it about the ice, and the worms, and apparently the very fact of being on Cantek, which turned the Earthmen sour? They didn't need to come here, but they came because they had the chance of making money.

Yet it appeared that the very process of making it drove them insane.

"I've studied marine biology," Skunder said in carefully conversational tones. "In particular, the bergworms and their life cycle. It's an important study on Cantek, more so since the freshwater crisis. Did you know that some worms can make up to forty journeys north in a lifetime? Their body is refrigerated in the berg as they head for warmer seas, then, when a certain latitude is reached and the berg is melted away, they spawn and make their way back, leaving the young to feed in the richer, warmer waters. The young worms only head south for the polar cap when they are mature; the males stay under the cap for the rest of their lives while the females mate, burrow into the edge of the cap, and wait, feeding all the time, for their section of ice to break free." Skunder was aware that his voice had risen; he was talking desperately in terror of this large Earthman with the dangerous shadow of fear in his eyes.

"You're too smart by half, Cantek," said Rosskidd coldly. "Follow me. We're going to have a talk with Erkelens." He swung away and struggled, feet sliding, up the sloping ice-tunnel.

Erkelens was sitting outside the dome, moodily eyeing the slowly revolving landscape. He looked up as they approached. Rosskidd seized Skunder by the elbow and propelled him before the captain. "Tell him what you told me." he commanded.

Skunder explained.

"So there's nothing we can do," observed Erkelens heavily when the Cantek had finished.

"I'm not so sure of that," said Rosskidd, with a meaningful glance at Skunder. In the open air, the tall man had gained confidence again; the fear was gone from his eyes to be replaced by a shrewd look.

"Have you got any ideas, Rosskidd?"

"No, but I think Skunder might have."

"Skunder?" The captain regarded the Cantek. "I thought you said it was a question of time?"

"That's right." Skunder wondered what was coming next, but Rosskidd did not enlarge upon his remark.

Later in the large dome, while Skunder slept outside, Rosskidd made his views plain.

"I don't trust that Cantek," he informed Erkelens.

"Skunder? He's OK. He's done the last three trips with me. A good man."

"Man?" Rosskidd laughed shortly. "How you can call a four-foot humanoid midget a man, I don't know, Erkelens. You've been here too long. You've gone native."

"What exactly have you got against the Canteks, Rosskidd?"

"Look." The big man leaned forward, his expression ominous. "You hired me to do a job and I'm doing it. So far I've done it well, I reckon, which is what I'm paid for. I give value for money. But I'm not paid to like the Canteks. Do you know what that superior little bastard did in the shaft? He started giving me a lecture about the worms, for Christ's sake. Told me he was a marine biologist."

"He is."

"By Cantek standards maybe, but he wouldn't get far on Earth. Who the hell do these people think they are? They're way behind the times. They still use internal combustion engines and they've polluted their atmosphere and sea. They're centuries behind Earth. And then that weird dwarf starts pulling the superior knowledge stunt on me."

Erkelens regarded his mate carefully. "Are you scared of the ice, Rosskidd?" he asked shrewdly. "Because if you are, you shouldn't be on this job. There's something about the ice; it gets you after a while. A man can get scared, permanently. I had trouble once, so I saw a doctor about it. He said this feeling comes on because we're in an environment of nonlife. There's nothing here, you see, except the ice, and the sea, and the sky; in these latitudes there are no birds, and no fish that I've ever seen. At least on a ship you'd have a large crew, a cat or two and rats, no doubt. But here, on the ice . . . Have you ever had the feeling, Rosskidd—when you're at the other end of the berg, or down in the tunnels by yourself, have you ever had the feeling that you're the only living being in the whole Galaxy? *Almost* the only living being, that is; but not quite. Because down there below you is the worm. It's just you and her, nothing else, Rosskidd; just you and the worm, alone in infinity and eternity; and you know you're no match for the worm. Have you ever felt like that, Rosskidd?"

"Damn you, Erkelens," muttered the other man.

"I just wanted to point out that all of us have our problems here. I've got mine, and Skunder's got his. But because we're scared, we don't start hitting out at each other. You're new to the bergs, Rosskidd, so we make allowances for you. But you've got to make allowances for us, too. We're stuck here for a long time, the three of us, and we've got to get along together. Now. Before we started all this, you were telling me you didn't trust Skunder. Perhaps you'll tell me why."

Rosskidd hesitated. "He seemed to give up easily," he said at last. "When the berg stopped he knew what the trouble was, but he didn't seem to want to do anything about it."

"He's the expert, you know," Erkelens pointed out gently. "This sort of thing has happened before. There's very little than can be done."

"I daresay, but I thought . . . I thought at the time, that maybe he was in league with Lejour. That he was delaying us deliberately."

Erkelens looked thoughtful. "I don't think so. He told us Lejour was around, remember? He needn't have done that. We didn't hear the helicopter."

Rosskidd mumbled something, unconvinced, and the two Earthmen began to prepare for bed. Erkelens was soon asleep, his breathing deep and regular, but Rosskidd tossed on the nightmare fringe of waking dreams for a long time. He kept seeing the ice beneath him as he lay on his stomach; it was as though the bed were not there; the ice was green and slowly changed to blue, bright phosphorescent blue, as the bergworm drove its way upward, vertically, questing hungrily for Rosskidd who was the only other living being in the Galaxy.

Erkelens was crouched over the screen. "I think she's turned," he said. "The trace has lengthened. Skunder, what do you think?"

The Cantek paced about the ice for a moment, expressionlessly. Rosskidd sniffed. "What's he supposed to be, telepathic?"

"Sort of," said Erkelens. "The Canteks have an affinity to animal life. You've noticed it already, haven't you? Skunder found us this worm; all we did was to plot the exact position."

The Cantek stopped pacing. "We shall be moving again within the hour," he informed them positively. "I can start drilling the control shaft again." He left them.

In fact the motion of the berg changed in fifty minutes; the spinning ceased and, to Erkelens' relief, they commenced moving in the right direction, heading west, hugging the coast-line. It would be some time before Skunder's control arrangements were complete; meanwhile, they were not losing any time.

Shortly before suppertime Rosskidd hurried to the dome to find Erkelens crouched outside preparing the meal. "There's a free berg ahead of us," he gasped. He was breathless; puffs of mist pulsed from his open mouth. "Could be Lejour. He hasn't got much of a start, after all."

"And Skunder said we had a good worm."

"He didn't say how good Lejour's worm was."

"We'll soon know. How far ahead is he?"

"About a mile."

Skunder was approaching them, a tiny, childlike figure on the white expanse. He glanced at the steaming pot, then at Erkelens. "Control shaft complete, Captain. Everything in order." He grinned nervously.

"Rosskidd's sighted Lejour. About a mile ahead of us. What are our chances?"

The Cantek started; he shielded his eyes and gazed across the sea, his expression unfathomable, while Rosskidd watched him closely. "I said we had a good worm," Skunder reminded them. "Lejour will have Alvo with him as pilot; he used him on the last trip. Lejour will see us, and make Alvo hurry the worm. Alvo is not a strong man. . . . I think, within the next week, Lejour's worm will be spent, or it will revolt and quit the berg. I feel sorry for Alvo. We will reach Alkar before them."

Rosskidd stared at Skunder. "What you're saying is, we shouldn't worry if Lejour draws ahead of us?"

"That is so."

Erkelens broke in hurriedly. "Look, Skunder. I don't want to teach you your own business, so let me put it like this—I wouldn't like to lose sight of Lejour, if you get my meaning. Let him draw ahead if you must, but not too far. I want to keep my eye on him."

"Tactfully put, Skipper," remarked Rosskidd.

Skunder looked from one Earthman to the other, then turned and made for his tiny sleeping quarters, unzipped the entrance and crawled inside.

"Looks like he's not eating," Rosskidd observed. "You've upset him, Erkelens."

The captain stared at his mate furiously. "When you've made a few more trips, Rosskidd, you might begin to understand. Meanwhile, just remember that there are three human beings on this berg, and another three on that berg ahead of us. And they are our enemies, and the sea is our enemy, and the sky and the bergworm are our enemies, and even our own minds. We're heavily outnumbered, Rosskidd, we three here. We don't want to increase the odds further."

Moodily, Rosskidd spooned a mouthful of stew, gazing at the silent minidome a few yards away.

For the next week the berg plowed through the gray ocean northward, leaving the glittering ice cap far behind, always keeping in sight the crystal flicker on the horizon which denoted the position of Lejour. The sea developed a sheen as they progressed: the fringes of pollution. One morning as Rosskidd and Erkelens were finishing breakfast they were alerted by a distant high-pitched whine.

Erkelens looked up in surprise. "Sounds like Lejour's helicopter," he remarked. "Heading this way."

"What do you suppose he wants?"

Erkelens grinned. "Well, there's always the chance that he's broken a leg, and his mate's coming to beg assistance. We're a long way from land, and his helicopter has no great range. I'm looking forward to this." He watched as the helicopter appeared, a winging beetle in the misty sky, hovered, and descended toward them to land in a fog of fine snow.

A figure emerged and strolled toward them unhurriedly. They remained seated. Lejour stood above them, a small man about the height of Erkelens. He greeted them. Erkelens looked up, as though surprised to see him. "Hello, Lejour," he said casually.

"I thought it must be you. When I saw you trailing behind me, I said to myself, that's Erkelens, bound for Alkar, and too late as usual." Lejour's tone was light and bantering; he glanced at Rosskidd.

"Rosskidd, meet Lejour." Erkelens introduced the two men who eyed each other warily. There was a lengthy silence; Erkelens and Rosskidd resumed their breakfast. "What's your problem, Lejour?" asked the captain at last, through a full mouth.

"You're the one with problems. Lagging behind a bit aren't you? You won't get much of a price at Alkar, once I've flooded the market."

"Always assuming you get there first. Which is an assumption I'm not making."

Lejour squatted on his haunches, bringing himself down to their level. "Now, look here Erkelens," he began in reasonable tones. "I don't see any point in our competing over this trip. We're cutting each other's throats. I've got a suggestion to make."

"I thought you might have."

Ignoring the sarcasm, Lejour continued: "We can make a killing over this thing. We both know the freshwater shortage at Alkar. So why not join forces; say, tell them that they have to accept both bergs at a fixed price, a little below the going rate, of course; they're not fools. But that way we'll both gain, instead of one of us taking the chance of getting next to nothing."

"You're the one who's taking that chance, Lejour. I'm confident of my price."

Lejour stood abruptly. "You're a damned fool, Erkelens. Racing like this, we could finish up with our worms quitting the bergs, and neither of us will make it."

"I'll make it," said Erkelens confidently.

Lejour glared at him, then spun around and started back for the helicopter. As he passed the minidome, Skunder emerged. The two men stood motionless for a moment, a frozen tableau on the ice as Lejour halted in mid-stride. They said nothing that Erkelens or Rosskidd could hear; they gazed at each other for an instant before Lejour resumed his walk to the helicopter. A moment later the machine roared into the sky and Skunder joined them, sitting on his heels and eating silently while the other two regarded him uncertainly.

"What do you make of that?" asked Rosskidd, when Skunder had finished and departed.

"Lejour's overtaxed his worm. He knows we can beat him to Alkar."

"I mean him and Skunder."

Erkelens sighed. "I wish you could forget this notion of yours. Skunder and Lejour worked together once. Lejour was surprised to see him here, maybe. I don't know. I don't see that it matters."

Rosskidd muttered something and walked away.

Later Erkelens met Skunder at the north end of the berg. The little Cantek was gazing out to sea. "Lejour's slowing down," he said. "We're closing on him."

"What exactly is between you and Lejour?" asked Erkelens.

Skunder scuffed his leather-bound feet in the snow and was silent. He looked at the Earthman, then at the sea again. He sniffed. "Smell that, Captain?" he asked.

Obediently Erkelens inhaled. A faint, thick smell came to him, cloying. "What is it?" he asked. The sea flowed past them, rainbow colored. "Pollution?"

Skunder sighed. "Another mistake by my people," he said. "You ought to keep up-to-date with what goes on, Captain. Cantek is not just a mindless planet which earns money for you to send home for a future memory of retirement. Cantek is a world where humanoids live and love and kill, and my people are just as greedy as yours, but younger. And in their greed they make mistakes, just like Earth did, years ago. Earth could prevent us making those mistakes if it wanted, but Earth will not help."

"You're feeling bitter today, Skunder. Was it seeing Lejour?"

"Possibly. It doesn't alter the facts. Your people have come to our planet to make money out of us. If you helped us progress to your level, there would not be so much money to be made. We would not, for example, have the freshwater problem, and the polluted seas and atmosphere. You have beaten the pollution problem on Earth, right?"

"We have. It took a long time and there was a lot of opposition, but we did it."

"And I expect before you achieved that, your ocean looked like this, sometimes."

Erkelens examined the water. Even from the height of the berg, he could discern the oiliness of the surface, the rainbow reflections. "It's spread this far south," he murmured. "In a decade it'll reach the ice cap. And then what? How can you get any rainfall, if the sea is unable to evaporate?"

"It's not quite that bad yet, Captain. This is from the new submarine oilfield. You remember, I mentioned it last trip? There was a big project, about five hundred miles from Alkar. Men were down there, living underwater in a big pressure dome, drilling, piping the crude oil to the coast."

"I remember." Erkelens gazed at the oil slick in horrified fascination.

"The disaster occurred last month. Nobody knows quite what caused it; maybe the dome fractured, maybe there was an explosion or an earthquake. All we know is that contact with the site was lost suddenly. Site!" Skunder laughed, shortly and bitterly. "It was more like a miniature city. The oilfield was going to supply the whole of Cantek for the next two hundred years, so they said. But contact was lost, as they put it, and suddenly the surface of the sea in this area was covered with a layer of oil inches, even feet thick. It's high-grade stuff. I wouldn't even light a cigarette until we're through, if I were you.

"But I can't get over the needlessness of it," the Cantek continued. "Earth doesn't use oil as a fuel anymore. Why should we?"

"I guess the World Government thinks the lesser-developed planets should make their own way forward," said Erkelens defensively. "We've had some bad examples, even on Earth itself in the old days, of what happens when you artificially accelerate the progress of a race."

"So we don't get our reactors and we don't get our uranium."

"Skunder," said Erkelens patiently, "Cantek still has a major war every twenty years. Let things settle down. Give yourself a chance. Handing out reactors to all your various governments would be like giving lasers to chimpanzees." He coughed uncomfortably as the insulting aspect of the simile struck him.

Skunder didn't reply, but gazed at the slowly heaving surface, brooding.

"We're closing on him," observed Rosskidd with satisfaction. "We're closing fast."

"His worm is tired," Skunder surmised. "He has driven it too hard."

It was two days later. The atmosphere was heavy with the clinging stench of oil, whipped past their faces by the driving northerly wind which had, over the past few hours, slowed the bergs almost to a standstill. Half a mile away was Lejour's berg; from time to time they could see the crew moving about, black ants on the translucent silver.

"Do you think his worm will leave him?" asked Erkelens hopefully.

"Not under this oil. The water will be dark, down there. The worms are scared. They will cling to familiar surroundings. You notice our own motion?"

The berg was rocking, an irregular movement which could not be attributed to the action of the sea. The giant worm was questing this way and that; they could imagine the cavernous mouth gaping as the head swung from side to side, seeking an end to the unnaturally black water. Nevertheless they continued to inch forward in a generally northerly direction. Skunder had advised against exercising too much control at this time; it was better to let the worm have her head until the oil was behind them.

"What's going on there?" asked Erkelens suddenly. The three tiny figures of Lejour's crew were grouped at the near end of their berg engaged in some sort of activity. A cascade of minute black dots fell slowly past the scintillating face of the berg. They saw no splash as the object hit the sullen water. Erkelens and Rosskidd regarded each other in some alarm. "The bastard's up to something," the captain said.

Suddenly the water at the base of Lejour's berg erupted into black and crimson spray; seconds later the thud of a detonation reached them.

"Trying to stir his worm up?" Rosskidd chuckled. "I suppose that's one way."

Erkelens and Skunder didn't reply. They watched as the fountain of water subsided. Through the thick black smoke which drifted toward them they could see a wide crimson glow spreading; then the dense fumes hid it from view.

"He's fired the sea!" Erkelens shouted. "The bastard's fired the sea! The wind will carry it toward us!"

"So?" Rosskidd was coughing, his eyes streaming. "We can sit it out in the dome."

"You don't understand," said Skunder quietly. "It could kill our worm."

"How? He's safe enough down there."

"I don't think so." Skunder was rubbing a cloth in the snow; he tied it around his lower face in an effort to filter out the fumes. "A worm can panic." His voice was muffled. "It's not entirely blind; there are light-sensitive cells above and behind the mouth. It's already nervous because of the oil."

The smoke was clearing as the blaze approached; the wind whipped the black fumes lower, beneath their feet and around the flanks of the berg like a thick swirling tide. Beyond, the flames had spread into a broad ribbon some three hundred yards wide. The berg trembled.

"The worm is frightened," said Skunder.

Rosskidd glanced around nervously. "What can we do?" he asked.

"Nothing. Just wait."

Crimson, yellow, boiling into jet black, the broad lake of fire swept toward them as they stood mesmerized on the lip of the berg. Beyond, Lejour's berg stood steady in calm water; they could see the minute figures of the crew, watching.

"Look!" A harsh cry from Rosskidd.

Fifty yards ahead a paleness appeared in the streaming black. A harsh sound reached them, a giant gasp, a tortured, racking inhalation. Heaving above the smoke, dripping cataracts of oily water from its segmented hide, the head of the bergworm appeared. Erkelens heard a low moan; Rosskidd was gazing at the monstrous apparition in horror, his hand clasped to his mouth. The head rose from the sea, higher, laboriously, swinging ponderously from side to side as the worm groaned in gigantic agony and the flames swept closer.

"She cannot get her head back underwater," Skunder cried. "The fire is too close."

Erkelens didn't hear. He watched as the flames approached; his lips moved as he silently implored the leviathan to save itself, to return to its natural element. But the fire was too close now, directly below the head of the monster as it reared farther from the water and the berg shuddered as great sinews strained in the corridors below. The neck and head were vertical now; the cavernous mouth gaped at the sky in mortal supplication. Fifty feet from the sea the monster rose like a lighthouse beside the berg, and the three men stepped back, appalled.

"She's going!" cried Skunder.

The berg itself was groaning as the tension increased, a trembling vibration transmitted into creaking cacophony. The flames were lapping around the column of the worm's neck; the head was shuddering with strain, tilting, falling in seeming slow motion, collapsing back into the blazing sea in a rising cascade of fire with a booming concussion, a giant thunderclap.

Rosskidd and Erkelens were flung to the ground as the berg heaved and lurched; only Skunder remained standing to witness the end. The huge tube writhed in the sea of flames; the head rose once more, slowly, barely clearing the surface, and emitted a vast, coughing exhalation, spewing from the cavern of its body a gout of blazing oil, then relaxed into motionlessness and sank slowly beneath the surface. The flames moved on, past the flank of the berg. The berg was still, dead.

Skunder walked away, leaving the two men lying in the snow.

Erkelens was the first to move; he rolled over, looked at the sky, sat up. He nudged Rosskidd, who still lay there, his head pillowed on his arms.

"OK, Rosskidd. You can get up now. It's all over."

Rosskidd groaned and turned over; he looked at the captain with the dregs of fear in his eyes. "God," he muttered.

"Take it easy. We're all right." Erkelens stood, brushing loose snow from his furs.

"I thought . . . I thought the berg was going to capsize. I've heard it doesn't take much to capsize a berg when it's been moving through warm waters. I thought we'd had it, Erkelens."

"So did I, as a matter of fact." Erkelens glanced at Lejour's berg, unscathed, moving slowly northward; then he turned and surveyed the blazing sea rolling into the distance. "Where's Skunder?" he asked suddenly.

"I don't know. He was here a minute ago. Have we lost the worm?"

"Yes." Erkelens shielded his eyes with his hand and gazed around the berg. "There he is!" he exclaimed. "Christ, he's swinging the submarine out! He's going over the side!"

Rosskidd laughed bitterly. "The little bastard's running out on us. We're stranded, we've got no worm, so he's teaming up with Lejour."

"I don't think so, somehow," said Erkelens.

Skunder depressed the lever and heard the click as the hooks disengaged. He thumbed the starter and coaxed the ancient pile into reluctant activity. Soon the turbine began to hum and the tiny submarine slid beneath the dark water. He switched on the floodlights, veered away from the viridescent ice-wall to his left, and headed north.

He remembered Valinda and felt the knot of hate in his

stomach as his thoughts slid to Lejour while a tiny corner of his mind registered the opaque green on the viewscreen as the water swallowed his lights at the limit of visibility. There were fish at these latitudes, hardy black sharks cruising on the fringes of the killing polar cold in which only the worms could live. They watched him curiously as he passed and their cold eyes glinted green and baleful in the glow of the floodlights. He remembered Valinda and the day she had saved his life with a well-aimed dart from the turret of Lejour's submarine. He had been inspecting a reluctant worm at close quarters and had not seen the shark as it circled above him, waiting its chance. But Valinda had seen it and he had felt a sudden, slight concussion; looking up, he saw the brute writhing and snapping at the dart projecting from its belly; blood trailed crimson in the water and he had thrashed his frantic way back to the submarine where Valinda held him close for a long time.

He thought of Lejour's face when he had seen him two days ago. The sudden shock of recognition and then a fear behind the Earthman's eyes. Lejour had remembered the day of their last meeting, when they had settled up Skunder's share of the contract price and the figure received by the Cantek had been exactly double what he had expected at the outset of the voyage. Lejour had made no demur about paying him Valinda's share; Skunder would have thought it was conscience money except for his conviction that Lejour was not the man to have a conscience.

"All yours, Cantek," he had said generously. "I'll be in touch when I get the next contract lined up."

Skunder had regarded him silently for a while, the money in his hand. It would have been a pointless gesture to refuse it, so he merely said: "Don't bother, Earthman. The next time you see me will be the last." It had sounded melodramatic at the time but he had seen Lejour's eyes widen slightly, allowing the fear to peep out.

Skunder recalled himself to the present, adjusted the trim of the craft and skimmed just below the surface, raising the periscope. A rainbow blur of oil slid down the screen, cleared, and he could see Lejour's berg, riding high before him. He altered course to leave it to starboard and retracted the periscope. After a few minutes he dived, circling back, moving in close to the jagged wall of ice. Soon, he saw the phosphorescent flank of the worm.

A tired worm, driven hard for many days, uneasy due to the unaccustomed blackness of the oil-blanketed water. Inside the berg, its flanks would be painful from the constant application of the scorching laser control.

It would be possible to persuade such a worm to leave the berg. A few well-placed mines about the rudimentary eyes . . . He eased forward, following the vast segments of the body, moving toward the mouth. The glowing shape ended abruptly; a scattering of pilot fish darted about the region of the mouth, the little blue fish which followed the leviathans in order to feed from the spawn, in due course themselves becoming food for the growing worms. Skunder traversed the area, sizing up the most advantageous position for the mines behind that yawning mouth which filled the viewscreen. Suddenly he checked, throttled back and increased the magnification on the screen, his attention caught by a dark blob within the glowing mouth itself. The shape jumped into close-up, sleek; somehow patient and watchful.

Lejour's submarine. Lurking within the very mouth, guarding the huge creature against just such an attack as Skunder envisaged. He wondered if Lejour himself was at the controls, but deemed it unlikely. In the time that he had worked for the Earthman, Skunder had never known Lejour to go below the surface; like most Earthmen, he was scared of the worm. He would have sent Alvo down.

Nevertheless, he had out-thought Skunder and the Cantek knew a moment of sick frustration. In order to plant the mines he would have to leave the submarine; he would be picked off easily by Alvo's darts. For a while he patrolled to and fro outside the circumference of the mouth while the enemy craft twisted in sympathy, keeping him in the center of its viewscreen.

A telltale light flashed on the control panel and Skunder dampened the miniature pile hastily; the reactor was beginning to overheat. He cursed Erkelens' ramshackle equipment; this was the worst moment for a breakdown to occur. Lejour's modern submarine, naturally, had automatic dampers. He cruised slowly away, around the rim of the mouth, followed by his watchful adversary. A dart clanged off his hull; a warning shot to remind him what the enemy could do if he tried to leave his craft to affix the mines.

He moved around the perimeter of the mouth, shadowed by the vigilant shape behind. He thought of Lejour on the surface of the berg, smiling grimly as the news of his futile attempt to cripple the worm was radioed back. He knew hate, frustrated and sickening.

And ahead, a ragged, star-shaped gash in the worm's lip, legacy of a bygone mine injury.

He veered away, his thoughts whirling, jetted a short distance into the open sea and turned, headed back, gained his bearings and stared at the scar as he approached.

Bergworms are long-lived; some make many voyages to and from the polar ice caps.

Again he saw Valinda swimming toward him; he saw the bright flash and jagged wound, just there, just *there*.

And Lejour smiling into the radio receiver.

He dragged at the damper control. The warning light flickered.

He drove forward.

Erkelens stood on the lip of the drifting berg, staring at the viscous sea; soon Rosskidd joined him.

"I've sent a distress signal," said the mate. "It seems there's a ship only a few miles away. They'll pick us up before long. They complained a bit about having to detour through the oil, but I made it clear we were Earthmen."

Erkelens glanced at him, then smiled bitterly.

"What about the berg?" resumed Rosskidd. "Do we just leave it here?"

"The luck of the game. This one's no use to anyone, now the worm's dead. It's not the sort of thing you can take in tow."

"That's true." Rosskidd was watching Lejour's berg as it moved steadily away. "What's that?" he asked, wondering.

Half a mile away, the glittering mass became suddenly indistinct, hazed with a corona of fine particles of snow and ice, refracting multicolored in the low sun. The sea around the base of the berg erupted slowly into incandescent spray.

"Christ!" whispered Rosskidd in awe. "He's breaking up!"

As though struck from above with a giant cleaver the berg split down the center, the halves rolling ponderously apart, and a vaulting spout of solid water leaped skyward from the widening gulf.

The rumble of a gigantic underwater explosion reached them, their berg trembled, they sat down abruptly in the snow and watched as the distant waterspout subsided and the sea quietened, became once more dark and somber, the twin peaks of ice jutting from the viscous surface like tombstones.

Rosskidd glanced at the captain; his eyes held a frightened, unspoken query.

Erkelens nodded. "Skunder had some grudge," he said. "I don't know what it was. Probably something which you or I wouldn't understand, but the Canteks are a volatile race. Always fighting wars. I'm not sure we'll ever get to the bottom of them."

They stood together on the gently rocking berg for a long time, watching the enigmatic horizon. Eventually, night fell.

Erkelens strolled back to the dome, leaving his mate standing alone under the stony stars.

"Where the hell is that ship?" asked Rosskidd of the planet Cantek, irritably.

THE GOLD AT THE STARBOW'S END

FREDERIK POHL

Any collection that purported to present the best of the year that did not contain this novella would be either a fraud or an example of very myopic mental vision. This is probably the best single piece that this very talented writer has produced in the last few years. If it is not this year's Hugo and/or Nebula winner, then something will have been drastically wrong with the ballot-counting.

Constitution One

Log of Lt-Col Sheffield N. Jackman, USAF, commanding U.S. Starship *Constitution*, Day 40.

All's well, friends. Thanks to Mission Control for the batch of personal messages. We enjoyed the concert you beamed us, in fact we recorded most of it so we can play it over again when communication gets hairy.

We are now approaching the six-week point in our expedition to Alpha Centauri, Planet Aleph, and now that we've passed the farthest previous manned distance from Earth we're really beginning to feel as if we're on our way. Our latest navigation check confirms Mission Control's plot, and we estimate we should be crossing the orbit of Pluto at approximately 1631 hours, ship time, of Day 40, which is today. Letski has been keeping track of the time dilation effect, which is beginning to be significant now that we are traveling about some 6 percent of the speed of light, and says this would make it approximately a quarter of two in the morning your time, Mission Control. We voted to consider that the "coastal waters" mark. From then on we will have left the solar system behind and thus will be the first human beings to enter upon the deeps of interstellar space. We plan to have a ceremony. Letski and Ann Becklund have made up an American flag for jettisoning at that point, which we will do through the Number Three survey port, along with the prepared stainless steel plaque containing the President's commissioning speech. We are also throwing in some private articles for each of us. I am contributing my Air Academy class ring.

Little change since previous reports. We are settling down nicely to our routine. We finished up all our post-launch checks weeks ago, and as Dr. Knefhausen predicted we began to find time hanging heavy on our hands. There won't be much to keep us busy between now and when we arrive at the planet Alpha-Aleph that is really essential to the operating of the spaceship. So we went along with Kneffie's proposed recreational schedule, using the worksheets prepared by the Nasa Division of Flight Training and Personnel Management. At first (I think the boys back in Indianapolis are big enough to know this!) it met with what you might call a cool reception. The general consensus was that this business of learning number theory and the calculus of statement, which is what they handed us for openers, was for the birds. We figured we weren't quite desperate enough for that yet, so we fooled around with other things. Ann and Will Becklund played a lot of chess. Dot Letski began writing a verse adaptation of *War and Peace*. The rest of us hacked around with the equipment, and making astronomical observations and gabbing. But all that began to get tiresome pretty fast, just as Kneffie said it would at the briefings. We talked about his idea that the best way to pass time in a spaceship was learning to get interested in mathematical problems—no mass to transport, no competitive element to get tempers up and all that. It began to make sense. So now Letski is in his tenth day of trying to find a formula for primes, and my own dear Flo is trying to prove Goldbach's Conjecture by means of the theory of congruences. (This is the girl who two months ago couldn't add up a laundry list!) It certainly passes the time.

Medically, we are all fit. I will append the detailed data on our blood pressures, pulses, etc., as well as the tape from the rocket and navigating systems readouts. I'll report again as scheduled. Take care of Earth for us—we're looking forward to seeing it again, in a few years!

Washington One

There was a lull in the urban guerrilla war in Washington that week. The chopper was able to float right in to the South Lawn of the White House—no sniper fire, no heat-seeking missiles, not even rock-throwing. Dr. Dieter von Knefhausen stared suspiciously at the knot of weary-looking pickets in their permitted fifty yards of space along the perimeter. They didn't look militant, probably Gay Lib or, who knew what, maybe nature-food or single-tax; at any rate no rocks came from them, only a little disorganized booing as the helicopter landed. Knefhausen bowed to Herr Omnes sardonically, hopped nimbly out of the chopper and got out of the way as it took off again, which it did at once. He didn't trouble to run to the White House. He strolled. He did not fear these simple people, even if the helicopter pilot did. Also he was not really eager to keep his appointment with the President.

The ADC who frisked him did not smile. The orderly who conducted him to the West Terrace did not salute. No one relieved him of the dispatch case with his slides and papers, although it was heavy. You could tell right away when you were in the doghouse, he thought, ducking his head from the rotor blast as the pilot circled the White House to gain altitude before venturing back across the spread-out city.

It had been a lot different in the old days, he thought with some nostalgia. He could remember every minute of those old days. It was right here, this portico, where he had stood before the world's press and photographers to tell them about the Alpha-Aleph Project. He had seen his picture next to the President's on all the front-pages, watched himself on the TV newscasts, talking about the New Earth that would give America an entire colonizable planet four light-years away. He remembered the launch at the Cape, with a million and a half invited guests from all over the world: foreign statesmen and scientists eating their hearts out with envy, American leaders jovial with pride. The orderlies saluted then, all right. His lecture fees had gone clear out of sight. There was even talk of making him the Vice Presidential candidate in the next election—and it could have happened, too, if the election had been right then, and if there hadn't been the problem of his being born in another country.

Now it was all different. He was taken up in the service elevator. It wasn't so much that Knefhausen minded for his own sake, he told himself, but how did the word get out that there was trouble? Was it only the newspaper stories? Was there a leak?

The Marine orderly knocked once on the big door of the Cabinet room, and it was opened from inside.

Knefhausen entered.

No "Come in, Dieter, boy, pull up a pew." No Vice President jumping up to grab his arm and slap his back. His greeting was thirty silent faces turned toward him, some reserved, some frankly hostile. The full Cabinet was there, along with half a dozen department heads and the President's personal action staff, and the most hostile face around the big oval table was the President's own.

Knefhausen bowed. An atavistic hankering for lyceum-cadet jokes made him think of clicking his heels and adjusting a monocle, but he didn't have a monocle and didn't yield to impulses like that. He merely took his place standing at the foot of the table and, when the President nodded, said, "Good morning, gentlemen, and ladies. I assume you want to see me about the stupid lies the Russians are spreading about the Alpha-Aleph program."

Roobarooba, they muttered to each other. The President said in his sharp tenor, "So you think they are just lies?"

"Lies or mistakes, Mr. President, what's the difference? We are right and they are wrong, that's all."

Roobaroobarooba. The Secretary of State looked inquiringly at the President, got a nod and said: "Dr. Knefhausen, you know I've been on your team a long time and I don't want to disagree with any statement you care to make, but are you so sure about that? They's some mighty persuasive figures comin' out of the Russians."

"They are false, Mr. Secretary."

"Ah, well, Dr. Knefhausen. I might be inclined to take your word for it, but they's others might not. Not cranks or malcontents, Dr. Knefhausen, but good, decent people. Do you have any evidence for such as them?"

"With your permission, Mr. President?" The President nodded again, and Knefhausen unlocked his dispatch case and drew out a slim sheaf of slides. He handed them to a major of Marines, who looked to the President for approval and then did what Knefhausen told him. The room lights went down and, after some fiddling with the focus, the first slide was projected over Knefhausen's head. It showed a huge array of Y-shaped metal posts, stretching away into the distance of a bleak, powdery-looking landscape.

"This picture is our radio telescope on Farside, the Moon," he said. "It is never visible from the Earth, because that portion of the Moon's surface is permanently turned away from us, for which reason we selected it for the site of the telescope. There is no electrical interference of any kind. The instrument is made up of thirty-three million separate dipole elements, aligned with an accuracy of one part in several million. Its actual size is an approximate circle eighteen miles across, but by virtue of the careful positioning its performance is effectively equal to a telescope with a diameter of some twenty-six miles. Next slide, please."

Click. The picture of the huge RT display swept away and was replaced by another similar—but visibly smaller and shabbier—construction.

"This is the Russian instrument, gentlemen. And ladies. It is approximately one quarter the size of ours in diameter. It has less than one-tenth as many elements, and our reports— they are classified, but I am informed this gathering is cleared to receive this material? Yes—our reports indicate the alignment is very crude. Even terrible, you could say.

"The difference between the two instruments in information-gathering capacity is roughly a hundred to one, in our favor. Lights, please.

"What this means," he went on smoothly, smiling at each of the persons around the table in turn as he spoke, "is that if the Russians say 'no' and we say 'yes,' bet on 'yes.' Our radio telescope can be trusted. Theirs cannot."

The meeting shifted uneasily in its chairs. They were as anxious to believe Knefhausen as he was to convince them, but they were not sure.

Representative Belden, the Chairman of the House Ways and Means Committee, spoke for all of them. "Nobody doubts the quality of your equipment. Especially," he added, "since we still have bruises from the job of paying for it. But the Russians made a flat statement. They said that Alpha Centauri can't have a planet larger than one thousand miles in diameter, or nearer than half a billion miles to the star. I have a copy of the Tass release here. It admits that their equipment is inferior to our own, but they have a statement signed by twenty-two academicians that says their equipment could not miss on any object larger or nearer than what I have said, or on any body of any kind which would be large enough to afford a landing place for our astronauts. Are you familiar with this statement?"

"Yes, of course, I have read it—"

"Then you know that they state positively that the planet you call 'Alpha-Aleph' does not exist."

"Yes, that is what they state."

"Moreover, statements from authorities at the Paris Observatory and the UNESCO Astrophysical Center at Trieste, and from England's Astronomer Royal, all say that they have checked and confirmed their figures."

Knefhausen nodded cheerfully. "That is correct, Representative Belden. They confirm that if the observations are as stated, then the conclusions drawn by the Soviet installation at Novy Brezhnevgrad on Farside naturally follow. I don't question the arithmetic. I only say that the observations are made with inadequate equipment, and thus the Soviet astronomers have come to a false conclusion. But I do not want to burden your patience with an unsupported statement," he added hastily as the Congressman opened his mouth to speak again, "so I will tell you all there is to tell. What the Russians say is theory. What I have to counter is not merely better theory, but also objective fact. I know Alpha-Aleph is there because I have seen it! Lights again, Major! And the next slide, if you please."

The screen lit up and showed glaring bare white with a sprinkling of black spots, like dust. A large one appeared in the exact center of the screen, with a dozen lesser ones sprinkled around it. Knefhausen picked up a flash pointer and aimed its little arrowhead of light at the central dot.

"This is a photographic negative," he said, "which is to say that it is black where the actual scene is white and vice versa. Those objects are astronomical. It was taken from our Briareus Twelve satellite near the orbit of Jupiter, on its way out of Neptune fourteen months ago. The central object is the star Alpha Centauri. It was photographed with a special instrument which filters out most of the light from the star itself, electronic in nature and something like the coronascope which is used for photographing prominences on our own Sun. We hoped that by this means we might be able actually to photograph the planet Alpha-Aleph. We were successful, as you can see." The flash pointer laid its little arrow next to the nearest small dot to the central star. "That, gentlemen, and ladies, is Alpha-Aleph. It is precisely where we predicted it from radio telescope data."

There was another buzz from the table. In the dark it was louder than before. The Secretary of State cried sharply, "Mr. President! Can't we release this photograph?"

"We will release it immediately after this meeting," said the President.

Roobarooba. Then the committee chairman: "Mr. President, I'm sure if you say that's the planet we want, then it's the planet. But others outside this country may wonder, for indeed all those dots look about alike to me. I wonder if Knefhausen could satisfy a layman's curiosity. *How* do we know that's Alpha-Aleph?"

"Slide Number Four, please—and keep Number Three in the carriage." The same scene, subtly different. "Note that in this picture, gentlemen, that one object, there, is in a different position. It has moved. You know that the stars show no discernible motion, of course. It has moved because this photograph was taken eight months later, as Briareus Twelve was returning from the Neptune flyby, and the planet Alpha-

Aleph had revolved in its orbit. This is not theory, it is evidence; and I add that the original tapes from which the photoprint was made are stored in Goldstone, so there is no question that arises of foolishness." *Roobarooba,* but in a higher and excited key. Gratified, Knefhausen nailed down his point. "So, Major, if you will now return to Slide Three, yes— And if you will flip back and forth, between Three and Four, as fast as you can— Thank you." The little black dot called Alpha-Aleph bounced back and forth like a tennis ball, while all the other star points remained motionless. "This is what is called the blink comparator process, you see. I point out that if what you are looking at is not a planet, it is, excuse me, Mr. President, the damnedest funniest star you ever saw. Also it is exactly at the distance and exactly with the orbital period we specified based on the RT data. Now, are there any more questions?"

"No, sir!" "That's great, Kneffie!" "Clear as a cow's ass to the stud bull." "I think that wraps it up." "That'll show the Commies."

The President's voice overrode them all.

"I think we can have the lights on now, Major Merton," he said. "Dr. Knefhausen, thank you. I'd appreciate it if you would remain nearby for a few minutes, so you can join Murray and myself in the study to check over the text of our announcement before we release these pictures." He nodded sober dismissal to his chief science advisor and then, reminded by the happy faces of his cabinet, remembered to smile with pleasure.

Constitution Two

Sheffield Jackman's log. Starship *Constitution.* Day 95.

According to Letski we are now traveling at just about 15% of the speed of light, almost 30,000 miles per second. The fusion thrust is operating smoothly and well. Fuel, power, and life-support curves are sticking tight to optimum. No sweat of any kind with the ship, or, actually, with anything else.

Relativistic effects have begun to show up as predicted. Jim Barstow's spectral studies show the stars in front of us are showing a shift to the blue end, and the Sun and the other stars behind us are shifting to the red. Without the spectroscope you can't see much, though. Beta Circini looks a little funny, maybe. As for the Sun, it's still very bright—Jim logged it as minus-six magnitude a few hours ago—and as I've never seen it in quite that way before, I can't tell whether the color looks bright or not. It certainly isn't the golden yellow I associate with type GO, but neither is Alpha Centauri ahead of us, and I don't really see a difference between them. I think the reason is simply that they are so bright that the color impressions are secondary to the brightness impressions, although the spectroscope, as I say, does show the differences. We've all taken turns at looking back. Naturally enough, I guess. We can still make out the Earth and even the Moon in the telescope, but it's chancy. Ski almost got an eyeful of the Sun at full light-gathering amplitude yesterday because the visual separation is only about twelve seconds of arc now. In a few more days they'll be too close to separate.

Let's see, what else?

We've been having a fine time with the recreational-math program. Ann has taken to binary arithmetic like a duck to water. She's involved in what I take to be some sort of statistical experimentation (we don't pry too much into what the others are doing until they're ready to talk about it), and, of all things, she demanded we produce coins to flip. Well, naturally none of us had taken any money with us! Except that it turns out two of us did. Ski had a Russian silver ruble that his mother's uncle had given him for luck, and I found an old Philadelphia transit token in my pocket. Ann rejected my transit token as too light to be reliable, but she now spends happy hours flipping the ruble, heads or tails, and writing down the results as a series of six-place binary numbers, heads for 1 and tails for 0. After about a week my curiosity got too much so I began hinting to find out what she was doing. When I ask she says things like, "By means of the easy and the simple we grasp the laws of the whole world." When I say that's nice but what does she hope to grasp by flipping the coin? she says, "When the laws of the whole world are grasped, therein lies perfection." So, as I say, we don't press each other and I leave it there. But it passes the time.

Kneffie would be proud of himself if he could see how our recreation keeps us busy. None of us has managed to prove

Fermat's Last Theorem yet or anything like that, but of course that's the whole point. If we could *solve* the problems, we'd have used them up, and then what would we do for recreation? It does exactly what it was intended to. It keeps us mentally alert on this long and intrinsically rather dull boat-ride.

Personal relationships? Jes' fine, fellows, jes' fine. A lot better than any of us really hoped, back there at the personal-hygiene briefings in Mission Control. The girls take the stripey pills every day until three days before their periods, then they take the green pills for four days, then they lay off pills for four days, then back to the stripes. There was a little embarrassed joking about it at first, but now it's strictly routine, like brushing the teeth. We men take our red pills every day (Ski christened them "stop lights") until our girls tell us they're about to lay off (you know what I mean, each of our individual girls tells her husband), then we take the Blue Devil (that's what we call the antidote) and have a hell of a time until the girls start on the stripes again. None of us thought any of this would work, you know. But it works fine. I don't even think sex until Flo kisses my ear and tells me she's getting ready to, excuse the expression, get in heat, and then like wow. Same with everybody. The aft chamber with the nice wide bunks we call Honeymoon Hotel. It belongs to whoever needs it, and never once have both bunks been used. The rest of the time we just sleep wherever is convenient, and nobody gets uptight about it.

Excuse my getting personal, but you told me you wanted to know everything, and there's not much else to tell. All systems remain optimum. We check them over now and again, but nothing has given any trouble, or even looked as though it might be thinking about giving trouble later on. And there's absolutely nothing worth looking at outside but stars. We've all seen them about as much as we need to by now. The plasma jet thrums right along at our point-seven-five Gee. We don't even hear it anymore.

We've even got used to the recycling system. None of us really thought we'd get with the suction toilet, not to mention what happens to the contents, but it was only a little annoying the first few days. Now it's fine. The treated product goes into the algae tanks, feces and urine together. The sludge from the algae goes into the hydroponic beds, but by then, of course, it's just greeny-brown vegetable matter like my father used to get out of his mulch bed. That's all handled semi-automatically anyway, of course, so our first real contact with the system comes in the kitchen. The food we eat comes in the form of nice red tomatoes and nourishing rice pilaf and stuff like that. (We do miss animal protein a little; the frozen stores have to last a long time, so each hamburger is a special feast, and we only have them once a week or so.) The water we drink comes actually out of the air, condensed by the de-humidifiers into the reserve supply, where we get it to drink. It's nicely aerated and chilled and tastes fine. Of course, the way it gets into the air in the first place is by being sweated out of our pores or transpired from the plants (which are irrigated direct from the treated product of the reclamation tanks), and we all know, when we stop to think of it, that every molecule of it has passed through all our kidneys forty times by now. But not directly. That's the point. What we drink is clear sweet dew. And if it once was something else, can't you say the same of Lake Erie?

Well. I think I've gone on long enough. You've probably got the idea by now: We're happy in the service, and we all thank you for giving us this pleasure cruise!

Washington Two

Waiting for his appointment with the President, Dr. Knef-hausen reread the communique from the spaceship, chuckling happily to himself. "Happy in the service." "Like wow." "Kneffie would be proud of himself"—indeed Kneffie was. And proud of them, those little wonders, there! So brave. So strong.

He took as much pride in them as if they had been his own sons and daughters, all eight of them. Everybody knew the Alpha-Aleph project was Knefhausen's baby, but he tried to conceal from the world that, in his own mind, he spread his fatherhood to include the crew. They were the pick of the available world, and it was he who had put them where they were. He lifted his head, listening to the distant chanting from the perimeter fence where today's disgusting exhibition of mob violence was doing its best to harass the people who were making the world go. What great lumps they were out there, with their long hair and their dirty morals. The heavens belonged only to angels, and it was Dieter von Knefhausen who had picked the angels. It was he who had established the selection procedures (and if he had done some things that were better left unmentioned to make sure the procedures worked, what of it?). It was he who had conceived and adapted the highly important recreation schedule, and above all he who had conceived the entire project and persuaded the President to make it come true. The hardware was nothing, only money. The basic scientific concepts were known; most of the components were on the shelves; it took only will to put them together. The will would not have existed if it had not been for Knefhausen, who announced the discovery of Alpha-Aleph from his radio-observatory on Farside(and gave it that name, although as everyone realized he could have called it by any name he chose, even his own) and carried on the fight for the project by every means available until the President bought it.

It had been a hard, bitter struggle. He reminded himself with courage that the worst was still ahead. No matter. Whatever it cost, it was done, and it was worthwhile. These reports from *Constitution* proved it. It was going exactly as planned, and—

"Excuse me, Dr. Knefhausen."

He looked up, catapulted back from almost half a light-year away.

"I said the President will see you now, Dr. Knefhausen," repeated the usher.

"Ah," said Knefhausen. "Oh, yes, to be sure. I was deep in thought."

"Yes, sir. This way, sir."

They passed a window and there was a quick glimpse of the turmoil at the gates, picket signs used like battle-axes, a thin blue cloud of tear gas, the sounds of shouting. "King Mob is busy today," said Knefhausen absently.

"There's no danger, sir. Through here, please."

The President was in his private study, but to Knefhausen's surprise he was not alone. There was Murray Amos, his personal secretary, which one could understand; but there were three other men in the room. Knefhausen recognized them as the Secretary of State, the Speaker of the House and, of all people, the Vice President. How strange, thought Knefhausen, for what was to have been a confidential briefing for the President alone! But he rallied quickly.

"Excuse me, Mr. President," he said cheerfully. "I must have understood wrong. I thought you were ready for our little talk."

"I am ready, Knefhausen," said the President. The cares of his years in the White House rested heavily on him today, Knefhausen thought critically. He looked very old and very tired. "You will tell these gentlemen what you would have told me."

"Ah, yes, I see," said Knefhausen, trying to conceal the fact that he did not see at all. Surely the President did not mean what his words said; therefore it was necessary to try to see what was his thought. "Yes to be sure. Here is something, Mr. President. A new report from the *Constitution*! It was received by burst transmission from the Lunar Orbiter at Goldstone just an hour ago, and has just come from the decoding room. Let me read it to you. Our brave astronauts are getting along splendidly, just as we planned. They say—"

"Don't read us that just now," said the President harshly. "We'll hear it, but first there is something else. I want you to tell this group the full story of the Alpha-Aleph project."

"The full story, Mr. President?" Knefhausen hung on gamely. "I see. You wish me to begin with the very beginning, when first we realized at the observatory that we had located a planet—"

"No, Knefhausen. Not the cover story. The truth."

"Mr. President!" cried Knefhausen in sudden agony. "I must inform you that I protest this premature disclosure of vital—"

"The truth, Knefhausen!" shouted the President. It was the first time Knefhausen had ever heard him raise his voice. "It won't go out of this room, but you must tell them everything. Tell them why it is that the Russians were right and we lied! Tell them why we sent the astronauts on a suicide mission, ordered to land on a planet that we knew all along did not exist!"

Constitution Three

Shef Jackman's journal, Day 130.

It's been a long time, hasn't it? I'm sorry for being such a lousy correspondent. I was in the middle of a thirteen-game chess series with Eve Barstow—she was playing the Bobby Fischer games, and I was playing in the style of Reshevsky—and Eve said something that made me think of old Kneffie, and that, of course, reminded me I owed you a transmission. So here it is.

In my own defense, though, it isn't only that we've been busy with other things. It takes a lot of power for these chatty little letters. Some of us aren't so sure they're worthwhile. The farther we get the more power we need to accumulate for a transmission. Right now it's not so bad yet, but, well, I might as well tell you the truth, right? Kneffie made us promise that. Always tell the truth, he said, because you're part of the experiment, and we need to know what you're doing, all of it. Well, the truth in this case is that we were a little short of disposable power for a while because Jim Barstow needed quite a lot for research purposes. You will probably wonder what the research is, but we have a rule that we don't criticize, or even talk about, what anyone else is doing until they're ready, and he isn't ready yet. I take the responsibility for the whole thing, not just the power drain but the damage to the ship. I said he could go ahead with it.

We're going pretty fast now, and to the naked eye the stars fore and aft have blue-shifted and red-shifted nearly out of sight. It's funny, but we haven't been able to observe Alpha-Aleph yet, even with the disk obscuring the star. Now, with the shift to the blue, we probably won't see it at all until we slow down. We can still see the Sun, but I guess what we're seeing is ultraviolet when it's home. Of course the relativistic frequency shifts mean we need extra compensating power in our transmissions, which is another reason why, all in all, I don't think I'll be writing home every Sunday, between breakfast and the baseball game, the way I ought to!

But the mission's going along fine. The "personal relationships" keep on being just great. We've done a little experimental research there too that wasn't on the program, but it's all OK. No problems. Worked out great. I think maybe I'll leave out some of the details, but we found some groovy ways to do things. Oh, hell, I'll give you one hint: Dot Letski says I should tell you to get the boys at Mission Control to crack open two of the stripey pills and one of the Blue Devils, mix them with a quarter-teaspoon of black pepper and about 2 cc of the conditioner fluid from the recycling system. Serve over orange sherbet, and oh boy. After the first time we had it Flo made a crack about its being "seminal," which I thought was a private joke, but it broke everybody up. Dot figured it out for herself weeks ago. We wondered how she got so far so fast with *War and Peace* until she let us into the secret. Then we found out what it could do for you, both emotionally and intellectually: the creative over the arousing, as they say.

Ann and Jerry Letski used up their own recreational programs early (real early—they were supposed to last the whole voyage!), so they swapped microfiches, on the grounds that each was interested in an aspect of causality and they wanted to see what the other side had to offer. Now Ann is deep into people like Kant and Carnap, and Ski is sore as a boil because there's no *Achillea millefolium* in the hydroponics garden. Needs the stalks for his researches, he says. He is making do with flipping his ruble to generate hexagrams; in fact, we all borrow it now and then, but it's not the right way. Honestly, Mission Control, he's right. Some thought should have been given to our other needs, besides sex and number theory. We can't even use chop bones from the kitchen wastes, because there isn't any kitchen waste. I know you couldn't think of everything, but still— Anyway, we improvise as best we can, and mostly well enough.

Let's see, what else? Did I send you Jim Barstow's proof of Goldbach's Conjecture? Turned out to be very simple once he had devised his multiplex parity analysis idea. Mostly we don't fool with that sort of stuff anymore, though. We got tired of number theory after we'd worked out all the fun parts, and if there is any one thing that we all work on (apart from our private interests) it is probably the calculus of statement. We don't do it systematically, only as time permits from our other activities, but we're all pretty well convinced that a universal grammar is feasible enough, and it's easy enough to see what that leads to. Flo has done more than most of us. She asked me to put in that Boole, Venn and all those old people were on the wrong track, but she thinks there might be something to Leibniz's "calculus ratiocinator" idea. There's a J. W. Swanson suggestion that she likes for multiplexing languages. (Jim took off from it to work out his parity analysis.) The idea is that you devise a double-vocabulary language. One set of meanings is conveyed, say, by phonemes —that is, the shape of the words themselves. Another set is conveyed by pitch. It's like singing a message, half of it conveyed by the words, the other half by the tune. Like rock music. You get both sets of meanings at the same time. She's now working on third, fourth, and nth dimensions so as to convey many kinds of meanings at once, but it's not very fruitful so far (except for using sexual intercourse as one of the communications media). Most of the senses available are too limited to convey much. By the way, we checked out all the existing "artificial languages" as best we could—put Will Becklund under hynotic regression to recapture the Esperanto he'd learned as a kid, for instance. But they were all blind alleys. Didn't even convey as much as standard English or French.

Medical readouts follow. We're all healthy. Eve Barstow gave us a medical check to make sure. Ann and Ski had little rough spots in a couple of molars so she filled them for the practice more than because they needed it. I don't mean practice in filling teeth; she wanted to try acupuncture instead of procaine. Worked fine.

We all have this writing-to-Daddy-and-Mommy-from-Camp-Tanglewood feeling and we'd like to send you some samples of our home handicrafts. The trouble is there's so much of it. Everybody has something he's personally pretty pleased with, like Barstow's proof of most of the classic math problems and my multimedia adaptation of *Sur le pont d'Avignon*. Its hard to decide what to send you with the limited power available, and we don't want to waste it with junk. So we took a vote and decided that the best thing was Ann's verse retelling of *War and Peace*. It runs pretty long. I hope the power holds it. I'll transmit as much of it as I can. . . .

Washington Three

Spring was well advanced in Washington. Along the Potomac the cherry blossoms were beginning to bud, and Rock Creek Park was the pale green of new leaves. Even through the *whap, whap* of the helicopter rotor Knefhausen could hear an occasional rattle of small-arms fire from around Georgetown, and the Molotov cocktails and tear gas from the big Water Gate apartment development at the river's edge were steaming the sky with smoke and fumes. They never stopped, thought Knefhausen irritably. What was the good of trying to save people like this?

It was distracting. He found himself dividing his attention into three parts—the scarred, greening landscape below; the escort fireships that orbited around his own chopper; and the papers on his lap. All of them annoyed him. He couldn't keep his mind on any of them. What he liked least was the report from the *Constitution*. He had had to get expert help in translating what it was all about, and he didn't like the need, and even less liked the results. What had gone wrong? They were his kids, handpicked. There had been no hint, for instance, of hippiness in any of them, at least not past the age of twenty, and only for Ann Becklund and Florence Jackman even then. How had they got into this *I Ching* foolishness, and this stupid business with the *Achillea millefolium*, better known as the common yarrow? What "experiments"? Who started the disgustingly antiscientific acupuncture thing? How dared they depart from their programmed power budget for "research purposes," and what were the purposes? Above all, what was the "damage to the ship"?

He scribbled on a pad:

> With immediate effect, cut out the nonsense. I have the impression you are all acting like irresponsible children. You are letting down the ideals of our program.
>
> Knefhausen

After running the short distance from the chopper pad to the shelter of the guarded White House entrance, he gave the slip to a page from the Message Center for immediate encoding and transmission to the *Constitution* via Goldstone, Lunar Orbiter and Farside Base. All they needed was a reminder, he persuaded himself, then they would settle down. But he was still worried as he peered into a mirror, patted his hair down, smoothed his moustache with the tip of a finger and presented himself to the President's chief secretary.

This time they went down, not up. Knefhausen was going to the basement chamber that had been successively Franklin Roosevelt's swimming pool, the White House press lounge, a TV studio for taping jolly little two-shots of the President with congressmen and senators for the folks back home to see, and, now, the heavily armored bunker in which anyone trapped in the White House in the event of a successful attack from the city outside could hold out for several weeks, during which time the Fourth Armored would surely be able to retake the grounds from its bases in Maryland. It was not a comfortable room, but it was a safe one. Besides being armored against attack, it was as thoroughly soundproof, spyproof and leakproof as any chamber in the world, not excepting the Under-Kremlin or the Colorado NOROM base.

Knefhausen was admitted and seated, while the President and a couple of others were in whispered conversation at one end of the room, and the several dozen other people present craned their necks to stare at Knefhausen.

After a moment the President raised his head. "All right," he said. He drank from a crystal goblet of water, looking wizened and weary, and disappointed at the way a boyhood dream had turned out: the Presidency wasn't what it had seemed to be from Muncie, Indiana. "We all know why we're here. The government of the United States has given out information which was untrue. It did so knowingly and wittingly, and we've been caught at it. Now we want you to know the background, and so Dr. Knefhausen is going to explain the Alpha-Aleph project. Go ahead, Knefhausen."

Knefhausen stood up and walked unhurryingly to the little lectern set up for him, off to one side of the President. He opened his papers on the lectern, studied them thoughtfully for a moment with his lips pursed, and said:

"As the President has said, the Alpha-Aleph project is a camouflage. A few of you learned this some months ago, and then you referred to it with other words. 'Fraud.' 'Fake.' Words like that. But if I may say it in French, it is not any of those words, it is a legitimate *ruse de guerre*. Not the *guerre* against our political enemies, or even against the dumb kids in the streets with their Molotov cocktails and bricks. I do not mean those wars; I mean the war against ignorance. For you see, there were certain sings—certain *things* we had to know for the sake of science and progress. Alpha-Aleph was designed to find them out for us.

"I will tell you the worst parts first," he said. "Number one, there is no such planet as Alpha-Aleph. The Russians were right. Number two, we knew this all along. Even the photographs we produced were fakes, and in the long run the rest of the world will find this out and they will know of our *ruse de guerre.* I can only hope that they will not find out too soon, for if we are lucky and keep the secret for a while, then I hope we will be able to produce good results to justify what we have done. Number three, when the *Constitution* reaches Alpha Centauri there will be no place for them to land, no way to leave their spacecraft, no sources of raw materials which they might be able to use to make fuel to return, no nothing but the star and empty space. This fact has certain consequences. The *Constitution* was designed with enough hydrogen fuel capacity for a one-way flight, plus maneuvering reserve. There will not be enough for them to come back, and the source they had hoped to tap, namely the planet Alpha-Aleph, does not exist, so they will not come back. Consequently they will die there. Those are the bad things to which I must admit."

There was a sighing murmur from the audience. The President was frowning absently to himself. Knefhausen waited patiently for the medicine to be swallowed, then went on.

"You ask, then, why have we done this thing? Condemning eight young people to their death? The answer is simple: knowledge. To put it with other words, we must have the basic scientific knowledge we need to protect the free world. You are all familiar, I si—I believe, with the known fact that basic scientific advances have been very few these past ten years and more. Much R&D. Much technology. Much applications. But in the years since Einstein, or better since Weizsäcker, very little basic.

"But without the new basic knowledge, the new technology must soon stop developing. It will run out of steam, you see.

"Now I must tell you a story. It is a true scientific story, not a joke; I know you do not want jokes from me at this time. There was a man named de Bono, a Maltese, who wished to investigate the process of creative thinking. There is not very much known about this process, but he had an idea how he could find something out. So he prepared for an experiment a room that was stripped of all furniture, with two doors, one across from the other. You go into one door, you go through the room, you walk out the other. He put at the door that was the entrance some material—two flat boards, some ropes. And he got as his subjects some young children. Now he said to the children, 'Now, this is a game we will play.

You must go through this room and out the other door, that is all. If you do that, you win. But there is one rule. You must not touch the floor with your feet or your knees or with any part of your body or your clothing. We had here a boy,' he said, 'who was very athletic and walked across on his hands, but he was disqualified. You must not do that. Now go, and whoever does it fastest will win some chocolates.'

"So he took away all of the children but the first one and, one by one, they tried. There were ten or fifteen of them, and each of them did the same thing. Some it took longer to figure out, some figured it out right away, but it always was the same trick: They sat down on the floor, they took the boards and the ropes, and they tied one board to each foot and they walked across the room like on skis. The fastest one thought of the trick right away and was across in a few seconds. The slowest took many minutes. But it was the same trick for all of them, and that was the first part of the experiment.

"Now this Maltese man, de Bono, performed the second part of the experiment. It was exactly like the first, with one difference. He did not give them two boards. He only gave them one board.

"And in the second part every child worked out the same trick, too, but it was of course a different trick. They tied the rope to the end of the single board and then they stood on it, and jumped up, tugging the rope to pull the board forward, hopping and tugging, moving a little bit at a time, and every one of them succeeded. But in the first experiment the average time to cross was maybe forty-five seconds. And in the second experiment the average time was maybe twenty seconds. With one board they did their job faster than with two.

"Perhaps now some of you see the point. Why did not any of the children in the first group think of this faster method of going across the room? It is simple. They looked at what they were given to use for materials and, they are like all of us, they wanted to use everything. But they did not need everything. They could do better with less, in a different way."

Knefhausen paused and looked around the room, savoring the moment. He had them now, he knew. It was just as it had been with the President himself, three years before. They were beginning to see the necessity of what had been done, and the pale, upturned faces were no longer as hostile, only perplexed and a little afraid.

He went on:

"So that is what Project Alpha-Aleph is about, gentlemen and ladies. We have selected eight of the most intelligent human beings we could find—healthy, young, very adventurous. Very creative. We played on them a nasty trick, to be sure. But we gave them an opportunity no one has ever had. The opportunity to *think*. To think for *ten years*. To think about basic questions. Out there they do not have the extra board to distract them. If they want to know something they cannot run to the library and look it up, and find that somebody has said that what they were thinking could not work. They must think it out for themselves.

"So in order to make this possible we have practiced a deception on them, and it will cost them their lives. All right, that is tragic, yes. But if we take their lives we give them in exchange immortality.

"How do we do this? Trickery again, gentlemen and ladies. I do not say to them, 'Here, you must discover new basic approaches to science and tell them to us.' I camouflage the purpose, so that they will not be distracted even by that. We have told them that this is recreational, to help them pass the time. This too is a *ruse de guerre*. The 'recreation' is not to help them make the trip; it is the whole purpose of the trip.

"So we start them out with the basic tools of science. With numbers: that is, with magnitudes and quantification, with all that scientific observations are about. With grammar. This is not what you learned when you were thirteen years old, it is a technical term; it means with the calculus of statement and the basic rules of communication: that is so they can learn to think clearly by communicating fully and without fuzzy ambiguity. We give them very little else, only the opportunity to mix these two basic ingredients and come up with new forms of knowledge.

"What will come of these things? That is a fair question. Unfortunately there is no answer. Not yet. If we knew the answer in advance, we would not have to perform the experiment. So we do not know what will be the end result of this, but already they have accomplished very much. Old questions that have puzzled the wisest of scientists for hundreds of years they have solved already. I will give you one example. You will say, 'Yes, but what does it *mean*?' I will answer, 'I do not know'; I only know that it is so hard a question that no one else has ever been able to answer it. It is a proof of a thing which is called Goldbach's Conjecture. Only a conjecture; you could call it a guess. A guess by an eminent mathematician some many years ago, that every even number can be written as the sum of two prime numbers. This is one of those simple problems in mathematics that everyone can understand and no one can solve. You can say, 'Certainly, sixteen is the sum of eleven and five, both of which are prime numbers, and thirty is the sum of twenty-three and seven, which also are both prime, and I can give you such numbers for any even number you care to name.' Yes, you can; but can you prove that for *every* even number it will *always* be possible to do this? No. You cannot. No one has been able to, but our friends on the *Constitution* have done it, and this was in the first few months. They have yet almost ten years. I cannot say what they will do in that time, but it is foolish to imagine that it will be anything less than very much indeed. A new relativity, a new universal gravitation—I don't know, I am only saying words. But much."

He paused again. No one was making a sound. Even the President was no longer staring straight ahead without expression, but was looking at him.

"It is not yet too late to spoil the experiment, and so it is necessary for us to keep the secret a bit longer. But there you have it, gentlemen and ladies. That is the truth about Alpha-Aleph." He dreaded what would come next, postponed it for a second by consulting his papers, shrugged, faced them and said: "Now, are there any questions?"

Oh, yes there were questions. Herr Omnes was stunned a little, took a moment to overcome the spell of the simple and beautiful truths he had heard, but then first one piped up, then another, then two or three shouting at once. There were questions, to be sure. Questions beyond answering. Questions Knefhausen did not have time to hear, much less answer, before the next question was on him. Questions to which he did not know the answers. Questions, worst of all, to which the answers were like pepper in the eyes, enraging, blinding the people to sense. But he had to face them, and he tried to answer them. Even when they shouted so that, outside the thick double doors, the Marine guards looked at each other uneasily and wondered what made the dull rumble that penetrated the very good soundproofing of the room. "What I want to know, who put you up to this?" "Mr. Chairman, nobody; it is as I have said." "But see now, Knefhausen, do you mean to tell us you're murderin' these good people for the sake of some Goldbach's theory?" "No, Senator, not for Goldbach's Conjecture, but for what great advances in science will mean in the struggle to keep the free world free." "You're confessing you've dragged the United States into a palpable fraud?" "A legitimate ruse of war, Mr. Secretary, because there was no other way." "The photographs, Knefhausen?" "Faked, General, as I have told you. I accept full responsibility." And on and on, the words "murder" and "fraud" and even "treason" coming faster and faster.

Until at last the President stood up and raised his hand. Order was a long time coming, but at last they quieted down.

"Whether we like it or not, we're in it," he said simply. "There is nothing else to say. You have come to me, many of you, with rumors and asked for the truth. Now you have the truth, and it is classified Top Secret and must not be divulged. You all know what this means. I will only add that I personally propose to see that any breach of this security is investigated with all the resources of the government, and punished with the full penalty of the law. I declare this a matter of national emergency, and remind you that the penalty includes the death sentence when appropriate—and I say that in this case it is appropriate." He looked very much older than his years, and he moved his lips as though something tasted bad in his mouth. He allowed no further discussion, and dismissed the meeting.

Half an hour later, in his private office, it was just Knefhausen and the President.

"All right," said the President, "it's all hit the fan. The next thing is: The world will know it. I can postpone that a few weeks, maybe even months. I can't prevent it."

"I am grateful to you, Mr. President, for—"

"Shut up, Knefhausen. I don't want any speeches. There is one thing I want from you, and that is an explanation. What the hell is this about mixing up narcotics and free love and so on?"

"Ah," said Knefhausen, "you refer to the most recent communication from the *Constitution*. Yes. I have already dispatched, Mr. President, a strongly worded order. Because of the communications lag it will not be received for some months, but I assure you the matter will be corrected."

The President said bitterly, "I don't want any assurances, either. Do you watch television? I don't mean *I Love Lucy* and the ball games; I mean news. Do you know what sort of shape this country is in? The bonus marches in 1932, the race riots in 1967—they were nothing. Time was when we could call out the National Guard to put down disorder. Last week I had to call out the Army to use against three companies of the Guard. One more scandal and we're finished, Knefhausen, and this is a big one."

"The purposes are beyond reproach—"

"Your purposes may be. Mine may be, or I try to tell myself it is for the good of science I did this, and not so I will be in the history books as the president who contributed a major breakthrough. But what are the purposes of your friends on the *Constitution*? I agreed to eight martyrs, Knefhausen. I didn't agree to forty billion dollars out of the nation's pockets to give your eight young friends ten years of gang-bangs and dope."

"Mr. President, I assure you this is only a temporary phase. I have instructed them to straighten out."

"And if they don't, what are you going to do about it?" The President, who never smoked, stripped a cigar, bit off the end and lit it. He said, "It's too late for me to say I shouldn't have let you talk me into this. So all I will say is you have to show results from this flim-flam before the lid blows off, or I won't be President anymore, and I doubt that you will be alive."

Constitution Four

This is Shef again and it's, oh, let me see, about Day 250. 300? No, I don't think so. Look, I'm sorry about the ship date, but I honestly don't think much in those terms anymore. I've been thinking about other things. Also I'm a little upset. When I tossed the ruble the hexagram was K'an, which is danger, over Li, the Sun. That's a bad mood to be communicating with you in. We aren't vengeful types, but the fact is that some of us were pretty sore when we found out what you'd done. I don't *think* you need to worry, but I wish I'd got a better hexagram.

Let me tell you the good parts first. Our velocity is pushing point four oh C now. The scenery is beginning to get interesting. For several weeks now the stars fore and aft have been drifting out of sight as the ones in front get up into the ultraviolet and the ones behind sink into the infrared. You'd think that as the spectrum shifts the other parts of the EMF bands would come into the visible range. I guess they do, but the stars peak in certain frequencies, and most of them seem to do it in the visible frequencies, so the effect is that they disappear. The first thing was that there was a sort of round black spot ahead of us where we couldn't see anything at all, not Alpha Centauri, not Beta Centauri, not even the bright Circini stars. Then we lost the Sun behind us, and a little later we saw the blackout spread to a growing circle of stars there. Then the circles began to widen.

Of course, we know that the stars are really there. We can detect them with phase-shift equipment, just as we can transmit and receive your message by shifting the frequencies. But we just can't see them anymore. The ones in direct line of flight, where we have a vector velocity of .34c or .37c (depending on whether they are in front of us or behind us) simply aren't radiating in the visible band anymore. The ones farther out to the side have been displaced visually because of the relativistic effects of our speed. But what it looks like is that we're running the hell out of Nothing, in the direction of Nothing, and it is frankly a little scary.

Even the stars off to one side are showing relativistic color shifts. It's almost like a rainbow, one of those full-circle rainbows that you see on the clouds beneath you from an airplane sometimes. Only this circle is all around us. Nearest the black hole in front the stars have frequency-shifted to a dull reddish color. They go through orange and yellow and a sort of leaf green to the band nearest the black hole in back, which are bright blue shading to purple. Jim Barstow has been practicing his farsight on them, and he can relate them to the actual sky map. But I can't. He sees something in the black hole in front of us that I can't see, either. He says he thinks it's a bright radio source, probably Centaurus A, and he claims it is radiating strongly in the whole visible band now. He means strongly for him, with his eyes. I'm not sure I can see it at all. There *may* be a sort of very faint, diffuse glow there, like the *gegenschein*, but I'm not sure. Neither is anyone else.

But the starbow itself is beautiful. It's worth the trip. Flo has been learning oil painting so she can make a picture of it to send you for your wall, although when she found out what you'd been up to she got so sore she was thinking of booby-trapping it with a fusion bomb or something. (But she's over that now, I think.)

So we're not so mad at you anymore, although there was a time when, if I'd been communicating with you at exactly that moment, I would have said some bad things.

. . . I just played this back, and it sounds pretty jumbled and confused. I'm sorry about that. It's hard for me to do this. I don't mean hard like intellectually difficult (the way chess problems and tensor analysis used to be), but hard like shoveling sand with a teaspoon. I'm just not used to constricting my thoughts in this straitjacket anymore. I tried to get one of the others to communicate this time instead of me, but there were no takers. I did get a lot of free advice. Dot says I shouldn't waste my time remembering how we used to talk. She wanted to write an eidetic account in simplified notation for you, which she estimated a crash program could translate for you in reasonable time, a decade or two, and would give you an absolutely full account of everything. I objected that that involved practical difficulties. Not in preparing the ac-count, I don't mean. Shucks, we can all do that now. I don't forget anything, except irrelevant things like the standard-reckoning day that I don't want to remember in the first place, and neither does anyone else. But the length of transmission would be too much. We don't have the power to transmit the necessary number of groups, especially since the accident. Dot said we could Gödelize it. I said you were too dumb to de-Gödelize it. She said it would be good practice for you.

Well, she's right about that, and it's time you all learned how to communicate in a sensible way, so if the power holds out I'll include Dot's eidetic account at the end. In Gödelized form. Lots of luck. I won't honestly be surprised if you miss a digit or something and it all turns into *Rebecca of Sunny-brook Farm* or some missing books of apocrypha or, more likely of course, gibberish. Ski says it won't do you any good in any case, because Henle was right. I pass that on without comment.

Sex. You always want to hear about sex. It's great. Now that we don't have to fool with the pills anymore we've been having some marvelous times. Flo and Jim Barstow began making it as part of a multiplexed communications system that you have to see to believe. Sometimes when they're going to do it we all knock off and just sit around and watch them, cracking jokes and singing and helping with the auxiliary computations. When we had that little bit of minor surgery the other day (now we've got the bones seasoning), Ann and Ski decided to ball instead of using anesthesia, and they said it was better than acupuncture. It didn't block the sensation. They were aware of their little toes being lopped off, but they didn't perceive it as pain. So then Jim, when it was his turn, tried going through the amputation without anything at all in the expectation that he and Flo would go to bed together a little later, and that worked well too. He was all het up about it; claimed it showed a reverse causality that his theories predicted but that had not been demonstrated before. Said at last he was over the cause-preceding-the-effect hangup. It's like the Red Queen and the White Queen, and quite puzzling until you get the hang of it. (I'm not sure I've gotten the hang of it yet.) Suppose he hadn't balled Flo? Would his toe have hurt retroactively? I'm a little mixed up on this, Dot says because I simply don't understand phenomenology in general, and I think I'll have to take Ann's advice and work my way through Carnap, although the linguistics are so poor that it's hard to stay with it. Come to think of it, I don't have to. It's all in the Gödelized eidetic statement, after all. So I'll transmit the statement to you, and while I'm doing that it will be a sort of review for me and maybe I'll get my head right on causality.

Listen, let me give you a tip. The statement will also include Ski's trick of containing plasma for up to 500K milliseconds, so when you figure it out you'll know how to build those fusion power reactors you were talking about when we left. That's the carrot before your nose, so get busy on de-Gödelizing. The plasma dodge works fine, although of course we were sorry about what happened when we converted the drive. The explosion killed Will Becklund outright, and it looked hairy for all of us.

Well, anyway. I have to cut this short because the power's running a little low and I don't want to chance messing up the statement. It follows herewith:

$1973^{354} + 331^{852} + 17^{2008} + 5^{47} + 3^{9606} + 2^{88}$ take away 78.

Lots of luck, fellows!

Washington Four

Knefhausen lifted his head from the litter of papers on his desk. He rubbed his eyes, sighing. He had given up smoking the same time as the President, but, like the President, he was thinking of taking it up again. It could kill you, yes. But it was a tension-reducer, and he needed that. And what was wrong with something killing you? There were worse things than being killed, he thought dismally.

Looking at it any way you could, he thought objectively, the past two or three years had been hard on him. They had started so well and had gone so bad. Not as bad as those distant memories of childhood when everybody was so poor and Berlin was so cold and what warm clothes he had came from the *Winterhilfe*. By no means as hard as the end of the war. Nothing like as bad as those first years in South America and then in the Middle East, when even the lucky and famous ones, the Von Brauns and the Ehrickes, were having trouble getting what was due them and a young calf like Knefhausen had to peel potatoes and run elevators to live. But harder and worse than a man at the summit of his career had any reason to expect.

The Alpha-Aleph project, fundamentally, was sound! He ground his teeth, thinking about it. It would work—no, by God, it *was* working, and it would make the world a different place. Future generations would see.

But the future generations were not here yet, and in the present things were going badly.

Reminded, he picked up the phone and buzzed his secretary. "Have you got through to the President yet?" he demanded.

"I'm sorry, Dr. Knefhausen. I've tried every ten minutes, just as you said."

"Ah," he grunted. "No, wait. Let me see. What calls are there?"

Rustle of paper. "The news services, of course, asking about the rumors again. Jack Anderson's office. The man from CBS."

"No, no. I will not talk to press. Anyone else?"

"Senator Copley called, asking when you were going to answer the list of questions his committee sent you."

"I will give him an answer. I will give him the answer Götz von Berlichingen gave to the Bishop of Bamberg."

"I'm sorry, Dr. Knefhausen, I didn't quite catch—"

"No matter. Anything else?"

"Just a long-distance call, from a Mr. Hauptmann. I have his number."

Hauptmann?" The name was puzzlingly familiar. After a moment Knefhausen placed it: to be sure, the photo technician who had cooperated in the faked pictures from Briareus Twelve. Well, he had his orders to stay out of sight and shut up. "No, that's not important. None of them are, and I do not wish to be disturbed with such nonsense. Continue as you were, Mrs. Ambrose. If the President is reached you are to put me on at once, but no other calls."

He hung up and returned to his desk.

He looked sadly and fondly at the papers. He had them all out: the reports from the *Constitution,* his own drafts of interpretation and comment, and more than a hundred footnoted items compiled by his staff, to help untangle the meanings and implications of those, ah, so cryptic sometimes reports from space:

"*Henle.* Apparently refers to Paul Henle (note appended); probably the citation intended is his statement, 'There are certain symbolisms in which certain things cannot be said.' Conjecture that English language is one of those symbolisms."

"*Orange sherbet sundae.* A classified experimental study was made of the material in Document Ref. No. CON-130, Para. 4. Chemical analysis and experimental testing have indicated that the recommended mixture of pharmaceuticals and other ingredients produce a hallucinogen-related substance of considerable strength and not wholly known qualities. 100 subjects ingested the product or a placebo in a double-blind controlled test. Subjects receiving the actual substance report reactions significantly different from the placebo. Effects reported include feelings of immense competence and deepened understanding. However, data is entirely subjective. Attempts were made to verify claims by standard I.Q., manipulative, and other tests, but the subjects did not cooperate well, and several have since absented themselves without leave from the testing establishment."

"*Gödelized language.* A system of encoding any message of any kind as a single very large number. The message is first written out in clear language and then encoded as bases and exponents. Each letter of the message is represented in order by the natural order of primes—that is, the first letter is represented by the base 2, the second by the base 3, the third by the base 5, then 7, 11, 13, 17, etc. The identity of the letter occupying that position in the message is given by the exponent: simply, the exponent 1 meaning that the letter in that position is an A, the exponent 2 meaning that it is a B, 3 a C, etc. The message as a whole is then rendered as the product of all the bases and exponents. *Example.* The word "cab" can thus be represented as $2^3 \times 3^1 \times 5^2$, or 600. ($=8 \times 3 \times 25$.) The name 'Abe' would be represented by the number 56,250, or $2^1 \times 3^2 \times 5^5$. ($=2 \times 9 \times 3125$.) A sentence like 'John lives,' would be represented by the product of the following terms: $2^{10} \times 3^{15} \times 5^8 \times 7^{14} \times 11^0 \times 13^{12} \times 17^9 \times 19^{22} \times 23^5 \times 29^{19} \times 31^{27}$ (in which the exponent '0' has been reserved for a space and the exponent '27' has been arbitrarily assigned to indicate a full stop). As can be seen, the Gödelized form for even a short message involves a very large number, although such numbers may be transmitted quite compactly in the form of a sum of bases and exponents. The example transmitted by the *Constitution* is estimated to equal the contents of a standard unabridged dictionary."

"*Farsight.* The subject James Madison Barstow is known to have suffered from some nearsightedness in his early school years, apparently brought on by excessive reading, which he attempted to cure through eye exercises similar to the 'Bates method' (note appended). His vision at time of testing for Alpha-Aleph project was optimal. Interviews with former associates indicate his continuing interest in increasing visual acuity. *Alternate explanation.* There is some indication that he was also interested in paranormal phenomena such as clairvoyance or prevision, and it is possible, though at present deemed unlikely, that his use of the term refers to 'looking ahead' in time."

And so on, and on.

Knefhausen gazed at the litter of papers lovingly and hopelessly, and passed his hand over his forehead. The kids!

They were so marvelous . . . but so unruly . . . and so hard to understand. How unruly of them to have concealed their true accomplishments. The secret of hydrogen fusion! That alone would justify, more than justify, the entire project. But where was it? Locked in that number-jumber gibberish. Knefhausen was not without appreciation of the elegance of the method. He, too, was capable of taking seriously a device of such luminous simplicity. Once the number was written out you had only to start by dividing it by two as many times as possible, and the number of times would give you the first letter. Then divide by the next prime, three, and that number of times would give you the second letter. But the practical difficulties! You could not get even the first letter until you had the whole number, and IBM had refused even to bid on constructing a bank of computers to write that number out unless the development time was stretched to twenty-five years. *Twenty-five years*. And meanwhile in that number was hidden probably the secret of hydrogen fusion, possibly many greater secrets, most certainly the key to Knefhausen's own well-being over the next few weeks. . . .

His phone rang.

He grabbed it and shouted into it at once: "Yes, Mr. President!"

He had been too quick. It was only his secretary. Her voice was shaking but determined.

"It's not the President, Dr. Knefhausen, but Senator Copley is on the wire and he says it is urgent. He says—"

"No!" shouted Knefhausen and banged down the phone. He regretted it even as he was doing it. Copley was very high, chairman of the Armed Forces Committee; he was not a man Knefhausen wished to have as an enemy, and he had been very careful to make him a friend over years of patient fence-building. But he could not speak to him, or to anyone, while the President was not answering his calls. Copley's rank was high, but he was not in the direct hierarchical line over Knefhausen. When the top of that line refused to talk to him, Knefhausen was cut off from the world.

He attempted to calm himself by examining the situation objectively. The pressures on the President just now: They were enormous. There was the continuing trouble in the cities, all the cities. There were the political conventions coming up. There was the need to get elected for a third term, and the need to get the law amended to make that possible.

And yes, Knefhausen admitted to himself, the worst pressure of all was the rumors that were floating around about the *Constitution*. He had warned the President. It was unfortunate the President had not listened. He had said that a secret known to two people is compromised and a secret known to more than two is not secret. But the President had insisted on the disclosure to that ever-widening circle of high officials —sworn, of course to secrecy, but what good was that?—and, of course, in spite of everything, there had been leaks. Fewer than one might have feared. More than one could stand.

He touched the reports from *Constitution* caressingly. Those beautiful kids, they could still make everything right, so wonderful. . . .

Because it was he who had made them wonderful, he confessed to himself. He had invented the idea. He had selected them. He had done things which he did not quite even yet reconcile himself to, to make sure that it was they and not some others who were on the crew. He had, above all, made assurance doubly sure by insuring their loyalty in every way possible. Training. Discipline. Ties of affection and friendship. More reliable ties: loading their food supplies, their entertainment tapes, their programmed activities with every sort of advertising inducement, M/R compulsion, psychological reinforcement he could invent or find, so that whatever else they did they did not fail to report faithfully back to Earth. Whatever else happened, there was that. The data might be hard to untangle, but it would be there. They could not help themselves; his commandments were stronger than God's; like Martin Luther, they must say *Ich kann night anders*, and come Pope or inquisition, they must stand by it. They would learn, and tell what they learned, and thus the investment would be repaid. . . .

The telephone!

He was talking before he had it even to his mouth. "Yes, yes! This is Dr. Knefhausen, yes!" he gabbled. Surely it must be the President now—

It was not.

"Knefhausen!" shouted the man on the other end. "Now, listen, I'll tell you what I told that bitch pig girl of yours, if I don't talk to you on the phone *right now* I'll have Fourth Armored in there to arrest you and bring you to me in twenty minutes. So listen!"

Knefhausen recognized both voice and style. He drew a deep voice and forced himself to be calm. "Very well, Senator Copley," he said, "what is it?"

"The game is blown, boy! That's what it is. That boy of yours in Huntsville, what's his name, the photo technician—"

"Hauptmann?"

"That's him! Would you like to know where he is, you dumb Kraut bastard?"

"Why, I suppose—I should think in Huntsville—"

"Wrong, boy! Your Kraut bastard friend claimed he didn't feel good and took some accrued sick time. Intelligence kept an eye on him up to a point, didn't stop him, wanted to see what he'd do. Well, they saw. They saw him leaving Orly Airport an hour ago in an Aeroflot plane. Put your big Kraut brain to work on that one, Knefhausen! He's defected. Now start figuring out what you're going to do about it, and it better be good."

Knefhausen said something, he did not know what, and hung up the phone, he did not remember when. He stared glassily into space for a time.

Then he flicked the switch for his secretary and said, not listening to her stammering apologies, "That long-distance call that came from Hauptmann before, Mrs. Ambrose. You didn't say where it was from."

"It was an overseas call, Dr. Knefhausen. From Paris. You didn't give me a chance to—"

"Yes, yes. I understand. Thank you. Never mind." He hung up and sat back. He felt almost relieved. If Hauptmann had gone to Russia it could only be to tell them that the picture was faked and not only was there no planet for the astronauts to land on but it was not a mistake, even, actually a total fraud. So now it was all out of his hands. History would judge him now. The die was cast. The Rubicon was crossed.

So many literary allusions, he thought deprecatingly. Actually it was not the judgment of history that was immediately important but the judgment of certain real people now alive and likely to respond badly. And they would judge him not so much by what might be or what should have been, as by what was. He shivered in the cold of that judgment and reached for the telephone to try once more to call the President. But he was quite sure the President woud not answer, then or ever again.

Constitution Five

Old reliable peed-off Shef here. Look, we got your message.
I don't want to discuss it. You've got a nerve. You're in a bad
mood, aren't you? If you can't say anything nice, don't say
anything at all. We do the best we can, and that's not bad,
and if we don't do exactly what you want us to, maybe it's
because we know quite a lot more than you did when you
fired us off at that blob of moonshine you call Alpha-Aleph.
Well, thanks a lot for nothing.

On the other hand, thanks a little for what little you did
do, which at least worked out to get us where we are, and I
don't mean spatially. So I'm not going to yell at you. I just
don't want to talk to you at all. I'll let the others talk for
themselves.

Dot Letski speaking. This is important. Pass it on. I have
three things to tell you that I do not want you to forget.
One: Most problems have grammatical solutions. The problem of transporting people from the Earth to another planet
does not get solved by putting pieces of steel together one at
a time at random, and happening to find out you've built the
Constitution by accident. It gets solved by constructing a
model (=equation (=grammar)) which describes the necessary circumstances under which the transportation occurs.
Once you have the grammatical model, you just put the metal
around it and it goes like gangbusters.

When you have understood this you will be ready for:
Two: There is no such thing as causality. What a waste of
time it has been, trying to assign "causes" to "events"! You say
things like, "Striking a match causes it to burn." True statement? No, false statement. You find yourself in a whole
waffle about whether the "act" of "striking" is "necessary"
and/or "sufficient" and you get lost in words. Pragmatically
useful grammars are without tenses. In a decent grammar
(which this English-language one, of course, is not, but I'll
do the best I can) you can make a statement like "There
exists a conjunction of forms of matter (specified) which
combine with the release of energy at a certain temperature
(specified) (which may be the temperature associated with
heat of friction)." Where's the causality? "Cause" and "effect"
are in the same timeless statement. So, *Three: There are no*

such thing as empirical laws. When Ski came to understand that, he was able to contain the plasma in our jet indefinitely, not by pushing particles around in brute-force magnetic squeezes but by encouraging them to want to stay together. There are other ways of saying what he does (="creates an environment in which centripetal exceed centrifugal forces"), but the way I said it is better because it tells something about your characters. Bullies, all of you. Why can't you be nice to things if you want them to be nice to you? Be sure to pass this on to T'in Fa at Tiantsin, Professor Morris at All Soul's, and whoever holds the Carnap chair at UCLA.

Flo's turn. My mother would have loved my garden. I have drumsticks and daffodils growing side by side in the sludgy sand. They do so please us, and we them: I will probably transmit a full horticultural handbook at a future date, but meanwhile it is shameful to eat a radish. Carrots, on the other hand, enjoy it.

A statement of William Becklund, deceased. I emerged into the world between feces and urine, learned, grew, ate, worked, moved and died. Alternatively, I emerged from the hydrogen flare, shrank, disgorged, and reentered the womb one misses so. You may approach it from either end; it makes no difference at all which way you look at it.

Observational datum, Letski. At time *t,* a Dirac number incommensurable with GMT, the following phenomenon is observed:

The radio source Centaurus A is identified as a positionally stable single collective object rather than two intersecting gas clouds and is observed to contract radially toward a center. Analysis and observation reveal it to be a Black Hole of which the fine detail is not detectable as yet. One infers all galaxies develop such central vortices, with implications of interest to astronomers and eschatologists. I, Seymour Letski, propose to take a closer look but the others prefer to continue programmed flight first. Harvard-Smithsonian notification service, please copy.

"Starbow," a preliminary study for a rendering into English of a poem by James Barstow:
   Gaggle of goslings but pick of our race

We waddle through relativistic space.
Dilated, discounted, despondent we scan:
But vacant the Sign of the Horse and the Man.
Vacant the Sign of the Man and the Horse,
And now we conjecture the goal of our course.
Tricked, trapped and cozened, we ruefully run
After the child of the bachelor sun.
The trick is revealed and the trap is confessed
And we are the butts of the dimwitted jest.
O Gander who made us, O Goose who laid us,
How lewdly and twistedly you betrayed us!
We owe you a debt. We won't forget.
With fortune and firmness we'll pay you yet.
Give us some luck and we'll timely send
Your pot of gold from the starbow's end.

Ann Becklund.
I think it was Stanley Weinbaum who said that from three facts a truly superior mind should be able to deduce the whole universe (Ski thinks it is possible with a finite number, but considerably larger than that). We are so very far from being truly superior minds by those standards, or even by our own. Yet we have a much larger number of facts to work with than three, or even three thousand, and so we have deduced a good deal.

This is not as valuable to you as you might have hoped, dear old bastardly Kneffie and all you bastardly others, because one of the things that we have deduced is that we can't tell you everything, because you wouldn't understand. We would help you along, some of you, if you were here, and in time you would be able to do what we do easily enough, but not at remote control.

But all is not lost, folks! Cheer up! You don't deduce like we deduce, but on the other hand you have so very much more to work from. Try. Get smart. You can do it if you want to. Set your person at rest, compose your mind before you speak, make your relations firm before you ask for something. Try not to be loathsome about it. Don't be like the fellow in the Changes. "He brings increase to no one. Indeed, someone even strikes him."

We've all grown our toes back now, even Will, although it was particularly difficult for him since he had been killed, and we've inscribed the bones and used them with very good effect in generating the hexagrams. I hope you see the point of what we did. We could have gone on with tossing coins or throwing the yarrow stalks, or at least with the closest Flo could breed to yarrow stalks. We didn't want to do that because it's not the optimum way.

The person who doesn't keep his heart constantly steady might say, "Well, what's the difference?" That's a poor sort of question to ask. It implies a deterministic answer. A better question to that is, "Does it make a difference?" and the answer to that is, "Yes, probably, because in order to do something right you must do it right." That is the law of identity, in any language.

Another question you might ask is, "Well, what source of knowledge are you actually tapping when you consult the hexagrams?" That's a better kind of question in that it doesn't *force* a wrong answer, but the answer is, again, indeterminate. You might view the *I Ching* as a sort of Rorschach bundle of squiggles that has no innate meaning but is useful because your own mind interprets it and puts sense into it. Feel free! You might think of it as a sort of memory bank of encoded lore. Why not? You might skip it entirely and come to knowledge in some other tao, any tao you like. ("The superior man understands the transitory in the light of the eternity of the end.") That's fine, too!

But whatever way you do it, you should *do* it that way. We needed inscribed bones to generate hexagrams, because that was the right way, and so it was no particular sacrifice to lop off a toe each for the purpose. It's working out nicely, except for one thing. The big hangup now is that the translations are so degraded, Chinese to German, German to English, and error seeping in at every step, but we're working on that now.

Perhaps I will tell you more at another time. Not now. Not very soon. Eve will tell you about that.

Eve Barstow, the Dummy, comes last and, I'm afraid, least.
When I was a little girl I used to play chess, badly, with very good players, and that's the story of my life. I'm a chronic over-achiever. I can't stand people who aren't smarter and better than I am, but the result is that I'm the runt of the litter every time. They are all very nice to me here, even Jim, but they know what the score is and so do I.

So I keep busy and applaud what I can't do. It isn't a bad life. I have everything I need, except pride.

Let me tell you what a typical day is like here between Sol and Centaurus. We wake up (if we have been sleeping, which some of us still do) and eat (if we are still eating, as all but Ski and, of course, Will Becklund do). The food is delicious and Florence has induced it to grow cooked and seasoned where that is desirable, so it's no trouble to go over and pick yourself a nice poached egg or clutch of French fries. (I really prefer brioche in the mornings, but for sentimental reasons she can't manage them.) Sometimes we ball a little or sing old campfire songs. Ski comes down for that, but not for long, and then he goes back to looking at the universe. The starbow is magnificent and appalling. It is now a band about 40° across, completely surrounding us with colored light. One can always look in the other frequencies and see ghost stars before us and behind us, but in the birthright bands the view of the front and rear is now dead black and the only light is that beautiful banded ring of powdery stars.

Sometimes we write plays or have a little music. Shef had deduced four lost Bach piano concerti, very reminiscent of Corelli and Vivaldi, with everything going at once in the tuttis, and we've all adapted them for performance. I did mine on the Moog, but Ann and Shef synthesized whole orchestras. Shef's is particularly cute. You can tell that the flautist has early emphysema and two people in the violin section have been drinking, and he's got Toscanini conducting like a *risorgimento* metronome. Flo's oldest daughter made up words and now she sings a sort of nursery-rhyme adaptation of some Buxtehude chorales; oh, I didn't tell you about the kids. We have eleven of them now. Ann, Dot and I have one apiece, and Florence has eight. (But they're going to let me have quadruplets next week.) They let me take care of them pretty much for the first few weeks, while they're little, and they're *so* darling.

So mostly I spend my time taking care of the kids and working out tensor equations that Ski kindly gives me to do for him, and, I must confess it, feeling a little lonely. I *would* like to watch a TV quiz show over a cup of coffee with a friend! They let me do over the interior of our mobile home now and then. The other day I redid it in Pittsburgh suburban as a joke. Would you believe French windows in interstellar space? We never open them, of course, but they look real pretty with the chintz curtains and lace tiebacks. And we've added several new rooms for the children and their pets (Flo grew them the cutest little bunnies in the hydroponics plot).

Well, I've enjoyed this chance to gossip, so will sign off now. There is one thing I have to mention. The others have decided we don't want to get any more messages from you. They don't like the way you try to work on our subconsciouses and all (not that you succeed, of course, but you can see that it's still a little annoying), and so in future the dial will be set at six-six-oh, all right, but the switch will be in the "off" position. It wasn't my idea, but I was glad to go along. I *would* like some slightly less demanding company from time to time, although not, of course, yours.

Washington Five

Once upon a time the building that was now known as DoD Temp Restraining Quarters 7—you might as well call it with the right word, "jail," Knefhausen thought—had been a luxury hotel in the Hilton chain. The maximum security cells were in the underground levels, in what had been meeting rooms. There were no doors or windows to the outside. If you did get out of your own cell you had a flight of stairs to get up before you were at ground level, and then the guards to break through to get to the open. And then, even if there happened not to be an active siege going on at the moment, you took your chances with the roaming addicts and activists outside.

Knefhausen did not concern himself with these matters. He did not think of escape, or at least didn't after the first few panicky moments, when he realized he was under arrest. He stopped demanding to see the President after the first few days. There was no point in appealing to the White House for help when it was the White House that had put him here. He was still sure that if only he could talk to the President privately for a few moments he could clear everything up. But as a realist he had faced the fact that the President would never talk to him privately again.

So he counted his blessings.

First, it was comfortable here. The bed was good, the rooms were warm. The food still came from the banquet kitchens of the hotel, and it was remarkably good for jailhouse fare.

Second, the kids were still in space and still doing some things, great things, even if they did not report what. His vindication was still a prospect.

Third, the jailers let him have newspapers and writing materials, although they would not bring him his books or give him a television set.

He missed the books, but nothing else. He didn't need TV to tell him what was going on outside. He didn't even need the newspapers, ragged, thin and censored as they were. He could hear for himself. Every day there was the rattle of small-arms fire, mostly far-off and sporadic, but once or twice sustained and heavy and almost overhead, Brownings against AK-47s, it sounded like, and now and then the slap and smash of grenade launchers. Sometimes he heard sirens hooting through the streets, punctuated by clanging bells, and wondered that there was still a civilian fire department left to bother. (Or was it still civilian?) Sometimes he heard the grinding of heavy motors that had to be tanks. The newspapers did little to fill in the details, but Knefhausen was good at reading betwen the lines. The Administration was holed up somewhere—Key Biscayne or Camp David or Southern California, no one was saying where. The cities were all in red revolt. Herr Omnes had taken over.

For these disasters Knefhausen felt unjustly blamed. He composed endless letters to the President, pointing out that the serious troubles of the Administration had nothing to do with Alpha-Aleph; the cities had been in revolt for most of a generation, the dollar had become a laughingstock since the Indochinese wars. Some he destroyed, some he could get no one to take from him, a few he managed to dispatch—and got no answers.

Once or twice a week a man from the Justice Department came to ask him the same thousand pointless questions once again. They were trying to build up a dossier to prove it was all his fault, Knefhausen suspected. Well, let them. He would defend himself when the time came. Or history would defend him. The record was clear. With respect to moral issues, perhaps, not so clear, he conceded. No matter. One could not speak of moral questions in an area so vital to the search for knowledge as this. The dispatches from the *Constitution* had

already produced so much!—although, admittedly, some of
the most significant parts were hard to understand. The Gödel
message had not been unscrambled, and the hints of its contents remained only hints.

Sometimes he dozed and dreamed of projecting himself to
the *Constitution*. It had been a year since the last message.
He tried to imagine what they had been doing. They would
be well past the midpoint now, decelerating. The starbow
would be broadening and diffusing every day. The circles of
blackness before and behind them would be shrinking. Soon
they would see Alpha Centauri as no man had ever seen it.
To be sure, they would then see that there was no planet
called Aleph circling the primary, but they had guessed that
somehow long since. Brave, wonderful kids! Even so they
had gone on. This foolishness with drugs and sex, what of it?
One opposed such goings-on in the common run of humanity,
but it had always been so that those who excelled and stood
out from the herd could make their own rules. As a child he
had learned that the plump, proud air leader sniffed cocaine,
that the great warriors took their sexual pleasure sometimes
with each other. An intelligent man did not concern himself
with such questions, which was one more indication that the
man from the Justice Department, with his constant hinting
and prying into Knefhausen's own background, was not really
very intelligent.

The good thing about the man from the Justice Department was that one could sometimes deduce things from his
questions, and rarely—oh, very rarely—he would sometimes
answer a question himself. "Has there been a message from
the *Constitution*?" "No, of course not, Dr. Knefhausen; now,
tell me again, who suggested this fraudulent scheme to you
in the first place?"

Those were the highlights of his days, but mostly the days
just passed unmarked.

He did not even scratch them off on the wall of his cell, like
the prisoner in the Chateau d'If. It would have been a pity
to mar the hardwood paneling. Also, he had other clocks and
calendars. There was the ticking of the arriving meals, the
turning of the seasons as the man from the Justice Department
paid his visits. Each of these was like a holiday—a holy day,
not joyous but solemn. First there would be a visit from the
captain of the guards, with two armed soldiers standing in the

door. They would search his person and his cell on the chance that he had been able to smuggle in a—a what? A nuclear bomb, maybe. Or a pound of pepper to throw in the Justice man's eyes. They would find nothing, because there was nothing to find. And then they would go away, and for a long time there would be nothing. Not even a meal, even if a meal time happened to be due. Nothing at all, until an hour or three hours later the Justice man would come in with his own guard at the door, equally vigilant inside and out, and his engineer manning the tape recorders, and his questions.

And then there was the day when the man from the Justice Department came and he was not alone. With him was the President's secretary, Murray Amos.

How treacherous is the human heart! When it has given up hope, how little it takes to make it hope again!

"Murray!" cried Knefhausen, almost weeping, "it's so good to see you again! The President, is he well? What can I do for you? Have there been developments?"

Murray Amos paused in the doorway. He looked at Dieter von Knefhausen and said bitterly, "Oh, yes, there have been developments. Plenty of them. The Fourth Armored has just changed sides, so we are evacuating Washington. And the President wants you out of here at once."

"No, no! I mean—oh, yes, it is good that the President is concerned about my welfare, although it is bad about the Fourth Armored. But what I mean, Murray, is this: Has there been a message from the *Constitution*?"

Amos and the Justice Department man looked at each other. "Tell me, Dr. Knefhausen," said Amos silkily, "how did you manage to find that out?"

"Find it out? How could I find it out? No, I only asked because I hoped. There has been a message, yes? In spite of what they said? They have spoken again?"

"As a matter of fact, there has been," said Amos thoughtfully. The Justice Department man whispered piercingly in his ear, but Amos shook his head. "Don't worry, we'll be coming in a second. The convoy won't go without us. . . . Yes, Knefhausen, the message came through to Goldstone two hours ago. They have it at the decoding room now."

"Good, very good!" cried Knefhausen. "You will see, they will justify all. But what do they say? Have you good scientific men to interpret it? Can you understand the contents?"

"Not exactly," said Amos, "because there's one little problem the code room hadn't expected and wasn't prepared for. The message wasn't coded. It came in clear, but the language was Chinese."

Constitution Six

Ref.: CONSIX T51/11055/*7
CLASSIFIED MOST SECRET

Subject: Transmission from U. S. Starship *Constitution.*

The following message was received and processed by the decrypt section according to standing directives. Because of its special nature, an investigation was carried out to determine its provenance. Radio-direction data received from Farside Base indicate its origin along a line of sight consistent with the present predicted location of the *Constitution.* Strength of signal was high but within appropriate limits, and degradation of frequency separation was consistent with relativistic shifts and scattering due to impact with particle and gas clouds.

Although available data do not prove beyond doubt that this transmission originated with the starship, no contraindications were found.

On examination, the text proved to be a phonetic transcription of what appears to be a dialect of Middle Kingdom Mandarin. Only a partial translation has been completed. (See note appended to text.) The translation presented unusual difficulties for two reasons: One, the difficulty of finding a translator of sufficient skill who could be granted appropriate security status; two, because (conjecturally) the language used may not correspond exactly to any dialect but may be an artifact of the *Constitution*'s personnel. (See PARA EIGHT, Lines 43-51 below, in this connection.)

This text is PROVISIONAL AND NOT AUTHENTICATED and is furnished only as a first attempt to translate the contents of the message into English. Efforts are being continued to translate the full message, and to produce a less corrupt text for the section herewith. Later versions and emendations will be forwarded when available.

TEXT FOLLOWS:
1 PARA ONE. The one who speaks for all [*Lt-Col*

2 *Sheffield H Jackman?*] rests. With righteous
3 action comes surcease from care. I [*identity*
4 *not certain, but probably Mrs Annette Marin*
5 *Becklund, less probably one of the other three*
6 *female personnel aboard, or one of their de-*
7 *scendants*] come in his place, moved by charity
8 and love.
9 PARA TWO. It is not enough to study or to do
10 deeds which make the people frown and bow
11 their heads. It is not enough to comprehend
12 the nature of the sky or the sea. Only through
13 the understanding of all can one approach wis-
14 dom, and only through wisdom can one act
15 rightly.
16 PARA THREE. These are the precepts as it is
17 given us to see them.
18 PARA FOUR. The one who imposes his will by
19 force lacks justice. Let him be thrust from a
20 cliff.
21 PARA FIVE. The one who causes another to
22 lust for a trifle of carved wood or a sweetmeat
23 lacks courtesy. Let him be restrained from
24 carrying out of wrong practices.
25 PARA SIX. The one who ties a knot and says, "I
26 do not care who must untie it," lacks foresight.
27 Let him wash the ulcers of the poor and carry
28 nightsoil for all until he learns to see the day
29 to come as brother to the day that is.
30 PARA SEVEN. We who are in this here should
31 not impose our wills on you who are in that
32 here by force. Understanding comes late. We
33 regret the incident of next week, for it was
34 done in haste and in error. The one who
35 speaks for all acted without thinking. We who
36 are in this here were sorry for it afterward.
37 PARA EIGHT. You may wonder [*literally: ask*
38 *thoughtless questions of the hexagrams*] why
39 we are communicating in this language. The
40 reason is in part recreational, in part heuristic
41 [*literally: because on the staff hand one*
42 *becomes able to strike a blow more ably when*
43 *blows are struck repeatedly*], but the nature
44 of the process is such that you must go through

45 it before you can be told what it is. Our steps
46 have trodden this path. In order to reconstruct
47 the Chinese of the *I Ching* it was first neces-
48 sary to reconstruct the German of the trans-
49 lation from which the English was made. Error
50 lurks at every turn. [*Literally: false apparitions*
51 *shout at one each time the path winds.*] Many
52 flaws mark our carving. Observe it in silence
53 for hours and days until the flaws become part
54 of the work.
55 PARA NINE. It is said that you have eight days
56 before the heavier particles arrive. The dead
57 and broken will be few. It will be better if all
58 airborne nuclear reactors are grounded until
59 the incident is over.
60 PARA TEN. When you have completed rebuild-
61 ing send us a message, directed to the planet
62 Alpha-Aleph. Our home should be prepared
63 by then. We will send a ferry to help colonists
64 cross the stream when we are ready.

The above text comprises the first 852 groups of the transmission. The remainder of the text, comprising approximately
7500 groups, has not been satisfactorily translated. In the
opinion of a consultant from the Oriental Languages Department at Johns Hopkins it may be a poem.

/s/ Durward S RICHTER

Durward S RICHTER
Maj Gen USMC
Chief Cryptographer
Commanding

Distribution: X X X BY HAND ONLY

Washington Six

The President of the United States (Washington) opened
the storm windows of his study and leaned out to yell at his
Chief Science Adviser. "Harry, get the lead out! We're waiting
for you!"

Harry looked up and waved, then continued doggedly plowing through the dripping jungle that was the North Lawn. Between the overgrown weeds and the rain and the mud it was slow going, but the President had little sympathy. He slammed down the window and said, "Damn that man, he just goes out of his way to aggravate me. How long am I supposed to wait for him so I can decide if we're gonna have to move the capital or not?"

The Vice President looked up from her knitting. "Jimbo, honey, why do you fuss yourself like that? Why don't we just move and get it over with?"

"Well, it looks so lousy." He threw himself into a chair despondently. "I was really looking forward to the Tenth Anniversary parade," he complained. "Ten years, that's really worth bragging about! I don't want to hold it the hell out in the sticks, I want it right down Constitution Avenue, just like the old days, with the people cheering and the reporters and the cameras all over and everything. Then let that son of a bitch in Omaha say I'm not the real President."

His wife said placidly, "Don't fuss yourself about him, honey. You know what I've been thinking, though? The parade might look a little skimpy on Constitution Avenue anyway. It would be real nice on a kind of littler street."

"Oh, what do you know? Anyway, where would we go? If Washington's under water, what makes you think Bethesda would be any better?"

His Secretary of State put down his solitaire cards and looked interested. "Doesn't have to be Bethesda," he said. "I got some real nice land up near Dulles we could use. It's high there."

"Why, sure. Lots of nice land over to Virginia," the Vice President confirmed. "Remember when we went out on that picnic after your Second Inaugural? That was at Fairfax Station. There was hills there all around. Just beautiful."

The President slammed his fist on the coffee table and yelled, "I'm not the President of Fairfax Station, I'm the President of the U. S. of A.! What's the capital of the U. S. of A.? Washington! My God, don't you see how those jokers in Houston and Omaha and Salt Lake and all would laugh if they heard I had to move out of my own capital?"

He broke off, because his Chief Science Advisor was coming in the door, shaking himself, dripping mud as he got out of his oilskin slicker. "Well?" demanded the President. "What did they say?"

Harry sat down. "It's terrible out there. Anybody got a dry cigarette?"

The President threw him a pack. Harry dried his fingers on his shirt front before he drew one out. "Well," he said, "I went to every boat captain I could find. They all said the same. Ships they talked to, places they'd been. All the same. Tides rising all up and down the coast."

He looked around for a match. The President's wife handed him a gold cigarette lighter with the Great Seal of the United States on it, which, after some effort, he managed to ignite. "It don't look good, Jimmy. Right now it's low tide and that's all right, but it's coming in. And tomorrow it'll come in a little higher. And there's going to be storms, not just rain like this, I mean, but you got to figure on a tropical depression coming up from the Bahamas now and then."

"We're not in the tropics," said the Secretary of State suspiciously.

"It doesn't mean that," said the Science Advisor, who had once given the weather reports over the local ABC television station, when there was such a thing as a television network. "It means storms. Hurricanes. But they're not the worst things; it's the tides. If the ice is melting then they're going to keep getting higher regardless."

The President drummed his fingers on the coffee table. Suddenly he shouted, "I don't *want* to move my capital!"

No one answered. His temper outbursts were famous. The Vice President became absorbed in her knitting, the Secretary of State picked up his cards and began to shuffle, the Science Advisor picked up his slicker and carefully hung it on the back of a door.

The President said, "You got to figure it this way. If we move out, then all those local yokels that claim to be the President of the United States are going to be just that much better off, and the eventual reunification of our country is going to be just that much more delayed." He moved his lips for a moment, then burst out, "I don't ask nothing for myself! I never have. I only want to play the part I have to play in what's good for all of us, and that means keeping up my position as the *real* President, according to the U. S. of A. Constitution as amended. And that means I got to stay right here in the real White House, no matter what."

His wife said hesitantly, "Honey, how about this? The other Presidents had like a Summer White House, and Camp David and like that. Nobody fussed about it. Why couldn't you do the same as they did? There's the nicest old farm house out near Fairfax Station that we could fix up to be real pretty."

The President looked at her with surprise. "Now, that's good thinking," he declared. "Only we can't move permanently, and we have to keep this place garrisoned so nobody else will take it away from us, and we have to come back here once in a while. How about that, Harry?"

His Science Advisor said thoughtfully, "We could rent some boats, I guess. Depends. I don't know how high the water might get."

"No 'guess'! No 'depends'! That's a national priority. We have to do it that way to keep that bastard in Omaha paying attention to the real President."

"Well, Jimbo, honey," said the Vice President after a moment, emboldened by his recent praise, "you have to admit they don't pay a lot of attention to us right now. When was the last time they paid their taxes?"

The President looked at her foxily over his glasses. "Talking about that," he said, "I might have a little surprise for them anyway. What you might call a secret weapon."

"I hope it does better than we did in the last war," said his wife, "because if you remember, when we started to put down the uprising in Frederick, Maryland, we got the pee kicked out of us."

The President stood up, indicating the Cabinet meeting was over.

"Never mind," he said sunnily. "You go on out again, Harry, and see of you can find any good maps in the Library of Congress where they got the fires put out. Find us a nice high place within, um, twenty miles if you can. Then we'll get the Army to condemn us a Summer White House like Mae says, and maybe I can sleep in a bed that isn't moldy for a change."

His wife looked worried, alerted by his tone. "What are you going to do, Jim?"

He chuckled. "I'm going to check out my secret weapon."

He shooed them out of his study and, when they were gone, went to the kitchen and got himself a bottle of Fresca from the six-pack in the open refrigerator. It was warm, of course. The Marine guard company was still trying to get the gas generator back in operation, but they were having little success. The President didn't mind. They were his personal Praetorians and, if they lacked a little as appliance repairmen, they had proved their worth when the chips were down. The President was always aware that during the Troubles he had been no more than any other Congressman— appointed to fill a vacancy, at that—and his rapid rise to Speaker of the House and Heir Apparent, finally to the Presidency itself, was due not only to his political skills and know-how, but also to the fact that he was the only remotely legitimate heir to the Presidency who also happened to have a brother-in-law commanding the Marine garrison in Washington.

The President was, in fact, quite satisfied with the way the world was going. If he envied Presidents of the past (missiles, fleets of nuclear bombers, billions of dollars to play with), he certainly saw nothing, when he looked at the world around him, to compare with his own stature in the real world he lived in.

He finished the soda, opened his study door a crack and peered out. No one was nearby. He slipped out and down the back stairs. In what had once been the public parts of the White House you could see the extent of the damage more clearly. After the riots and the trashings and the burnings and coups, the will to repair and fix up had gradually dwindled away. The President didn't mind. He didn't even notice the charred walls and the fallen plaster. He was listening to the sound of a distant gasoline pump chugging away, and smiling to himself as he approached the underground level where his secret weapon was locked up.

The secret weapon, whose name was Dieter von Knefhausen, was trying to complete the total defense of every act of his life that he called his memoirs.

He was less satisfied with the world than the President. He could have wished for many changes. Better health, for one thing; he was well aware that his essential hypertension, his bronchitis, and his gout were fighting the last stages of a total war to see which would have the honor of destroying their mutual battleground, which was himself. He did not much mind his lack of freedom, but he did mind the senseless destruction of so many of his papers.

The original typescript of his autobiography was long lost,

but he had wheedled the President—the pretender, that is, who called himself the President—into sending someone to find what could be found of them. A few tattered and incomplete carbon copies had turned up. He had restored some of the gaps as best his memory and available data permitted, telling again the story of how he had planned Project Alpha-Aleph and meticulously itemizing the details of how he had lied, forged and falsified to bring it about.

He was as honest as he could be. He spared himself nothing. He admitted his complicity in the "accidental" death of Ann Barstow's first husband in a car smash, thus leaving her free to marry the man he had chosen to go with the crew to Alpha Centauri. He had confessed he had known that the secret would not last out the duration of the trip, thus betraying the trust of the President who made it possible. He put it all in, all he could remember, and boasted of his success.

For it was clear to him that his success was already proved. What could be surer evidence of it than what had happened ten years ago? The "incident of next week" was as dramatic and complete as anyone could wish. If its details were still indecipherable, largely because of the demolition of the existing technology structure it had brought about, its main features were obvious. The shower of heavy particles—baryon? perhaps even quarks?—had drenched the Earth. The source had been traced to a point in the heavens identical with that plotted for the *Constitution*.

Also there were the messages received, and, take them together, there was no doubt that the astronauts had developed knowledge so far in advance of anything on Earth that, from two light-years out, they could impose their will on the human race. They had done it. In one downpour of particles, the entire military-industrial complex of the planet was put out of action.

How? How? Ah, thought Knefhausen, with envy and pride, that was the question. One could not know. All that was known was that every nuclear device—bomb, powerplant, hospital radiation source or stockpile—had simultaneously soaked up the stream of particles and at that moment ceased to exist as a source of nuclear energy. It was not rapid and catastrophic, like a bomb. It was slow and long-lasting. The uranium and the plutonium simply melted in the long, continuous reaction that was still bubbling away in the seething lava lakes where the silos had stood and the nuclear power plants had generated electricity. Little radiation was released, but a good deal of heat.

Knefhausen had long since stopped regretting what could not be helped, but wistfully he still wished he had the opportunity to measure the total heat flux properly. Not less than 10^{16} watt-years, he was sure, just to judge by the effects on the Earth's atmosphere, the storms, the gradual raising of temperature all over, above all by the rumors about the upward trend of sea level that bespoke the melting of the polar ice caps. There was no longer even a good weather net, but the fragmentary information he was able to piece together suggested a world increase of four, maybe as many as six or seven degrees Celsian already, and the reactions still seething away in Czechoslovakia, the Congo, Colorado, and a hundred lesser infernos.

Rumors about the sea level?

Not rumors, no, he corrected himself, lifting his head and staring at the snake of hard rubber hose that began under the duckboards at the far end of the room and ended outside the barred window, where the gasoline pump outside did its best to keep the water level inside his cell low enough to keep the water below the boards. Judging by the inflow, the grounds of the White House must be nearly awash.

The door opened. The President of the United States (Washington) walked in, patting the shoulder of the thin, scared, hungry-looking kid who was guarding the door.

"How's it going, Knefhausen?" the President began sunnily. "You ready to listen to a little reason yet?"

"I'll do whatever you say, Mr. President, but as I have told you there are certain limits. Also I am not a young man, and my health—"

"Screw your health and your limits," shouted the President. "Don't start up with me, Knefhausen!"

"I am sorry, Mr. President," whispered Knefhausen.

"Don't be sorry! What I got to judge by is results. You know what it takes to keep that pump going just so you won't drown? Gas is rationed, Knefhausen! Takes a high national priority to get it! I don't know how long I'm gonna be able to justify this continuous drain on our resources if you don't cooperate."

Sadly, but stubbornly, Knefhausen said: "As far as I am able, Mr. President, I cooperate."

"Yeah. Sure." But the President was in an unusually good mood today, Knefhausen observed with the prisoner's paranoid attention to detail, and in a moment he said: "Listen, let's not get uptight about this. I'm making you an offer. Say the word and I'll fire that dumb son-of-a-bitch Harry Stokes and make you my Chief Science Advisor. How would that be? Right up at the top again. An apartment of your own. Electric lights! Servants—you can pick 'em out yourself, and there's some nice-looking little girls in the pool. The best food you ever dreamed of. A chance to perform a real service for the U. S. of A., helping to reunify this great country to become once again the great power it should and must be!"

"Mr. President," Knefhausen said, "naturally, I wish to help in any way I can. But we have been all over this before. I'll do anything you like, but I don't know how to make the bombs work again. You saw what happened, Mr. President. They're gone."

"I didn't say bombs, did I? Look, Kneffie, I'm a reasonable man. How about this. You promise to use your best scientific efforts *in any way you can*. You say you can't make bombs; all right. But there will be other things."

"What other things, Mr. President?"

"Don't push me, Knefhausen. Anything at all. Anything where you can perform a service for your country. You give me that promise and you're out of here today. Or would you rather I just turned off the pump?"

Knefhausen shook his head, not in negation but in despair. "You do not know what you are asking. What can a scientist do for you today? Ten years ago, yes. Even five years ago. We could have worked something out maybe; I could have done something. But now the preconditions do not exist. When all the nuclear plants went out— When the fertilizer plants couldn't fix nitrogen and the insecticide plants couldn't deliver—When the people began to die of hunger and the pestilences started—"

"I know all that, Knefhausen. Yes or no?"

The scientist hesitated, looking thoughtfully at his adversary. A gleam of the old shrewdness appeared in his eyes.

"Mr. President," he said slowly. "You know something. Something has happened."

"Right," crowed the President. "You're smart. Now tell me; what is it I know?"

Knefhausen shook his head. After seven decades of vigorous

life, and another decade of slowly dying, it was hard to hope again. This terrible little man, this upstart, this lump—he was not without a certain animal cunning, and he seemed very sure. "Please, Mr. President. Tell me."

The President put a finger to his lips, and then an ear to the door. When he was convinced no one could be listening, he came closer to Knefhausen and said softly:

"You know that I have trade representatives all over, Knefhausen. Some in Houston, some in Salt Lake, some even in Montreal. They are not always there just for trade. Sometimes they find things out, and tell me. Would you like to know what my man in Anaheim has just told me?"

Knefhausen did not answer, but his watery old eyes were imploring.

"A message," whispered the President.

"From the *Constitution*?" cried Knefhausen. "But no, it is not possible! Farside is gone, Goldstone is destroyed, the orbiting satellites are running down—"

"It wasn't a radio message," said the President. "It came from Mount Palomar. Not the big telescope, because that got ripped off too, but what they call a Schmidt. Whatever that is. It still works. And they still have some old fogies who look through it now and then, for old times' sake. And they got a message, in laser light. Plain Morse code. From what they said was Alpha Centauri. From your little friends, Knefhausen."

He took a sheaf of paper from his pocket and held it up.

Knefhausen was racked by a fit of coughing, but he managed to croak: "Give it to me!"

The President held it away. "A deal, Knefhausen?"

"Yes, yes! Anything you say, but give me the message!"

"Why, certainly," smiled the President, and passed over the much-creased sheet of paper. It said:

PLEASE BE ADVISED. WE HAVE CREATED THE PLANET ALPHA-ALEPH. IT IS BEAUTIFUL AND GRAND. WE WILL SEND OUR FERRIES TO BRING SUITABLE PERSONS AND OTHERS TO STOCK IT AND TO COMPLETE CERTAIN OTHER BUSINESS. OUR SPECIAL REGARDS TO DR. DIETER VON KNEFHAUSEN, WHOM WE WANT TO TALK TO VERY MUCH. EXPECT US WITHIN THREE WEEKS OF THIS MESSAGE.

Knefhausen read it over twice, stared at the President and read it again. "I—I am very glad," he said inadequately.

The President snatched it back, folded it and put it in his pocket, as though the message itself was the key to power. "So you see," he said, "it's simple. You help me, I help you."

"Yes. Yes, of course," said Knefhausen, staring past him.

"They're your friends. They'll do what you say. All those things you told me that they can do—"

"Yes, the particles, the ability to reproduce, the ability, God save us, to build a planet—" Knefhausen might have gone on cataloging the skills of the spacemen indefinitely, but the President was impatient:

"So it's only a matter of days now, and they'll be here. You can imagine what they'll have! Guns, tools, everything— and all you have to do is get them to join me in restoring the United States of America to its proper place. I'll make it worth their while, Knefhausen! And yours, too. They—"

The President stopped, observing the scientist carefully. Then he cried "Knefhausen!" and leaped forward to catch him.

He was too late. The scientist had fallen limply to the duckboards. The guard, when ordered, ran for the White House doctor, who limped as rapidly to the scene as his bad legs and brain soaked with beer would let him, but he was too late too. Everything was too late for Knefhausen, whose old heart had failed him . . . as it proved a few days later (when the great golden ships from Alpha-Aleph landed and disgorged their bright, terrible crewmen to clean up the Earth), just in time.

TO WALK A CITY'S STREET

CLIFFORD D. SIMAK

We think of Clifford Simak as a writer of pleasant fantasies of the future, as a novelist who sees the universe as filled with goblins and not very frightening spooks, as a gentle visionary. In this short story, you might think so for a while, but you will be wrong.

Joe stopped the car.

"You know what to do," he said.

"I walk down the street," said Ernie. "I don't do nothing. I walk until someone tells me it is time to stop. You got the other fellows out there?"

"We have the fellows out there."

"Why couldn't I just go alone?"

"You'd run away," said Joe. "We tried you once before."

"I wouldn't run away again."

"The hell you wouldn't."

"I don't like this job," said Ernie.

"It's a good job. You don't have to do anything. You just walk down the street."

"But you say which street. I don't get a pick of streets."

"What difference does it make what streets you walk?"

"I can't do anything I want, that's the difference that it makes. I can't even walk where I want to walk."

"Where would you want to walk?"

"I don't know," said Ernie. "Any place you weren't watching me. It used to be different. I could do what I wanted."

"You're eating regular now," said Joe. "Drinking regular, too. You have a place to sleep each night. You got money in your pocket. You have money in the bank."

"It don't seem right," said Ernie.

"Look, what's the matter with you? Don't you want to help people?"

'I ain't got no beef against helping people. But how do I know I help them? I only got your say-so. You and that fellow back in Washington."

"He explained it to you."

"A lot of words. I don't understand what he tells me. I'm not sure I believe what he tells me."

"I don't understand it, either," said Joe, "but I have seen the figures."

"I wouldn't know even if I seen the figures."

"Are you going to get started? Do I have to push you out?"

"No, I'll get out by myself. How far you want I should walk?"

"We'll tell you when to stop."

"And you'll be watching me."

"You're damned right we will," said Joe.

"This ain't a nice part of town. Why do I always have to walk the crummy parts of all these crummy towns?"

"It's your part of town. It's the kind of place you lived before we found you. You wouldn't be happy in any other part of town."

"But I had friends back there where you found me. There was Susie and Jake and Joseph, the Baboon and all the other people. Why can't I ever go back and see my friends?"

"Because you'd talk. You'd shoot off your mouth."

"You don't trust me."

"Should we trust you, Ernie?"

"No, I guess not," said Ernie.

He got out of the car.

"But I was happy, see?" he said.

"Sure, sure," said Joe. "I know."

There was one man sitting at the bar and two sitting at a table in the back. The place reminded Ernie of the place where he and Susie and Joseph, the Baboon, and sometimes Jake and Harry used to spend an evening drinking beer. He climbed up on a stool. He felt comfortable and almost as if he were back in the good old days again.

"Give me a shot," he said to the bartender.

"You got money, friend?"

"Sure, I got money." Ernie laid a dollar on the bar. The bartender got a bottle and poured a drink. Ernie gulped it down. "Another one," he said. The man poured another one.

"You're a new one," the bartender said.

"I ain't been around before," said Ernie.

He got a third drink and sat quietly, sipping it instead of throwing it right down.

"You know what I do?" he asked the bartender.

"Naw, I don't know what you do. You do like all the rest of them. You don't do nothing."

"I cure people."

"Is that so?"

"I walk around and I cure people when I walk."

"Well, great," said the bartender. "I got the beginning of a cold. So cure me."

"You're already cured," said Ernie.

"I don't feel no different than when you walked in here."

"Tomorrow. You'll be all right tomorrow. It takes a little time."

"I ain't going to pay you," said the bartender.

"I don't expect no pay. Other people pay me."

"What other people?"

"Just other people. I don't know who they are."

"They must be nuts."

"They won't let me go home," said Ernie.

"Well, now, ain't that too bad."

"I had a lot of friends. I had Susie and Joseph, the Baboon—"

"Everyone got friends," the bartender said.

"I got an aura. That is what they think."

"You got a what?"

"An aura. That is what they call it."

"Never heard of it. You want another drink?"

"Yeah, give me another one. Then I got to go."

Charley was standing on the sidewalk outside the joint, looking in at him. He didn't want Charley walking in and saying something to him, like get going. It would be embarrassing.

He saw the sign in an upstairs window and darted up the stairs. Jack was across the street and Al just a block or so ahead. They would see him and come running, but maybe he could get to the office before they caught up with him.

The sign on the door said: Lawson & Cramer, Attorneys-at-law. He moved in fast.

"I got to see a lawyer," he told the receptionist.

"Have you an appointment, sir?"

"No, I ain't got no appointment. But I need a lawyer quick. And I got money, see."

He brought out a handful of crumpled bills.

"Mr. Cramer is busy."

"What about the other one? Is he busy, too?"

"There isn't any other lawyer. There used to be—"

"Look, lady, I can't fool around."

The door to the inner office came open and a man stood in it.

"What's going on out here?"

"This gentleman—"

"I ain't no gentleman," said Ernie. "But I need a lawyer."

"All right," said the man. "Come in."

"You're Cramer?"

"Yes, I am."

"You'll help me?"

"I'll try."

The man closed the door and went around the desk and sat down.

"Have a chair," he said. "What is your name?"

"Ernie Foss."

The man wrote on a yellow pad.

"Ernie. That would be Ernest, would it?"

"Yeah, that's right."

"Your address, Mr. Foss."

"I ain't got no address. I just travel around. Once I had an address. I had friends. Susie and Joseph, the Baboon, and—"

"What seems to be the trouble, Mr. Foss?"

"They're holding me."

"Who's holding you?"

"The government. They won't let me go home and they watch me all the time."

"Why do you think they're watching you? What have you done?"

"I ain't done nothing. I got this thing, you see."

"What thing? What have you got?"

"I cure people."

"You can't mean you're a doctor."

"No doctor. I just cure people. I walk around and cure them. I got an aura."

"You have what?"

"An aura."

"I don't understand."

"It's something in me. Something I put out. You got a cold or something?"

"No, I haven't a cold."

"If you had, I'd cure you."

"I tell you what, Mr. Foss. Why don't you go out into the outer office and have a seat. I'll be back with you right away."

As he went out the door, Ernie saw the man reaching for the phone. He didn't wait. He went out the door and into the hall as fast as he could manage. Jack and Al were waiting for him there.

"That was a stupid thing you did," Joe said to Ernie.

"He didn't believe me," Ernie said. "He was reaching for the phone. He would have called the cops."

"Maybe he did. We thought he might. That's why we got out of there."

"He acted as if he thought maybe I was crazy."

"Why did you do it?"

"I got my rights," said Ernie. "Civil rights. Ain't you ever heard of them?"

"Of course we have. You have your legal rights. It was all explained to you. You're employed. You're a civil servant. You agreed to certain conditions of employment. You're being paid. It's all legal."

"But I don't like it."

"What don't you like about it? Your pay is good. Your

work is light. You just do some walking. There aren't many people who are paid for walking."

"If I am paid so good, why do we always stay in crummy hotels like this one?"

"You aren't paying for your room and food," said Joe. "You're on an expense account. We take care of it for you. And we don't stay in good hotels because we aren't dressed for it. We'd look funny in a good hotel. We'd attract attention."

"You guys dress like me," said Ernie. "Why do you dress like me? You even talk like me."

"It's the way we work."

"Yeah, I know. The crummy part of town. And that's all right with me. I never was nowhere but the crummy part of town. But you guys, I can tell. You're used to dressing in white shirts and ties and suits. Suits all cleaned and pressed. And when you aren't with me, you talk different, too, I bet."

"Jack," said Joe, "why don't you and Al go out with Ernie and have a bite to eat. Charley and me will go later on."

"That's another thing," said Ernie. "You never go into any place or out of any place together. You make it look as if you aren't all together. Would that be so we aren't noticed, too?"

"Oh," said Joe, disgusted, "what difference does it make?"

The three of them left.

"He's getting hard to handle," Charley said.

"Wouldn't you know," said Joe. "There is only one of him and he has to be a moron. Or damn close to one."

"There is no sign of any other?"

Joe shook his head. "Not the last time I talked with Washington. Yesterday, that was. They're doing all they can, of course, but how do you go about it? A statistical approach is the only way. Try to spot an area where there is no disease and once you find it, if you ever find it, try to spot the one who's responsible for it."

"Another one like Ernie."

"Yes, another one like Ernie. You know what? I don't think there is another one like him. He's a freak."

"There might be another freak."

'The odds, I'd think, would be very much against it. And even if there were, what are the chances they'll find him? It was just dumb, blind luck that Ernie was located."

"We're going at this wrong."

"Of course we're going at it wrong. The right way, the

scientific way is to find out what makes him the way he is. They tried that, remember? For damn near a year they tried. All sorts of tests and him bitching every minute. Wanting to go back to Susie and Joseph, the Baboon."

"They might have quit just at the time when they might have found . . ."

Joe shook his head. "I don't think so, Charley. I talked with Rosenmeir. He said it was hopeless. A thing has to get real bad for a man like Rosy to admit that it is hopeless. It took a lot of soul searching to decide to do what we are doing. He couldn't be kept in Washington for further study when there was so little chance of learning anything. They had him. The next logical step was to make some use of him."

"But the country is so big. There are so many cities. So many ghettos. So many pestholes. So much misery. We walk him down a few miles of street each day. We parade him past hospitals and old folks' homes and . . ."

"And don't forget. For every step he takes there may be a dozen people who are made well, another dozen people who won't contract the ailments they would have gotten if it hadn't been for him."

"I don't see how he can help but realize that. We've told him often enough. He should be glad of it, of a chance to help."

Joe said, "I told you. The man's a moron. A little selfish moron."

"You have to see it his way, too, I suppose," said Charley. "We jerked him away from home."

"He never had a home. Sleeping in alleys and flophouses. Panhandling. Doing a little stealing when he had the chance. Shacking up with his Susie when he had a chance. Getting a free meal now and then from some soup kitchen. Raiding garbage cans."

"Maybe he liked it that way."

"Maybe he did. No responsibility. Living day to day, like an animal. But now he has a responsibility—perhaps as great a responsibility, as great an opportunity as any man ever did. There is such a thing as accepting a responsibility."

"In your world, perhaps. In mine. Maybe not in his."

"Damned if I know," said Joe. "He has me beat. He's a complete phony. This talk of his about a home is all phony, too. He was only there for four or five years."

"Maybe if we let him stay in one place and brought people to him, on one pretext or another. Let him sit in a chair, without being noticeable, and parade them past him. Or take him to big meetings and conventions. Let him live it up a little. He might like it better."

"This was all hashed out," said Joe. "We can't be noticed; we can't stand publicity. Christ, can you imagine what might happen if this became public knowledge? He brags about it, of course. He probably was telling them all about it in that dive he stopped off at this afternoon. They paid no attention to him. The lawyer thought that he was crazy. He could stand on a rooftop and yell it to all the world and no one would pay attention. But let one hint come out of Washington . . ."

"I know," said Charley. "I know."

"It's being done," said Joe, "the only way it can be done. We're exposing people to good health, just the way they are exposed to disease. And we're doing it where the need of it is greatest."

"I have a funny feeling, Joe."

"What's that?"

"We may be doing wrong. It sometimes doesn't seem quite right to me."

"You mean going blind. Doing something and not knowing what we are doing. Without understanding it."

"I guess that's it. I don't know. I am all confused. I guess we're helping people."

"Ourselves included. The exposure we are getting to this guy, we should live forever."

"Yes, there's that," said Charley.

They sat silent for a moment. Finally Charley asked, "You got any idea, Joe, when they'll end this tour? It's been going for a month. That's the longest so far. The kids won't know me when I get home if it isn't soon."

"I know," said Joe. "It's tough on a family man like you. Me, it doesn't matter. And I guess it's the same with Al. How's it with Jack? I don't know him well. He's a man who never talks. Not about himself."

"I guess he's got a family somewhere. I don't know anything about it, just that he has. Look, Joe, would you go for a drink? I have a bottle in my bag. I could go and get it."

"A drink," said Joe, "is not a bad idea."

The telephone rang and Charley, who had started for the door, stopped and turned around.

"It might be for me," he said. "I called home a while ago.

Myrt wasn't there. I asked little Charley to have her call. I gave both room numbers, just in case I was here."

Joe picked up the phone and spoke into it. He shook his head at Charley. "It's not Myrt. It's Rosy."

Charley started for the door.

Joe said, "Just a minute, Charley."

He went on listening.

"Rosy," he finally said, "you are sure of this?"

He listened some more. Then he said, "Thanks, Rosy. Thanks an awful lot. You stuck out your neck calling us."

He hung up the phone and sat, staring at the wall.

"What's the matter, Joe? What did Rosy want?"

"He called to warn us. There is a mistake. I don't know how or why. A mistake is all."

"What did we do wrong?"

"Not us. It's Washington."

"You mean about Ernie. His civil rights or something.

"Not his civil rights. Charley, he isn't curing people. He is killing them. He's a carrier."

"We know he is a carrier. Other people carry a disease, but he carries—"

"He carries a disease, too. They don't know what it is."

"But back there in his old neighborhood, he made all the people well. Everywhere he went. That is how they found him. They knew there must be someone or something. They hunted till they—"

"Charley, shut up. Let me tell you. Back in his old neighborhood they're dying like flies. They started a couple of days ago and they still are dying. Healthy people dying. Nothing wrong with them, but they're dying just the same. A whole neighborhood is dying."

"Christ, it can't be, Joe. There must be some mistake. . . ."

"No mistake. It's the very people he made well who are dying now."

"But it doesn't make sense."

"Rosy thinks maybe it's a new kind of virus. It kills all the rest of them, all the viruses and bacteria that make people sick. No competition, see? It kills off the competition, so it has each body to itself. Then it settles down to grow and the body is all right, because it doesn't intentionally harm the body, but there comes a time . . ."

"Rosy is just guessing."

"Sure Rosy is just guessing. But it makes sense to hear him tell it."

"If it's true," said Charley, "think of all the people, the millions of people . . ."

"That's what I'm thinking of," said Joe. "Rosy took a chance in calling us. They'll crucify him if they find out about the call."

"They'll find out. There'll be a record of it."

"Maybe none that can be traced to him. He called from a phone booth out in Maryland somewhere. Rosy's scared. He is in it up to his neck, the same as us. He spent as much time with Ernie as we did. He knows as much as we do, maybe more than we do."

"He thinks, spending all that time with Ernie, we might be carriers, too?"

"No, I guess not that. But we know. We might talk. And no one can talk about this. No one will be allowed to talk about this. Can you imagine what would happen, the public reaction . . ."

"Joe, how long did you say Ernie spent in that neighborhood of his?"

"Four or five years."

"That's it, then. That's the time we have. You and I and all the rest of us, maybe have four years, probably less."

"That's right. And if they pick us up, we'll spend those years where there won't be any chance of us talking to anyone at all. Someone probably is headed here right now. They have our itinerary."

"Then let's get going, Joe. I know a place. Up north. I can take the family. No one will ever think of looking."

"What if you're a carrier?"

"If I'm a carrier, my family has it now. If I'm not, I want to spend those years—"

"And other people . . ."

"Where I'm headed there aren't many people. We'll be by ourselves."

"Here," said Joe. He took the car keys out of his jacket pocket and tossed them across the room. Charley caught them.

"What about you, Joe?"

"I have to warn the others. And, Charley . . ."

"Yeah?"

"Ditch that car before morning. They'll be looking for you.

And when they miss you here, they'll watch your family and your home. Be careful."

"I know. And you, Joe?"

"I'll take care of myself. As soon as I let the others know."

"And Ernie? We can't let him—"

"I'll take care of Ernie, too," said Joe.

RORQUAL MARU

T. J. BASS

Here is a solid instance of scientific projection——a world of the future utterly different from ours——a product of genetic engineering. Now tampering with the genes is something that will derive from the work of the Twentieth Century but its effect (if and when it is put to use) may be vastly different from the fantasies of charmingly handsome supermen that may be utilized someday to beguile the public into its acceptance.

A thundering surf drowned the forlorn screams of sand-locked *Rorqual Maru*. Brine-tossed grains of olivine and calcite buried her left eye, blocking her view of the sky. Uranus had marched thirty times through the constellations while the island's changing beaches had slowly engulfed her tail. Six hundred feet of her shapely hull lay hidden under a silted and rooted green hump of palm and frond. Now the sea was completing her interment, using cemented shell grit and granulated porphyritic basalt from ancient lava flows.

As the eyelid of sand darkened her world. *Rorqual* wept over her irretrievable, wasted years. She was a harvester without a crop—a plankton rake abandoned by Earth Society when the seas died. Her search of the continental shelves had proved futile: marine biota, negative.

Her sisters had quietly sunk, littering the bottom with their skeletons. She had selected this island for her grave, hoping to keep her carcass visible for possible salvage.

Although her long ear heard nothing she believed that man still lived in his Hive. If he should ever return to see she wanted to serve. She longed for the orgasmic thrill of feeling man's bare feet on the skin of her decks. She missed the hearty hails, the sweat and the laughter. She needed man.

Deep in the Hive a dispenser called out, "Wake up. Wake up. Enjoy, Enjoy."

Fat old Drum, a forty-eight-inch and balding Nebish, sat up in his cot and glanced around the cubicle. Pleasures of retirement awaited him after two grueling years in the musicians' caste. He was younger than most retirees—aged nineteen—and wealthy, for he had earned enough CBQ for this private six-foot cubicle and a flavor with every meal. He was vigorous also—possessed of a clear lens and eight good teeth. Some eleven more years remained on his life span.

"Welcome to the awake state, suave citizen," chortled dispenser. "Today's distribution is well above calorie-basic. The screen scene looks promising. Select two flavors and refresh while your gourmet meal is prepared. Two glorious flavors on this glorious day."

"Pink and green?" mumbled Drum hesitantly.

"Those are whole categories," reminded dispenser. "Which pink? Which green?"

Frugal citizens were often unsophisticated in matters of luxuries. Drum had invested a large part of his credits for retirement. He had qualms about adjusting his consuming habits upward.

"I'll start with pink-one and green-one and work my way down the menu—try them all," he said, feigning excitement.

When he stepped out of the refresher he found seven, soft, bag-like packets in the edible chute—five gray, one pink and one green.

"Savor the flavor," sang dispenser.

Humming a cheerful tune, Drum took his utensils from the

cupboard and ceremoniously arranged the Hive's pseudo-consommé, -soufflé and -parfait: liquids, pastes and puddings. All stable foodstuffs. No perishables. Dispenser selected a pulsing geometric visual with sonics to soothe subcortical neu-rones during the meal. Drum tried a generous bite of the green paste and experienced a tart shock—more color than a flavor—that faded quickly into the usual dull pap. He frowned; his appetite jaded. Where were the pleasures of retirement?

Dispenser detected his irritation and changed channels. Son-ics flexed. Drum's bio-electricals showed negative happiness.

"Some residual job fatigue remains in you," rationalized dispenser. Lights dimmed. "A nap will invigorate you. Lie down, please."

Audio switched to woodwinds and strings. Drum's cot vi-brated.

> *Hear the bacon frying,*
> *Crackling in the heat.*
> *Just smell those aromas,*
> *Good enough to eat . . .*

Drum awoke to choking synthe-smoke and the *clang, clang, clang* of a ranchwagon triangle. The viewscreen carried an old historical still showing rolling green hills dotted with squarish blobs of fauna, simple wooden artifacts—hut, fence and tools—and a bright blue sky. He sat up, relaxed and smiling. This new odor did excite him. Olfactory luxuries were quite rare. He hurried to the chute but found only three tube sand-wiches—soft, gray sticks. He frowned.

"One is laced with bacon," offered dispenser.

Drum forced a grin and picked it up—bland paste with a rare crunchy particle. The flavor was more that of burned grease than of any delicacy. Shrugging, he packed the other sticks into his kit.

"Where do you wish to go, beloved citizen?"

"To visit Grandmaster Ode."

"Sorry," said dispenser, "but commuter density is three point two per square yard on the spiral—four point one in tubeways. Rush hour. It would be better to wait until between shifts for your recreational travel."

Drum sat down slowly. Commuter priority had gone with his job. Now he couldn't even walk around when density was above two. Shrugging off his disgust, he called Ode on the screen.

"Got time for a game?" he queried as he unrolled his chess board.

The grandmaster smiled out of the screen. He did not comment on Drum's abrupt manner, for he understood the status changes of retirement.

"Pawn to queen-bishop-four." said Ode.

Drum moved the worn pawn and studied the position for an unusually long time. He moved woodenly until the tension level of the middle game position washed away his depression. He rode into the battle on his knight. Rooks clashed magnificently. A pawn-fork took the survivor. A nervous king fidgeted in his castled position until his reign was ended by a pair of bishops. For the moment the game took on a meaning bigger than life itself.

On the following morning Drum awoke a bit more philosophical. He was about to accept his new status for what it really was, but dispenser had other plans.

"Let me see a view of the jammed tubeways," said Drum. "I want to appreciate the quiet of my cubicle."

The screen remained blank—on standby.

Drum smiled.

"What is commuter density? Three? Four?"

A dry female appeared on the screen. She had an air of efficiency about her that Drum didn't like. Her thin lips and gaudy smock clashed.

"Recertification time," she said, her smile pasted on.

Drum's mouth opened and closed.

"Society has run a bit short of calories," she explained. "Water table dropped three centimeters in our sector and the harvest reflected it. We'll be cutting back on the warm, consuming population for a while. Please vote for those citizens with whom you want to share next year. Hurry, now. Your friends need your vote to avoid being put into Temporary Suspension—TS. Remember, you must not vote for yourself or your clone litter mates. No blood prejudice is allowed."

Drum smiled nervously. He had done this before, but he did not enjoy it. He used to vote for his conductor, a Venus attendant and a job mate—but now he was more concerned with the plumbing and the air in his little cubicle.

"My votes go to my friend Grandmaster Ode, this city's

Tinker, and the pipe caste member who keeps my refresher working."

The screen switched to geometric dance, then printed out an order for his own Temporary Suspension.

The thin-mouthed female reappeared long enough to announce: "You failed to receive your necessary three votes, so it is TS for you."

"But I'm retired," he objected. "My calories and quarters are paid up for life."

The screen blanked. Dispenser's voice answered his plea. "Recertification has nothing to do with wealth. The only criterion is love. Without love there can be no license for life."

"My funds—"

"Your retirement funds remain in your name while you are in TS. When harvests improve you'll be rewarmed. Hurry. You are to report to the clinic immediately. The air you are breathing belongs to somebody else."

The signs read: VS LEFT, TS RIGHT.

Drum lined up with the unloved TS candidates of mixed ages. On his left was the line of cachectic, sick, elderly citizens hoping to survive Voluntary Suspension long enough to be awakened when their physical problems could be solved. Drum knew how hopeless the statistics were.

Grandmaster Ode joined him in line.

"You didn't manage enough votes either?" asked Ode.

Drum shook his head. "I wish all those damn embryos weren't protected by future job requisitions. It would be much less traumatic just to lower the birth rate for the duration."

Ode shook his head.

"Those future jobs keep the Hive going. If no Tinkers were born today the shortage would be felt ten years from now— we would have no trainees. Of course, if job quotas drop the embryos lose their protective vote like anyone else."

A job hawker walked between the lines shouting, "Get your job vote here. Work outside your caste. Many rewarding positions available. Apply now."

"Let's chance it. I'd try anything to avoid TS." said Drum.

Ode was reluctant to leave his caste, but Drum pulled him out of line with a rough grip on his arm.

"Two volunteers right here," shouted Drum, raising his hand.

The hawker gave them each a voucher. They showed it to

the first optic they came to. The CO (the Class One meck that balanced the books for Earth Society) confirmed their unfrozen assets. The jobs were in the Sewer Service—dark, wet work.

The glowing meteor trail lit the night sky. Strange celestial voices tugged at *Rorqual*'s long ear. Booming mushrooms of plasma pocked the dark ocean. *Rorqual*'s consciousness flickered as her sensor thresholds were violated. She sucked the Big H from the sea to feed her growing belly fires. Her strength returned. Flexing and squirming, she began to worm her flanks out of the imprisoning silt. Warmth filled her hull. Her deep dish eyes rose out of the blinding olivine and gazed into the lagoon. The waters had changed. Incoming spectra were fuzzed by nanoplankton.

She pulled away from the island. Roots and vines snapped. Tree trunks split. She reentered the sea, carrying a hump of vegetation firmly locked into her back by gnarled woody roots. Salty, wind-blown spray followed the roots through damaged plates and burned her vitals—until layers of electroplating and oxides crusted over the sensitive, exposed circuits.

Joyfully she toiled the straits—raking and pumping. Only faint traces soiled her membrane filters during the first year, but her chromatographs identified all the amino acids. Protein had returned to the sea. Growth bloomed. During the second season larger creatures were caught on her rakes—soft copepods, heteropods with bizarre delicate shells, chaetognaths and dinoflagellates. Earth Society would be pleased with her harvest. Man would be pleased.

In ancient undersea ruins an occasional building meck survived and maintained its air pocket. It survived to serve a noncitizen, the Benthic—a marine hominid that filled one of the niches abandoned by the Hive. The Benthics were a sullen, thick-necked race. The concept of territorial integrity was strong in their culture. They lived in small family units separated by miles of open ocean.

Big Opal glanced around her ten-fathom nest. The fruit bin was low. She had scarcely enough for an offering to the Deep Cult. She would have to be the one to raid the Gardens again, since her mate had lost a leg in the meteor shower. An astrobleme-induced tsunami had shifted a mountain of debris, trapping him in the ruins. His left foot had been badly crushed and had gone purulent—it had to be amputated. The burden of feeding the family had fallen on Opal's broad shoulders.

"I must swim up to the Gardens," said Opal, patting her two young children. Clam, her oldest, was an adult.

Ray nodded. He and the children watched her climb down through a toothy rent and swim up past the swaying transparent walls—her pink breasts and buttocks shimmering through the cloudy waters. Since the meteor shower there had been a drop in visibility.

Opal swam leisurely among the ruins. Most had died and wore an opaque shroud of marine scum, but some buildings lived and offered her the hospitality of their bubbles. She approached a tall, mushroom-shaped dwelling whose walls glowed with life-giving air, heat and light—Halfway House. She bobbed up in the living room pool.

"Welcome," said a wizened, hairy Benthic—the Listener.

She climbed, dripping, up the ramp to where he sat among his wires—the communication web. He held a bowl of water and appeared worried.

"What do you hear from the surface?" she asked.

"Nothing yet, but I fear I have seen a harbinger of evil—the krill."

He held up a red crustacean. It flipped back into the bowl.

"The krill have returned?" she exclaimed.

He nodded gravely.

"Why, that's wonderful. I've seen them in the murals—good food from the seas. We'll never have to go up into the Gardens again. What's wrong?"

A tear started down Listener's wrinkled face. He pointed to his communication web. "The Hive will see the krill, too. It will come to harvest the seas again and drive us out. Our children will have no place to hide—no place."

Opal was stunned. The Benthics had lived here for generations. She knew the Hive had built the ruins in the distant past, but she never dreamed it would return. The ocean was the refuge of her people. She jumped up and shook her fist at the ceiling.

"We'll fight the damned Hive," she muttered.

Several fathoms overhead the surf dulled with soupy green and yellow blooms—diatoms, algae and salps. After one sleep Opal swam up to the Gardens and stole her share of the harvest. Agro-mecks trundled about their chores, ignoring her. At dusk she tied her melons into a raft and rode the rip current toward Halfway buoy. A few stars blinked down at her. The western horizon still glowed a faint blue when a silhouette appeared against it—nearly a quarter mile long, low and dotted with trees.

It was right in her path.

An island where no island should be. The current carried her up to the smooth, slightly granular beach. With her raft vine in one hand she examined the trees—jumbled leaves, trunks and vines—natural enough. She tied her raft and began to explore the shoulder-high brush under the palm canopy. She found a hillock at one end of the beach. At first she thought it was just a heap of boulders, but it was hollowed out. Inside she found glowing ornaments and bright, blinking stones. The floor was littered with small tools, seaweed and pinching crabs.

Rorqual trembled at the touch of bare feet. The huge harvester tried to speak, but air molecules did not respond—she could make no sound, managed only a flimsy printout that resembled an obscure falling leaf to Opal. Excitedly *Rorqual* tried an offering. Chewing cellulose mulch into a hydrocarbon, solution, the meck polymerized and extruded a small tool. Opal picked it up—curious. Next the meck formed a small doll in the likeness of the wet, naked guest. It was rubbery and translucent—a tough polymer.

Opal's curiosity was quenched abruptly by what she saw through the porthole. The island had a wake—it was moving! She cursed and ran, diving overboard without her melons.

Three Benthics sat in Halfway, watching the shadow pass overhead.

"That's it. It is looking for me," Opal whispered.

"A floating island?" asked her son. Clam, her eldest, had come to see what had delayed her.

Listener shook his head.

"The Leviathan," he said, blinking beady eyes under shaggy brows. "The Deep Cult had studied them in old ballads and murals. It is not an island. It is a creature that gathers krill for the Hive—a giant mutation of the finback whale. Did you notice the control cabin?"

Opal nodded. "A little room?"

"Attached to the back of the skull," he explained. "The Hive must have had hookups between machines and the hapless creature's brain and muscles. The Hive crew could steer it anywhere, ignoring its usual migrations. We don't know how they bred them."

"A sea creature controlled by the Hive," mumbled Opal. She didn't at all like the idea.

Two fat Nebishes, Drum and Ode, entered the sewer meck's control room. The wall was covered with pulsing flow diagrams; lights indicated water levels, gate status and silt/surface ratios.

"Welcome, trainees," said the meck, a voice in the wall.

"What jobs are open?" Drum asked, sitting down slowly. "I'm trained in music. Ode is grandmaster—"

"Wet crew," snapped the meck. "You're late. Your boots and shovels are out in the landing—through that hatch. Since my dredge died there has been an endless amount of shoveling to do."

"But our backgrounds—" objected Drum.

Ode touched his arm. "We'll take it. We need the vote."

"Wear the belts and helmets so I can keep an eye on you in the pipe," instructed the meck.

They splashed along the thirty-foot-diameter pipe, guided by the eerier bioluminescence of *Panus stipticus* mycelia growing in the drying sludge high on the walls. Sewer meck directed pencils of light from their belts.

"There's a weir," said Drum's belt.

Drum and Ode paused and shoveled at the silt dam. A lightbeam focused on a horned slug the size of Ode's foot.

"Pick it up," said his belt.

Ode nudged the slug cautiously with his shovel.

"What is it?"

"Sewer slug—a gastropod. Flavors."

"Edible?" asked Ode.

"Good perishable flavors," said his belt. "Fringe benefits of the wet crew. Put it in Drum's belt pail."

As they worked their way down the tube the belts pointed out other delicacies: snap larvae, worms, fungus balls and slime pods. When they approached the tidal sump the air took on a brackish odor and marine photobacteria glowed bluegreen in the men's footprints.

"Don't walk out on the delta," warned Ode's belt. "It is too soft and drops off rapidly."

Ode strained his eyes across the sump.

"I can't see across. How wide is it?"

"About three hundred feet," said his belt. "My lights won't carry that far."

"There seems to be something out there that is closer than three hundred feet," said Ode.

Drum heard the lapping of small waves against an obstruction about thirty feet into the darkness. His belt's lights pulsed. He caught a brief glimpse of a mottled wet wall.

"That is not supposed to be there," said his belt. "My sensors indicate a large disturbance. Hurry to the out hatch."

The two Nebishes climbed a service ladder to the barracks —to bright lights and warm air. Drum pulled off his boots. The skin of his feet was white and badly wrinkled, but there were no blisters or sores. He sorted through his pail of edibles. A snap larva swam on small oar bristles.

"What's the tithe?" asked Ode.

"Fifty percent," said his belt. "Drop half your perishables down the flavor chute to Synthe. Divide up the fluid and grit also."

They paid their tithes and sat back while several of the regular wet crew members showed them how a handful of live creatures added an entire new dimension to the pseudo-consommé.

"I call this my sewer bouillabaisse," said the Nebish with the spoon. "You stir it carefully so you don't fragment the little creatures—keep them whole so you know exactly what you are eating."

The Synthe chute passed through a sorting meck. Each species had its own peculiar flavor. The meck indexed these and also passed the creature census report along to the boys in Bio who were struggling with data on extinct species.

"New species?" asked the meck.

Its companion teck awoke, glanced into the viewer, reached in and gave the glob a squeeze.

"No. Just half a sewer slug."

The meck went back to sorting. At shift's end Harry-the-courier brought contraband bamboo for the teck's weaving and picked up the spec bottles on the way to Bio.

"The tiny vial has an old otolith," said the teck. "That new wet crew must have dug real deep."

Harry nodded and trotted off.

"Another fossil otolith," he announced as he entered the

labs at Bio. Wandee, an unpolarized fem teck, was bent over her bubbling tanks.

"Put it down and take a look at this," she said.

Harry leaned over her shoulder. The viewer contained amorphous blobs of green. The water looked scummy to him.

"Algae?"

"No," she said, smiling. "A flagellate—only no flagella. The gene spinner finally identified the flagellar codons and built this creature's DNA without it."

"How are you coming with the marine biota?"

"Slow. We're still mapping the DNA of freshwater diatoms and algae. But less than five percent of the code has been cracked. We did find the eye spot—and now the flagella. I even have one synthetic creature that will live in seawater but must return to fresh water to reproduce."

"What does the spinner say?" asked Harry. "How close are we?"

Wandee straightened up and wiped her hands.

"Spinner's WIC/RAC has come up with a lot of 'what ifs' and 'random association' theories, but I'd need a lot more personnel and floor space to follow them all up. We're just time-sharing now. I can try out a couple of likely maps each week, but there are actually millions of possibilities. It would be easy if we just had one marine protozoan to map and decode. Getting membrane pumps to work against hypertonic solutions after evolution has selected a life form for a freshwater environment takes an entirely different set of enzymes—RNA and DNA. It's slow."

She walked Harry over to the fossil otolith. They placed it in the hood for analysis and sat down for a glass of foamy. The flimsy printout had a red "attention" trim.

"This is no fossil," she said breathlessly. "It is contemporary!"

"Impossible."

They both studied the images on the viewer. The isotopes were in contemporary ratios. There was no evidence of leaching, ion drift or mechanical wear.

"I know it is impossible," she said. "But there was a real live bony fish in the sewer recently."

Arc lights crackled in the pipes as the teams of samplers spread out and began their netting and digging.

"Bring some nets down here by the delta."

"What's that smell?"

"Oh, oh. I don't think we'll be needing those nets."

Attracted by the voices, *Rorqual Maru* cruised down the sump toward the delta. Her hundred-and-fifty-foot beam was half as wide as the sump. Before her drifted a spongy wall of brine-soaked biscuits. The Nebishes backed away as her towering, barnacled hull nosed gently into the mud. Baleful optics gazed while pails were nervously filled.

"Plankton," chirped Wandee. "Look at this printout. There are over a hundred species here that have been labeled extinct."

Harry flaked another biscuit into the sorting meck.

"How could it have happened? Where did all these come from?"

Wandee shrugged. The meck passed the question along to the CO—the Class One meck also had neural connections with all the continents. In a few hours Harry had his answer.

"Meteor shower," said CO. "The marine biota reappeared three point two years afterward. An astrobleme must have opened an atoll or other landlocked body of salt water where these species had survived."

Harry nodded.

"It is lucky that whatever caused the sea death in the first place was no longer active," he said.

"Doesn't look like it. Things are really flourishing. Lots of food out there now."

"Who will harvest it?"

The platoon of orange-suited insignia wearers crept into the SS barracks and nudged Ode. As the grandmaster opened his eyes the ensign handed him a captain's coveralls.

"Whom do you want?"

"You, Captain—sir," said the ensign curtly. "You have been named to command. We'll voyage on plankton rake *Rorqual Maru*—the whale ship. CO's orders, sir."

Ode glanced around at the placid, young faces of his crew—barely mature children. He pulled on the coveralls and thick-soled boots. His belt was wide and ornate. Drum sat up on his cot and watched the drafting of Captain Ode. He shook his head slowly. He wondered why a grandmaster would be commissioned to pilot a rake. Did the reason lie in his military experience on the chess board—or the simple fact that Ode had been first to spot the vessel?

"Good luck," said Drum sadly.

"Smile," said Ode. "It is an honor to captain the first vessel returning to the sea. A turning point for the Hive. More food for all. They'll be opening the shipyards and building copies of *Rorqual*. We'll all have a great time."

"Be careful, anyway," cautioned Drum. "You aren't used to being Outside. No one knows very much about the seas these days—"

Captain Ode waved his friend to silence and marched off with his crew.

Priorities were juggled as the Hive attempted to get the shipyards working again. Meck brains were taken from dispensers, doors and every manner of machine. They were carted up and delivered to the flooded, corroded ruins by the sea. Crane and lathe robots were heaped into a rusted mass with twisted girders, cables, plates and other scrap gear. The Nebish work crews found their jobs impossible. Everything was too heavy or too sharp. Tinkers and pipes were pulled from their cities for a while—and returned when efforts at the yards failed.

The CO sent requisitions to the gene spinner for laborers with broader shoulders and thicker skins. It would be many years before a finished ship slid down the ways.

Drum took a detail of citizens Outside to string the long ear in an effort to establish contact with Captain Ode. The detail wore the closed-environment suits, but "outside phobia" tightened Drum's chest as soon as they stepped into the spacious Gardens. Bright sun glinted off gaudy flowers. Leafy plants hushed human voices and cut off men's views of one another. Three workers—each finding himself alone in such a wide open space—collapsed in their agoraphobia and died.

The towers of the long ear stood on a hill and reached up into the sky. Glassy insulators clung to spider-web-thin struts. The structure appeared delicate, swaying in the wind. More than half the crew was unable even to approach the towers. Many of the men who made the climb only lasted a few hours before dropping to the ground in heaps of fractures. Replacements arrived. Spools were creaking at the base of the towers as wires were strung up and down the antennae. Stretcher teams jogged back and forth with their splinted burdens. Fresh details were sent out at dusk to spell the survivors. They worked through the night, swaying against a star-strewn sky. Darkness erased most of the landmarks so the Nebish, limited by his helmet light, worked more comfortably.

Several days later Drum realized where the structure got its name—an oblong dish, a rabbit's ear, was slowly taking shape.

Captain Ode lost six crew members to agoraphobia. Another dozen or so were in various stages of catatonia.

Rorqual raked well. Her hold already bulged with a hundred thousand tons of food for the Hive.

The alarm siren called Ode's attention to the viewscreen. The deep scanner had picked up a Benthic silhouette and the nets were bringing it in. For a while Ode thought the captive might be canal sirenian or pinniped, but as it was brought closer he saw that it was humanoid, naked and primitive. The crane extruded a soft polymer net and gently dragged the body up on the deck. The crew shuddered at the size of the brine-soaked hulk: six feet long—two feet taller and a hundred pounds heavier than a Nebish. It wore a rope belt, had leathery burnt-sienna skin and large five-toed feet. The crew scattered, wet boots squeaking.

The Sharps Committee met and issued Captain Ode a curved blade. He walked up to the Benthic and nudged it with his boot. It was cold, stiff—lifeless. As a precaution Ode cut the left carotid artery. The blood was purple and jellylike. Eight Nebishes carried the Benthic down to the freezer. Ode reported it as a fossil hominid, theorizing that it had thawed out of some glacier and drifted down in a bottom arctic current.

The CO bounced Ode's report back to Drum with more data. The five-toeds were classified as extinct—fossils—but the Benthic was no fossil. Jellylike blood was quite recent and the inner lining of the cut artery was still white—the intima was not yet stained. Drum called Captain Ode over the long ear.

"So you finally got the communicator working." Ode grinned. "What's new in the shipyards?"

"Nothing going on at all here," said Drum. "But we are a little worried about you—and that Benthic beast you pulled in yesterday."

"An interesting fossil." Ode shrugged. "But you should see our harvest—"

"That's no fossil," warned Drum. "Maybe the meteors

brought back the five-toed hominids, too—or maybe they've been out there all along. Anyway—they are dangerous."

"Nonsense." Ode laughed. "Why, everyone knows—"

Sirens announcing the approach of another Benthic beast interrupted him. *Rorqual*'s course held steady until the beast climbed aboard—then the contact with the bare feet sent shudders through the whole ship.

"Sharps Committee—" Ode shouted.

Panic broke out on deck. Boots squeaked and slipped. The crew scattered. Two men fell overboard. Others fled into the trees and below decks. Only two from the Sharps Committee made it to the captain's office. They fumbled their keys into the weapons' locker, but two of the keyholes were still empty. The door wouldn't budge.

"Defend the ship," shouted the captain. "Use any weapon you can find."

The siren continued to rise and fall—bewailing the ship's fate. Even knives and forks were locked up. The reluctant squads that climbed back out onto the deck were carrying such useless things as spools, drinking jugs and chairs—nonweapons. The brine-soaked, naked beast towered over them, puzzled. Someone threw a four-inch bolt at him. It missed, but it clarified the situation in his mind. He lunged into the little Nebishes, kicking and flailing. Soon the decks were splattered with rose-water blood and five-toed footprints. Captain Ode was still tugging on the door to the weapons' locker when the Benthic dismembered him.

Drum cursed his helplessness as he monitored the one-sided battle. The Benthic was not even wounded, yet he had slain the entire ship's complement. He tracked red below decks until he found the frozen body of the other Benthic. This seemed to satisfy him. He weighted it with tools and jumped into the ship's wake with it.

A furious Drum stomped in on the Hive committee meeting.

"Why does *Rorqual* have to remain neutral? We lost the whole crew to a creature the ship could have dispatched with one swat of the crane."

The Security representative, a fat compromising neuter, turned piggish eyes to him and spoke slowly, didactically. "Your ship is equipped with the WIC/RAC genius circuit. I understand this enables it to survive in very hostile environments. However, we learned a long time ago that our genius machines must never be given the option of killing a hominid of any kind. It might discover a good reason to kill all of us."

Other committee members nodded. Even the CO, one mentioned, used a citizen to push the button that actually executed capital offenders.

Drum sat down, mumbling, "Then why send a crew at all? The ship harvests pretty well alone."

"The *Rorqual Maru* must be manned at all times," ordered CO. "She takes long voyages and gets lonely. To permit her to sail alone is to invite a commandeering by the Benthics."

The teck from Synthe stood up.

"The plankton clouds are widespread. I'm sure we can plot a course that avoids areas controlled by the Benthics."

"And," said Wandee from Bio, "we are working on the genes of a new prototype citizen who will be able to fight the Benthics. A stronger, bigger citizen—who will also fill the job requirements at the shipyards."

"Big enough to handle a Benthic with his bare hands?" asked Security.

Wandee nodded.

"Why—his body would be classified as a weapon. How would you insure his loyalty?"

"Just as certain ants insure the loyalty of their warriors. We'll design him so he can't feed himself."

Drum was shocked. "Do you mean—no esophagus or no hands? Something like that?"

Wandee smiled. "Oh, nothing so crude. He won't even notice anything amiss. We'll delete one of his key metabolic pathways so he'll be dependent on a special diet only the Hive can give him. Without it he'll sicken and die."

Drum shuddered. He was sorry he had asked. A tied-off esophagus could be corrected by a friendly Tinker. What could the poor warrior do about a defective enzyme system if he wanted to quit his job? Nothing.

"Here is a copy of the traits we hope to program into the genes of our warrior," said Wandee and handed him a clipboard.

Drum glanced at the list.

"Sounds good, but will it walk?" he asked.

"Walk, run, swim—and fight," said Wandee.

Drum was skeptical.

"How can you be sure? Just last year spinner couldn't

construct a gene map for marine protozoa. Now you think you can spin us a superman?"

The clipboard was passed around the table. The battle gear it listed was impressive: heavy bone and muscle, a fast reflex time, high pain threshold, potent neurohumoral axis. . . . None of the committee members really understood the details of gene spinning. Wandee wanted to quiet Drum's objections without exposing the other complacent Nebishes at the table to a lot of disturbing new terms they might not understand. Drum had an exceptional grasp of matters beyond his specialty and more—he had an open mind.

"Growing the prototype warrior is entirely different. We do not have to build an entirely unknown gene—as we were trying to do with marine biota. Human genes have been mapped many times and about twenty percent of the map is pretty well understood. Enough for us to design certain broad traits we are interested in. We will use the known map of the most primitive human we have on file—Larry Dever—from before the Era of Karl. We will have some of his alpha renal nuclei in suspension. By using his chromosomes—and deleting what we don't want—we have relatively few genes actually to assemble."

"Assemble a Larry Dever?" asked Drum.

"Modified. We'll grow an augmented Alpha Renal Nucleus of Larry Dever—an ARNOLD—with the traits listed."

The chairman had dozen off. He awoke with a start.

"You two can continue this discussion down in the spinner labs. Meeting adjourned."

Drum marveled at Wandee's deft manipulations. The meiotic renal cell was spilled into the sorting chamber filling the screen with X- and V-shaped chromosomes. She selected those to be augmented: a large D acrocentric #13; two B submetacentrics #4 and #5 and an F metacentric #19. They were moved into the cutting chamber. Her electron pencil carved as she talked.

"We'll cut off half of these long arms at the secondary constriction—a good landmark. Remove those little satellites —and take off the short arms from this late replicator. Careful of that centromere. There, now—plenty of room for translocating the synthetic chromatids from the spinner's bath."

The bath (a soup of purines and pyrimidines) contained the enzyme *reverse transcriptase*—the RNA-dependent DNA polymerase. (RNA molecules act as templates for the replication of DNA genes.) Spinner assembled the RNA template: GCAUGGAUCUU—guanine, cytosine, adenine, uracil, guanine, etc. When added to the soup a DNA gene replicated: CGTACCTAGAA—cytosine, guanine, thymine, adenine, cytosine, etc. Each grouping of three bases formed one codon (or letter) in the genetic message.

"This appears to be an excessive amount of the Grube-Hill gene," suggested Drum. He had been studying spinner's screen where the molecular activity was being simulated.

"A triple dose of gristle." Wandee smiled. "Our ARNOLDS will be real mechanized-armor bucks with triple calcium, collagen, phosphatase and growth hormone."

Drum nodded, frowned. "But what is this sequence? It does not translate."

"The Hive safety factor—a nonsense sequence where the gene locus for amino-acid synthesis should be. The bases have been scrambled to UAA, UAG and UGA, which do not translate at all. The ARNOLDS will be unable to synthesize six of the amino acids you and I can manufacture from the inorganic constituents in our diet. For ARNOLD, alanine, aspartate, glutamate, glycine, serine and tyrosine will be essential—along with the other nine all of us need in our diet. ARNOLD's diet must contain these fifteen essential amino acids or he'll become protein-deficient, weaken and die."

Drum was silent. He felt uneasy about building the ARNOLD—a human who would lay down his life for the Hive, not realizing that the Hive had implanted in him this molecular time bomb that would kill him if he became separated from the Hive. Drum felt himself to be more of an enemy to ARNOLD than the Benthic beast.

A codon GAG was changed to CAC, substituting the histidine letter for a glutamine—another nonsense sequence closing the transaminase "back door" to one of the amino acids. ARNOLD would not be able to get his amino acids even from his Kreb's cycle.

Playing with the Watson-Crick structures was tedious work, but soon Wandee had several clones working on the prototype ARNOLD DNA.

"We can sort the cells out of culture on the basis of their Grube-Hill content. Those with a lot of phosphatase fluoresce the brightest with this labeled substrate. We'll embryonate about a thousand of the triple GH's first."

Wandee hovered over the foaming nutrients and plated the placental matrix with the first hundred cells that showed chorionic tendencies (villi and gonadotropins). Soon the embryos were visible under the magnifier.

Wandee seemed pleased.

"Size and length of tail are good indexes at this stage," she said. "But I like to rely almost entirely on the Organ of Zuckerkandl—the chromaffin tissue near the inferior mesenteric artery. It is a good index of the neurohumoral axis. Autonomic tone, sex organs and adrenal medulla function can usually be predicted by studying the O. of Z."

Drum nodded. "And how many toes?"

"Oh, they'll all be five-toed, of course."

Twenty thick-necked, hairy infants survived Wandee's critical culling. They were tested repeatedly and the six most vigorous were turned over to Mullah. The rest went to shipyard nurseries on high job priority.

> *Warrior human beings*
> *Under Hive's control—*
> *Spinner made your genes.*
> *Who made your soul?*

Tangled girders and crusted plates were the tapestries for Listener's eulogy on the funeral raft. Benthics crowded around the weighted body. They were gathered in the far bubble of a torn tubeway overlooking the yawning blackness of the abyss. The body drifted for a long moment. Then it began to sink slowly, accompanied by a halo of zooplankton fighting over its nitrogen treasures.

"The Leviathan is not a whale?" asked Listener.

"A ship," said Clam. "I was all over her insides. I saw no sign of an organ or a muscle of any kind—just rooms and machines."

"But this machine—it showed signs of life after you had driven the crew away?"

"Yes. I heard and felt things I didn't understand. But I'm certain it knew I was there. It opened doors for me and followed me with little eyes in the walls."

"And it didn't try to harm you." Listener smiled. "Wonderful. I'll bet the Leviathan is a friendly ship."

"But it killed Peter," objected Clam. "The nets caught him at fifteen fathoms and pulled him up until the pops got him."

"Perhaps that was an accident," suggested Listener. "A surface machine like the Leviathan may not know about the pops. That is one of the secrets of the Deep Cult. I think we should try to capture the Leviathan. Perhaps we can learn to talk to it."

Opal said, "It might be able to protect us from the Hive."

The Benthics passed the word along the reef. The ocean would be theirs.

Young ARNOLD buckled on his harness while the workmen loaded his two-wheeled cart. He munched on the crust of 15-amino-acid bread. All his food was handed to him by his supervisor. He leaned into the straps. Wheels creaked. It was a two-hour run to the top of the spiral.

Citizens were already lined up at the dispenser when he arrived. The pressure had fallen again and they would have had to go down to shaft base for their calorie basic if it weren't for ARNOLD's training runs.

"Good time, ARNOLD," said the workman who had ridden in the cart. He climbed down and handed ARNOLD a yellow-4 sweet.

ARNOLD squatted in his harness, chewing his treat. He was only six years old, but was already the size of an average citizen. His powerful calf muscles tingled after the workout. Soon he would be trained to work in the shipyards, they had told him. The work was important—clearing rusted debris. He was a very bright ARNOLD. He understood everything real fast. His mentors hardly ever had to use the whip anymore.

That night he slept under his cart at the loading docks. He had lots of room to stretch out. The workers on the shift made hardly any noise at all. His chains were real long—a light new alloy. He was fed his special 15-AA bread six times a day. He had lots to eat and grew fast.

Drum sat on the edge of the wagon and offered ARNOLD an orange-3 sweet bar.

"All of us are Reincarnationists," said Drum, speaking slowly. "We believe in the transmigration of the soul. Our souls lived in other bodies, even other creatures, before inhabiting our present ones. We go to the chapel and try to feel some experience from a previous life. We learn to understand ourselves better—become better citizens. Would you like to do that, ARNOLD?"

ARNOLD nodded.

"You may find that you weren't always a draft animal," said Drum.

ARNOLD grinned. He did not understand what Drum meant.

An appointment was made with Mullah.

ARNOLD appeared at the chapel with Drum at his elbow. He was almost two feet taller than the average citizen as he walked down the aisle, his chains going *ching, ching, ching*. The walls of the chapel were covered with the Darwinian Transmigration from amoeba through invertebrates, lower vertebrates and finally the highest animal—the four-toed Nebish. The robed Mullah directed ARNOLD to put down his chains and stretch out on the heavily telemetered couch. The links clattered noisily to the floor. Four meditecks tubed and wired him to the sensory tape machine for a review of his phylogenetic tradition—his leptosoul.

"Let's see if we can establish a common language between the tapes and ARNOLD," said Mullah. They watched the encephalogram as a combination of drugs and midbrain trickle current suppressed ARNOLD's consciousness.

"It will take several sessions before leptosoul imagery is clear. The symbols we will start with are basic: itch, thirst, hunger, sleep, sex—things like that. The itch is useful in localizing a sensory message. It is better than pain or heat or cold, because the itch stimulates you to do something other than simple withdrawal. The itch gets you to scratch. Notice the readouts. He is getting a good response to both central and peripheral itching."

Drum watched the ARNOLD get exposed to thirst, probably one of the oldest phylogenetic memories dating back to the time life left the seas. Hypertonic fluids bathed key receptors, making him physiologically thirsty. Neurological thirst came with steriotactic sonic stimulation of the thirst center in the brain stem. Psychological thirst was induced by images of dust, dry leaves, skeletons and a distant lake mirage. Heat and a throat itch brought physical thirst. AR-NOLD writhed and suffered 4-D thirst. The thirst stimuli were turned off and cool hypotonic fluids were flushed into his stomach.

"Hunger can be a bit dangerous," warned Mullah. "When we sag his blood glucose under forty milligrams we run the risk of causing brain damage. We lost several citizens early this month during this step. The tubes empty his stomach and pucker the rugal folds with cold water. Insulin drops the blood sugar. The hunger center in the brain stem is stimulated and the itch is located in the mouth."

ARNOLD experienced visions of skeletons familiar to him from the thirst sequence, only this time he wanted to stuff his mouth with meat pies and sponge cakes. The stimuli were stopped and relief came in a visual image of the hand of the Hive carrying pies and cakes.

Mullah looked up.

"Sex is an important warrior drive. We can use it for imprinting and motivating other lesser drives. A mature male is the best engineered warrior in terms of muscle and bone. Testosterone, you know. For this imagery we localize the itch in the genital region and the neural stimulus in the basal ganglia. We can program a variety of sexual encounters for imprinting. The last symbol is sleep. The itch is a bright red asterisk behind the eyelids. Neural stimuli play with his alpha rhythms."

"That seemed to be a good session," commented Drum.

Mullah nodded.

"Since he is to be a warrior, we might as well offer him a little vivid imagery to take home with him."

Stag ARNOLD perched on a low fir limb, reigning over beautiful speckled Frost Gray hens. They scratched and pecked in musty humus. He smelled aromatic pine needles and saw glistening grubs. The power of his spur stubs made him cock of the knoll. The day before he had knocked a great yellow cat from this very limb. The sex urge pulled him from his perch. He swooped down on a pretty little hen and grabbed her by the short feathers. She squawked and struggled, but he pinned her to the ground, mated and strutted off with a cavalier air. Flustered, she preened her disarray. Crowing, he returned to his perch. . . .

The leptosoul experience left young ARNOLD puzzled. Residual euphoria made him want to crow. As he gathered up his chains he stared at the links for a long time. They seemed out of place now that he had relived part of a regal back-

ground. He, ARNOLD, had been a king—a feathered warrior—a game fowl.

Drum watched the giant leave. He shook his head slowly,
saying, "Poor ARNOLD. The Hive has a big job for you."

"I think he is equipped for it," said Mullah.

Drum eased himself down on the edge of the couch. Raising
ARNOLD had drained him. One lens had clouded over and
all his teeth were gone. He had little time left.

"ARNOLD has a big job," continued Drum, "and he can
never retire."

"Why?"

"The safety factor. We programmed his genes so he can't
make fifteen amino acids. He can never live on calorie basic.
In fact, he can live on nothing in the Hive except his own
special fifteen-AA crusts. If he lacks just one of those amino
acids his protein synthesis stops. He sickens and dies rather
horribly—swollen with edema fluids, bleeding, ulcerating,
paralyzed."

Mullah said, "But if he works he will eat. Everyone does his
share—some do more. Look at yourself, Drum. Once you
stepped outside your caste the Hive had you doing everything
and anything to keep your Recertification job vote. You're the
oldest out-of-caste laborer I've ever seen. ARNOLD won't
have it any tougher than that."

"Unless he becomes obsolete. He's very specialized, as you
well know."

Big Opal cautioned her adventurous daughter White Belly
to stay away from South Abyss.

"Leviathan has been sighted there. Leave her to the males.
Clam is taking his mussel scrapers there today. You work
North Reef."

White Belly nodded reluctantly and swam north. She had
been a surface baby—born in Halfway House. She had spent
much of her youth swimming around buoys and soaking up
solar UV. Melanocytes darkened. Her freckled, brown back
and pale abdomen had given her her name.

Born too late for raiding the Gardens—the Hive was once
again active Outside—she was now being denied the excitement of hunting the Leviathan.

Drum studied the ocean charts. The years of raking had
given the Hive a good picture of plankton distribution along

the shelf where upcurrents carried nutrients from the ocean floor. Benthic beasts were also located on the shelf—in the flooded ruins of old Rec Centers around the twenty-fathom range.

ARNOLD was ten years old now. His years in the shipyards had hardened his body. His visits to the chapel had strengthened his leptosoul.

Capon ARNOLD roosted with other fat-bottomed neuter birds—neither cock nor hen. Each had his own mush cup and water. ARNOLD was restless. His soul remembered when food had flavors and hens were speckled. He tried to stir up his roostmates by pushing them away from their mush and eating it himself. They wouldn't fight. They just lowered their heads. He gained weight rapidly and invited an early ax.

END OF TAPE. NEW LEPTOSOUL: BATTLECOCK.

Battlecock ARNOLD was all testicular valor and iron spur. His days of secret training in the keep had hardened his body and strengthened his wind. A hundred times a day he had been tossed by the *hand*. Each time he flew back to his windowsill to look out into the hen yard. His diet removed extra water and fat from his body: Twelve kernels of corn, chopped cooked meat, chopped lettuce, wheat germ, honey and peanut butter. When his irons were tied over his spurs he knew someone would die. Odors of blood, tobacco and whiskey told him that other *hands* were there with their cocks. He rested comfortably in his handler's arms until the time came to fight. He was placed in the pit with a Claret. Twice they went up and locked irons. Each time they were tenderly disengaged and placed back in the pit. ARNOLD was blind now. He had taken some iron in the skull. He couldn't see the Claret, so he waited. When the Claret attacked he knew just where it was.

ARNOLD went up, striking out with his spurs. He felt the Claret's iron in his belly and left wing. Then his own iron crunched cartilage and diced myocardium. When they were disengaged this time he was held in the arm and petted by the *hand*. He heard the Claret's last coughs.

When ARNOLD's orbital hematoma subsided the hens were his. He was brood cock now—under wire—with three of the most feminine Frost Gray hens. The big hen tried to shoulder him away from the water, but he gave her a resounding peck. He was king. Soon all three would be setting handsome clutches of eggs.

One morning the wind brought a faint answer to his crowing. There was another cock on the other side of the ridge. He couldn't wait for the chicken wire to be lifted.

"This wire is the only thing that keeps you alive," mumbled ARNOLD.

"Wonderful," commented Mullah. "Notice how real these leptosoul experiences have become for him. He is 'ARNOLD the battlecock' in his subconscious. These 4-D sensory dreams have more significance than his dull routine of real life."

Drum studied the feedbacks to see if ARNOLD was showing maximum effects. There was still room for improvement.

"Let's step it up next time. We'll run through these tapes with more energy—enhance the ax pain in the Capon sequence, build up his euphoria and sexual stimuli after the battlecock win."

"When does he sail?" asked Mullah.

"Soon. Perhaps on his eleventh birthday. His testosterone levels are high enough. Epiphyses are closing. He'll be ready."

"Yes. I'm sure he'll do fine."

A sullen Clam stalked on South Reef. Warm body tickling sensors—his presence activated ancient circuits, and fields of waving, man-sized umbrellas welcomed him. He swam toward Leviathan's trawling lane pausing at two-fathom umbrellas to fill his lungs. Ahead of him the reef sprang to life. Meck pumps filled the umbrella air pockets. Snap electrolysis spiked the air with oxygen. Clouds of marine scum and overflow bubbles rose from the writhing shapes—cyber barnacles that had survived the twenty-seven centuries to serve the rare fugitive Benthic.

Clam waited at the edge of the reef. Behind him the umbrellas quieted. He watched the surface overhead. A dark sky spat big drops into the choppy water. Leviathan's whale-shape approached trailing nets. Clam left his air pocket and grabbed the fine mesh netting. In a moment he was on the rain-spattered deck. His boarding caused pandemonium this time The siren initiated a regular cadence of squeaking boots. Rows of Nebish crew members lined up, carrying shoulder-high netting—walking fences. Clam leaped onto the cabin roof.

Thunder rolled. Hump palms rustled in the wind. ARNOLD stepped out of the foliage and studied the Benthic—a hundred yards away. Both were six-foot giants; half again as high as the other crew Nebishes. Clam was dark-skinned, naked. ARNOLD wore standard coveralls with a wide, studded belt, but his big bare feet made flat sounds like Clam's.

"Hello," shouted Clam, waving.

ARNOLD silently motioned for the net fences to be lowered and advanced slowly across the rows of wet mesh. Clam glanced around for a possible attack from behind. The nose of the ship had no hatch. Beyond the hump the crane worked casually on heavy plankton netting. Only the deck crew and ARNOLD seemed to notice him.

"I can let you live," offered Clam, "if you give me this ship."

A cock crowed in ARNOLD's subconscious.

Clam couldn't believe the fury of the attack. The ARNOLD had sprinted across sixty yards of open deck and leaped on him—kicking, biting and elbowing. They tumbled down onto the deck. ARNOLD's teeth were crunching deep into Clam's left forearm. A wave carried the fighters off the nose of the ship and the huge maw sucked them into the rakes. AR-NOLD's fingers closed on Clam's throat. The Nebish netters draped the pair with sticky tangle-foot mesh. Clam clawed at ARNOLD's fingers as his sensorium clouded. The tunnel vision frightened him. He found ARNOLD's left middle finger and quickly bent it back—breaking it with a *snap*. He clung to the stump twisting it hard. ARNOLD's grip slipped. Clam vaulted back into the sea, dragging the netting and three drowning Nebishes.

Drum wheezed and patted ARNOLD on the forearm. A banjo-splint held the damaged finger along with all four fingers in a fanlike position.

"Good warrior. You did well. You are only eleven years old and you defeated the Benthic beast, saving the ship. The sea is open to the Hive."

ARNOLD smiled and nodded. He accepted the accolades and returned to the shipyards. When his injuries healed he'd captain again.

Drum took the battle report down to the chapel.

"We'll have to step up his battle conditioning, use those heavy tapes—Dan-with-the-golden tooth."

Mullah programmed his leptosoul meck.

"How far do you want to go with this? I've got one where Dan allows his head to be cut off so he can fight two battles at the same time. His head wins and then flops into the second pit where his body is holding the second contestant. He wins both fights, naturally."

Drum shook his head.

"No, keep the battle physiology plausible in human terms. We want ARNOLD to use a little judgment. In name at least —and by the grace of some learning-tape conditioning—he'll be captain of the ship. He's programmed for a little judgment —not much."

Dan worked the cold femur back in his mouth. Molars cracked it open and the rusty marrow and crumbling bone distended his gastric rugal folds, loading his hepatic lymph with iron and calcium ions. Dan sniffed the dirt, wondering where the other old bone was buried. *Cluck. Cluck.* His wards, the feathered friends in the coop, were upset.

Ears up, he watched the scrub pine. A massive intruder appeared—black and hairy—walking on its hind paws. The intruder had long claws and sharp white teeth. It was twenty times his size. Dan froze to quiet his chain. The intruder was intent on the succulent coop dwellers. It failed to notice the circle of dead grass that marked chain's end. As its big left hind paw entered the circle Dan leaped and sank his teeth into the black shaggy hide. Tendons jumped under his fangs. A hot tibia split. The intruder was down—howling. Claws and teeth ripped Dan's hide open, snapping his spine and spilling his intestines. Dan tightened his jaw as darkness swallowed him up.

Dan's leptosoul floated above the gory scene. The bulky intruder limped off with a distinctive lump on its left ankle—Dan's head. The baying of a pack of hounds and a rifle sound finished Dan's job on the intruder.

ARNOLD snorted, strode out of the chapel. Drum was impressed. He stayed behind to study the tapes.

"What was this creature— this Dan-with-the-golden-tooth?"

Mullah smiled eagerly. "These are the most aggressive lepto-soul tapes we have. I think the subject was a small meat-eating pet that worked for man—protecting him against varmints big and small. He was so aggressive he had to be muzzled to be bred."

"Why? Couldn't he recognize a female?"

"Yes, but apparently he fought anything that came into his territory. Fought for wagers, too. But the beast obviously could not tell a bet from a stud fee, so he had to subdue any female he met to be safe."

"It certainly worked. Look at ARNOLD's adrenergics."

Mullah frowned. "I hope this doesn't endanger his Hive loyalty. Adrenergics like that in a citizen would make him a candidate for the psych clinic."

Drum wheezed and sat down. His jaw ached.

"We needn't worry about ARNOLD's loyalty. He can't live without the Hive's fifteen-AA bread."

Mullah nodded, reminded of the safty factor in ARNOLD's genes. Then he noticed Drum's discomfort.

"Life span coming to an end? Want me to call VS?"

Drum shook his head. He would live out his span warm.

Opal changed Clam's bandage. The toothmarks in his fore-arm had gone purulent, were draining cloudy pink fluids. The arm was swollen to twice its size and the fingers would not move. Fever racked his body.

"He still smells foul," complained sister White Belly.

"If that arm doesn't improve by tonight I'll have to ampu-tate," said Opal.

"He needs hot packs and hot broth," said White Belly.

"We can't go to the beach and build a fire. The Hive would find us."

Young White Belly brooded and swam alone. She found herself at Halfway, where she had been born. She told Listener about Clam's injury.

"We must get him down into the squeeze where the air is thicker. His infection sounds anaerobic. *Clostridia* type of gangrene. Oxygen will cure it down in the squeeze. Come with me."

They dragged the delirious Clam from bubble to bubble as they descended into the abyss.

"Don't come any farther. If you aren't used to it, the thick air will give you the fits or the giggles. I'll take Clam to that dome down there to the left. He'll have air and fresh water. If he isn't better in twelve hours there is nothing more we can do," explained Listener.

He towed a limp Clam down another ten fathoms and they disappeared into a pale glowing dome. White Belly waited in a cliffside umbrella. The oxygen made her feel a little giddy, but she controlled her silly impulses as she stood watch over her brother's dome. A strange humanoid creature visited the dome. It had wide lacy wings like a butterfly—one of the Deep Cult that lived off the Benthics' offerings. Opal came down and tugged White Belly back to the upper level.

"We must stay home for one day after visiting the squeeze or the pops will get us," said Opal. "Then you must do Clam's chores. He was harvesting the South Reef. But, beware of Leviathan."

White Belly toyed with the fragments of polymer netting that Clam had brought back.

"What was that big thing on Leviathan? Another Benthic like us?" she asked.

Opal shook her head.

"No, child. Listener says it is an ARNOLD. The Hive can build people as easily as you or I can draw their pictures. They wanted a big one to fight us—so they grew a big ARNOLD in a bottle. Without a mother. Just a bottle."

White Belly sharpened her abalone iron.

ARNOLD sat by Drum's sickbed as the teck removed the banjo-splint.

"See, Drum," ARNOLD said, flexing. "I'm fine."

Drum grinned weakly, "Good boy. Now go back to *Rorqual* with those extra cyber panels I gave you. Wire the ship to talk to you. Tell it to warn you if the Benthic beasts appear. Make friends with the ship. It is a good harvester. Take care of it and it will take care of you."

ARNOLD patted the old man's shoulder. As he left he paused in the anteroom. A battery of Hive personnel huddled around a temporary communications center. Wandee sat among a group of tecks, reading Drum's bio-electricals.

ARNOLD towered over the group with a pained expression.

"He's stable by the charts," said Wandee. "The CO wants you to know that the Hive is doing everything it can for him."

ARNOLD nodded. He picked up the cyber panels and

carried them to the docks where *Rorqual* prepared for her next voyage.

Once on board, ARNOLD set to work at splicing the new panels in place. Learning tapes had prepared him. He crawled between walls, moving the thick, fluffy insulation around to make room for the new units. When he was finished he patted the wall.

"There you are, old girl. You should be able to work your lingual readout now. What do you say?"

"Hello, bare feet."

ARNOLD glanced down, smiling. He was the only crew member without boots.

"Wonderful, you sound fine. What else?"

"Clear my hump."

"Clear it?"

"Yes," said *Rorqual*, "the electrolyte spray burns."

"The sea mist—does it really hurt?"

"It burns," said the ship. "Clear my hump and close my plates. The wind-blown electrolyte burns and ages me."

"Right away, old girl. You machine a nice double-bladed ax for me and I'll get right to work on your hump trees."

Although the *Rorqual* was far out to sea, the ax looked like a weapon to Hive Security. The committee was called into session. They opened channels to *Rorqual* and the CO.

"Why wasn't the Sharps Committee informed prior to the blade's manufacture?" asked Security.

"It is a tool," said *Rorqual*.

"Does the ARNOLD intend to put it in the arms locker immediately?" asked the chairman.

The screen focused on a deck optic. A storm had blown up and a dark, heavy rain splattered into the hump vegetation. ARNOLD sang as he chopped. Wood chips were flying. The question was repeated. The wind carried away the words.

"What?" asked ARNOLD.

"Do you intend—" began the chairman. His words were choked off by his view of another figure moving behind ARNOLD—a wet, naked Benthic.

A siren.

ARNOLD turned, ax in hand, to meet the lunge of White Belly—breasts, hips and a voluminous mane. Ax and abalone iron *clicked* and *clacked*. Her iron sliced across his chest, cutting fabric and chipping thick studs. Her left hand was on the ax handle above his. She stabbed and sliced with the iron—opening his coveralls. He caught her mane in his left hand and they rolled on the wet deck. Lightning flashed. Wood chips and wet leaves clung to her warm, moist body, giving it a speckled appearance.

(Something went *cluck, cluck*.)

Her blade sank into his side, releasing a well of thick dark blood.

The screen before Drum's deathbed focused on the struggling pair.

"He's wounded." Drum watched the main project of his lifetime hang in the balance.

"Just a knife in the *latissimus dorsi*," reassured CO after a study of the bio-electricals. "He's fine, but needs encouraging words. Tell him to chop off her head."

Drum moaned in his orthopnea. The deck scene was obscured by the misty rain, but ARNOLD seemed vigorous enough.

"He seems to be doing fine," wheezed Drum.

"But he's not killing her," objected the CO. "I can't get involved, being a meck—but you understand our mission here. Tell him to fight."

Drum could not understand why the CO was dissatisfied with ARNOLD's performance. It was clear that he had the Benthic subdued. He had it down on the deck. A good grip on its mane—oh, yes! He wasn't fighting. He was copulating. The Benthic was a female.

Drum chuckled, wheezed and coughed.

"Humor?" asked CO.

"It's those Dan-with-the-golden-tooth leptosoul tapes. Dan never could tell a bet from a stud fee."

ARNOLD stepped away from a prone White Belly and pulled her weapon from his *latissimus* with a cavalier air, tossed it aside. She scrambled into a crouched position—eyes blazing. Her speckled skin excited him. He took a step toward her.

"Touch me again and I'll kill you," she growled.

He paused, thinking. Odd, but the threat meant absolutely nothing to him. He continued to advance. She glanced around for her iron. It was too far away. Turning, she dove into the sea.

"Why?" asked CO.

"Copulins," said *Rorqual*. "She was reeking of male sex attractant—the primate sexual pheromones. I ran a few whiffs of her body odor through my chromatographs and came up with the simple aliphatic acids: acetic, propionic, isobutyric, butyric, isovaleric and isocaproic—the constituents of copulins. ARNOLD has an intact rhinencephalic-hypothalamic pathway. He couldn't control himself."

The committee reviewed the behavior of their marine gladiator.

"Nose plugs. All he needs is nose plugs and he will do just fine."

But ARNOLD did not do just fine. He stood on the deck a long time before returning to the work on the hump trees. The work went slowly, but smoothly. With one eye on the seas he chopped and directed the removal of twisted plates with their medusa-heads of roots. New plates were brought in by the crane. *Rorqual*'s skin was slowly healed. The ship was grateful.

Drum was aroused from an agonal stupor by the Mullah and Wandee.

ARNOLD had defected, they told him.

Drum blinked. He could not grin, though he wanted to. A line of saliva trailed down his chin.

"He turned off *Rorqual*'s communicator. We guess that he is searching for the Benthics. Psychteck reviewed the optic records and thinks he is sexually imprinted on her. Something about being imprinted on speckled hens at the chapel. The Benthic was speckled with freckles."

Drum moved slightly, whispering, "Why pick on me?"

"You're his father figure," said Mullah. "Wandee spun his genes, but you took him to chapel and spent a lot of time with him. He'll listen to you."

Drum shook his head. "If he wants to be free—"

"But he will just die," moaned Wandee. "He must return for his Hive fifteen-AA bread."

"You told him?"

"Yes, but he doesn't believe us. He might believe you."

Drum was propped up with pillows.

"Just talk slowly," said Wandee. "The CO will record it and broadcast it every few minutes. *Rorqual* isn't sending— but it may have its long ear on, listening."

"ARNOLD—son—" Drum coughed. "We made your genes. We gave you a powerful body and a good mind. The best in the Hive. I know you want to be free, but you can't be. The Hive asked us to design your metabolism so you'd be dependent on the special fifteen-AA bread. Without it you'll sicken and die. Believe me—son."

Rorqual opened a channel to Drum. ARNOLD was not in view. The ship spoke.

"ARNOLD doubts your words, Drum. Perhaps I can relay your message in terms he can understand, but I, too, find it difficult to understand why he needs a special bread. All humans have some essential amino acids."

Wandee interrupted. "Here is the list. ARNOLD has six more essential amino acids than other humans. He must return."

Rorqual studied the list: alanine, aspartate, glutamate, glycine, serine and tyrosine.

"I understand," said the ship. "Now I shall try to explain it to ARNOLD. Somehow I shall make him comprehend."

The screen darkened. Drum's tired face went cyanotic at the same time. Bio-electricals flattened. His mind struggled against the enclosing void. He had had one more question to ask, but he was unable to get it past his cool lips. He had wanted to ask—how many amino acids were in plankton?

The Hive never saw *Rorqual Maru* or her ARNOLD again. Benthic sightings became almost nonexistent. Muscular and lesser ARNOLDS waited in shipyards with their heavy tools, but Hive allocations for raking were held up in the committee. Their experience with ARNOLD had left too many questions unanswered. The added marine calories had not been worth all the expense.

CHANGING WOMAN

W. MACFARLANE

*Sympathetic magic is as old as human-
ity——and where something like that per-
sists it may be that there is something to
it that science should investigate. In any
case, this is presented as a science fiction
work which touches upon that most primitive of beliefs. We know that individuals
influence history——the question is can they
also influence geology?*

SAN FRANCISCO (UPA) A spokesman for the UC
Geophysical Group said today: "An 8.4 Richter with a
Mercalli X-XI is not incompatible with observed effects,
however localized. The San Andreas Fault goes out to sea
at the mouth of Alder Creek, 85 air miles to the south.
The so-called 'Red Lady' branch fault must be regarded
as hypothetical, though stresses between the Pacific and
Continental crustal plates. . ."

Girl Cloud-Walking said, "A job on the California coast?"
She turned on her high stool and looked through the window

down the canyons of Chicago fading into quiet snow a couple of blocks away. She was a plump woman with small feet and long, blunt-fingered hands. Her hair was shining crow color and braided into a coronet. "They get a little hysterical out there."

"Birdeena Ora Oza Yadon, sweetie—" Her boss was hesitant.

"Are you using your forked or unforked tongue?"

"Deena, from us you get six months' leave of absence. From the Mundy Foundation you get double pay plus all expenses. That's much wampum, my lady Indian friend. Work in big wigwam. You get food and lodging thrown in."

"Forked, I think. Maybe I'll phone Rand McNally for a job. What do you get out of this?"

"Nothing but trouble. You are the best collagist in the business, but Mrs. Arlis Mundy owns thirty-eight percent of Aero Precision Survey. Who's to replace you? Do you know how much that eighty-two mile Indiana State highway was out? Sixteen inches."

"So how did they measure it? With a string?"

"They said laser triangulation."

"The benchmarks were painted fat and I have some reservations about that print-drying process. We've got to get deeper into the materials. I'm not sure the errors canceled. Now look, John—"

"Don't put me off, Birdeena."

She glanced around the room where she had worked for the past three years. It was familiar and comfortable to her —the tilted drawing board, the 4x12 table, the K&E tools, her desk with the calculator and phone and hideaway typewriter, the tall files and the ranks of flat files for air photos. This was a web of precision and rationality and beauty. This had been a safe and growing place.

"Well, John?" There were spiders that cast a silk web into the air and drifted off with the wind. She smiled faintly at the idea of herself as a fat spider flying to California.

"Hell with it," he said suddenly. "Let the woman squeal. If she don't like it bad enough, we'll both phone Rand McNally." He had a wife and children in Oak Park, but he meant it. He was a tough-minded Syrian with an appreciation of his own worth.

"Not to be hasty," she said. "Maybe it's time to go."

Girl Cloud-Walking never questioned the provenience of

decisions forming themselves from the sum of her life. She felt no need to justify the quiet satisfaction of mathematics or her pleasure in the precise detail of engineering draftsmanship. Her father had been a high-iron man and followed construction. She had had a year of college in Virginia and another in Nebraska. When she had had enough college she had found this job in Chicago.

"Baby, you are so precisely my bag of tea I hate to see you go." He was troubled. "You might not come back, Deena. You might like it out there."

"Might," she said. *"How can I tell until I go to Cairo or Cathay/Whether or not, this blessed spot is blessed in every way?* Old Indian saying by Edna St. Vincent Millay."

"Sure," he said sadly. "I mean, ugh."

Four days later Birdeena Ora Oza Yadon flew from O'Hare to San Francisco International. She was met and made to feel a Very Important Person by the pilot of the Beech Queen Air, who flew her north along the coast and ducked under a rolling fog bank, to land south of Cape Mendocino on an abrupt airstrip carved in the timber of a valley behind the first ridge, paralleling the fog-blotted breakers.

"What are you?" she asked the pilot.

"Almost a foolish man, but not quite. Otherwise we'd have to land thirty miles away." He grinned. "Blackfoot."

"Jicarilla Apache. My mother is Navaho. Friends or enemies?"

"Brand-new," he said and taxied the Queen Air to a hangar. "I don't think we ever met historically." He ran to a door and she sat with her hands in her lap. She could not see the tops of the redwoods behind the hangar in the drizzling fog. The great doors opened from the center. He fastened a towbar to the nose wheel and hauled the plane into the brightly lighted building with a towmotor. It was an amazing place with great laminated beams and enough shop to build a scratch airplane.

He carried her luggage to a four-wheel drive station wagon parked in front of a rubber-tire roller and beside a full-size motor grader. They drove outside into the rain and fog and he punched a code on a dash-mounted radio control. The doors of the hangar closed and the lights turned off.

"Extra special, first class."

"Well, what do you do with all the money there is?"

"Build a quarter-million-dollar hangar. Then you lay a

twenty-four-foot asphalt road. That runs along the strip. That runs into a rain forest, that's what."

"Right on. You can afford spectacular temper tantrums."

"The Mundy Foundation is a temper tantrum?"

"It's my latest theory."

"What do you do here?"

"Oh, I'm airplane driver and head custodian—systems maintenance engineer. You'll stay warm at the house because of the dam and generator, two thirty-thousand gallon propane tanks and fifty thousand gallons of diesel. We got backup systems on backup systems. The last time I tried to figure, the investment in this hysterical complex was two point eight million iron men."

"Because Mrs. Foundation is in a snit?"

The station wagon shuddered as they left the forest and followed a cut through a ridge. The surf boomed somewhere in the fog. Rain lashed the windows. Scud creamed across the road in wavy lines.

"This outfit has paid me more money in the last five years than I expect to see in the next ten." He raised his voice against a drumbeat of rain. "I'm still going back to Montana and cowboy. Trouble is, I know everything about this place —but what it's about."

They drove into a wide paved area sheltered by rock walls and a roof. The asphalt was black with wind-driven rain. A door lifted in response to the radio control and they drove through a short tunnel to a garage. A dozen cars were·parked herringbone around a glassed-in central office. A man stood by the door, laughing at another struggling into foul-weather gear.

"Hey, Marty, the bridge farside screwed up again. Mesi Stevens is stuck over there." He leaned against a red XKE Jaguar and pulled on his boot.

"Damn it," said the pilot. "We got to go underground with that line. ˙Ed, this is Birdeena Yadon, new tech staff. Ed Fukahara, electric genius and troubleshooter." He introduced Birdeena to Doc Crowell in the glass office. He was a bony blond man with white snaggle teeth who said he would have a key and ID card for her tomorrow morning.

Birdeena followed the pilot to an elevator. "Who is Mesi Stevens?" she asked. "Is this a league of nations?"

"Mesi is our darkroom genius. All the people who work here are extra special. I'd like to know how much it cost to

pick the permanent staff. They interviewed me three days before I skinned by. A fancy kind of selection and it sure works."
The door opened to a 40x60 room, thick with carpet and
interest.

"What do they choose for?" asked Birdeena, looking up at
him.

"You tell me after supper," he said and led her through
chairs and planters and bookcases and tables to meet the
housekeeper, Rose Chiappetta. She was at the far end of the
room with her finger on a switch. Soft primrose-colored drapes
marched across black, rain-running windows. She welcomed
Birdeena and took her to her room. It was luxurious and
comfortably snug.

The people she met at dinner seemed curiously open to her,
like moon-shot commentators revealed as perceptive men
removed from the banalities of TV by the occasion and their
own intelligence. Her new associates did not put on a front.
They had sober self-esteem. They were courteous from
strength and helpful and friendly.

And something worth knowing was the pilot's name. Martin
Sanderson . . . might just catch . . . a plump little watermelon
. . . out of the air—she smiled drowsily and resolved to continue her new negative response to the deep-frosted chocolate
cake Paul Maniatti, the cook, made.

Girl Cloud-Walking went to sleep that night with a feeling
of integrity and immediate security, like going up green in
her mother's old riddle. What goes up green and comes down
red?

She met Arlis Mundy next morning in the drafting loft.

Arlis Mundy looked like the Queen of Hell. She was tall
and regal in a vermilion knit dress and soft, cerise, ankle-high
boots.

"Birdeena Ora Oza Yadon, how nice you could come to
work with us."

Birdeena was shy but not self-conscious. Arlis Mundy's
charm put her at ease, though she observed the nakedness of
the hips under the knit dress and the faint, minuscule awk-
wardness with which this imperial woman moved. It was an
almost imperceptible flaunting of the joints, a ghost of hesi-
tancy that might be taut control or a conscious check of
wracking forces.

She took Birdeena through her austere office—orange and

black and white—to a balcony overlooking an enormous cube
of space. It took in one entire end of the building, five stories
tall. There were no windows. The temperature was controlled
and the humidity constant. A series of composite air photos
were racked one behind another, flown from the ceiling on
overhead tracks. To the left was a montage of weather satellite
shots of the entire Earth, sixteen by forty feet, in a clever
Homolosine equal-area projection, an intricately cut orange
peel spread flat. To the right was the coast of California from
San Francisco to the Sierras and south to San Diego bay and
the Mexican border. The photos were mounted on high density
overlay with plywood web support trusses behind. Girl Cloud-
Walking felt the hanging panels were desolate, scuffed and
pushed to discard.

They walked down stairs to the lowest of the three bal-
conies. "Our project is to create the most accurate photo-
montage possible," said Mrs. Mundy. "The scale is one to
three-sixteenth-eight-oh-five or five miles to the inch." She
hesitated. "What is your secret name, dear? We'll be working
together for some months."

"Deena. My parents are not reservation. They called me
Deena."

"Well then, Deena, reducing a curved surface to a plane
has not proven altogether satisfactory. I'm told on good
authority that a circle is a polygon with an infinite number
of sides, so we shot along thirty-four degrees, twenty minutes
from the New Mexico border west and laid the strip to the
west as well. We reached the coast with errors obvious. What
happened was not exactly what I had in mind."

Her hair was wheat gold, her face a triangle with a high
wide brow. Her skin was white and smooth, her mouth small
and crimson above a pointed chin. "There's no precedent for
original research—obviously," she said. "So we shall try another approach with control inherent. This is it."

In the center of the floor was a dome fifty feet across, rising
not quite five feet at the center. The precisely patterned
circumference was eight feet off the floor.

"A representational slice of the Earth," said Arlis Mundy.

A carpeted platform projected from the lowest balcony. At
the far end was a hip-high control standard. She stepped
aboard and flicked a switch and checked a dial. She pushed
a toggle.

The platform ran out from the balcony on triangular steel

columns with a hushed purr of motors and gearing. It was dead steady. She touched another control and the platform sank to within two inches of the dome surface. "You might call this a plotting chair or a layout cradle. You'll be working off it." She flexed her knees. There was not the faintest quiver. She shook the control standard with both hands. No movement at all. She hiked her skirt and kicked a leg over the standard with a dancer's improbable leap and lash and faced Birdeena.

Her voice was level. *"Similia similibus curantur,"* she said. "Like things are—let us say—cured by like. The principle is, like produces like and the part stands for the whole. This is where we map the United States as it has never been done before."

She touched the controls and the platform rose and carried her smoothly toward Birdeena, who stood stolidly on the balcony as the Empress of Hell in red loveliness rode the air to her. She wondered why she had not seen the color of Arlis Mundy's eyes before. They had no color. They were gray as fog.

Birdeena Yadon worked twenty-two days straight before Martin Sanderson lifted her chin with a curled forefinger and asked if she would like to go to San Francisco. "Avoid excess," he said. "If the Great Spirit wanted you to work all the time he never would have invented Saturday and Sunday."

She blinked like a woman half out of a dream. "Oh, dear," she said. "Mesi Stevens has Springfield, Illinois to do again. He doesn't know who slipped the scale but that's what happened. I was checking along forty degrees north and found it."

"Then let him grope by himself in the darkroom. Moderation is a lovely virtue. Let's go now."

She took a deep breath. "Yes, please."

It was a sparkling day as they taxied to the end of the strip for takeoff. She admired the tall trees on either side and asked why shorter ones had been left beyond the end of the runway. He said the brush down to the rocky riverbed was for contingencies, the trees for emergency.

"Life is very, very dangerous," he said. "You should try to maintain orderliness in areas not subject to control." He ran up the engines. "The wingspan is fifty feet three inches and the trees are maybe twenty feet apart. We land at over eighty miles an hour. If the brakes fail or power quits on takeoff, I have those trees to go between. Ripping off wings is one way to stop."

They took off and banked over the ocean. The Mundy Foundation was an architect's rendering on the shelf above the tumbling cliffs. The maproom at the far end was blind. Girl Cloud-Walking tightened her seatbelt and asked, "What degree of latitude is Los Angeles?"

"About thirty-four, maybe a little north. Why?"

"Earthquakes."

"We can do anything here just as good as they can in LA," he said, "but don't worry about our little home. It's steel frame with plywood in sheer panels. The rock on the outside is for pretty. It's a nonstructural facade with lots of rebar in it. You might tip over the Mundy Foundation, but it won't collapse. How do you like your job by now?"

"Cartographer's heaven." She said there was not a trace of expediency—unlike the experience of the old man of Thermopylae, everything here was done properly—though she felt like the top of an iceberg. An enormous amount of work had been done before she arrived and she was in the sunshine, sparkling. "I walk past all those empty tables and the dark communications center and I work in the drafting loft with only Nancy Kaneshige to help and we rattle around."

"Deena, I asked how you like it."

"Yes." She turned to face him in the high, thin sunshine. "Did you ever hunker down to look at the iridescent colors of oil on water? Ever surprise a skunk when the sun was low and the high fan of a tail was haloed black and white and gold? Were you ever really greedy with a box of your mother's chocolates?"

"Sounds like you have mixed emotions."

"I get a very Indian feeling out of this, those thousands of color photographs, the file systems, the loft, the layout tables, the arched assembly sections. It makes amazing good sense—until you wonder why." She said shyly, "I thought you were going to Montana and cowboy."

"I thought I might stick around for a while. Up by the border it gets mighty pretty by June—a very good month."

They separated in San Francisco and met for a late lunch at the Mark Hopkins. She thought the Top of the Mark very grand. It justified the chrysanthemum rust dress she bought a size smaller than her old size at the Emporium. She sat quietly by a window overlooking the world. She was deeply pleased with Marty Sanderson, hawk-elegant in her eyes. How well did she know him? She felt far better than she knew.

"How much does this cost?" she whispered.

"A couple of boxes of thirty-ought-six cartridges," he whispered back. "A case of ten-thirty oil." His eyes twinkled. "A small wiener pig."

They flew up the coast in companionable silence and Deena only raised her eyebrows when they did not put down at the strip behind the Mundy Foundation. "Thought you might like to see Humboldt Bay and Eureka," he said. "They massacred Indian women and children there a hundred-something years ago." She could not read his face as they overflew the sawmills and the bar and the long bay. "Get lots of rain. Better see it while it's clear." They banked over Arcata and flew south. "I've got an Indian feeling, too," he said. "If you meet a bear by mistake, the best thing to do is nothing. If that doesn't work, run away." He did not look at her. "We're mixed up with a crazy paleface, Deena. Maybe we should run away to Montana."

"Why the to-ing and fro-ing?" she asked carefully. "The best of both worlds is barely good enough for us—even if it takes maintaining order in an area not subject to control."

In the busy days that followed Birdeena took mental notes. She had not been so formal since college. What she wanted to remember, she remembered. What she forgot, she forgot. The notes were mosaic pieces she turned slowly in her mind to see if they made a pattern.

Marty Sanderson told her, "Mrs. Mundy leased six Constellations and flew in front of winter last year." Connies made the best photographic platforms. They flew the contiguous United States in east-west strips during September and October.

Paul Maniatti said, "Come on and see some day, Deena. There are caves dug in this hill behind us. We could eat for three years before we opened one sack of corn or beans. It's all refrigerated and the bulk stuff is CA sealed. Controlled Atmosphere, nitrogen or helium or something. How about a piece of cake?"

Mesi Stevens confirmed her opinion of the air photos. "I was with the ESSA, the Coast and Geodetic for twelve years. They never put together a series like this. The planning took eighteen months. There were four men in the comm center with radio and direct teletype to field stations. Result—brilliant negatives, good overlap, no cloud cover."

Doc Crowell said, "The drawbridge works fine now. If you come back late at night just put your card in the slot and turn the key. It's pretty fair security. Park the roller and grader on the airstrip and you need a chopper to get in. You can't land a boat at the bottom of the cliffs. On foot it's a long old walk in tough old country. A very careful setup. There's no such thing as complete security, but this comes close."

Nancy Kaneshige said, "How did you guess? We are missing Cape Mendocino to Point Delgada. They're not in the prints or the duplicate prints and Mesi doesn't have the negatives. Do you suppose Mrs. Mundy has them?" Birdeena said not to bother yet.

When Martin Sanderson asked her if she would like an ice cream soda at Garberville she said, "Yes, indeed I would." She leaned back comfortably on the car seat beside him as they drove over the bridge and through the woods to the rutted public road.

"Have you concluded any conclusions?" he asked.

"Human nature is neither good nor evil," she said. "What happens is what counts. You'd better take what people say literally. More often than not they tell you true. Do you know, Marty, I feel all high-school girlish going for a soda?"

"That's too much to untangle at once." He pulled off where the road was wide. He put both hands on her shoulders and shook her gently. "Speak slowly in short words."

"Sure, Marty. Arlis Mundy doesn't like the world. She wants to do something about it. She doesn't like the United States most, because she knows it best. The *why* could be hubris and three unsatisfactory husbands. It's surprising how much time you can waste with *why* when the house is burning down. Hubris is overweening pride. And she is using the most advanced technology for old and dark purposes. Marty, I think I'll have a strawberry soda—"

He popped a smacking kiss on her mouth to get her attention and succeeded beyond expectation. It was Girl Cloud-Walking who caught her breath and murmured, "Besides, she does violence to the principle of duality—oh, my goodness—men and women belong together and complement each other—" She surfaced again flushed and rosy. "So when the first good maps were being made, things were horribly stirred up and they called it the Renaissance. And with the blank spaces filled in—will you leave a girl no secrets?—the First World War came along. And air photography went on between the wars and a little more was stolen—"

"What was stolen?" he asked in a muffled voice.

"The soul of the Earth."

"Oh, no."

"Yes. And things settled down again until satellites and radio photos and the air-caught film drops and especially those in color—when you come right down to it, do you think the people have souls whose pictures are most taken?" She had his attention on two levels and he slowly disengaged the action on one. "Presidents, ballplayers, movie people," she went on a little breathlessly. "I'm not sure television counts unless it's recorded—"

"Primitive superstition," he snorted. "Soul stealing!"

"Bad things happen. Did you hear about the airliner on the Kansas-Nebraska border? They blamed CAT. That means—"

"Clear Air Turbulence, I know."

"What you don't know is it happened when the very first montage was done. I'm extending from an arbitrary center, forty degrees north, ninety-eight degrees west. Arlis Mundy was on the platform with me. There was a fly buzzing around. I don't know how it got in. She caught the fly out of the air with a snatch of her hand. She is very quick. The plane did a cartwheel over Burr Oak, Kansas."

"I'm getting thirsty," he said.

"Marty, what are we going to do?"

"The second thing that comes to mind is Garberville."

"You don't believe me?"

"What do you want me to do? I'll do it."

"I want to get into Arlis Mundy's office some day when you take her flying. I don't think her flat maps correlated enough. I want a key. What I don't want is to see the rest of the country as far out in left field as she is."

"Birdeena Ora Oza Yadon, Girl World Saver?"

"It's not because I asked for the job—it's just because if I quit somebody else will put the map together. Honest and truly, I'm my-heart-is-in-my-throat afraid. Let's go get that soda."

So when Mrs. Mundy flew to San Francisco three days later Deena found the negatives in an orange-colored file cabinet. She took them to Mesi Stevens who said he would be happy to blow them up for her, just for the change. She hid the prints in the middle of Texas and returned the negatives. When Mrs. Mundy was away again, she made collage with all her skill and precision.

> OKLAHOMA CITY (UPA) Earthquake at Harrah! Town devastated! Violent shocks recall 1811 New Madrid disaster!"

If Birdeena was patient, Marty Sanderson was not. The earthquake in the Midwest bothered him. He got Paul Maniatti to fix a picnic lunch and took Birdeena past the airstrip and up the road a mile beyond the dam. She was sparkling but he was troubled. They walked along the narrow lake and spread lunch above a pleasant cove.

"It's wicked superstition," he said.

"Have another piece of chicken."

"Deena, the earthquake's only logical. There's a banana-shaped belt running north-south from the middle of Oklahoma through Kansas into southeast Nebraska. Just because they had a Richter three point four at Oklahoma City doesn't mean Arlis Mundy had anything to do with it."

"These home-cured olives are good."

"Nobody believes you can steal a soul by photography."

"Seen any pictures of Howard Hughes lately? Marty, there are more ham sandwiches."

"You are out of your Indian mind!"

"Over you," she said shyly. He groaned in exasperation. "Tell you what, Marty. Let me take a sneaky peek. That unfortunate woman is up all hours and I've noticed things happening in the morning. Before dawn is an awful time if you've been up all night, hating."

"I'll make you a deal," he said. "I'll get the as-builts out of my files. We'll both take a look and see what goes on. I don't agree with you and I don't like any part of this—"

"I'm glad you can come," she said simply. "I'm scared."

The next morning he scratched on her door at 4:00 A.M. She was dressed in blue jeans and a black sweater. He had a roll of corrected blueprints in his hand.

"Here you are," he said, "but we can't go this morning. I got a call last night after you'd gone to bed. I've got to pick up a couple of Internal Revenue Service men along with the Foundation's tax attorney. Eight o'clock in San Francisco. I want to run a check on the plane before I take off. OK, Denna?"

"Anything you want is all right with me." He grinned at her broadly, kissed her soundly and went out softly.

She studied the blueprints. She took her courage and her flashlight and went up stairs she had never seen before. She climbed a ladder to a black attic. There was a catwalk through a wilderness of rafters and insulation and steel trusses. Ducting ran like rectangular snakes. Every forty feet she came to a solid partition with a door. Bundles of wire followed the catwalk on one side, conduit and pipes on the other. The place was cold and black and quiet.

She opened a final door. Blocky, louvered shapes were droning. There was a *hisk* and whine of moving air. Stacks for the heating and ventilation units ran through the roof. A relay clicked and her heart turned over when a motor stopped. Beyond the machinery was the enormous, unpartitioned and solid-decked attic of the map cube. The trusses and girders were heavier. She stepped carefully over electric motors and gearbox assemblies. They were the support system for the overhead tracks of the vertical maps. She walked a line of nailheads with the utmost caution to a drum of cable.

She lifted a trapdoor. It was an inspection panel for the tracks. Then she lifted a two-foot square of ceiling module. She lay on her stomach. The view was puzzling. She moved away from the obstruction of the tracks and saw the sliced-off portion of the Earth way and away below.

It would accommodate the central section of the North American continent at the determined scale. In the very center were the color air photos of her montage. They took the shape of a webbed X with the corners filled in at Arlis Mundy's direction. Birdeena had been precisely on the Geodetic Survey's control points as they were plotted. It could be a handsome job, she thought rather ruefully.

Something moved on the blank world around the cross. It lurched with a horrible grace away from the mapped area, a preposterous shrunken midget, a child's drawing with a head and legs but no torso. The legs went front and back from her direct overhead view. The figure spun and leaped over the montage. It sank to the surface on the other side and stretched out with the head near the edge of the map.

It was Arlis Mundy. She wore an ice-green leotard. She crossed her legs and sat in ferocious concentration. Was she thinking hate at the world? Panic? Hysteria? She moved her head in a curious forward rocking motion. She was blowing gently over a corner of Missouri.

Half an hour later Birdeena stood in her shower and asked herself a little shakily if she felt like God, looking down on Earth. She dressed again and went for an early breakfast. The radio that morning had a news filler about the jet stream swinging south. Birdeena decided she was looking from Earth down into Hell.

When Marty Sanderson flew in with the IRS men, Arlis Mundy took them to the map room. "The spherical surface is built with the octagonal sections in question ribbed for strength and precision assembly." Each piece was turned to a thousandth's tolerance by a profile-milling machine. Yes, it was expensive. And it rotates and that wasn't cheap. The architectural engineers wrote the specs. Certainly other construction was considered, screeded casting plaster, a fiberglass section from a concave form . . . .

"But the cost!" said an IRS man.

"The government is concerned with expense?" She turned her head away and Birdeena saw her instant silent scream—all the muscles of her neck corded. She resumed control and turned back to the men. "The contract, the earnest money, the progress payments, the receipted bills are filed in my office. My attorney will be with you. I won't." She left the room.

Birdeena saw Marty at lunch. He said Arlis Mundy inspected the Queen Air while he was out on the airstrip, regrading and rolling a hollow. He told Birdeena he expected orders to bring an ax and fly east, so Arlis Mundy could chop down the Washington Monument.

When Birdeena went back to work, laying out nylon fiber paper on which the collage was tissue-fixed in curvature by a special dry-mount press, she saw Arlis Mundy in the comm room, speaking into a microphone.

Arlis Mundy turned off the radio and said to Denna, "I missed them on the ground. The invoices must go out today. Will you run this envelope over to the strip and give it to Marty Sanderson?"

Doc Crowell said he would drive her. They arrived at the hangar just as the Queen Air appeared over the treetops with flaps down, sideslipped and landed. Halfway along the field a cloud of mist trailed behind the right wheel. The plane

stumbled forward on the tricycle gear—and did not slow.
Crowell spun dirt onto the runway. He said something about
too fast to stop, too slow to take off and it would sure as hell
flip if Marty tried to turn. Birdeena folded the envelope of
invoices and put it into her purse.

Sanderson chose to go between his trees but he could not
manage to hit dead even. The left wing tore off with a
wrenching squall and leapfrogged through the brush into the
rocky stream. The fuselage pivoted on the other wing. It
crumpled. The stub reached for the sky. The wreck slammed
to the ground. Sanderson flung open the door and threw out
two men. They got up and walked dazedly. He hung a third
out of the cabin, dropped to the ground and slung him over his
shoulder. They all staggered away and were in a stumbling
run when the gasoline hissing on hot metal went *whoomp*
and a billowing ball of flame rose higher than the tree.

They tumbled into the wagon smelling of blood and singed
hair and shock. At the hangar Crowell phoned the house and
the U.S. Forest Service about the fire. Birdeena ripped a clean
rag for Marty to hold on the jagged cut from temple to ear
while she mopped his bloody face with a wet towel.

He said, "Ruptured brake line. Switches off but it burned.
Too bad. Give a pretty to see if it was cut and taped. Oh,
well."

She said, "Press harder. And be more careful. The life you
save is not entirely your own anymore."

Arlis Mundy braked her XKE to a stop and said she would
drive the men to the hospital. Crowell would direct the fire
crew. She drove the wagon with two men in shock beside her.
Marty was in the back, steadying the unconscious man.

Birdeena mopped his blood from her dress. She watched a
green pumper arrive and water down the wreck. She washed
her face and hands. She got her purse and opened the envelope. It had invoices in it, all from the files, a year and a
half old.

Dinner was quiet. Arlis Mundy came in and had a cup
of coffee with the staff. She said one of the IRS men had a
broken pelvis. The other was burned and the doctor suspected
internal injuries. Her attorney had a dislocated shoulder and
bruises and Marty Sanderson had twelve stitches in his head
and was resting uneasily. He wanted to get out. She flicked her
upper lip with a pointed tongue.

Girl Cloud-Walking awoke at two that morning with a quiet heart. She dressed as she had the night before and climbed to the attic. She thought of Changing Woman, a favorite figure among the Holy People of the Navahos. Changing Woman taught the People to control wind, lightning and storms and how to keep all forces in harmony with each other. She developed ways of doing things that were partly practical and partly magical. Girl Cloud-Walking removed the inspection panel and looked at the world below. A naked figure was dancing there. All restraint was gone. It was a dance of indecent triumph.

She put back the ceiling panel. She replaced the trapdoor, returned through the attics and down the ladder. She walked the silent corridors to the loft. She turned on all the lights. Without haste and without waste motion she took the montage Mesi Stevens had blown up for her and fixed it together. She laid it out on the curved surface and the edges were lifted.

Of course, she thought practically. One of the large tables was very slightly arched. It should approximate the scale almost precisely. It was a brilliant color montage with every detail in fine contrast. She could see the airstrip, the road and the house. She fixed it to the table and shoved it into proper orientation. She clenched her fist above her head and caught her breath. She thumped the map softly. Nothing happened. She bent and blew gently. Birdeena straightened to listen—no wind at all outside. She kicked off her shoes and climbed to the table top. She bent and blew fiercely this time.

The door to the office slammed open. Hell's own Queen stood there in fiery orange wrapped. Her eyes were a mad gray fog.

Of course. Girl Cloud-Walking understood. It was a matter of intent. In sorrow, in compassion, in absolute determination she brought her heel down on the Mendocino coast.

The building rocked and shuddered.

Changing Woman danced and the world reeled under her and the Empress of Hell screamed soundlessly and screamed again. She wheeled to her office, a shadow seeker from the light, and the desk charged down the rocking floor. The door slammed shut of itself and sprang open again. Changing Woman saw her through both open doors, standing on the balcony, then flying and flying—as Girl Cloud-Walking herself was flying from the table in the jolting, punching, rumbling earthquake. Mr. Richter would admire this one.

Deena was not surprised to wake by firelight. The electricity had gone with Arlis Mundy. The world was askew but steady now. The fire was licking at the photo files. Fire had no malicious intent. A door pushed open with a crash. Marty Sanderson stood there looking like the Sun, husband to Changing Woman.

Changing Woman dwelt in a wondrous house on western waters. She was ever young and ever radiant in beauty. But Marty had a lopsided bandage on his head and Girl Cloud-Walking said "Aie!" when he picked her up.

And she was content as he carried her through the shambles of the building, Birdeena Ora Oza Yadon, a safe little watermelon as the fire crackled and grew and roared behind them.

GARBERVILLE (our local correspondent) The energy released during an earthquake is sufficient to run a battleship at full speed for 46,000 years or raise a cubic mile of rock 6,000 feet into the air. "Nonsense!" says a UC Geophysical scientist. "It is impossible to put any comparative numerical value on a force that shifts 'solid' earth twenty feet vertically." He deplored hysteria and rumors that "exotic machinery" found in the ashes of the Mundy Foundation could have any connection with the tragedy that took the life of a great and generous woman.

"WILLIE'S BLUES"

ROBERT J. TILLEY

Science fiction fans number among their ranks a large number of music buffs and devotees of this century's various pop cults. Here, in a story which could well qualify for any fine selection of "mainstream" fiction, is a sensitive and knowing novelette that combines the nostalgia of the jazz age with the savvy of the time travel technique.

Thursday, September 17th, 1936
Room 24, Taylor House Hotel, Florence, South Carolina

The drive here gave me my first real chance to see rural America, 1936 style. Incredibly restful, almost too much so. I found myself dozing at the wheel a couple of times, a highly dangerous thing to do. The car has behaved itself pretty well, but I still can't get used to actually having to steer the damn thing myself.

Florence is nothing special, what I've seen of it so far; could be any small town. The Freemont hall where they're playing tonight is right down the street from here, half a block away on the other side. They've got posters outside, confirming the date I got from the booking agency, so at least I'll be spared hanging around here any longer than I have to.

Not much traffic down there at the moment, certainly no band buses in sight, so it looks as though they're still on their way from Portland.

Come on, Willie Baby.

Friday, September 18th, 1936
Room 24, Taylor House Hotel,
Florence, South Carolina

It's a little after 2:00 A.M., and I've just finished rewriting history.

I still can't grasp it. I thought I was coming here to plug the gaps in our own records, but instead I've been finding out just what they mean at the transfer center when they talk about the past, present and future being interlinked in ways that we haven't even begun to understand yet.

I feel drunk. I suppose the whiskey has something to do with it, but it's more emotional than alcoholic. To find out that you're a part of something like this, a *real* part—

Good God. Can it really mean that without my intervention he would have spent the rest of his life skulking around in musical vacuums like Curry's crowd? Surely it couldn't be! A talent like that would be bound to get kicked out into the open by *something*. It just isn't—

But—what *else* could have done it?

I must get this down in detail now, before I go to bed. I might have lost some of it by morning if I don't. Hell, my head feels as if its one ambition is to float up and nestle against the ceiling. I shouldn't think my chances of getting hold of any coffee are very bright, either. This place is like the rest of the town, lights out by one o'clock at the very latest. Better try walking around. I only hope the fellow underneath is asleep by now—*and* that he sleeps heavy.

First impressions. A small man who looks like an apologetic version of his photographs, playing in a pretty bad band. The acoustics were abominable, but even so it was possible to tell that the records made at the time hadn't lied. The whole thing was a scrappy echo of what the Curry band of five or six years earlier had done so well, and the crowd knew it, too. This is only a medium-sized country town, but even a semi-rural bunch like that listen to the radio and know the difference. They applauded, but it was more good manners than enthusiasm.

He took no solos. All the tenor breaks were handled by Claude Perry, playing a thin pastiche of what Joe Pitman was doing with them before he went off to make it on his own. And Turnhill just sat there, blowing when the sheets told him to; a musician doing a job. I really wanted to scream. The whole thing was insane, with something uniquely unreal about it; ghosts, mimicking echoes from a glorious past, with the only real talent there confined to section work. Ludicrous. I'd been running the machine, but I didn't waste thread when it became obvious that Turnhill wasn't going to be given any space at all.

It finished just after twelve and I went outside with the rest of the crowd, fetched the car, and parked it across from the front of the hall. It was raining, something that I thought of at the time as a lucky break, but I see it a little differently now, of course. It was an ingredient, in exactly the same way that I was; a scheduled event that could no more have failed to happen than I could have prevented myself from being here right now, talking into this microphone.

Anyway, he came out on his own, the last one to leave. The rest of them had already beat it to different parts of town, towing local girls with them. He was wary when I hailed him and offered him a lift, but he didn't have a topcoat and it was raining pretty steadily by then. He got in the back, gave me directions, and off we went.

To put him at his ease, I went straight into my electronics engineer/jazz buff from Baltimore routine; how I'd beeen passing through town when I'd seen the posters advertising Jerome Curry and his Famous Band, and decided to stay over for the night, and so on. I went on to say that I'd heard him once or twice with Benny Case when I'd been in Michigan a couple of years before, and couldn't understand why he wasn't getting any solo space with Curry.

He said his style hadn't fitted in too well, and I didn't find that too hard to believe. Curry had been good about it, though, he said, keeping him on the while he worked on his tone. He'd bought a new mouthpiece to help him thicken it up a little, the way they'd specified he should.

I felt an uncomfortable prickling around the scalp at that point, the first hint that things weren't as I'd expected them to be. The statement itself was bad enough, of course, but what really worried me was the offhand way that it was delivered. Here was the man who was going to have more influence on the distilling of the music than anybody else in its entire history, placidly telling me that he was in the process of mutilating the most sublime instrumental tone I ever heard, and talking about it in the same way that he might have discussed wearing a different kind of hat.

The conversation died completely for maybe half a minute while I digested this, or tried to, and then I asked him what his plans were, whether he intended sticking with Curry or perhaps trying his luck in surroundings that might offer him a little more scope.

I'd expected at least a glimmer of discontent in his answer, some small hint of restiveness, but again, nothing, and this time my hair really rose. He made some vague remark about New York, a new cooperative band, but it was obviously a straight lie, prompted by what was left of his vanity. He didn't really want to try his luck in New York, or anywhere else. It was impossible to imagine a more ludicrous candidate for revolution, but there he was; a man who honestly seemed to think that he'd found his slot and was staying in it as long as he could, thickening up his tone the way they'd told him to and glad of the chance to commit such a crime.

We reached where he was staying, and I stopped the car, wondering what the hell was going on. Although I still had no inkling that I was in any way essential to the pattern of events, I did have the feeling at that point that to let him go without trying to work on him in some way, soften him up a little, would be a mistake. So, on the spur of the moment, as he was getting out of the car, I asked him if he'd like to come over here for a drink.

He didn't dither too much this time. I'd more or less established my credentials by then, and the place he was booked into was a drab, unwelcoming hole. He said thanks, sat down again, and we headed back into town.

His relief at my invitation had been pretty obvious, and I began to get a bit more of the picture. He was twenty-six years old, a professional musician for ten of these, but despite that he was still a small-town boy from Oklahoma, still painfully shy, and the fact that his head had gradually filled with ideas and sounds like nobody else's had proved to be no asset in his present employment. It must have been an almost traumatic experience in some ways, after painfully building himself a minor reputation in territory bands; the chance of playing with a name band on the skids when Curry found himself stuck for a tenor in midtour, the reactions of the older, relatively established musicians, gradually corroding what little confidence he'd ever had, until finally this; a small, confused, tired man, gratefully snapping up the stale crumbs that they threw his way.

It was murder, pure and simple. But somewhere along the way I knew that he was going to hear the Sam Lacey band, and that was to be the turning point. I sweated with relief when I remembered that, knowing it for a solid fact that had been entered in the history books a long, long time before I was even born, something that, no matter what was said and done prior to the event, had actually happened.

Feeling better, I asked him if he'd heard the Lacey band, and he said he hadn't. He'd met Lacey, though, had gigged with him a few times around Scranton, but he didn't know anything about him getting his own group together.

It was right then when it hit me, and I still don't really know why. It was as though I'd turned a page in an until then incomprehensible story and suddenly found myself looking at the key to the whole thing, the piece of the puzzle around which everything else fitted and without which none of what was happening right then would have made any sense at all; my actual trip back to this time, the two days in Kansas City, when I'd visited the Blackjack Club, our meeting that evening, my choice of "profession"; all of them slipping smoothly into place and making beautiful sense, without a seam showing anywhere.

What had happened up until then had shaken me, but this was something else again. It frightened me then and it frightens me now, because it's confirmed a suspicion that I've had all my life and which I've deliberately avoided thinking about too much, for the simple reason that I didn't want to run the risk of convincing myself that it really was so. But it's happened, and there's no going back. In short, what it means is that free will is just an expression, a myth founded on vanity and wishful thinking; that every single mote in the universe is committed to exist in time and space only according to the specification. The interaction of time that they talked about at the transfer center is even more of an involved fact than they perhaps dream, and my mind is still blundering along after the concept, unable to get more than an occasional and all too brief grip on it. Dear Jesus—every step that I take around this room, every movement that I've ever made, every syllable that I'm saying right now; all of it indelibly printed on the circuit, each inflection a response that it's impossible to break or even bend, just a little.

Where did I get to? Fetched him back here, right. I sat him down and poured drinks and gradually got him to open up about himself, prompting him every time he started to slow down and crawl back into his shell. It's on thread, and it'll make an interesting exercise in sifting fact from fiction when I get around to working on it. He was a pretty pathetic character in a lot of ways at that point, but I can't honestly say that I spent a lot of time feeling sorry for him. After all, how do you feel pity for a god that you know is standing on the threshold of his kingdom? If he'd been given the choice, I don't think he would have hesitated for a minute in choosing the way that he was destined to go, and I doubt that there are many people who would really want to trade long-lived anonymity for that kind of glory, however brief.

We drank and talked for about half an hour, and then I went over to my suitcase and fooled around, making it look as though I had the recorder in there instead of my jacket pocket. I dug out the thread with the Lacey band on it, changed it with the one I'd been using during the evening, and then showed it to him. I told him it was something I'd been working on for a while, an experimental model, but I hadn't been able to iron out a few bugs just yet so that it would be marketable. I stuck it between us on the carpet, switched on, and then sat back, confidently waiting for the big awakening.

It didn't take long for it to dawn on me that his reactions were hardly those of a man who was at long last seeing the light at the end of the tunnel. I hadn't expected him to leap to his feet shouting "Eureka!" or anything like that, but all I was getting was guarded approval, completely in character with what had gone before. He drank and tapped his foot, and every so often he would smile a little and say that this or that was OK. He did criticize the tenor player—he said he thought he was a little busy for that kind of outfit—but even this came out of a kind of apology, as though he thought I might bounce back at him for having the nerve to put down somebody that I personally might think was pretty good.

Again, I couldn't believe it. I sat there, staring at him, my piece of history shriveling like a deceptively bulging paper bag that had been holding nothing but air after all. The situation had degenerated into pure nightmare this time. There might have been the faintest shadow of wistfulness somewhere in his eyes, but it didn't disturb the other things that I saw there. He was still small, still frightened; too smart to take any real notice of siren songs like the one he was hearing then, too battered by experience to consider venturing from his small corner to add his own voice to it.

After a while, there was a knock on the door. It was the manager, asking me to cut the noise down in response to a complaint from the room underneath. I apologized, and when he'd gone I switched off the machine and sat down again feeling like the biggest damn fool in all creation.

It seemed to be a total impasse. I thought that I'd stumbled across the real facts as opposed to the inevitable distortions of historic records, but now it looked as though I'd simply jumped to the wrong conclusions, probably steered there by some childishly vain part of my subconscious. But the records had been wrong, anyway. He'd heard Lacey now, and if he were all fired up to race off to Kansas City, he certainly had me fooled. It's always been common belief, supposedly backed by his own testimony, that he'd heard the band on the radio and straightaway wired them, offering Lacey his services. But the moment of encounter had come and gone, and he was still the same vaguely shifty nonentity that he'd been before; liking what he'd heard, that had been obvious enough, but showing not the slightest sign that he'd been stirred sufficiently to even consider leaving Curry of his own volition.

He hadn't been fired, that was pretty certain. There's an interview that Curry gave to *Downbeat* magazine in the nineteen-forties, where he confirmed that Turnhill had walked out on the band during a tour, this tour. So *something* had yanked him up out of his rut and set him running, but whatever it was it wasn't Lacey's music. There was another ingredient that hadn't shown itself yet, lurking somewhere just along the way; something so potent that it had reached right down through the fear and shattered confidence and ignited what was buried somewhere there underneath it all. And then I got it, my second and conclusive flash of realization, and my immediate reaction was "My God, I can't possibly do it."

The reason for this was simple enough. I've broken a cardinal rule laid down by the transfer people, and at that moment the fear of possible resulting restrictions being placed on the rest of my program if it was found out was all that concerned me. But gradually I began to get it in proportion, because it was obvious that this was going to be the only possible way to stir him from the awful apathy that was pinning him down. And again, I saw that this was further evidence that the transfer people still don't really appreciate what they're tampering with. The rule itself is clear and on the face of it perfectly reasonable and logical, but only because the workings of time still aren't understood and probably never will be completely. When they say that apart from essential equipment absolutely nothing originating further along the time-line must be taken back, their reasoning is just plain wrong. The rule is pointless, because any such action and its results have already happened. The pattern is set, and if some lunatic, in a misguided attempt to benefit humanity long before it's due, is going to bring back the formula for curing cancer a hundred years before it's found, then it's simply not going to work. It couldn't. Something would be bound to stop it, even if the ingredients for periducium were available now, which I guess they are; lab equipment that hasn't been invented yet, or maybe something even more obvious. But whatever it was, the line would break down somehow, because everything has its place in the sequence, and there it stays.

I'm starting to ramble again. Walk and concentrate, that's all I must do right now.

My cancer cure was on thread, tucked away at the bottom of my suitcase, but this one was on schedule, I knew it. My reasons for compiling it and bringing it along had been simple enough, or so I'd thought at the time. By putting the absolute cream on one spool, the very best of the music that had ever been issued commercially, I felt that I was taking along the equivalent of a favorite book, one that you can pick up and reread any time you feel the need for something familiar in an alien place. But now I knew the real reason, and I almost laughed out loud at the sheer contrary poetry of it.

The visit of the hotel manager had shaken him quite a bit. There'd been no one at the desk when we'd come in; so I'd helped myself to my key, and although I'd instinctively had the sense to hold the conversation in the doorway so that he hadn't been seen, the simple fact of his being there at all, a Negro in a white man's hotel room late at night, the setting for a disturbance even as minor as the one we'd made, had stirred him to a kind of fear that only people of his time and circumstance could really understand.

Thanks to my prolonged silence, he was on his feet and muttering that he had to go by the time I'd more or less sorted out my own confusion. I poured him another drink and said there was just one more thing I wanted him to hear, get his opinion on. I kept the conversation going while I dug out the spool, saying that I'd picked it up on a K.C. waveband on a recent trip and thought it pretty fine, but didn't have any idea who it could be. Maybe he'd know. He fidgeted and sneaked glances at his watch and the door, but he obviously didn't want to cause offense by beating it out of here in too much of a hurry. I reset the spool, taking the tone control right back so that the sound would be a little muddy and, I hoped, more authentic, put the recorder on the dresser this time, turned the volume down a little, and switched on.

It got him, almost from the first bar; not hooking him completely, but enough to stop his dithering around, as though he'd had most of his motor reflexes switched off. It's a track that I've probably played more than any other and it's never failed to electrify me, but the circumstances then were magnifying its power to a pitch that it had never reached before. Lacey's opening solo, the simplest and probably the most effective one he ever recorded, with that filigree of single notes in the fifth and sixth bars and the final bump he gives to the chord in the tenth; in a way, it was hitting me as hard as it was hitting him. And when the tenor came in with that sublime descending figure, laying it across the twelfth bar and then pushing into the second chorus, it was as though he'd suddenly been kicked in the solar plexus.

He bent at the knees and sank back onto his chair again, leaning forward the whole time. He looked almost sick, jaw hanging, sweat showing around his nose and mouth. His feet stayed still to start with, but then they began to move; gently, barely lifting off the floor, but he could no more have kept them still than he could have flown. It was the moment of revelation, all right; a kind of aural surgery that was showing him his own piece of genius underneath all the muck that had accumulated around it and stifled it to near-extinction.

My own feelings at this juncture were pretty mixed, and they still are. "Willie's Blues" was the finest thing he ever committed to record, but I couldn't help remembering that it had been his last recording, too, made when he must have

been a pretty sick man. To be his savior, that was fine. But
what would have happened if I hadn't been? Would he have
lived longer? Would he have ever gotten started on his no-
torious overindulgence in just about every single thing that it
doesn't pay to overindulge in, after diving straight into the
deep end of the pool that he'd been scared to even dip his
toe in all those years? He might have married, raised a family,
got out of the music business altogether; found a less demanding slot for himself somewhere, a life where he might even
have been happy in the low-keyed way that most people are
at least a part of the time.

I'm just being maudlin about this, I guess. He could just
as easily have been knocked down by a car or got himself
killed in the war, anything at all, really. No, I didn't exactly
do him a complete disservice, and it's on the record that he'll
live the time he has left right up to the hilt, something that
only happens to the handful who find themselves deified in that
special way.

The music finished, and he sat there like a statue for maybe
ten, fifteen seconds without speaking. Then he asked me who
it was, in a gritty kind of whisper, like someone struggling to
surface from a deep trance. I said I didn't know. Static, I im-
probably lied, had cut in just as it had finished, and in fiddling
around with the station dial I'd lost it for good.

He believed me, I suppose, because he had no real choice.
He got up and began pacing around, not speaking, his face still
dull with shock. I said I guessed that Kansas City was throwing
up a lot of good new people just then and that it must have
been a tough job keeping up with everything that was happening there and elsewhere. He said he guessed so, but he hadn't
really heard me. He was still listening to the music inside his
head, struggling to accept the fact of something that even in
his wildest dreams he'd never believed could really exist outside his own imagination.

He paced some more, and then he wandered to the door,
saying that he had to go, that they had a long haul the next
day and he'd better snatch some sleep before getting back on
the road. I don't recall him saying anything while I drove him
back to his rooming house, just thanks and so long when we
got there, and then he went inside without looking back.

And that's about it. God, I'm beat. As far as he's concerned
it's been like opening the door to another world, his personal
vision of Paradise. For me, it's different, and simply knowing

the finish while I went through all those incredible prelimi-
naries hasn't made it the kind of experience that I'm in any
hurry to go through again.

And how about the sixty-four billion dollar paradox? Without me, would it have happened at all? Any of it, or any of
the things that developed from it? Or would he have stayed
right where he was, fouling up his tone until the sounds and
shapes were buried for good and all, turning him into a walking graveyard for some of the most sublime music to grace
a part of history that wasn't exactly notable for either sub-
limity or grace?

Go to bed, Palmer. Even if I had a clear head I wouldn't be
able to dent that one, and right now I couldn't think my way
through the alphabet.

Good night, Willie baby. The shadows aren't going to be
around again for quite a while now, and you've got songs to
sing. Sweet dreams, and I'll be seeing you.

Saturday, February 6th, 1937
Room 31, Brooks Hotel, Kansas City

It turns out that the great night was cold and misty, and I
mean cold. This room has a radiator that makes a hell of a
lot of noise but works well enough in its own way; so I'm
getting this down while I thaw out.

It *was* a great night, and not just because of its historical
significance. The thread I made has done it even less than
justice, I'm sure, but I guess that was inevitable. The place
was jammed to the doors; great atmosphere, but it meant that
the music suffered, and I was only able to pick them up from
one side of the room, right next to a particularly vocal bunch
of customers, who'll have come over loud and clear, I imagine.

But what a band it is now! It could be argued that they're
still rough—collectively, that is—but that would be finicking
for its own sake. It was incredible, like the pulse of the
universe. And Willie—

I'm going to be hearing him under better conditions than
this, of course, but even through all that damned extraneous
racket there was something special there tonight. It was the
sheer poise of the man and what he could produce in a hectic
setup like that which impressed me so much. Smoke and noise
all around him, people yelling in his face, and it was as if he
really were off in a world of his own. He had to be, I guess,
or else it just wouldn't have ben possible to create that kind

of subtly intricate and beautifully controlled line. I don't know whether or not he was high, or even if he's really on anything much yet, but I suppose it was likely, with Clay there and so much hinging on the way he reacted.

But how he *swings!* Across the beat, behind it, juggling it like a man with six hands and all the time in the world; the most beautiful natural of them all, now that he's found his way. It makes me sweat, just thinking about it. A touch of parental pride, no doubt.

The Blackjack hasn't changed since my first visit, despite the increase in business. It's the usual kind of trap; longish and thin, and with a crowd in there you can't really hear much of what's happening if you're at the back of the room. The band was still jammed up in the top left-hand corner, and if there'd been more than nine of them the management would have had to chop a piece out of the bar, something I don't imagine they'd have seriously considered doing.

I got as close as I could, up against the side wall about four or five yards away, and with just enough clearance to get some kind of fix on them. It was an exhausting business, though, and I've got a pretty good idea now what it must feel like to be a sardine caught up in an earthquake, if such a thing is conceivable. I didn't actually see Clay until I was leaving, but the bunch hovering around the table nearest to the band and laughing too much and too loud gave me a pretty good idea of where he was.

Most of the time, of course, I kept my eyes on Willie. It's hard to believe that this poker-faced, totally assured man is only five months older than he was at the time of our first meeting; difficult, in fact, to believe that he's the same person at all. The telescoping of the two occasions has underlined it, of course, but even so it's an almost ludicrous transformation. He generates the kind of detached arrogance that only a few people ever really achieve; complete and utter self-confidence, the kind that's impregnable because its foundations are built on a virtually unshakable belief in what they can do. In actual physique he's hardly altered at all, but I have the impression of someone twice the size he was. It's Lacey's band, and in a deceptively self-effacing way he has the aura of a leader about him, but the spotlight is almost exclusively reserved for Willie, and already he's pretty close to being infallible, the personification of all that's good and right in the music.

The evening ended a little differently to what I'd expected.

It certainly hadn't been part of my plans to actually meet up with him again, not at this stage, but that's what happened. The session had finished, and Clay, all smiles, was button-holing Willie as I squeezed my way out; so it came as some-thing of a surprise when I found him grabbing my arm, fifty yards or so away from the club.

He told me he'd spotted me in the crowd just before the close, and asked what I was doing in K.C. I said hello, and told him I'd been passing through on my way from Baltimore and had made a point of looking in at the Blackjack because I'd heard from a local acquaintance that he was playing there with Lacey, news, I said, that had come as something of a surprise after what he'd said at our first meeting.

It didn't rattle him one bit. He just gave me an appraising kind of look, and then he told me about Leonard Clay show-ing up from New York that evening and how he was back there at the club talking business with Lacey at that moment; so I'd been right there on the spot when the big break had come. I congratulated him, saying that it had obviously been a smart move whichever way you looked at it, his leaving Curry, and that in that case I'd certainly be seeing him again soon as the company I worked for had just opened a New York office, and I hoped to fix things so that I spent a fair amount of my time there.

He said that would be fine, and then he asked the question that had been his sole reason for following me outside and which had kept him standing there in a thin band-jacket in a temperature that couldn't have been too many degrees above zero, the way it felt to me. He asked if I'd ever got a lead on the tenor player on that last thing I'd played him, the one that I said I'd picked up on a Kansas City station.

I said I hadn't, acted surprised, and asked him if he'd drawn a blank, too. He stared at me for a moment before answering, the only outward trace of uncertainty that he showed, and then he said, no, he hadn't been able to locate him, either. But what he couldn't understand, he said, was that nobody else in the region had ever heard of anyone who was playing along remotely similar lines to his own, let alone the caliber of musician that he'd described to knowledgeable locals. Was I sure it had been a K.C. station, or could it have been coming from somewhere else?

I felt I had to let him off the hook a little at this point. I could see that the situation had reached a stage where its plausibility was rubbing a little thin, and some sort of explanation, at least a possibility, was needed to bolster it up again. He'd already given me a suitable opening, but I didn't want to appear too eager to go along with the first suggestion that was made; so I said I was pretty sure it had been local, although it had been too long ago to swear with absolute certainty. Maybe, I suggested, it had been some kid who'd managed to get himself a little air time before he got knocked down by a truck, something like that.

He wouldn't buy that one at all. He said, no, that kind of playing was too mature for any kid to have produced, and besides, if anything like that had happened it would have been talked about. What we'd heard, he said, had been music with a lot of years and experience behind it; adult music, that consisted of a lot more than just technical virtuosity and an individual sound. I said that in that case it must have come from somewhere else, that I must have misread the dial setting at the time, which in turn had probably been the reason why I hadn't been able to relocate the station. In all probability, I said, he'd be turning up in New York one of these days if he hadn't already; so they'd be almost bound to meet eventually.

He said he supposed so. He was shivering quite a lot by then; so I said I had to go, that I'd look him up in New York when I was there and maybe we could have a drink sometime. He said OK, we shook hands, and I came back here, not too sorry that the conversation was over. Quite apart from finding myself in a situation where I'd had to come up with some convincing lies at extremely short notice, something that I'm not normally too good at, this whole business is beginning to make me uneasy, almost squeamish in a sense. The effect of that business in Florence, when he was virtually shown his own soul—how did it really hit him? It must have been a pretty cataclysmic encounter, stirring up echoes of a very special kind; from the future instead of the past, showing him not just what might have been, but what in fact *could* be.

It's a relief to know that he's at least going to hang onto his sanity, because no crazy man could have cut "Willie's Blues." But although this whole thing is out of my hands and I'm only going through motions that have been delegated to me, I'm still having trouble with my conscience. Stupid, really.

Every time I start thinking like this I get a headache, and it isn't to be wondered at. At least it can't be as bad as the one they're suffering from at the transfer center, ever since I turned in my report on my first trip. I must say they took it quite well, considering that it came from a layman, but it's obviously given them a lot of rethinking to do.

My headache isn't going to improve if I stick by this radiator. It sounds as though there's somebody inside the damned thing, trying to break out with a hammer. Home, James, and I hope the climate there is the same as it was when I left, 70° in the shade.

Wednesday, May 12th, 1937
Room 104, Spicer's Hotel, New York

One more for the books, and this one qualified for the battle of the century, all five solid hours of it. Just watching and listening is exhausting enough, but that's the amazing thing. They thrive on it; not exactly unaided in a lot of cases, admittedly, but the level of coherence rarely seems to suffer.

Pitman got back from France today, and it was obvious from the way he walked into the place—Cummings' Playhouse —that he was out to get Willie. The word must have got around, because the crowd was a little different; quite a lot of older faces, and some familiar ones that hadn't been seen too much lately, I gathered; Petey Small, Jay Collins, Edgar Brown, all the people that Willie's blown down during the last month or so.

I have to hand it to Pitman, though, it was hardly a no-contest. Like a lot of other people there, I imagined that his European trip would have slowed him down a little, especially after playing with some of those rhythm sections, but he's a genuine giant, no question about it. The stuff comes steaming out in a torrent, and his control is really quite superlative, but the sheer power that he puts into it was what undid him tonight. It was bull versus panther; direct energy spending itself against subtlety and fantastically judged pacing, and I guess the result was inevitable. Five hours of blowing the way Pitman did would have decimated a mastodon, and to be fair he hasn't had any real competition to speak of for the past year or so.

But even if he'd been physically up to it, I doubt that it would have ended any other way. The ragged edges were really beginning to show toward the finish—"Blue Lou" especially—and there's an element of frustration about his last few choruses. He played the last hour with his coat off and his shirt open right down to his trousers, and it was like a wet rag. Even his pants were soaked. By the time he quit, he was drained, blown out.

I can't find words for Willie right now. I've never really believed that it was possible for any of these people to actually produce the kind of sustained virtuoso performances that they were credited with, but at this particular point in time I have to accept that, on occasions at least, it did happen. He genuinely does seem to have no limits; not only that, his sense of form and continuity is absolutely incredible at this stage. One thing is becoming very obvious: "Willie's Blues" might have been the greatest thing he ever put on a commercial recording, but in fact he matched it time and again, and at far greater length.

He's still showing no real signs of wear, although the stories about his private doings are pretty hair-raising, some of those I've heard. I had a drank with him afterward, and I was amazed at his condition. He wasn't even sweating, and Pitman had gone out of there like a wet sponge. Every time we meet I expect him to mention "the other guy," but he never does. But he's still waiting for him, I can tell. He has that look in his eye, the one that says that there's still one more mountain out there somewhere, and he won't really feel that he's made it until he's stuck right up there at the top with no company in sight. Pitman was a milestone, but to Willie he's still well short of the peak, and after tonight I guess he won't be alone in thinking that.

Thus are the mighty fallen, for the time being, at least. But Pitman's lucky, if only he knew it. Another twenty-six years for him, another fifteen months for Willie. It's a strange, hard world.

Tuesday, June 14th, 1938
Room 88, Spicer's Hotel, New York

A complication of a kind; not drastic, but it's something that I've been expecting for a long time, and I'm only surprised it didn't happen sooner.

He played a radio date with the band last night, and I met him afterward in a bar called Sutton's, a place where musicians generally go after broadcasts. He had a cold, and he asked if he could come over here to put his feet up for an hour or so instead of going on to play somewhere. He said his throat was pretty sore, but he didn't want to go home just then.

Right off I had an idea of what he was really after, but there would have been no point in stalling. We came back here and had a couple of drinks and talked, and after a while he asked if I still had the gadget, as he called it.

I said that I didn't, that I was still having trouble with it and I'd left it back in Baltimore until I had a chance to really work on it, get it right before I tried to market it again. He didn't like that. He stared at me, the kind of stare that suspects all kinds of nameless subterfuge but can't make up its mind exactly what it could be. I tried to get the conversation going again, but he didn't want to talk. He hadn't even wanted my company, and now that he'd failed to get what he came for he wasn't going through any more pretense that he did. He finished his drink without speaking, and said he was going. I said I hoped the cold would clear up soon, and that I'd be seeing him. He replied in just about as noncommittal a way as it's possible to without actually spitting in your eye, and went.

As I say, it wasn't too much of a surprise. He's been very withdrawn with me on my last couple of trips, and it isn't hard to see why. He thinks of me now as the one person who'll be able to say who's the original and who's the plagiarist when "the other guy" does eventually turn up! What a tangle. I suppose it's almost tragic in its way, but I must admit that it has its funny side as well.

It would be interesting to know just how closely he actually connects me with what's been happening to him, though. The fact of our always meeting at the really crucial times and in such widely spaced locales must have got him speculating by now, surely. He suspects something, but whether or not it goes beyond some kind of sleight-of-ear, for God only knows what bizarre purpose, I can't imagine. He certainly doesn't think I'm his fairy godmother, anyway.

Bad joke. Less than four weeks to go now. It's too bad about his cold, which is genuine enough. If he knew how precious time was to him, he'd have spent the whole evening blowing somewhere instead of wasting it on an abortive business like his call here.

For the thousandth time I'm almost tempted to shoot the works and tell him. Almost, but not quite. I stretched the rules once, but only because there was no other way. He's on his own, and that's how it'll have to stay.

Friday, September 10th, 2078
Lewiston, Maine

It won't ever be possible to record this in a truly objective way, but I can't put it off forever. I suppose I've been hanging onto the hope that time would at least blunt the edges before I tackled it, but if it does then it's an imperceptibly slow process. It's been over two months now, and the details are still as sharp and clear as if it were only yesterday. Maybe this will help to clear my thinking, which is still very confused. It may even help me to find answers of a kind, although this seems less than a possibility at the moment.

I'll try to keep off the why's and wherefore's this time, too. I still can't make up my mind just how much sense my speculations on the first couple of threads made, if they made any at all. This thing is so complex that it only emphasizes our inability to understand even our own time and place, if such an expression means anything anymore. If only—

I'm getting bogged down already. Straight facts, inasfar as that's going to be possible.

He still didn't look really sick during the last few days, not even particularly tired. I'd expected to find him showing real signs, but even after the marathon at the Joyland, when he took on all the big guns and shot them to pieces like a flock of sitting quail, he looked pretty much as he had ever since K.C.; a little more pouchy under the eyes, maybe, but nothing more. But I was still of two minds how to wind things up. The actual product of the Consort session was on record, which was all that really counted, and the idea of actually witnessing his collapse had always been distasteful, really nothing more than an exercise in morbid curiosity that I'd already pretty well decided I could do without.

In the event, I went to West 44th Street on the evening of July 8th, stationed myself in a hamburger joint opposite the studios, and waited there; a halfhearted gesture of farewell, I admit, but one that I felt compelled to make. On the aural evidence he'd been in complete control at the session, and yet he'd died almost immediately afterward. So it was curiosity that pulled me there; really, a partial resurgence of the unhealthy inquisitiveness that I'd rejected earlier, but which I found didn't repel me in quite the same way in its modified form.

It was a long wait, almost an hour and a half. I got a couple of mildly curious looks from the counterman after a while, but every so often I bought a fresh coffee and carried on checking the traffic across the way while it gradually got dark outside. Cee Hall arrived first and unloaded his kit from a cab, and Charlie Williams turned up with his bass ten minutes or so afterward. Willie and Lacey and a couple of girls arrived twenty minutes later, sharing a cab.

It wasn't really possible to gauge his complexion in that light, but if anything he looked more relaxed and cheerful than he normally did as he paid off the cab while Lacey and the girls went on inside. He had good reason to be happy, I suppose; his first recordings under his own name, with just about the best supporting talent available, and he must have been particularly pleased about getting Lacey to duck his Swingtone contract and play the date. He always was the perfect accompanist for him, and they never jelled better than on the two tracks that they were going to cut that night.

I sat there for a minute or two after he'd gone into the studio, wondering about it, but more relieved at that moment than curious. It really did look as though it were going to be as clean as could be reasonably expected, which at least meant that there would be no gradual enfeebling decline to be borne and fretted over, the kind of ending that had no place in the existence of a comet as bright as he had been.

Cheered, in a bleak kind of way, I left and walked back to the hotel; a longish pull, but I wanted to take a final look at the town by night, because this was the place and the time that for me summed up most of the attractions of the era. But my principal feeling when I finally walked in off the street was one of relief. I'd suddenly become obsessed with the idea that I had no right to be there at all; that despite the facts of history the setting and myself were two different kinds of incompatible shadow, intermingling only to the extent that oil and water do; touching at the surface, but nothing more. It's a contradiction, I know, but it was very real just then, and it has at least a suggestion of logic on its side. Different kinds of experience and thought and feeling, all born of the circumstances of their time; how can such things ever do more than just show their skins to the stranger? The concept of such a fusion has an unreal quality about it, one that I somehow think I shall never be able to accept completely.

I settled my account with the usual excuse that I'd probably have to leave at very short notice in the morning, and went up to my room. I got rid of excess clothing down the laundry chute at the end of the corridor, packed, and put on the transfer suit.

As I checked and set the power packs on the suit and my case, I had this nagging thought that the thing was finishing all wrong, that a flat ending simply didn't fit in with the spirit of what had happened during the past few weeks. The dying fall is the right close to lots of encounters, but not this one, I was sure. It had been excitement and discovery right from the start, the kind of experience that demanded a statement summarizing all that was best in what I'd found.

I dug out the spool with "Willie's Blues" on it, fitted it, and ran it back to the program number, put the recorder back in the case and switched to play. Then I activated both power packs, sat down on the edge of the bed, and listened.

It's music that I've heard God alone knows how many times, and it's one of the few pieces that has stood the test of frequent repetition, the only real test as far as I'm concerned. I must know every note, almost every nuance of what's played, and yet it always sounds as though it's being created right at the very moment of my listening to it. It's a genuine miracle of a kind, dovetailed so perfectly that there isn't a note or a beat that isn't an essential part of its structure. But it was sad music then, despite its buoyancy, because it was a requiem, shadowed by the things I knew about its creation.

I had my head lowered; so I didn't see the door open as they were working through the final bars. But then the latch clicked shut, and I looked up, and there he was, leaning against it and staring at me with wide, blank eyes. And then the music cut out, and the only sound in the room was his breathing; a ragged, grating, desperate noise that filled my head and choked off my own breath as if my heart had suddenly been grabbed by a huge, cold hand.

I can't for the life of me imagine what he thought or felt at that God-awful moment. I can list my own reactions easily enough—disbelief, fear, and then pity and remorse when the truth of what must have happened and was happening right then hit me. But as for him, I simply don't know, and his reading of the implications of what he saw is going to remain a mystery that I have no particular desire to solve.

How was it possible for me to have been so completely blind for so long? I've always thought of myself as a reasonably intelligent person, but intelligence is the ability to think past the surface of events and see the reality that lies underneath. I hadn't done this at all. I'd been too flattered by the importance of my role as catalyst to see that I wasn't simply showing him the road to tragically short-lived glory and enduring legend. In effect, what I'd done was implant something in his mind; something that, when the time came for him to create that particular pattern of sound, would strike through him with all the awful force of an internal explosion, devastating his reason and triggering the physical disaster that his abuse of his body had already paved the way for.

The clues had all been there. The detailed reports of his death told how he'd recovered from the initial attack sufficiently to leave the building on his own, brushing aside all offers of help, and had finally been found in an alley an hour or so later, where he'd apparently collapsed for the last time. Remembering these things now was like the revelatory moments I'd experienced when we first met, the sudden flashes of insight that showed the puzzle neatly interlocking, a beautifully tooled exercise in cause and effect. But until that moment I'd seen no link, no unifying thread to tie them all together and show the whole picture. Like any scavenger, or dumb, brainless bird, I'd seen only the bright side of the coin, all the time blind to the shadows on its reverse. But even when it isn't out in plain view, the balancing factor is never really absent, always there, always visible to eyes with thought and imagination behind them.

He was already far gone when he came into the room; wet, graying face, weak movements that he couldn't coordinate properly anymore. Whatever it was he'd expected to find there, it couldn't have been what was actually waiting for him; a man dressed in a black, skintight suit, with a control-box of some kind strapped to his chest; a crazy, unbelievable portrait in smoke that was fading even as he watched it. It was like kicking a man who's already three-quarters of the way over a cliff edge, providing the final impetus to his fall. As I moved away, with everything breaking up into the extraordinary grained effect that occurs during the period of actual transfer, dots and flecks that dance and multiply and hurt your eyes, I saw him reach out a hand; whether to try to grab me and hold me there or to push me away I've never been able to decide.

He was posed like that, shrinking and dying and dissolving into a billion pieces when the blackout pulled me under.

He didn't actually die right then, not in the true physical sense, He must have had just enough strength left to scramble away from the nightmare, only to find himself in a dark, grimy place where he fell again and escaped from it forever. But even without my unwitting final assistance, it would still have happened, not right then, but soon. He was sick, possibly without his even knowing it, and the way he pushed himself, squeezing life for all it was worth, meant that there was only one possible ending.

But what was he thinking while he ran? Even if he'd had the time or the strength to consider it rationally, did he have the kind of imagination that could link the pieces together and accept a proposition as farfetched as the truth would have seemed in his own time? I can't imagine that he would, or could. I think he died frightened and confused, after suddenly finding himself in the middle of a situation that defied everything he knew and understood, destroyed by an assault on his mind and body that it had been impossible for him to anticipate or defend himself against. Poor Willie. It must have been a terrible moment for him there in the recording studio, when time suddenly overlapped and he found himself transmitting his contribution to the echoes that had stayed in his memory ever since his one hearing of them; recognizing them, knowing them to be impossible, but committed to their completion; sounds that came from the past but were being made in the present, originating there.

I killed him. I can say it now without actually flinching; externally at least; so perhaps I've found what I was hoping to find when I started this personally prescribed therapy. The images are still there, but I think they've lost a little of their sharpness now. I suppose it means that I've learned to accept what I've known all along but, because of my final role, just couldn't bring myself to acknowledge; that the pattern was set and that my own part in it was an immutable fact that all the cursing and railing and struggling in the world wouldn't have canceled out. It's a familiar pattern, too, on reflection—not exactly exclusive to people who hear unique sounds or possess unique vision or who mold language to suit the singular rhythms that fill their minds, but they seem to fit it more easily than most. But how many of them, I wonder, have been directed by people like myself—wide-eyed, narrow-visioned trippers who blunder through time like clumsy children, totally unaware of the real effect that they are having on people and history? I daren't think of some of the possible implications, not even now.

But why *me*? Perhaps it's a kind of compensation for a total lack of creative talent, history's method of making the achievement a collective thing in an oblique and cruel kind of way. I'll just have to learn to be grateful for having been the chosen recipient of this particular apple with the shiny skin and the big dark worm inside, ignore the sugar content in my feelings and applaud the monstrous humor of the powers of creation with the wry detachment that I guess it deserves.

Not easy, but necessary, now. And I have a feeling it's something we're all going to have to learn.

LONG SHOT

VERNOR VINGE

*We have had a lot of automated space
ship stories, but this one is different. On
the surface it could be said that there
isn't a human character in it. But to insist
on that would be sheer folly.*

They named her Ilse, and of all Earth's creatures, she was
to be the longest lived—and perhaps the last. A prudent tor-
toise might survive three hundred years and a bristle-cone pine
six thousand, but Ilse's designed span exceeded one hundred
centuries. And though her brain was iron and germanium
doped with arsenic, and her heart was a tiny cloud of hydrogen plasma, Ilse *was*—in the beginning—one of Earth's creatures: she could feel, she could question, and—as she
discovered during the dark centuries before her fiery end—
she could also forget.

Ilse's earliest memory was a fragment, amounting to less
than fifteen seconds. Someone, perhaps inadvertently, brought
her to consciousness as she sat atop her S-5N booster. It was
night, but their launch was imminent and the booster stood
white and silver in the light of a dozen spotlights. Ilse's sharp

223

eye scanned rapidly around the horizon, untroubled by the glare from below. Stretching away from her to the north was a line of thirty launch pads. Several had their own boosters, though none were lit up as Ilse's was. Three thousand meters to the west were more lights, and the occasional sparkle of an automatic rifle. To the east, surf marched in phosphorescent ranks against the Merrit Island shore.

There the fragment ended: she was not conscious during the launch. But that scene remained forever her most vivid and incomprehensible memory.

When next she woke, Ilse was in low Earth orbit. Her single eye had been fitted to a one hundred and fifty centimeter reflecting telescope so that now she could distinguish stars set less than a tenth of a second apart, or, if she looked straight down, count the birds in a flock of geese two hundred kilometers below. For more than a year Ilse remained in this same orbit. She was not idle. Her makers had allotted this period for testing. A small manned station orbited with her, and from it came an endless sequence of radioed instructions and exercises.

Most of the problems were ballistic: hyperbolic encounters, transfer ellipses, and the like. But it was often required that Ilse use her own telescope and spectrometer to discover the parameters of the problems. A typical exercise: determine the orbits of Venus and Mercury; compute a minimum energy flyby of both planets. Another: determine the orbit of Mars; analyze its atmosphere; plan a hyperbolic entry subject to constraints. Many observational problems dealt with Earth: determine atmospheric pressure and composition; perform multispectrum analysis of vegetation. Usually she was required to solve organic analysis problems in less than thirty seconds. And in these last problems, the rules were often changed even while the game was played. Her orientation jets would be caused to malfunction. Critical portions of her mind and senses would be degraded.

One of the first things Ilse learned was that in addition to her private memories, she had a programmed memory, a "library" of procedures and facts. As with most libraries, the programmed memory was not as accessible as Ilse's own recollections, but the information contained there was much more complete and precise. The solution program for almost any ballistic, or chemical, problem could be lifted from this "library," used for seconds, or hours, as an integral part of

Ilse's mind, and then returned to the "library." The real trick was to select the proper program on the basis of incomplete information, and then to modify that program to meet various combinations of power and equipment failure. Though she did poorly at first, Ilse eventually surpassed her design specifications. At this point her training stopped and for the first—but not the last—time, Ilse was left to her own devices.

Though she had yet to wonder on her ultimate purpose, still she wanted to see as much of her world as possible. She spent most of each daylight pass looking straight down, trying to see some order in the jumble of blue and green and white. She could easily follow the supply rockets as they climbed up from Merritt Island and Baikonur to rendezvous with her. In the end, more than a hundred of the rockets were floating about her. As the weeks passed, the squat white cylinders were fitted together on a spidery frame.

Now her ten-meter-long body was lost in the webwork of cylinders and girders that stretched out two hundred meters behind her. Her programmed memory told her that the entire assembly massed 22,563,901 tons—more than most ocean-going ships—and a little experimenting with her attitude control jets convinced her that this figure was correct.

Soon her makers connected Ilse's senses to the mammoth's control mechanisms. It was as if she had been given a new body, for she could feel, and see, and use each of the hundred propellant tanks and each of the fifteen fusion reactors that made up the assembly. She realized that now she had the power to perform some of the maneuvers she had planned during her training.

Finally the great moment arrived. Course directions came over the maser link with the manned satellite. Ilse quickly computed the trajectory that would result from these directions. The answer she obtained was correct, but it revealed only the smallest part of what was in store for her.

In her orbit two hundred kilometers up, Ilse coasted smoothly toward high noon over the Pacific. Her eye was pointed forward, so that on the fuzzy blue horizon she could see the edge of the North American continent. Nearer, the granulated cloud cover obscured the ocean itself. The command to begin the burn came from the manned satellite, but Ilse was following the clock herself, and she had determined to take over the launch if any mistakes were made. Two hundred meters behind her, deep in the maze of tanks and beryllium girders, Ilse felt magnetic fields establish themselves, felt hydrogen plasma form, felt fusion commence. Another signal from the station, and propellant flowed around each of ten reactors.

Ilse and her twenty-thousand-ton booster were on their way.

Acceleration rose smoothly to one gravity. Behind her, vidicons on the booster's superstructure showed the Earth shrinking. For half an hour the burn continued, monitored by Ilse, and the manned station now fallen far behind. Then Ilse was alone with her booster, coasting away from Earth and her creators at better than twenty kilometers a second.

So Ilse began her fall toward the sun. For eleven weeks she fell. During this time, there was little to do: monitor the propellants, keep the booster's sunshade properly oriented, relay data to Earth. Compared to much of her later life, however, it was a time of hectic activity.

A fall of eleven weeks toward a body as massive as the sun can result in only one thing: speed. In those last hours, Ilse hurtled downward at better than two hundred and fifty kilometers per second—an Earth to Moon distance every half hour. Forty-five minutes before her closest approach to the sun —perihelion—Ilse jettisoned the empty first stage and its sunshade. Now she was left with the two-thousand-ton second stage, whose insulation consisted of a bright coat of white paint. She felt the pressure in the propellant tanks begin to rise.

Though her telescope was pointed directly away from the sun, the vidicons on the second stage gave her an awesome view of the solar fireball. She was moving so fast now that the sun's incandescent prominences changed perspective even as she watched.

Seventeen minutes to perihelion. From somewhere beyond the flames, Ilse got the expected maser communication. She pitched herself and her booster over so that she looked along the line of her trajectory. Now her own body was exposed to the direct glare of the sun. Through her telescope she could see luminous tracery within the solar corona. The booster's fuel tanks were perilously close to bursting, and Ilse was having trouble keeping her own body at its proper temperature.

Fifteen minutes to perihelion. The command came from Earth to begin the burn. Ilse considered her own trajectory data, and concluded that the command was thirteen seconds premature. Consultation with Earth would cost at least sixteen minutes, and her decision must be made in the next four seconds. Any of Man's earlier, less sophisticated creations would have accepted the error and taken the mission on to catastrophe, but independence was the essence of Ilse's nature: she overrode the maser command, and delayed ignition till the instant she thought correct.

The sun's northern hemisphere passed below her, less than three solar diameters away.

Ignition, and Ilse was accelerated at nearly two gravities. As she swung toward what was to have been perihelion, her booster lifted her out of elliptic orbit and into a hyperbolic one. Half an hour later she shot out from the sun into the spaces south of the ecliptic at three hundred and twenty kilometers per second—about one solar diameter every hour. The booster's now empty propellant tanks were between her and the sun, and her body slowly cooled.

Shortly after burnout, Earth offhandedly acknowledged the navigation error. This is not to say that Ilse's makers were without contrition for their mistake, or without praise for Ilse. In fact, several men lost what little there remained to confiscate for jeopardizing this mission, and Man's last hope. It was simply that Ilse's makers did not believe that she could appreciate apologies or praise.

Now Ilse fled up out of the solar gravity well. It had taken her eleven weeks to fall from Earth to Sol, but in less than two weeks she had regained this altitude, and still she plunged outward at more than one hundred kilometers per second. That velocity remained her inheritance from the sun. Without the gravity well maneuver, her booster would have had to be five hundred times as large, or her voyage three times as long. It had been the very best that men could do for her, considering the time remaining to them.

So began the voyage of one hundred centuries. Ilse parted with the empty booster and floated on alone: a squat cylinder, twelve meters wide, five meters long, with a large telescope sticking from one end. Four light-years below her in the well of the night she saw Alpha Centauri, her destination. To the naked human eye, it appears a single bright star, but with her telescope Ilse could clearly see two stars, one slightly fainter and redder than the other. She carefully measured their position and her own, and concluded that her aim had been so perfect that a midcourse correction would not be necessary for a thousand years.

For many months, Earth maintained maser contact—to pose problems and ask after her health. It was almost pathetic, for if anything went wrong now, or in the centuries to follow, there was very little Earth could do to help. The problems were interesting, though. Ilse was asked to chart the nonluminous bodies in the Solar System. She became quite skilled at this and eventually discovered all nine planets, most of their moons, and several asteroids and comets.

In less than two years, Ilse was farther from the sun than any known planet, than any previous terrestrial probe. The sun itself was no more than a very bright star behind her, and Ilse had no trouble keeping her frigid innards at their proper temperature. But now it took sixteen hours to ask a question of Earth and obtain an answer.

A strange thing happened. Over a period of three weeks, the sun became steadily brighter until it gleamed ten times as luminously as before. The change was not really a great one. It was far short of what Earth's astronomers would have called a nova. Nevertheless, Ilse puzzled over the event, in her own way, for many months, since it was at this time that she lost maser contact with Earth. That contact was never regained.

Now Ilse changed herself to meet the empty centuries. As her designers had planned, she split her mind into three co-equal entities. Theoretically each of these minds could handle the entire mission alone, but for any important decision, Ilse required the agreement of at least two of the minds. In this fractionated state, Ilse was neither as bright nor as quick-thinking as she had been at launch. But scarcely anything happened in interstellar space, the chief danger being senile decay. Her three minds spent as much time checking each other as they did overseeing the various subsystems.

The one thing they did not regularly check was the pro-grammed memory, since Ilse's designers had—mistakenly—judged that such checks were a greater danger to the memories than the passage of time.

Even with her mentality diminished, and in spite of the caretaker tasks assigned her, Ilse spent much of her time contemplating the universe that spread out forever around her. She discovered binary star systems, then watched the tiny lights swing back and forth around each other as the decades and centuries passed. To her the universe became a moving,

almost a living, thing. Several of the nearer stars drifted almost
a degree every century, while the great galaxy in Andromeda
shifted less than a second of arc in a thousand years.

Occasionally, she turned about to look at Sol. Even ten
centuries out she could still distinguish Jupiter and Saturn.
These were auspicious observations.

Finally it was time for the midcourse correction. She had
spent the preceding century refining her alignment and her
navigational observations. The burn was to be only one
hundred meters per second, so accurate had been her perihelion impulse. Nevertheless, without that correction she
would miss the Centauran system entirely. When the second
arrived and her alignment was perfect, Ilse lit her tiny rocket
—and discovered that she could obtain at most only three-
quarters of the rated thrust. She had to make two burns
before she was satisfied with the new course.

For the next fifty years, Ilse studied the problem. She tested
the rocket's electrical system hundreds of times, and even fired
the rocket in microsecond bursts. She never discovered how
the centuries had robbed her, but extrapolating from her
observations, Ilse realized that by the time she entered the
Centauran system, she would have only a thousand meters
per second left in her rocket—less than half its designed
capability. Even so it was possible that, without further complications, she would be able to survey the planets of both
stars in the system.

But before she finished her study of the propulsion problem, Ilse discovered another breakdown—the most serious
she was to face:

She had forgotten her mission. Over the centuries the pattern of magnetic fields on her programmed memory had
slowly disappeared—the least used programs going first.
When Ilse recalled those programs to discover how her reduced maneuverability affected the mission, she discovered
that she no longer had any record of her ultimate purpose.
The memories ended with badly faded programs for biochemical reconnaissance and planetary entry, and Ilse guessed
that there was something crucial left to do after a successful
landing on a suitable planet.

Ilse was a patient sort—especially in her cruise configura-
tion—and she didn't worry about her ultimate purpose, so
far away in the future. But she did do her best to preserve
what programs were left. She played each program into her

own memory and then back to the programmed memory. If the process were repeated every seventy years, she found that she could keep the programmed memories from fading. On the other hand, she had no way of knowing how many errors this endless repetition was introducing. For this reason she had each of her subminds perform the process separately, and she frequently checked the ballistic and astronomical programs by doing problems with them.

Ilse went further: she studied her own body for clues as to its purpose. Much of her body was filled with a substance she must keep within a few degrees of absolute zero. Several leads disappeared into this mass. Except for her thermometers, however, she had no feeling in this part of her body. Now she raised the temperature in this section a few thousandths of a degree, a change well within design specifications, but large enough for her to sense. Comparing her observations and the section's mass with her chemical analysis programs, Ilse concluded that the mysterious area was a relatively homogeneous body of frozen water, doped with various impurities. It was interesting information, but no matter how she compared it with her memories she could not see any significance to it.

Ilse floated on—and on. The period of time between the midcourse maneuver and the next important event on her schedule was longer than Man's experience with agriculture had been on Earth.

As the centuries passed, the two closely set stars that were her destination became brighter until, a thousand years from Alpha Centauri, she decided to begin her search for planets in the system. Ilse turned her telescope on the brighter of the two stars . . . call it Able. She was still thirty-five thousand times as far from Able—and the smaller star . . . call it Baker—as Earth is from Sol. Even to her sharp eye, Able didn't show as a disk but rather as a diffraction pattern: a round blob of light —many times larger than the star's true disk—surrounded by a ring of light. The faint gleam of any planets would be lost in the diffraction pattern. For five years Ilse watched the pattern, analyzed it with one of her most subtle programs. Occasionally she slid occulting plates into the telescope and studied the resulting, distorted, pattern. After five years she had found suggestive anomalies in the diffraction pattern, but no definite signs of planets.

No matter. Patient Ilse turned her telescope a tiny fraction of a degree, and during the next five years she watched Baker.

Then she switched back to Able. Fifteen times Ilse repeated this cycle. While she watched, Baker completed two revolutions about Able, and the stars' maximum mutual separation increased to nearly a tenth of a degree. Finally Ilse was certain: she had discovered a planet orbiting Baker, and perhaps another orbiting Able. Most likely they were both gas giants. No matter: she knew that any small, inner planets would still be lost in the glare of Able and Baker.

There remained less than nine hundred years before she coasted through the Centauran system.

Ilse persisted in her observations. Eventually she could see the gas giants as tiny spots of light—not merely as statistical correlations in her carefully collected diffraction data. Four hundred years out, she decided that the remaining anomalies in Able's diffraction pattern must be another planet, this one at about the same distance from Able as Earth is from Sol. Fifteen years later she made a similar discovery for Baker.

If she were to investigate both of these planets she would have to plan very carefully. According to her design specifications, she had scarcely the maneuvering capability left to investigate one system. But Ilse's navigation system had survived the centuries better than expected, and she estimated that a survey of both planets might still be possible.

Three hundred and fifty years out, Ilse made a relatively large course correction, better than two hundred meters per second. This change was essentially a matter of pacing: it would delay her arrival by four months. Thus she would pass near the planet she wished to investigate and, if no landing were attempted, her path would be precisely bent by Able's gravitational field and she would be cast into Baker's planetary system.

Now Ilse had less than eight hundred meters per second left in her rocket—less than one percent of her velocity relative to Able and Baker. If she could be at the right place at the right time, that would be enough, but otherwise . . .

Ilse plotted the orbits of the bodies she had detected more and more accurately. Eventually she discovered several more planets: a total of three for Able, and four for Baker. But only her two prime candidates—call them Able II and Baker II—were at the proper distance from their suns.

Eighteen months out, Ilse sighted moons around Able II. This was good news. Now she could accurately determine the planet's mass, and so refine her course even more. Ilse was now less than fifty astronomical units from Able, and eighty from Baker. She had no trouble making spectroscopic observations of the planets. Her prime candidates had plenty of oxygen in their atmospheres—though the farther one, Baker II, seemed deficient in water vapor. On the other hand, Able II had complex carbon compounds in its atmosphere, and its net color was blue-green. According to Ilse's damaged memory, these last were desirable features.

The centuries had shrunk to decades, then to years, and finally to days. Ilse was within the orbit of Able's gas giant. Ten million kilometers ahead her target swept along a nearly circular path about its sun, Able. Twenty-seven astronomical units beyond Able gleamed Baker.

But Ilse kept her attention on that target, Able II. Now she could make out its gross continental outlines. She selected a landing site, and performed a two hundred meter per second burn. If she chose to land, she would come down in a greenish, beclouded area.

Twelve hours to contact. Ilse checked each of her subminds one last time. She deleted all malfunctioning circuits, and reassembled herself as a single mind out of what remained. Over the centuries, one third of all her electrical components had failed, so that besides her lost memories, she was not nearly as bright as she had been when launched. Nevertheless, with her subminds combined she was much cleverer than she had been during the cruise. She needed this greater alertness, because in the hours and minutes preceding her encounter with Able II, she would do more analysis and make more decisions than ever before.

One hour to contact. Ilse was within the orbit of her target's outer moon. Ahead loomed the tentative destination, a blue and white crescent two degrees across. Her landing area was around the planet's horizon. No matter. The important task for these last moments was a biochemical survey—at least that's what her surviving programs told her. She scanned the crescent, looking for traces of green through the clouds. She found a large island in a Pacific sized ocean, and began the exquisitely complex analysis necessary to determine the orientation of amino acids. Every fifth second, she took one second to reestimate the atmospheric densities. The problems seemed even more complicated than her training exercises back in Earth orbit.

Five minutes to contact. She was less than forty thousand kilometers out, and the planet's hazy limb filled her sky. In the next ten seconds she must decide whether or not to land on Able II. Her ten-thousand-year mission was at stake here. For once Ilse landed, she knew that she would never fly again. Without the immense booster that had pushed her out along this journey, she was nothing but a brain and an entry shield and a chunk of frozen water. If she decided to bypass Able II, she must now use a large portion of her remaining propellants to accelerate at right angles to her trajectory. This would cause her to miss the upper edge of the planet's atmosphere, and she would go hurtling out of Able's planetary system. Thirteen months later she would arrive in the vicinity of Baker, perhaps with enough left in her rocket to guide herself into Baker II's atmosphere. But, if that planet should be inhospitable, there would be no turning back: she would have to land there, or else coast on into interstellar darkness.

Ilse weighed the matter for three seconds and concluded that Able II satisfied every criterion she could recall, while Baker II seemed a bit too yellow, a bit too dry.

Ilse turned ninety degrees and jettisoned the small rocket that had given her so much trouble. At the same time she ejected the telescope which had served her so well. She floated indivisible, a white biconvex disk, twelve meters in diameter, fifteen tons in mass.

She turned ninety degrees more to look directly back along her trajectory. There was not much to see now that she had lost her scope, but she recognized the point of light that was Earth's sun and wondered again what had been on all those programs that she had forgotten.

Five seconds. Ilse closed her eye and waited.

Contact began as a barely perceptible acceleration. In less than two seconds that acceleration built to two hundred and fifty gravities. This was beyond Ilse's experience, but she was built to take it: her body contained no moving parts and—except for her fusion reactor—no empty spaces. The really difficult thing was to keep her body from turning edgewise and burning up. Though she didn't know it. Ilse was repeating —on a grand scale—the landing technique that men had used so long ago. But Ilse had to dissipate more than eight hundred times the kinetic energy of any returning Apollo capsule. Her maneuver was correspondingly more dangerous, but since her

designers could not equip her with a rocket powerful enough
to decelerate her, it was the only option.

Now Ilse used her wits and every dyne in her tiny electric
thrusters to arc herself about Able II at the proper attitude
and altitude. The acceleration rose steadily toward five hundred gravities, or almost five kilometers per second in velocity
lost every second. Beyond that Ilse knew that she would lose
consciousness. Just centimeters away from her body the air
glowed at fifty thousand degrees. The fireball that surrounded
her lit the ocean seventy kilometers below as with daylight.

Four hundred and fifty gravities. She felt a cryostat shatter,
and one branch of her brain short through. Still Ilse worked
patiently and blindly to keep her body properly oriented. If
she had calculated correctly, there were less than five seconds
to go now.

She came within sixty kilometers of the surface, then rose
steadily back into space. But now her velocity was only seven
kilometers per second. The acceleration fell to a mere fifteen
gravities, then to zero. She coasted back through a long ellipse
to plunge, almost gently, into the depths of Able II's atmosphere.

At twenty thousand meters altitude, Ilse opened her eye
and scanned the world below. Her lens had been cracked,
and several of her gestalt programs damaged, but she saw
green and knew her navigation hadn't been too bad.

It would have been a triumphant moment if only she could
have remembered what she was supposed to do *after* she
landed.

At ten thousand meters, Ilse popped her paraglider from
the hull behind her eye. The tough plastic blossomed out
above her, and her fall became a shallow glide. Ilse saw that
she was flying over a prairie spotted here and there by forest.
It was near sunset and the long shadows cast by trees and hills
made it easy for her to gauge the topography.

Two thousand meters. With a glide ratio of one to four, she
couldn't expect to fly more than another eight kilometers.
Ilse looked ahead, saw a tiny forest, and a stream glinting
through the trees. Then she saw a glade just inside the forest,
and some vagrant memory told her this was an appropriate
spot. She pulled in the paraglider's forward lines and slid
more steeply downward. As she passed three or four meters
over the trees surrounding the glade, Ilse pulled in the rear
lines, stalled her glider, and fell into the deep, moist grass. Her

dun and green paraglider collapsed over her charred body so that she might be mistaken for a large black boulder covered with vegetation.

The voyage that had crossed one hundred centuries and four light-years was ended.

Ilse sat in the gathering twilight and listened. Sound was an undreamed-of dimension to her: tiny things burrowing in their holes, the stream gurgling nearby, a faint chirping in the distance. Twilight ended and a shallow fog rose in the dark glade. Ilse knew her voyaging was over. She would never move again. No matter. That had been planned, she was sure. She knew that much of her computing machinery—her mind—had been destroyed in the landing. She would not survive as a conscious being for more than another century or two. No matter.

What did matter was that she knew that her mission was not completed, and that the most important part remained, else the immense gamble her makers had undertaken would finally come to nothing. That possibility was the only thing which could frighten Ilse. It was part of her design.

She reviewed all the programmed memories that had survived the centuries and the planetary entry, but discovered nothing new. She investigated the rest of her body, testing her parts in a thorough, almost destructive, way she never would have dared while still centuries from her destination. She discovered nothing new. Finally she came to that load of ice she had carried so far. With one of her cryostats broken, she couldn't keep it at its proper temperature for more than a few years. She recalled the apparently useless leads that disappeared into that mass. There was only one thing left to try.

Ilse turned down her cryostats, and waited as the temperature within her climbed. The ice near her small fusion reactor warmed first. Somewhere in the frozen mass a tiny piece of metal expanded just far enough to complete a circuit, and Ilse discovered that her makers had taken one last precaution to insure her reliability. At the base of the icy hulk, next to the reactor, they had placed an auxiliary memory unit, and now Ilse had access to it. Her designers had realized that no matter what dangers they imagined, there would be others, and so they had decided to leave this backup cold and inactive till the very end. And the new memory unit was quite different from her old ones, Ilse vaguely realized. It used optical rather than magnetic storage.

Now Ilse knew what she must do. She warmed a cylindrical tank filled with frozen amniotic fluid to thirty-seven degrees centigrade. From the store next to the cylinder, she injected a single microorganism into the tank. In a few minutes she would begin to suffuse blood through the tank.

It was early morning now and the darkness was moist and cool. Ilse tried to probe her new memory further, but was balked. Apparently the instructions were delivered according to some schedule to avoid unnecessary use of the memory. Ilse reviewed what she had learned, and decided that she would know more in another nine months.

THUS LOVE BETRAYS US

PHYLLIS MACLENNON

The ways of the primitive mind are strange enough here on Earth——Miss MacLennon is a world traveller who knows (currently she is in Central Africa researching a novel). But however primitive humans may be or might have been, the logics of primitive non-human intelligences may be very dangerous to deduct. Similarities of culture might prove to be strictly surface aspects.

It's a strange, sad, lonely world, is Deirdre, forever enshrouded in mists that never lift. There is no day or night. The same dim silvery light seeps always from the pewter sky, casting no shadows and annulling time. The thick, moist atmosphere blots up all sound and muffles the winds into fainthearted breezes hardly strong enough to sway the pendent branches of the black-barked trees that droop like widows weeping over graves, or rustle the transparent leaves that well from their stems like tears about to fall.

Men have not yet encroached here. Perhaps they never will, but the planet has been charted and described, and research ships have landed. The first of them, the *Magus*, was lost with all hands elsewhere in the system. She stopped at Deirdre before she disappeared and left one man behind, a biologist, her sole survivor; he more than half mad when the search party found him.

When the star Selina was first listed, the *Magus* was ordered to call there for a brief preliminary survey on its way to a more urgent task. Of the system's seven worlds, only one showed life, and Alex Barthold was dropped off to investigate it while the ship made a routine evaluation of the other six.

It was common practice, and he had been left thus before, on worlds more hostile than this one appeared to be. Informed of his assignment, he set up his shelter, checked equipment and supplies, and reported to the captain that everything was in order with the matter-of-factness of habit; nevertheless, when the ship had signed off, he stood at the viewport of the plastic dome to watch her leave with the same involuntary pang of abandonment he had felt the first time and would always feel, no matter how certain he was that he would survive and they would come back for him. The lights on the distant hull glowed faintly through the eternal fog. They were all he could distinguish of the *Magus*; but when the boosters flared, they seared the fog away, and he could see her hoist herself up and squat for a moment on her cushion of flame, like a fat old lady catching her breath before forcing herself into space. She vanished, and the boggy earth quivered beneath his feet in the after-shock like something alive.

He was alone.

He had looked forward to this respite from the cramped quarters of the ship. The dome seemed almost vast in comparison, and there would be relief from the tensions inevitably produced by the confinement and total lack of privacy, the constant noise, the personal frictions that could not be avoided. He would be able to go for long walks, with real gravity tugging at his boots. There would be living things to look at that no man had seen before; and even though the myriad fungus spores that formed the nuclei of the mist droplets forced him to wear a protective suit and filter mask, there was fresh, living air to breathe, untainted by the reek of hot

metal, lubricants, and human bodies that no recycling process
could ever quite remove. He arranged the few personal be-
longings he was allowed to bring with him to give the dome
an aura of familiarity, put on his suit, stepped through the
inner hatch into the lock, and sealed the door behind him
with anticipation; but when he opened the outer hatch and
stepped onto the virgin soil of Deirdre, it was an anticlimax.

He found no sense of freedom. Fog swallowed him, a
milky vagueness in which no object more than ten feet away
was clearly seen, which thickened beyond that into a barrier
that moved as he moved, walling him in, softly threatening,
impenetrable because he could never reach it to test what it
was made of. As he stepped forward, dark skeletons of trees
flowed into sight. What lurked beyond them? Behind him the
outline of the dome was already blurred, as if it melted in
the mist. He was suddenly unreasoningly afraid to walk away
from it, to leave the reassurance of the warm golden light that
beckoned from the viewports. The compass on his gauntlet
swung erratically in the weak magnetic field. He dared not
depend on it to guide him, but he had the FoolFinder. He
bent down and touched the buttons on the heels of his boots.
At each step he took, a drop of fluorescent stain would be
released to mark his trail. It showed up cold blue-green like
insect phosphorescence against the rich tapestry of moss beneath his feet. Only after he had walked around enough to
convince the child within him that he could not get lost did
he dare move out of visual contact with the shelter.

. . . He did not like Deirdre.

It was not dead. That would have been less disquieting than
the waiting stillness that enveloped him. He felt as though
something unseen paced him behind the screen of mist, just
at the limit of his vision. Drifting on currents beyond his
comprehension, the fog thickened and thinned in response to
its own will, shaping wraiths of its own substance that seemed
solid enough to touch, and then dissolving them as he came
closer as if it teased him purposely.

He tried to lose himself in work, but here too Deirdre
taunted him. Never had he seen a world so limited in the
variety of its flora and fauna. It teemed with life, but most of
it was the same. The plants that carpeted the earth in regal
splendor were curious forms of algae and lichens, but he
could find no true plants. Even the trees were closely related
to the mosses, as far as he could tell, and though mosses of

such size and toughness were extraordinary, they were all alike. The animal life was equally limited in type—nothing beyond creeping insects, two or three arthropods, and several coelenterates, none larger than a football, and all sluggish enough to make him drowsy watching them.

His specialty was not to have one, to know a little about every aspect of biology; but he did not know any one area of it well enough to make the detailed, exhaustive studies later investigators would undertake, and he came so rapidly to the end of what he was equipped to do that the time he had to wait until the ship returned began to stretch into infinity before him. Bored, restless, increasingly uneasy, he went for long walks, going further and further from the dome in fruitless quest of something new to look at; but Deirdre was everywhere the same. He might have been on a treadmill in some dim, forgotten Limbo. The same dark trees swam up and disappeared behind him, the same fog constantly enshrouded him, the same thick moss sprang back beneath his feet; and in the pale, pearly light, like an eternal dawn, it seemed that Time did not exist. There was only *here, and now,* and the present would never end. He found himself checking his chronometer constantly, but it, too, seemed to have been affected: minutes turned into hours, what seemed like half a day was measured as an hour. The dreamlike atmosphere imbued him more and more with a sense of unreality. He blamed it on nerves, on his own more than half illusory sensations; but he could not overcome the developing conviction that something was there, hiding in the mist, just out of sight, seeing him although he could not see it—or them. In the course of his monotonous explorations, he sometimes thought he caught a glimpse of movement from the corner of his eye; but when he turned, there was never anything: a wisp of mist, veils thicker than it had been, but only mist that faded into mist. It frightened him. He grew anxious away from the shelter of the dome, the instruments companionably ticking, the warm, dry air, the light. He ceased to venture out and sealed himself in against the ghostlines of Deirdre to wait for the *Magus'* return.

. . . It was too long. Why did she take so long? They could not have forgotten him. At chronometer noon every twenty-four hours he sent off his I-am-alive-and-well signal. The code-burst acknowledgement came from the computer, he knew; but someone had to log it. If he did not report, if he

signaled an emergency they would notice and come back for
him . . . unless something had happened. The ship could be
an empty shell, all her crew dead, wandering derelict among
the stars. . . . Or perhaps they had never meant to come back
for him. Perhaps they had always meant to leave him here
alone. There were supplies enough for ten men. Why had
they left so much? They always did, he knew that; but still . . .
They had told him "ten days to two weeks"; it was ten days
by the instruments; and no sign of the *Magus,* no word from
her at all.

. . . They couldn't abandon him. He didn't really believe
they would. Someone would come for him, eventually; and
though, each time he signaled, he was tempted to sound a
false emergency that would hurry them, the penalty for that
was too severe to risk, as yet.

. . . It was too long. When at last the ship sent back no
answer to his daily message, he was not surprised. He had
known it wouldn't, he had felt it in his bones, each day the
chattering response had startled him more, so sure had he
become that it would not be given; and as he tapped his code
call out, and repeated it, and repeated it again, and still no
answer came, he felt a sick satisfaction now that his fears
had been realized. He had suspected that he was somehow
doomed to this murky hell of solitude and uncertainty. He
had been dropped out of life, shunted aside into nowhere,
cursed for crimes committed in the past. . . . What crimes,
what misdeeds warranted such punishment? He thought back,
and they were many, trivial once, but looming larger now:
crimes of omission as well as of commission; people he had
hurt, unknowing or uncaring; tasks he had slighted; responsi-
bilities he had slid out from under—the list was endless. In
this gray, haunted world, his self confronted him and there
was no escape. He could not face himself, so naked and alone.

In the back of his head some shred of sanity reminded him
that he would not be left here forever; sooner or later another
ship would come, no matter what had happened to the *Magus.*
He knew that; but, sure as he was of it, he did not believe it.
The time would come—but there was no Time on Deirdre.
Nothing ever ended. He was trapped in an eternal present;
the chronometer lied, and not a day had passed since the
Magus had taken off. . . .

But there *would* be a ship. It would materialize out of the
fog, and men would step out of it and check the beacon to see

how long it had been sending its plaintive cry into the void.
Where would he be then? What would he be? Would they
know that a man had been left here by himself? Would they
think to look for him? He sealed the logs he had kept to date
and carried them to the beacon. The FoolFinder would disappear in time. Compass headings would be useless; still he
tried to work them out, to devise some way to tell them
where to find him. From spare parts he jury-rigged a small
homing device for the dome and hooked it into his power
pack. Then there was nothing more he could do, except fight
to retain sanity; for he could feel his mind slipping away.

He played films, he played tapes, at high volume, drowning
himself in them to shut out awareness of Deirdre—or rather,
the realization that there was nothing there, that what he
shut out was nothingness, emptiness . . . and looked within
himself and saw his soul draw closer and closer in upon itself,
shrinking into a hard, bright jewel at the center of his being
that not even he could touch, hiding itself away; and he was
afraid.

The hemisphere of his shelter was no longer a refuge. It was
a trap. There was no safety in it, only a danger greater than
any he had known, and of a different kind, harder to fight
because it lay within himself, a part of his own essence.
Driven to escape, he suited up and fled into the spectral landscape where the fog-figures beckoned. He saw them almost
clearly now: pale, childish shadows slipping behind the trees,
always just at the limit of his vision, as if they knew he sought
them, and mocked him, teasing, whispering, "I am here, but
you will never reach me."

They withheld themselves, and he pursued them, surer and
surer that they were concrete. They *had* to be. . . . There was
one that seemed to wait. He could—not quite—distinguish its
slender man-shape, mist-colored, but not mist. As he approached, it drew away, eluding him; yet still it led him on.
He followed patiently, keeping his distance so as not to
frighten it; and as it seemed to sense that he would not press
too closely, its caution lessened. It moved forward stealthily,
but with purpose, intent upon some errand of its own, pausing
from time to time to look and listen, though its wariness
seemed not to be of him. Each time it hesitated, he approached
it nearer, until he could see it clearly.

. . . It was beautiful. Under translucent skin, blue-white as
watered milk, shapes of internal organs pulsed in faint tints of

blue and green and gold. Poised, its back to him, it was a statue carved from living opal; then it turned its head. He shrank away. Such faces he had seen in dreams of ghosts, when, childlike, he shuddered at the dark: white; featureless, except for round, fathomless black eyes like peepholes into Hell. It did not fear him. The slight relaxation of its posture told him that, although it still was timid. It was not hostile. If it had been, it would have attacked before. How could he fear it, when it appeared almost to trust him?

It was real. It was alive. It studied him intently, and he marveled that it should be so bold. How must he look to it? A snouted monster nearly twice its size, lumbering blindly through its territory, breath soughing through the filter mask —in its nightmares, if it had them, could it imagine anything so alien?

It was alive, and near him . . . not much less human than an ape. If he could win its confidence, befriend it . . . he would not fear it. He stretched his hands out, palms upward. It slid away, a supple, darting movement like a snake's putting itself beyond his reach, yet staying with him. It looked at him and turned, as if in invitation. Taking the gesture so, he followed as it wandered through the trees. Watchful, it seemed to scout for enemies, but not to count him one. He felt himself obscurely flattered by this tenuous companionship, like walking with a cat that accompanies because it chooses, not at command. When they came to the village, it had somehow maneuvered him into the lead, so that he entered first and realized with shock just where he was: in an inhabited place.

. . . Or one that had been inhabited. He stared, dumbstruck, at the crude, boxlike dwellings huddled around him, for dwellings they must have been. Hacked out of a coarse, fibrous stuff like hardened peat, they had doors, but no windows. He went into one of them and saw scattered on the floor objects designed for uses he could only guess at, and they were real. For a brief panic-stricken moment he had thought himself hallucinating, but these huts were no illusion. As material as his own familiar shelter, they had been constructed by sentients who knew the use of tools; but the builders were no longer there. Where had they gone, and why? When had they left? A lifetime ago, or only as he came? There was no way of knowing.

The being that had led him there stood waiting, as if impatient to go on. He followed once again, wondering where it wished to take him, until they came upon a wide depression in the ground like nothing he had seen before on Deirdre. Scattered pools of condensed moisture dimpled the moss, surrounded by a profusion of large, bulbous lichens quite unlike those he had already found and taken samples of. The mist-child gathered some of these and ate, cramming food into a lipless mouth stretched like a seam across the empty face, continually glancing at the clouded edges of the clearing as if it feared attack. Its suspicion was contagious. Alex found himself peering around, not knowing what he looked for, thinking of predators, and thus unprepared to see another man-thing hurl itself from among the trees upon its feeding victim. On impulse, he thrust himself between the attacker and its prey. It skidded to a stop, and pulled back, snarling. As he advanced on it, it darted toward the trees, then whirled to face him. Something evil glittered in its paw. He had no choice now but to face it down; he raised both arms and roared. It bolted into the secret safety of the fog.

Behind him, the creature he protected crouched huddled in upon itself, head buried in its arms, shivering like a dog expecting to be beaten. He bent and placed his hand upon its back, wanting to reassure it. It shrieked—in fear, or pain?—and oozed flat to the ground as if it deliquesced. What should he do? He dared not leave it. The enemy still watched. He could not see it, but he felt its hating eyes upon him. He waited. The mist-thing sprawled abandoned at his feet, a rag doll waiting to be painted and dressed into a semblance of humanity. Beneath its hide the delicate colors pulsed and wavered, then grew stronger as it returned to consciousness. The outer integument tensed. It flowed upright, peered into the mist, and shuddered. Alex would have left it then, but as he retraced his course by gleaming flecks of FoolFinder, it slunk behind him as if it found safety in his presence; and when they reached the dome, it sought to interpose itself between him and the hatch so that he could not enter. He motioned it aside. When it refused to move, he stretched out his hand to touch it, and it pulled back, whimpering, far enough for him to reach the release. The hatch irised open. As he stepped inside, the aggressor, who had stubbornly pursued them, slid from the mist and launched itself at them. The mist-thing dashed inside, cowered behind him, moaning in panic, heedless of any but the imminent danger, and Alex slapped the hatch shut, then automatically pulled the lever to turn on the fungicide. Spray hissed from the nozzles all around them, foaming as it struck upon their bodies; and the beast went wild. The lock was barely big enough for two, and as it dashed itself from wall to wall, Alex was forced to seize it to keep it from hurting itself. It turned upon him then. It threw its paws up. Tentacle-digits furled back, and from the center of them, like an ugly flower, a long, sharp tooth flashed forth, serrated on the edges, wickedly pointed. They stood, body to body, frozen an instant, human eyes and Deirdran locked on each other. The spray clicked off, and as if that were a signal, both relaxed. Alex sighed with relief. The thing was as slippery as wet glass—he could not have held it—strong as an octopus and if he had known about its hidden weapons, he would never have dared to touch it.

As he stripped his suit off and draped it on the hooks, the mist-thing pressed its back against the wall and watched, more curious than afraid. Either it was more intelligent than he had suspected, or he was too strange for it to fear him. In either case, now that it was inside and disinfected, he could not open the hatch to let it out without contaminating the lock again; and so he left it there, opened the inner seal, and stepped into the shelter to go about his business, such as it was. He logged the day's events, prepared his meal and ate it, all the while conscious of another presence. Almost transparent, it slipped into the room, an incorporeal substance drifting along the wall like ectoplasm, not quite touching what it studied, lipless mouth half open as if it sniffed or tasted the unfamiliar atmosphere and new, pungent odors. The process of eating over, he slipped a reel of film into the viewer and settled back to watch it—but more to observe the reaction of his visitor. The sounds and the shifting patterns on the screen meant nothing to it, he could see that; but it coiled itself down onto the floor beside him, glancing from the viewer into his face and back, as if it sought some explanation. . . .

He hardly dared to hope, but there was nothing lost by trying. He turned the film off, waited a moment, then tapped himself on the chest.

"Alex."

His throat was tight; the word came out half croak, half whisper. He tried again.

"Alex," he repeated, pointing to himself; and—

"Sessiné," it answered.

They were friends.

It was as simple and as natural as that, a relationship that grew from that first small seed of understanding and bound them together in a kind of sharing Alex did not attempt to analyze. There was no need. Sessiné was there. Slowly, in halting steps, he learned to communicate with "him," as language-bound to sex identification, he thought of his outwardly genderless companion. He had no hope of ever reproducing the half-whispered, bubbling sounds made by the Deirdran, but Sessiné picked up a smattering of Galactic and enriched it constantly as Alex talked to him; and talk he did. In the unmeasured hours they passed together, he confided to this alien being things he had never told to anyone of his own kind, male or female. It listened patiently, deep eyes fixed on his, attentive, whether it knew the meaning of his words or not; and he felt that it did understand, that on an unspoken level it knew his loneliness and shared it, so that he was no longer by himself.

Perhaps the love that grew in him for this inhuman creature was largely based on gratitude. How deep that gratitude was! To hear a voice not his own, pronouncing words that he had not invented, framing thoughts not his; to know a living, sentient presence near him always—although he could not often bring himself to touch it. The texture of its cold, rubbery flesh recalled too sharply how alien it was. He did not wish to be reminded that it was not like him, but made of a different substance, born on a world of which he knew too little. He wanted to learn more, and Sessiné tried to teach him; but much of what the mist-child told him was as far beyond his comprehension as his own maunderings must have been to it. The pattern of life on Deirdre as Sessiné described it baffled him. He wanted to go back to the village, to observe and cross-check some of the apparently conflicting information given him. He could not even guess the level of intelligence. If he could meet others, he might be better able to judge; but Sessiné refused to guide him there, telling him it was useless.

"They are not there," he insisted. "You come, they go. They see . . . these marks—" He pointed to the slight corrugations of the protective suit. "They think are many brands, you are one of those who do not stop to kill. It happens sometimes. But Sessiné comes close when you do *so*—" He imitated Alex collecting specimens. "You look at other things;

you do not see Sessiné. I look, and I think that those are
not brands on you. You have no brand at all. I know you
may not kill, but those others do not know that, and they are
afraid."

"Brand?" Alex was puzzled.

"As in the film you showed me. But we are not like those
beasts; we go by ourselves to the Place at the Time of Branding, and we are not afraid when the Oldest marks our skin
with the water that burns." He held his arm out proudly for
inspection. Alex had briefly noted the narrow scar and taken
for granted it was the result of accident. He examined it now
with more care and saw with revulsion how the gelatinous
tissue had been seared away in a deep groove, rough-edged
and charred.

"That was done *deliberately*? But . . . why?"

Sessiné was surprised by his reaction.

"It is true I am not big, not strong. I am easy to kill. But"—
he groped to express a concept Alex had not taught him words
for— "out of myself I made others like me . . . you understand? When that was done, at the next Time of Branding I
went to the Place. Now this mark says that I must kill or one
will kill me. . . . You do not understand? It is so: with no
brand at all, I may not kill, none may kill me. With many
brands—*so*"—he indicated that both arms would be striped
from wrist to shoulder— "I do not kill, none may kill me.
. . . But Sessiné will not have many brands," he said, apparently resigned to the idea. "At the next Time, one will come
to the Oldest to show him this"—he pointed to the scar—
"that he has cut from me, and the Oldest will burn on his arm
that he has killed this one."

"But *why*?" Alex was horrified. To destroy life was repel-
lent to him. He did it when he had to: for food, if necessary;
to collect specimens for research; in self-defense, if there
were no other way; but to kill wantonly, merely for the record,
as these people seemed to do, was an act that shocked him
deeply.

Sessiné was clearly puzzled by his ignorance.

"It must be so. How else could it be?"

They stared at each other in silence, Alex aware as he had
not been before of the gulf between them. Sessiné tried to
explain; he seemed to sense Alex's repugnance and to want
to dispel it.

"It is good so," he urged him to believe. "Those who have

killed many times grow tired of the taste of death. They have no wish to kill, and none may kill them. Where they want to go, they go. What they want to do, they do. They lie down to sleep and know that they will awaken. They feed, and if another comes they eat together; they need not run with the food sour inside them. They may be together with another as Sessiné is now with Alex. That is very good. Is it not so?"

"Yes. It is so," Alex admitted. It *was* good to be together with Sessiné, and he was touched and shyly pleased to hear the Deirdran say that it seemed good to him as well. It was a pleasure Sessiné was not likely to survive to enjoy with one of his own kind, he realized. On their excursions to the feeding ground, he noted that Sessiné grew increasingly less cautious, feeling himself secure in Alex's presence; and as his carelessness increased, Alex was compelled to be more watchful.

He knew that they were spied on, that every time they left the dome a hidden enemy trailed them—but never more than one, since only one could claim the brand Sessiné bore. That one must be more brave or else more desperate than its fellows to risk the threat that Alex posed; and, like Sessiné, it might someday conclude that threat was empty. If it should attack . . . he would be forced to kill it. He had no choice. The tight-beam ultrasonic handgun he always carried now was vicious in its effect at full intensity, but he dared not turn it down; for once the thing came at them, he could not give it a second chance. One opening in his suit to let the fungus in would do for him, and Sessiné could never hold his own in battle; he was so sure of this himself that he would submit without struggle to the blades of an assassin. He could not let that happen. If either of them should die, the other was lost.

For Sessiné, the matter was simple enough: he would be killed as soon as he lost his protector. For Alex, the prospect was more frightening. He did not like to think about it. . . . A ship would come. Only on Deirdre the present never ended; on other worlds it fled into the past. The silence of the *Magus* would be noted, her course followed until some remnant, some wreckage or survivors had been found. The seekers would trace her path here to the beacon, and they would look for him, his life or death a question they must answer; and when the found him . . . When? If nothing marked the flow of Time, it might as well be never. Without companionship he knew that he could not endure this never-ending *now*.

Those who **had lived in** the village had not yet been branded, and although Sessiné insisted the huts had been abandoned since he came there, he still had hopes of making contact with some other Deirdrans. He had no trade goods, but he collected a few things he thought might catch their interest: bright, shining wire, gaudy scraps of plastic, a small flashlight, colored pens and paper. He left them in the center of the village and went back now and then to see if they had been touched.

On one such tour of inspection, he decided it would be his last. His trinkets lay as he had left them, the wire corroded, the paper mildewed, mold tracing the convolutions of his fingerprints across the gleaming plastic like an arcane message no one here could read, or wanted to. With disappointment verging on despair, he gave up hope. He would have only Sessiné . . . but where was he? In the brief seconds during which he had let his attention wander the fool had disappeared, probably heading toward the feeding ground alone, so overconfident had he grown of late. Alex swore silently and ran to find his friend, but those few seconds were what the enemy had waited for. As Alex burst from in between the huts, he saw two figures struggling on the ground. He shouted, fell upon them, tore them apart, and flung one to each side before they knew he was there. Sessiné lay where he had fallen, cowed, whimpering, arms wrapped around his head. Not so the attacker. As Alex turned to face it, it launched itself at him. He saw it vividly as it hurtled toward him: the opal-hued translucence of its body, its outstretched arms, one branded to the shoulder, the other almost to the elbow—and the tooth-daggers, deadly ivory, pointed at his chest.

He slapped the plastic sheath; the gun leaped to his hand. The enemy was upon him. He pushed the gun into its belly and fired. The ultrasonics shook it apart. He pushed it from him. It stood upright a moment, the tension of its skin still holding it together, its insides shivered into jelly; then it slid shapeless to the ground, a bag of skin, its substance liquefied inside it.

Sessiné stepped from behind him.

"At the Time of Branding, many will fear me when I show this."

He bent over the dead creature and with a grunt of satisfaction sliced away the brands that had adorned its arms, when they were arms.

As his palm-dagger slashed into the skin, the nauseous mess

within gushed forth. Alex had to vomit; he could not control it. He tore his faceplate open just in time and blurted out the contents of his stomach until dry retching produced no more than drops of bitter bile. Relieved, the spasms over, he straightened up and took a deep, clean breath—only to be shocked by a new, more personal horror: he breathed the raw air of Deirdre, and it smelled of Death.

Death was the close companion of men who traveled space. They died predictably, in accidents, and in strange, ugly, painful ways that no one knew of until they happened. But he had known. Still on the ship, before he had set foot on the planet itself, he had seen the cultures under their sealed covers swarm almost instantly with fungi as the voracious spores from the air samples settled on them. The surface of Deirdre was nothing but mold, one solid blanket of it. The animals that lived on it were safe only because their surfaces were too acid for it; but his skin, his lungs, his mouth and nose and eyes, provided ideal conditions. He had known that, and he had forgotten it, and that was how men died.

Cold sweat broke out all over him, even on his arms and legs, and his knees turned to water. His fingers trembled; he pushed the faceplate home but could not close the catch. There were fungicides and antibiotics in the dome, ample supplies of them for just such an accident as this, but could he reach them? How much time did he have? He was shaking, too weak with fear to walk; but with Sessiné to help, he could still make it. The mist-creature stood several feet away from him, fondling his trophies. He stretched his hands toward him.

"Sessiné!"

It seemed that he did not hear him, that he slid away, starting to fade into the mist.

"Sessiné!"

He heard. He looked at him, blank face unreadable.

"Help me!"

He could hardly breathe, his eyes were filming over—but surely that was his imagination, the fungus could not have taken hold so fast. He felt himself waver, sank to the ground, reaching out. . . .

"You are killed."

His voice was cold and flat; he stated a fact that was of no importance to him.

"No ... not yet. Not yet! Help me to walk, help me get to the dome. I'll be all right if I get there."

"No. You are killed," he repeated. "Others watch. They see that you are weak; they do not fear you now. If Sessiné stays with you, one will kill him."

"No one will kill you! I will kill them first; I have the gun!"

It lay on the ground where he had dropped it when he started to vomit. He wormed toward it, but even as he spoke Sessiné had seen it and picked it up. The alien handled the small weapon carefully, and Alex could have sworn he smiled.

"With this, Sessiné will kill many. At the next Time of Branding, all will fear him."

"You fool! You don't even know how to use it!"

"It has a button. All your things have buttons to make them do what you want. Sessiné can use it."

He turned away. He really meant to leave him there to die alone. There was no doubt of that.

Alex coughed. His throat felt full of slime; his words pushed bubbling through it.

"You stinking, soulless hunk of protoplasm! Why don't you shoot me while you're at it? You need the practice!"

He didn't even bother to look back at him.

"You have no brand," he stated and vanished in the fog.

Alex stared after him, numb with disbelief. He could not leave him now, he *could* not, when it would take so little effort to save him! . . . But he had done so.

"Don't go! Please don't leave me!" he screamed soundlessly. He closed his eyes against the tears that filled them and felt that he dropped through a black, bottomless abyss, desperate, reaching out for something to hold onto; but there was nothing there, nothing to cling to, nobody to save him. . . .

. . . Except himself. He would not die, he *would not*! Rage flooded him, and he drew strength from it.

"I'll make it without you, you bastard! Who the hell needs you? You're not even human! Fifty brands I need before they'll talk to me? Then fifty brands I'll have—and yours will be the first!"

It was too hard to struggle to his feet, and if he did he knew that he would fall. But he would make it. On hands and knees, on his belly, if he had to; but he would get there. It wasn't all that far, the fungus couldn't kill him that fast, he

wouldn't let it. He only imagined that he suffocated. Although his breath came hard, he still was breathing. . . .

He started forward. He and Sessiné had come this way so
often, they had begun to leave a trail. Along the shadow of a
path drops of FoolFinder still glistened. He would not get
lost. He crawled, and as he crawled he talked sometimes to
Sessiné in his head, to remind himself that he had something
still to live for, something that he must do:

*"That gun won't last forever . . . but while it lasts, use it,
you son of a bitch—use it, and keep yourself alive until I can
come after you. Because I'm going to. I'm going to get you.
. . . I'm going to cut that goddamn brand off you and stuff
it down your miserable throat. . . ."*

His lungs were filling, his eyes and nose and mouth, even
his ears were all encrusted. Sick and tired and aching everywhere, he sank flat to the ground to rest, and he was crying.
The hot, salt tears cleared out his eyes and nose a little. He
had not even tried to close his faceplate—what did it matter
now? He forced himself up as far as he was able and coughed
and coughed and coughed, bringing up great lumps of green
slime from his lungs. He was exhausted; he could not go on.
. . . He fell back to the earth and thought of Sessiné, who
could have helped him. . . . Flat on his belly, he dug his
elbows into the yielding moss, pulled himself forward, braced
his feet, pulled himself forward. . . . His eyes were clouding
over; he had to blink and blink again to keep them clear so
he could distinguish the path; he had to stop and cough from
time to time to clear his lungs, but he kept breathing. In his
mind's eye, even more clearly than he saw the trail, he saw a
strip of transparent skin and a thin black scar etched on it. He
crawled to reach it, concentrating on it, blotting out the pain
from his chafed elbows, his tortured lungs. He inched himself
forward, stopped to cough and wipe his burning eyes, inched
himself forward. . . .

. . . There was no time, no distance, only slow, hurting
movement. It would have been so easy to give up, to sink into
the spongy moss, let it enfold him, wrap itself gently around
him and make him one with it. . . . He thought of it; the
thought was sweet; but part of himself watched, as from a
distance, and coldly, detachedly, would not let it happen.
God, how he wanted to die! But he would not.

. . . The dome was there. Warm light streamed from the
viewports; inside were rest and safety and means to kill the

tenacious fibers that wove into his flesh and sucked his strength away. Three feet above him, on the dull gray plastic surface, the metal plate to touch to reach that haven twinkled, remote, unfeeling as a star. He squeezed himself against the place where the hatch would open, forced his feet under him, and, remembering Sessiné, pushed himself upward until his hand lay on it. The hatch irised open to receive him, and he fell through into the womb that was the lock.

Pain. Fever. Nausea. Delirium.

. . . He was well and strong. He suited up and left the dome and found the feeding ground. He lay in ambush until Sessiné appeared; sprang at him, caught him, choked him, the lipless mouth wide open, screaming, the deep-set eyes popped out like grapes squeezed from their skins. . . . But was it Sessiné?

. . . He found the Place of Branding; it swarmed with Deirdrans weaving in a slow dance like mummies resuscitated by a necromancer. Sessiné swaggered forward to be branded, carrying a slimy bundle of fresh trophies. As he stretched his arm out to be honored, Alex let fly at him with a needlegun, and from a thousand tiny wounds his inner stuff spewed out as he sank screaming to the ground. . . . But was it Sessiné?

. . . He found the village. Sessiné sat in the central clearing, surrounded by smaller versions of himself, boasting of his exploits. Alex dragged him away, crushed the life from him as he screamed for mercy. . . . But was it Sessiné?

They found him screaming in the dome, screaming and screaming. The medic who was with them listened to him for a while, then quietly disposed of the little heap of unspeakable things he found beneath the bunk. There was no need for anyone to know about them, he decided.

Especially not Alex.

Attention:

DAW COLLECTORS

Many readers of DAW Books have written requesting information on early titles and book numbers to assist in the collection of DAW editions since the first of our titles appeared in April 1972.

We have prepared a several-pages-long list of all DAW titles, giving their sequence numbers, original and current order numbers, and ISBN numbers. And of course the authors and book titles, as well as reissues.

If you think that this list will be of help, you may have a copy by writing to the address below and enclosing fifty cents in stamps or coins to cover the handling and postage costs.

DAW BOOKS, INC. Dept. C
1301 Avenue of the Americas
New York, N.Y. 10019

Presenting MICHAEL MOORCOCK
in DAW editions

The Elric Novels

☐ ELRIC OF MELNIBONE (#UW1356—$1.50)
☐ THE SAILOR ON THE SEAS OF FATE (#UW1434—$1.50)
☐ THE WEIRD OF THE WHITE WOLF (#UW1390—$1.50)
☐ THE VANISHING TOWER (#UW1406—$1.50)
☐ THE BANE OF THE BLACK SWORD (#UW1421—$1.50)
☐ STORMBRINGER (#UW1335—$1.50)

The Runestaff Novels

☐ THE JEWEL IN THE SKULL (#UW1419—$1.50)
☐ THE MAD GOD'S AMULET (#UW1391—$1.50)
☐ THE SWORD OF THE DAWN (#UW1392—$1.50)
☐ THE RUNESTAFF (#UW1422—$1.50)

The Oswald Bastable Novels

☐ THE WARLORD OF THE AIR (#UW1380—$1.50)
☐ THE LAND LEVIATHAN (#UW1448—$1.50)

Other Titles

☐ LEGENDS FROM THE END OF TIME (#UY1281—$1.25)
☐ A MESSIAH AT THE END OF TIME (#UW1358—$1.50)
☐ DYING FOR TOMORROW (#UW1366—$1.50)
☐ THE RITUALS OF INFINITY (#UW1404—$1.50)

DAW BOOKS are represented by the publishers of Signet and Mentor Books, THE NEW AMERICAN LIBRARY, INC.
